PIA FIDELIS

PIA FIDELIS

Book I

THE TWO KINGDOMS

By

Steven O'Reilly

Hartwell Publishing Company

Atlanta / Snellville, GA

Edited by Fiona Mclaren
Cover design and map design by Rafael Andres

Library of Congress Control Number: 2019915965

ISBN 978-1-7341260-1-3 (Paperback)
ISBN 978-1-7341260-2-0 (Hardback)
ISBN 978-1-7341260-0-6 (e-book)
ISBN 978-1-7341260-3-7 (Audio)

Published by Hartwell Publishing Company
P.O. Box 2163
Lawrenceville, Georgia 30046

Ad Maiorem Dei Gloriam

Beatae Mariae Virgine Honore

In Memoriam

my mother (Jane), father (James) and brother Chris

And

To my wife Margaret

CONTENTS

The Creed of the Council of Nicaea (325 AD)

"We believe in one God, the Father Almighty, Creator of all things visible and invisible; and in one Lord Jesus Christ, the Son of God, only begotten of the Father, that is, of the substance of the Father, God of God, light of light, very God of very God, begotten, not made, being of the same substance with the Father, by whom all things were made in heaven and in earth, who for us men and for our salvation came down from heaven, was incarnate, was made man, suffered, rose again the third day, ascended into the heavens, and He will come to judge the living and the dead. And in the Holy Ghost.

Those who say, There was a time when He was not, and He was not before He was begotten, and he was made of nothing (i.e., He was created), or who say that He is of another hypostasis, or of another substance (than the Father), or that the Son of God is created, that He is mutable, or subject to change, the Catholic Church anathematizes."

Chapter 1

The Throne of Satan

(Pergamum, 351 AD)

Julian traveled the dark streets of Pergamum as the call of a watchman, echoing in the distance, signaled the end of the third watch. The city slept, neither candle nor lantern shining from closed residences and shops to illuminate his path. With even the lights of the heavens veiled by thick storm clouds, Julian clung to the walls of buildings, feeling his way along like a blind man. A rumble of thunder and several bright flashes of lightning came in quick succession. Atop the acropolis which loomed over the city, temples and colonnades of white marble, invisible in the darkness a moment before, now appeared a ghostly apparition suspended in the sky. Julian's eyes widened as he beheld the sight.

The great temples and altar of Pergamum! he thought. He then snickered. *And Paul, the disciple of the Galilean, dared to call you the Throne of Satan.*

A faint murmur, or so he thought, came from behind. He paused and peered down the street whence he'd come. He shook his head. *It's your imagination, Julian. You heard nothing. You are not being followed.* Goaded on by self-reproach, he continued on his way, only to stop after a few more steps. This time the patter of bare feet upon the stone of the opposite sidewalk couldn't be mistaken. "Who is there?"

No response came.

Julian quickened his pace, shooting frequent glances over his shoulder as he went. He thought he discerned the shape of someone—or some *thing*—on the opposite sidewalk. He clutched his chest as his heart raced. The shape moved and stopped when he

1

did, only to melt away into the darkness when he tried to focus his eyes upon it. Going another hundred feet, he halted again. He stepped to the edge of the sidewalk.

"Is it a dog?" he muttered. The young man closed his eyes, focusing his attention to listen for any sound in the night. Nothing. Opening his eyes, he recoiled with a loud gasp. Two large canine-like eyes, glowing red, stared back at him from across the narrow street. A hand took firm hold of his cloak from behind and yanked him back until he collided against the stone frame of a door.

"You are late, Prince Julian," said a voice in the darkness.

"Priscus? Is that you?" asked Julian, sweat dripping on his brow.

"Yes, Prince. It is I."

"I lost my way in the dark."

"Have you been followed? Any sign of imperial spies?"

"No . . . but—"

"But what?" asked Priscus.

"I saw the eyes of a dog . . . they glowed red—like hot embers."

"Where? When?"

"Across the street. Just now, before you grabbed hold of me."

Priscus emerged from the shadows. A few inches taller than Julian, who was of average height, he stepped to the edge of the sidewalk for a look. "The dogs of Hecate. You must have seen one."

Julian turned to his companion, his voice quivering with uncertainty as he formed his words. "The dogs of Hecate?"

"Her guardians and messengers—restless souls and daemons," said Priscus. "She must know you seek her this night. She beckons to you." A howl came from up the street. Priscus looked in the direction whence the sound had come. Then, with an eager gleam in his eye, he faced Julian. "It is a sign of her approach."

Rays of moonlight poured through a break in the clouds, shining on the street and a square a short distance ahead of them. His face now discernible, Priscus, a bearded man in his mid-thirties, glanced into the eyes of Julian and back toward the moon. "The torch of Hecate lights the way. Look!" Like a wave upon the shore, the light of the full moon advanced across the stone pavement as the clouds drew back. The glow washed across the square, making visible everything that it touched—first a flight of marble steps and then, rising along them like the tide, the columns and portico of a temple. "There! The Temple of Hecate—goddess of the crossroads between the worlds!"

"Perhaps we should leave this place," said Julian.

"You wanted to witness a prodigy of the gods. Did you not?"

Julian gave a slow, grudging nod. "Yes."

"Turn back now; it is your choice—but I cannot guarantee that you will witness another," said Priscus. He gave a friendly pat on the young man's shoulder. "Courage, Prince Julian! Follow me."

Priscus and Julian crossed the square and ascended the temple steps to the portico. Reaching the top, they were met by the sight of a dozen or more men standing in several small groups.

"I recognize these men," said Julian. "They are fellow students from the school of Eusebius."

"They, too, are here to witness Maximus perform a prodigy," said Priscus, as they passed through their midst.

The two stood before the entrance of the temple. Two brass doors, fifteen feet in height, stood closed before them. Julian observed an old man in his seventies with a long gray beard walking amongst the groups of students, speaking to each for a few moments before moving on to the next.

"It is Master Eusebius!" said Julian.

Priscus snickered. "Of all men, I would not have expected the old philosopher to come."

The old man approached them. His gaze seemed to examine Julian as if to take stock of his character.

Julian brought a trembling hand to his pudgy face. "Master Eusebius! It is you!" He fiddled with his well-manicured beard, following its bristling, dark hairs along the jawline to the chin, where it came to a finely-trimmed point. Acting more like a child, surprised by a parent while misbehaving, he gave a brief, furtive glance to Priscus, as if hoping for support.

"It is I, fool that I am to be out at this hour—three hours past midnight," said Eusebius. He considered the doors of the temple and shook his head. "In this of all places." He turned and glared at Julian. "I had thought you to be a serious student of philosophy."

Julian winced at his words.

Priscus snickered. "You mock the prince, but you are here

3

tonight, Master Eusebius. How is that? Are you here as a teacher or as a seeker of knowledge?"

"Maximus was once a pupil of mine, long ago," said Eusebius. "When I learned he had spread word among my students that he would display his power at this temple tonight, I wanted to see how many of them were fool enough to come. I came to convince those of whom I could to leave, and to watch over the rest—that they not be led into folly by a sorcerer." Eusebius glanced around the portico at the young men. "Too many of them are vain seekers of curiosities."

Priscus stepped forward, coming toe-to-toe with the older man. "Tonight is a quest for knowledge—no less so than the time spent in your boring lectures during the day, philosopher."

"A temple dedicated to Hecate—goddess of ghosts, daemons, and sorcery?" said Eusebius with a sneer. "There is no knowledge to be found here. Not for the living, at least." He placed his hand on the shoulder of Julian. "Forget this quest, Prince. It is not too late to reconsider. Have no part in these practices. The oddity and strangeness of them will not satiate the thirst for true knowledge— it will, instead, consume you with an endless, idle curiosity. No good can ever come of it. It can only lead to one's destruction."

A loud moan emanated from the great brass doors. Julian, who was only a few feet from the doors, froze where he stood. The other students retreated across the portico. A few fled the square and disappeared into the night.

Eusebius rolled his eyes at those cowering near and behind the row of columns. "Do you think it the goddess groaning at you? Superstitious fools! It is only the inner bolt sliding back."

Julian ran his figures over the brass reliefs on the doors, which depicted various gods and strange, mythic animals. He focused on one relief at eye level, a robed female holding two torches. He traced the female form with the tips of his fingers. "Hecate," he whispered to himself. As soon as he had said this, the door opened inward a few inches, revealing a faint glow of yellow, orange, and red from within the temple.

Eusebius grabbed Julian by the forearm. "Turn back, Prince. As the darkness steals away the sight from your eyes, pursuit of this evil will only darken your intellect. Let common sense and the good be your guide. Leave with me now. You will be glad for it in the light of day."

Julian looked into the kind eyes of the old philosopher as he considered his words. He turned his eyes back to the door, where his hand still rested on the cold form of the goddess. Doubt swept across his face. For a moment, he was lost in thought. The prince took a deep breath and let out a sigh of relief. Then, nodding in acknowledgment of the wisdom of the philosopher's words, he withdrew his hand from the door. The philosopher reached out to the young man to now guide him away.

Priscus forced his way between Julian and Eusebius. He pressed his hands against the great door. His face lit by the faint glow from within the temple, he fixed his eyes on Julian. "Remember your quest, my prince."

Priscus pushed with great effort against the door, its metallic creaks and groans echoed within the temple and across the portico as it opened. The students shrunk back several steps, ready to flee. However, when the door had swung open all the way, the students gathered at the threshold to peer inside as morbid fascination edged out fear for the moment. The temple's nave had the appearance of a road, paved with limestone blocks, on either side of which the floor was made of inlaid marble. A statue of a woman, over twelve feet in height, atop a pedestal that was the height of a man, dominated the apse of the temple. Dressed in a flowing robe of black cloth, she held aloft two unlit torches in her hands. Two wide braziers containing small fires were set upon tripods on either side of the statue, their dancing flames casting strange shadows against the curved, recessed wall of the apse.

"Enter!" came a commanding male voice, which resounded from deep within the temple. "The goddess Hecate welcomes you!"

Julian and the other students wondered in amazement upon hearing it. Although their curiosity was rekindled, Julian and the others looked to each other to see whether any one of them could summon the courage to do as the voice invited.

Unafraid, Priscus moved several steps within the entrance. He turned around to the others. "Let go of your fear. Follow me." His eyes then met Julian's. "My prince, you may not have another chance."

Julian nodded. *This is why I have come,* he thought, as he plucked up the nerve. He proceeded with cautious steps into the temple. The other students followed his example, proceeding slowly, scanning the shadows for any sign of danger.

Priscus led the group forward, their sandals echoing on the limestone blocks as they went. For security, the young prince remained close by the side of his mentor, Priscus, who—in his late thirties—Julian also viewed as a big brother. Pillars and side altars lined both sides of the temple. Obscured by shadows, it was not possible to tell to which gods these were dedicated. As the men neared the apse, closer inspection of the statue on the pedestal showed it was not the figure of one woman, but of three—their backs and shoulders against one another, as if conjoined.

"Hecate—goddess of the three aspects," said Priscus, as he and Julian continued around the statue to examine it.

The female figures, their skin painted a pale, deathly white and having eyes of dark stone, held aloft an unlit torch in each hand. Their flowing black robes rippled with a cold breeze that blew into the temple. The rounded wall of the apse, covered with a mosaic of two diverging roads that disappeared into the horizon, created the effect of the statue standing at an intersection where each of the female figures gazed down one of three roads, either one of the two depicted in the mosaic, or the one leading from the entrance to the temple.

Julian turned to Priscus. "Whence came the voice we heard?" he asked. "There is no one here."

A loud clang and thud reverberated throughout the temple. Julian, his heart racing at the unexpected noise, hurried around to the front of the statue and found the rest of the group staring wide-eyed back toward the entrance doors which now stood shut.

"The doors closed by themselves!" explained one student to Priscus, as he appeared from around the pedestal of the statue. "There was no one there!"

"You fool, it was only the wind!" said Eusebius.

"But the breeze was blowing into the temple," said Julian.

"Sit!" commanded the same mysterious voice they had heard. No longer distant, it came from behind them—only feet away. The men turned to see a man in the hooded robe of a philosopher

6

standing beside the pedestal.

"Please, sit," he said, gesturing to stools arranged in a semicircle on either side of the road. When all had taken a seat, the stranger pulled back the hood, revealing the gray-bearded face of a man of fifty years.

Priscus stood to greet him. "Maximus, old friend! There is someone I want you to meet." He glanced back at Julian. "My prince, he is the one I have told you about—Maximus of Ephesus."

Maximus bowed to Julian. "I am honored that you are here tonight, my prince." His eyes fell upon Eusebius, who sat next to Julian. "Eusebius of Myndus? My master of old. I am also honored by your presence."

"Do not think to flatter yourself, Maximus," said Eusebius. "I have not come for myself—or for your so-called demonstration of power. I came to watch over my students . . . that their curious minds not be led away into absurdities as was yours." Saying this, his eyes fell upon Julian.

The attention of Maximus also now focused on the young prince, who felt his soul the center of a tug of war between the two minds. "You know only Plato and Socrates of old," he replied to Eusebius. "You have set boundaries around your knowledge of this world."

"What else is there beside reason and logic? These are enough."

"Other things—other realities."

"Other realities?" Eusebius scoffed. He shot a glance at the statue towering above them. "Such as that?"

"Such as learning the secrets and power of the gods. The gods have longed worked marvels in this city, founded by the people of Arcadia, land of Pan. In the Asclepion of this city, the gods communicate with the sick and heal them with serpents."

"You speak of dreams—not reality."

"No. More than dreams. I speak of seeing them and speaking with them."

Julian's eyes opened wide, nodding in approval at the prospect of communing with the gods. *What secrets or future events might they reveal to me? What doors to worldly power might they open?* The half dozen other students who had remained to this point stood in respectful silence, listening with great interest, but none appeared to fully understand the nature of the dispute.

Maximus studied the prince. "I see that you are interested in that of which I speak. You have come tonight because you thirst for something more than what Eusebius and his philosophy can show you."

Julian nodded.

"He speaks nonsense, my Prince—pay no mind to him!" said Eusebius.

"Tonight, my Prince, I will give you but a foretaste of what the gods offer to those that seek them," said Maximus. "Observe what shall come to pass in a few moments before your eyes." He covered his head with the hood of his cloak and approached a small altar at the base of the pedestal. His back to the observers, he then recited a series of whispered incantations.

A breeze snaked through the temple once more. "What marvel is this?" Julian whispered to Priscus. "The door is closed, yet the air moves and grows colder." He studied the statue of Hecate. Whereas before her face, though carved and painted with great detail, was only lifeless stone, she now appeared to have color in her skin and to even breathe. The head of Hecate tilted, fixing its eyes on Julian—looking straight at him. A slight smile appeared on her face.

The other spectators gasped as this prodigy, each rising from their seats, ready to flee. Eusebius tumbled backward over his stool. A cackling laugh of a female emanated from the statue and echoed throughout the cavernous space. Several of the students broke for the entrance.

Maximus held up his hands, trying to calm the onlookers, even as the statue's laughter continued. "Do not be terrified by what you are witnessing! All is under my command." He pointed to one of the statue's many outstretched arms. "See, even at my word the goddess will light the torches."

At once, the six torches in the hands of the multiform statue burst into flames. The low, flickering fires in the braziers exploded outward and upward to a great height; the flames seeming to touch the coffered ceiling. The whole inner temple was bathed in a red hue. Julian, paralyzed with fear by the spectacle that had unfolded before him, now felt his attention drawn to a statue in the side altar to his left. The horned god Pan, with the upper body of a man and the hindquarters of a goat, appeared to stare back into the prince's eyes.

The others fled the temple, leaving behind Priscus, Julian, and Eusebius, who was still on the floor where he had fallen. Maximus mumbled more incantations. The torches held by Hecate extinguished, seemingly by themselves, and the great flames in the braziers withered away until the fires returned to their former size. As the light diminished, much of the temple, the statue of Pan included, were once again hidden in shadow.

Julian gazed at the face of Hecate. The statue once again appeared to be lifeless stone, its eyes focused on a point on the invisible horizon. "Did you sense the presence of the goddess?" asked Julian.

"It arrived with the chill in the air," said Priscus. He gripped the arm of the prince. "The goddess looked right at you!"

"And into my soul."

Maximus pulled back his hood. "The gods favor you, my Prince. They have a greater plan for you."

Eusebius struggled to his feet. "Young Prince, you must not marvel at these prodigies—even as I marvel not. Rather, the purification of the soul is of greater importance in this life. This comes through knowledge of the Good and the practice of virtue, not through the practice of magic and sorcery."

Maximus's lanky frame convulsed in laughter. "Marvel not? Old man, how can you say this after what you have seen?" he asked. He now turned to Julian. "This night you have seen my power and what I can teach you. What has Eusebius, this old philosopher, taught you that can match this demonstration?"

"Do not listen to him, Julian," said Eusebius. "Do not follow this man. Maximus was my student long ago. I cast him aside because he was vain and arrogant. Self-deluded by his genius and eloquence, he long ago forsook true philosophy and impetuously resorted to the acts of a madman—such as you have witnessed just now." He stretched out his hand and took hold of Julian by a forearm.

Julian glanced with doubt first to one and then to the other, unsure of what to believe or whom to follow.

Maximus now stood before the prince. "True philosophy? Can reason or logic show you the things I have shown you this night?"

His eyes are gazing into my soul, Julian thought to himself. His heart pounded as the sorcerer seemed to assert control over his will.

Eusebius tightened his grasp of Julian's arm. "Follow the path of reason and logic which leads to knowledge of the Good. Be on guard against such men as Maximus who try to raise themselves by engaging in occult rites and practices to command powers not their own by nature. Beware of these impostures of witchcraft and magic which cheat the senses with lying signs and darken the intellect." He pointed an accusing finger at Maximus. "These are the works of conjurors—who are insane men led astray by the exercise of earthly and material powers."

The attention of Maximus remained fixed on the prince. "What need have I for eloquence to respond to Eusebius? My demonstration of power speaks for itself. My deeds you have seen with your own eyes." He glared at the old philosopher. "Prince Julian has free will. He will decide for himself who he will follow."

"Prince Julian—choose!" said Eusebius.

Julian's posture stiffened as his eyes darted back and forth between the philosopher and sorcerer. He brought his hands to his forehead, as if in pain, as he debated within himself what to do. *Eusebius offers me the pursuit of truth, the Good and virtue. He is well known and respected for his wisdom, derived from the study of the great philosophers. I am lucky to be under his tutelage.* He swallowed. *But Maximus is shrouded in mystery; the source of his abilities not yet clear. Yet, he promises access to hidden knowledge of the dark arts, possessed by only a few, as well as power over the material world, by communing with the gods and daemons. Is that something I should so easily turn away?*

Then, after a long moment, Julian dropped his hands to his sides. Calm now returned to his face. He smiled at the old philosopher.

Eusebius nodded. He shot a quick glance at Maximus and smirked in triumph. He grabbed Julian's cloak and began to tug at it. "Then let us leave this place at once, my Prince."

But, as the prince stared at Eusebius, Julian's smile melted away. His gentle gaze transformed into a cold stare. He shook off the old philosopher's grip. "Farewell and devote yourself to your books, old man. But I thank you, Eusebius. You have shown me the man I was in search of—this Maximus of Ephesus, a master of the occult arts who is worthy to instruct me."

***

The clattering of hooves echoed through the narrow streets of Pergamum. City residents busy with their daily errands watched as a column of cavalry passed by, the midday sun reflecting off of the armor-clad riders. Pedestrians hurried onto the sidewalks to make way. The column of men and horses came to a halt before the gates of a villa.

"Open the gate," shouted the captain at the head of the column.

There was no response.

The officer dismounted and strode up to the gate and tested it. It gave way, opening at his touch. He entered a large courtyard within the walls and approached the house where he found several guards asleep near the steps of the entrance. One of them, a centurion, sat on a stool, snoring as he leaned back against a pillar.

The captain scowled at the sight. "Centurion!" he shouted, as he kicked the legs of the chair out from beneath the centurion who toppled to the ground with a loud thud that woke both him and his companions. They all scrambled to their feet to confront the intruder.

"What is going on?" shouted the centurion, still disoriented from his nap. He tried to reach for his sword, but several soldiers from the column who had run over to aid their commanding officer restrained him. Now more alert, a flash of recognition crossed the face of the centurion. Before him stood a young officer wearing a cuirass, polished like silver, and a black-plumed helmet and cape. "Captain. You startled me."

"Where is he?" asked the captain in a firm tone.

"Prince Julian? Inside, sir. I think."

"You think?" the captain said with disgust. The captain beckoned to one of his junior officers. "Decurion, wait here while I check on the prince." He ascended the steps to the house and paused. "Have those men flogged."

The captain pounded on the door. Without waiting for a response, he pushed it open. He went down a hallway that opened into a large open-air atrium. In its center, sat a shallow, ten-by-twenty-foot pool. At one end of it, a fountain with a seashell-shaped basin spilled water into the pool, which, reflecting the sunlight, projected the ripples onto the deep-red interior walls of the atrium.

A male servant of about forty years, wearing a knee-length tunic, came running around the corner and collided with the captain, who then grabbed the heavyset slave by the collar and pushed him up against the wall.

"Forgive me, sir," said the servant. "I was rushing to answer the door. But I see you let yourself in the villa."

The captain released his grip on the servant. He took off his helmet, revealing the sweaty and matted black hair beneath it. The officer stuffed the helmet against the chest of the servant to hold and then walked over to the fountain and splashed water on his face. "Where is your master, the prince?"

"He is out in the peristyle with guests."

The officer splashed more water onto his face, neck, and hair. Across the pool, a mosaic on the wall which depicted Pan caught his attention. Marcus cupped water into his hands and drank. When he had finished, he grabbed his helmet back from the servant. "Take me to him. At once."

The servant brought the soldier to a door that led out to a peristyle, an outdoor space enclosed by a surrounding wall and colonnade. Julian reclined in the shade, resting with his eyes shut. Maximus and Priscus were seated nearby.

"I shall announce you," insisted the servant, as he skirted around the officer to get ahead of him.

Julian, his eyes still closed, shook his head, which rested on a pillow. "I told you. Do not disturb us!"

The captain pushed aside the servant. "I shall announce myself."

The prince opened his eyes and saw the officer standing before him. "I know you," said Julian, as he straightened himself in his seat. His knuckles turned white as he gripped the arms of the chair. "Captain Marcus Scudillo?" said Julian, a slight tremble in his voice.

The captain saluted.

12

The prince turned to Maximus and Priscus. "Captain Marcus is a friend of my brother, Gallus. Is that not correct, Marcus?"

"Prince Gallus and I trained together in Antioch," said the captain, as he stood before them resting his helmet between the crook of his left arm and side, while with his other hand he gripped the handle of his sword, which hung from its belt on his right.

"Marcus, to what do I owe the pleasure of a visit of a captain of the Imperial Guard?"

"Emperor Constantius sent me to fetch you back to Constantinople."

Julian jumped up from his seat. "To fetch me back? What have I done?"

"Fear not, Prince Julian. This errand is a happy one. Your brother, Prince Gallus, is to wed."

"My brother wed? To whom?"

"The Emperor is giving the hand of his sister—your cousin Constantina—to Gallus in marriage."

Julian sank back into his chair. He sighed as his posture relaxed. "So, I am not being arrested?"

"No, my Prince," said Marcus. "I am to bring you back immediately to Constantinople for the wedding. Prince Gallus recommended me for this task." The captain studied Maximus and Priscus. He raised an eyebrow as he did so. "Also, at the personal and private request of your brother—I am to make sure you have not gotten yourself into any trouble."

Julian's body stiffened as he gripped the arms of the chair. "Trouble?"

"You have not introduced me to your guests, my Prince," said Marcus.

"My apologies, Captain," said Julian. "These are my instructors. Maximus of Ephesus and Priscus of Epirus."

"Prince Gallus said your instructor was Eusebius of Myndus."

The Prince averted his eyes. "Oh, Eusebius . . . yes . . . well . . . I recently changed instructors." He rose from his seat and approached Marcus. "When shall we leave for Constantinople, Captain?"

"Tomorrow at sunup," said Marcus. "We have a long ride ahead of us. My troop of men and their horses must rest." He then bowed. "And now, if you will excuse me, Prince Julian, I must see to their care." Marcus saluted and exited the peristyle.

***

Julian returned to his seat beside Maximus and Priscus. He sighed and let out a nervous laugh. "It is only a wedding."

"I thought the captain rather rude and disrespectful," said Priscus. "He barged into your quarters as if he owned it, paying no mind whatsoever to the dignity of your rank and family."

"There is much I have not yet told you about the history of my family and its treatment at the hands of the Emperor," said Julian.

Maximus listened, stroking his gray beard as he did. "But why, my Prince, did you believe you might be arrested just now?"

"My anxious temperament gets the best of me at times," said Julian. He finished his wine. "I fear the discovery of my secrets. The soldiers the Emperor has assigned to me are meant as much to watch me as to protect me while I pursue my studies. They are more like spies than bodyguards. Fortunately enough for me, there is more drunkard in them than spy."

Julian stood to pour himself and his guests another cup of wine. "I keep them well supplied with all the wine and women they would care to have. All to keep their attention occupied with other things—everything else but me. You know what would happen if my secrets were discovered? But perhaps you are right, Maximus. I have taken these precautions. There is no reason I should fear arrest. I have been careful. Yes?"

"Be at peace, Prince Julian," said Maximus. "Your secrets are safe with us."

***

Captain Marcus exited the house to rejoin his troop. The courtyard echoed with the crack of a whip and the cries of a man in pain as the captain's sentence upon the sleeping soldiers was carried out.

As the captain stood and watched, the decurion approached and saluted him.

Marcus gave an approving nod. "They're getting what they deserve."

"Orders, Captain?" asked the decurion.

"The troop will overnight on the grounds of the villa," said Marcus. "We leave for Constantinople in the morning. See to the men and their horses."

"And you, sir?"

"I return after dark," said Marcus. "I have inquiries to make in the city regarding Prince Julian. Prince Gallus is interested in knowing what occupies his brother's time here in Pergamum."

Chapter 2

Rumors of War

(Rome, Late Spring, 351 AD)

Tribune Gaius Marius Septimus, wearing a leather cuirass and red-plumed helmet, sat astride a gray warhorse behind a large villa. A handsome man of twenty-five years, Septimus rode the animal around a small courtyard. A golden-haired dog kept pace with them, barking and wagging its tail as it dodged in and out from underneath the horse.

After several circuits, Septimus brought the horse to a halt near the foot of a terrace which stood ten feet above the ground. He glanced up to see several men and women observing him from above. "What is your opinion, General Marcellinus?" Septimus said to the oldest of the men watching him, a man in his early sixties with thinning gray hair.

Marcellinus, wearing a scarlet toga with a golden wreath embroidered around the neck, set his goblet of wine down on the railing. He stepped closer to the edge of the terrace for a better view of the horse. "A beautiful animal, Tribune Marius. What do you call him?"

Septimus patted the horse on the neck. "I have given him a name befitting a noble horse—I call him 'Ulysses.'" He addressed the other men standing near the general, both in their early thirties. "Leontius? Silvanus? What say you both?"

"What did you pay for the animal?" asked Silvanus, who wore the leather cuirass of a soldier, to which was attached a blue cape. His chiseled features cut a dashing appearance, which captivated

16

the attention of the two young women who had accompanied him for the evening, and who clung to either side of him. One of the young ladies played with his long black hair which reached to his shoulders, making curls of it with her finger, while the other woman was content to wrap her hands about a muscular bicep.

"I bought him for a half a million sesterces in the forum a fortnight ago."

"A half-million sesterces for a horse?"

"From a Thessalian who assured me that Ulysses was of the line of Bucephalus."

Silvanus chuckled. "And you believed him?"

Silvanus turned to Leontius, who stood along the railing. "Imagine that! A horse from the line of Bucephalus—the great horse of Alexander the Great!'

Leontius laughed. "Oh, my dear friend, Septimus. You were swindled! I have never heard of a Thessalian horse trader who does not claim to own a horse descended from Bucephalus." He was a man of plain appearance, with a crooked nose broken long ago in battle. He was already bald on top, and what hair he had left, which wrapped his head like a wreath, was already gray. Without charisma or flare for the opposite sex, he could only admire from afar his friend Silvanus's way with the women.

"You are too cynical," said Septimus.

"You are too trusting," replied Leontius.

"The Thessalian assured me the horse is a clever one . . . already knowing many commands and tricks."

"For a half-million sesterces he had better be as clever as his namesake!" said Silvanus.

"Watch this," said Septimus. He let go of the reins and held his hands to his sides. He leaned forward to address the horse. "Back!" The horse did nothing. "Back!" commanded Septimus, now with a louder voice. The animal stepped forward. The tribune stopped the horse. He let go of the reins, again. "Forward!" he commanded. The horse moved backward.

Silvanus turned to Leontius. "You command the garrison of Rome. Do a favor for our young tribune Marius—have this Thessalian hunted down, arrested, and flogged. There might still be hope of recovering some of the sesterces our dear friend paid for this dumb creature."

"I will not give up Ulysses," said Septimus. "He is a clever horse. You will see."

"Very well," said Silvanus with a chuckle. "But I will never let you buy a single horse for my cavalry."

"Have the horse of your choice, Septimus," said General Marcellinus. "This one—if you must. But, do not let this clever horse get you killed. Civil war will soon be upon us. I can ill afford to lose a good officer."

"So, you believe there will be civil war?" asked Septimus.

Marcellinus furrowed his brow. "Emperor Magnentius has sent messengers to Emperor Constantius offering peace between the Eastern and Western empires. Common sense suggests this is the wisest course for both sides. Both East and West are under the shadow of many threats—barbarians and Parthians. It would be folly to weaken the empire through civil war and to bring upon our civilization the deprivations that accompany it."

"All things are wretched in civil wars," said Septimus.

"Quite right, Tribune," replied the general as he adjusted a bit of the toga draped over his left arm. "Words for the wise from Cicero. Let us hope the Emperors are wise." He then held up his hand in a halting gesture. "But let us talk no longer of war this day, we will upset the other guests. We are here to celebrate the engagement of Tribune Gaius Marius Septimus to the beautiful Lady Marciana."

"Yes, indeed!" said Leontius. "One thing is certain—Septimus had better luck in his choice of a woman than in his choice of a horse."

***

"Guests will arrive at any moment—where is he?" asked Lady Camilia, a Roman matron in her sixties, as she ran her fingers through her gray hair. She hurried from room to room within the spacious Roman villa while several servant girls tried to keep pace with her. She turned to one. "Check with the cooks. The meats and fish must be ready within the hour." She turned to another. "Have the wine brought out now." She continued to rush on but paused again and brought her hands to her cheeks. "Oh no . . . the musicians!"

"They have arrived, Lady Camilia," announced a young servant girl of twenty. "They await you in the atrium."

"Thank the gods!"

Rushing through the atrium, Camilia passed a man in his early sixties wearing a bright white toga with a wide purple stripe. He sat on a bench reading a scroll in the shade beside the shallow pool. She took no notice of him.

"Where is the senator?" she called out to no one in particular. Her eyes then fell upon the half dozen musicians dressed in powder-blue tunics, who huddled together just inside the atrium. She beckoned to them with a wave. "Hello. There you are. Follow me. I will show you where you are to set up in the banquet hall." Again, she rushed past the man on the bench without taking notice of him. "Where is the senator? Where is my husband?" She guided the musicians to the banquet hall. There she passed them off to a servant girl. "Show them where they are to perform. I must find the senator."

Camilia hurried back through the atrium. She spied the man on the bench. "Senator Gaius Marius, where have you been?"

He kept his eyes on the scroll he was reading. "My dear, Camilia, I have been here the whole time."

"How can you sit there, oblivious and unconcerned, with all that is happening around you? We are holding an engagement celebration for our son, Septimus. Over a hundred guests ... senators ... generals ... noblemen and ladies from the great families of Rome. Marciana—his bride-to-be—and her family."

The senator tilted his head to his wife and then stood, his movement slow and reluctant. Over six feet tall and trim, he appeared at least ten years younger than his sixty-plus years. Crow's feet formed at the corners of his eyes as a bemused expression came over his face. "And?"

"And ... where is he?"

There came several knocks on the main door that echoed from the vestibule.

Camilia glared at her husband. "The first guests are here! Septimus is late for his own engagement party! It would not surprise me if he were late for his own wedding."

19

The senator called to an old male servant standing nearby. "Eumaeus, let the guests in."

Camilia waved to the guests as they entered the villa. "It is as I feared. Marciana and her family have arrived and Septimus is not here to greet his future in-laws," she whispered to her husband.

Marius took her hand. He smiled. "All will be fine, dear."

Eumaeus announced the first guests as they entered the atrium. Lady Tertia, a widow in her sixties, was followed by her son, Cyprian, and eldest daughter, Domitia—both in their forties. While Cyprian had a pleasant and cheerful countenance, Domitia, a Vestal Virgin, appeared to have a frown chiseled into her face. She wore the white tunic and palla of a priestess of Vesta. Beneath her veil, wool braids of white and red wrapped around her head.

Camilia gave the older woman a polite hug. "Lady Tertia, so good to see you again."

The senator bowed when he greeted Domitia. "Glad to see they let you out of the temple for the evening." The remark drew a soft elbow to his side from his wife. She lowered her eyebrows as she shot him a glance as if to say 'How could you say such a thing?'

Eumaeus announced the last of the group to enter. "Lady Marciana Quarta, daughter of the late Admiral Anicetus and Lady Tertia." The young Marciana, who bore a strong resemblance to her mother, was a beautiful woman of twenty-three years with brunette hair in shoulder-length curls. She wore a light-yellow tunic that shimmered like gold.

Lady Camilia embraced her. "Marciana, you are as lovely as ever."

Tertia cleared her throat. She frowned. "I do not see Septimus."

"He is here, somewhere," Camilia said with a quiver in her voice. "We were just searching for him."

"Not here to greet his future bride? Hmm."

Marciana winked at Camilia. "Pay no mind to my mother. If I know Septimus, he is working with that new horse of his. Attempting to teach it new tricks."

***

The senator and Lady Camilia led the guests out on to the

20

terrace. There they joined the general, Silvanus and his two lady friends, and Leontius at the railing watching Septimus on his horse.

"Gaius Marius Septimus, there you are!" said Camilia.

Septimus saw his audience had grown to include his future in-laws, including Domitia, who glowered at him. Fixing his eyes on Marciana, he grinned.

"Septimus, how could you disappear like that?" Camilia asked. "Not only are guests arriving—but here is your lovely bride-to-be and your future in-laws. There you are sitting on a smelly horse!"

Septimus prodded his horse forward a few feet. "I am sorry, mother."

Marciana leaned over the railing. She raised her hand to her forehead in a mock military salute. "Hail, Gaius Marius Septimus—tribune of the Roman Legions!"

In response, the horse bent one of its front legs and lowered himself as if to bow before Marciana. The tribune took off his helmet, which revealed his light brown hair, and made a wide sweeping gesture with his arm. "Hail, Lady Marciana!"

The senator clapped. "A fine new trick, Ulysses."

"Well, I do not know about that," said Marciana, a coquettish twinkle in her eyes and a lilt in her voice. "Bowing? It does not seem a proper, practical trick to teach a warhorse."

Silvanus laughed. "We have had our doubts about this horse as well," he said, as he hugged his two lady friends even closer to him. "Have we not?" he said, then he kissed each one of them in turn. His two female companions giggled at his rhetorical question, but it was doubtful they had paid any attention all along to anything or anyone else but Silvanus.

Septimus feigned a frown. "Not practical, you say?" He jumped down from Ulysses. "How dare you!" he exclaimed as he bounded up the marble steps toward Marciana. She let out a shriek of laughter as he caught her up in his arms. The two embraced and kissed.

Septimus addressed his small audience on the terrace. "You want to see a practical horse trick? I have trained Ulysses to return to the stable on his own."

Silvanus chuckled. "Do you really think you should? We saw the results of your last attempts."

Septimus looked down from the terrace at his horse. "Ulysses, dismissed!" he called out as he pointed to the stable. He then turned to Marciana and gazed into her brown eyes. He leaned forward and kissed her. "Impressed?" he asked as their lips parted.

Marciana raised her eyebrows. "With the horse or with the kiss?"

"The kiss . . . wait . . . no . . . the horse. If you put the question *that* way—both, I guess."

Septimus followed Marciana's gaze to the courtyard below. His shoulders slumped. Ulysses had not budged an inch. "All right, we will have to work on that."

Marciana giggled. "You are lucky to be a better kisser than you are a horseman. Had I preferred horsemanship to kisses, I never would have consented to marry you."

Tribune Marius walked to the bottom of the steps. He whistled and gestured to Ulysses to come. Instead, the horse trotted away while the dog ran at once to the tribune's side. Septimus hung his head. He walked up the steps. He glanced at Eumaeus as he passed him. "Make sure Ulysses makes it back to the stable," he said in a low voice. When he reached the top of the steps, he found Marciana and the others laughing at his difficulties with the horse.

The senator beckoned to the guests on the terrace to follow him. "Come! Let us give the young ones a few moments alone together before they must greet their other guests."

"And, please, let there be no talk of war this day," said Camilia.

***

Alone at last, Septimus and Marciana strolled to the edge of the terrace, which had an excellent view of the grounds. Beyond the courtyard, hedged gardens of red, white, and yellow flowers were in full bloom. Stone-paved pathways wound their way under arched lattices covered in flowering vines and past rows of greenery. Fountains and statues of the gods set upon travertine pedestals dotted the well-manicured landscape. Groves of pine and cypress trees encompassed the grounds.

"Happy?" he asked.

She rested her head against his chest. "The happiest girl in

Rome!"

"Only *in Rome?*"

"What do you mean?"

"You said you are the *happiest girl in Rome*,"

"Yes."

"But not that you are the *happiest girl in the empire*."

Marciana rolled her eyes. "Men and their egos! May the gods spare us women from them. Very well then—I am the happiest girl in the entire empire." She squinted in thought. "But . . . then again . . . perhaps you would prefer I said the happiest girl in the entire *world*, rather than just one mere empire?"

"Yes, much better."

The tribune reached inside his cloak and pulled out a necklace of gold and precious stones. "Now that I know you are the happiest woman in the whole world—for I would not accept less— I present this to you as a token of my love and of our engagement." He stood behind her and placed it around her neck. "Something for you to wear on our wedding day."

Marciana examined the necklace studded with blue sapphires. "Septimus, it is beautiful!" She hugged him.

***

The engagement celebration was held in the villa's banquet hall, a large room with a thirty-foot vaulted and coffered ceiling, and walls and floor covered with inlaid marble in geometric patterns. Several steps down from this level was a spacious dining area where low sofas surrounded a dozen large tables. The aromas of roasted beef, pork and fish, fruits and spices pervaded the hall. Lively music from lyres and flutes sounded in the background as some of the guests danced along while others reclined on cushioned sofas as dozens of servants rushed to bring platters of food and wine to them. Yet, despite the gaiety of the occasion, here and there in the hall, despite Camilia's hope and plea, one could hear whispered talk among the nobles of a coming war

Silvanus observed Domitia sitting at the other end of the table, frowning as she drank her wine. He leaned over one of his lady friends seated on his left to speak with Septimus. "Domitia has not so much as smiled at you all night," he whispered.

"She never smiles at anyone," replied Septimus.

"Not only her, but I have noted your future mother-in-law, Lady Tertia, sitting at the next table. She appears dissatisfied with everything."

Septimus looked over at the next table where Marciana's mother sat with the senator, Lady Camilia and General Marcellinus. There, Lady Tertia sat with a blank, disinterested expression on her face.

"The cause of her dissatisfaction cannot be the hospitality of the House of Marius," said Silvanus. He chuckled. "It must be you, poor Tribune! I do not believe your in-laws like you,"

Septimus glanced at Marciana, who sat beside him, to make sure she wasn't listening to their conversation. "I believe she is unhappy with the suddenness of the engagement and the fact the marriage is next week."

It was at this point that General Marcellinus rose to his feet to address those gathered in the hall. He straightened his scarlet tunic. He then held out his cup for a servant to fill it with more wine. "Last year, Emperor Magnentius ordered me to Rome with a force of cavalry and infantry to put down the insurrection of Nepotian, who had declared himself Emperor of the West after the death of Constans. Nepotian had seized control of the city with a mercenary army of gladiators and criminals. Silvanus—my right arm as I call him—and Leontius were my lieutenants. Both friends of old."

The guests applauded the two soldiers.

"Let us honor the memory of Tribune Cassius, who commanded one of my legions—the Third Italica—and lost his life in the Battle of Rome," said Marcellinus. He blessed himself with the sign of the cross. "God rest his soul." He paused for a moment of silence for the fallen soldier. "When Cassius was killed at a moment of supreme crisis, it was Septimus who assumed acting command of the legion. Through his personal bravery, he saved this legion during an ambush and defeated the gladiators. All know the story—now almost mythic—that his legionaries circulate of how he defeated two gladiators in single combat."

Septimus turned red and shook his head at the scattered applause.

"I heard it was five gladiators—not two!" shouted Silvanus,

giving a wink to one of his lady friends after he did so.

"And it was not in single combat—I heard he fought the gladiators all at the same time!" said Leontius.

The hall erupted with loud cheers.

Septimus continued to shake his head and hold up his hands in protest. "The legionaries have exaggerated the story in the retelling. It was nothing like that! In great part, it is myth. Believe me." But the cheering drowned out his voice. He turned to Silvanus and Leontius. "You two are not helping—you must know the tale has grown in the retelling."

The two only grinned, enjoying his discomfort and embarrassment.

Leontius grew serious. "What I know is you saved my life that day. I will forever be in your debt."

Septimus saw that Marcellinus had come over to their table and now stood behind him. The general gave a wink to Marciana.

Septimus raised an eyebrow at his bride-to-be. "Oh, no—what have you two arranged?"

Marciana kissed him on the cheek and then stood. She rushed to the entrance of the banquet hall. There she waved to someone out of sight. She then signaled Marcellinus with a nod.

The general placed a hand on Septimus's shoulder as he addressed all present. "Therefore, in recognition of these feats, I come bearing two gifts on this great and happy day on which we celebrate the engagement of Lady Marciana and Tribune Gaius Marius Septimus. First, following the victory over the gladiators, by which Septimus freed the city of Rome from the tyranny of Nepotian the Usurper, the legionaries of Third Italica acclaimed him 'Romanus.' So, bowing to the wish of the legion, the Roman Senate voted to award Septimus the agnomen of *Romanus*."

Shouts of "Hail, Septimus Romanus!" echoed in the hall.

Septimus turned red. He shook his head as his eyes met those of his father, Senator Marius. "You did this." *It is a rare thing to be awarded an agnomen, by the Roman Senate no less,* he thought to himself. He scanned the room. Red marbled columns, spaced at intervals along the inner walls, alternated with niches containing statues of notable ancestors of the Marii family—senators, generals, and consuls—going back four centuries to the days of the Republic.

Observing these ancestors, Septimus winced. *Romanus. "Conqueror of Rome"? It was a just minor insurrection, a glorified riot. This is a terrible mistake. I am not worthy of such an honor.*

Marcellinus invited Septimus to stand. "Last of all, the Emperor, upon my recommendation, and with the approval of the Senate and the people of Rome, has appointed Septimus the legionary commander of Third Italica."

Marcellinus raised his cup. "Therefore, a toast! I present to you for the first time—Tribune Gaius Marius Septimus Romanus, commander of the Third Italica."

While the guests gave the tribune a standing ovation, Marciana entered the hall. When Septimus caught sight of her, he forgot the pain of embarrassment, and the grimace he wore because of it faded away. Now his face beamed with affection as his eyes followed Marciana across the room until she took her place again by his side. She kissed him. "I am so proud of you."

Eumaeus and another slave who had followed behind her set a stand on the floor in the center of the banquet hall. The stand was draped with a large cloth that hid its contents.

When the shouts and cheers faded away, Marciana approached the covered stand which stood higher than she. "The senator and Lady Camilia must be very proud of their son tonight—as am I." She glanced at Septimus. "Close your eyes." She then addressed the seated guests. "I was hard-pressed for ideas for an engagement gift for Tribune Marius. And as the ladies know, it is hard to find a present for a man. But when General Marcellinus confided in me this great news, it gave me the idea I needed."

Marciana pulled off the cover to reveal the uniform of a legionary commander. The silver armor, draped with a bright scarlet cloak and topped with a plumed helmet, sparkled in the torchlight. "Here is my gift to my Septimus Romanus. Something for him to wear on my wedding day." She kissed him on the cheek. "Open your eyes!"

The tribune looked at the gift. He ran his hands over the molded breastplate and examined the greaves, wrist plates, and sword.

Marciana, holding her hands together, pressed them to her chin in anticipation of his reaction. "I hope you like it. I know nothing of armor. Leontius helped me."

Septimus hugged Marciana. "I love it! It is magnificent. Thank you, my love."

She stood on her toes as he held her, straining to reach closer to whisper into his ear. "This gift is for our wedding day and parties, nor for battle. Nothing must happen to you. You must not go away if there is war. Ever. Promise me?"

Septimus drew his head back, his face colored with uncertainty. "Marciana," he replied, her name stumbling from his lips. He breathed in slow as he thought, about to say more, when he was interrupted.

"I propose a toast," said Leontius, as he stood and held up his cup. "We have, thus far this evening, heard from General Marcellinus, who sang the praises of Septimus Romanus."

"Please do not call me that," said Septimus.

"Nonsense!" said Leontius. He held up his hand. "Be quiet, Tribune Marius; you know I outrank you. I could have you thrown into the Tullianum." He walked over and stood between Septimus and Marciana. He then addressed himself to the guests. "Let us not lose sight on this occasion, when there are rumors of war, that the skills of a soldier—such as Septimus—or of Mars, the dread god of war himself, are not the most powerful forces in the world. It is true that with the martial skills heroes are made, battles won, and nations conquered." Leontius put his arms around both Septimus and Marciana. "Yet, I submit to you that the influence of Venus, goddess and patroness of love and passion, is more subtle and powerful. Venus over Mars—how can that be, you might ask. Do we not have it on the authority of the great poet, Virgil, that *love conquers all*? And what better example of these words do we have tonight than this couple?" He looked at the bride-to-be. "The beautiful Marciana is more dangerous than our Septimus. When the tribune saw her that first time by the Acqua Virgo, he fell in love with her at first sight. He was defenseless. Though our Septimus has vanquished many foes in combat, he was helpless against the beauty, charms, and wit of Marciana—the most beautiful and fairest of all Roman maidens! This evening, we have hailed Septimus as 'Romanus'—conqueror of Rome. But, let us not forget . . . while it was Septimus who conquered Rome, it was Marciana who conquered Septimus."

Leontius lifted his cup. "To Lady Marciana and Septimus! Love conquers all."

"Love conquers all!" cheered the guests as they joined in the toast.

Septimus and Marciana interlocked their arms as they drank from their cups. After taking their sips, he gazed into her eyes and they kissed.

When their lips parted, the tribune caught sight of a legionary at the entrance to the banquet hall. He was a tall, muscular man wearing scaled armor over a white tunic, grieves, and a blue cloak. Nine large silver medallions, awards from his service, covered the chest and stomach of his armor. He wore a helmet with a transverse crest with red plumes and carried a three-foot-long vine staff in one hand—each a sign of the military rank of centurion. Appearing to be about forty years of age, his face had a rough, weathered look of a seasoned veteran with many years of service in the legions. Scars on his arms were visible, and his nose had a slight bend to it from a break long ago.

The smile melted away from the tribune's face. "Longinus," he muttered to himself.

Marciana followed the eyes of the tribune to the legionary. The color drained away from her face. "I recognize him. That is one of your centurions, is it not? What is he doing here?"

The servant Eumaeus approached Septimus. "Tribune Marius, there is a centurion here. He wishes to speak with you and General Marcellinus on a matter of great urgency."

Septimus grimaced. "Have him wait for us in the library."

***

Marcellinus led Septimus, Silvanus, and Leontius into the senator's library. There stood the towering figure of the centurion.

"Longinus, I fear you are not here for the celebration," said Marcellinus.

The centurion saluted. "I am afraid not, sir," he said in a deep voice. He reached into a haversack slung over his shoulder. He produced a scroll which he handed to the general. "A dispatch

28

came by ship to Ostia. A message from Emperor Magnentius."

While the general read the message, Longinus turned to Septimus. "My apologies, Tribune Marius. I did not wish to interrupt your engagement party."

Septimus replied with a grim nod.

Marcellinus looked up from the message when he had finished reading it.

"War?" asked Silvanus.

Marcellinus nodded. "The bulk of the Eastern army has crossed the Hellespont. It must be in Sirmium by now." The general walked over to a map on the wall. "Magnentius is marching into Pannonia. Our Emperor intends to lay siege to Mursa Major and capture it to use as a base of operations. The Emperor has ordered all legions to join him there as soon as possible." Marcellinus handed the message to the officers to read, with Septimus being the last to review it. "The Emperor has canceled all leave. Officers are to return to their units without delay or exception."

The general looked at the young tribune. "I am sorry Septimus—for you and Marciana both. Unfortunately, we must now put our personal affairs aside."

Septimus nodded.

The general faced each of the officers in turn as he issued his own orders for them. "Silvanus, you and I will make overland and rejoin the bulk of our legions encamped near Aquileia. Leontius, you are to stay here in Rome as prefect of the city garrison to maintain order—and to ensure the allegiance of the city to Magnentius. Septimus, you must rejoin your legion near Ostia and then march at best speed to join us at Mursa Major."

Septimus lowered his eyes. *Marciana.*

"I am sorry for you, Septimus," said Marcellinus. "War is never convenient." The general departed with Silvanus to prepare for their journey.

"I, too, am sorry for you and Marciana," said Leontius, who then followed the general out of the room.

Septimus still held the message from Magnentius in his hands. He read it again.

Longinus broke the silence. "Your orders, Tribune?"

Septimus glanced up from the scroll. "Go. At once. Hire a boat to take us down the Tiber tonight to Ostia."

The door to the library burst open. Marciana rushed in, her eyes red and welled up with tears. Seeing the centurion, she scowled at him. "You were not invited here this evening."

Longinus bowed. "My apologies, Lady Marciana—I was just leaving." He looked to Septimus. "I will make the arrangements," he said as he departed.

When the centurion had gone, Septimus took Marciana's hands into his own. "Marciana, you should not have been so rude to the centurion. He is doing his duty."

"He is a Christian . . . a harbinger of grave tidings," she said. "Silvanus told me the news on his way out."

"My love, please do not speak that way of the centurion."

"I know the general is a Christian, too . . . I like him, but why would he give you command of a Christian legion? You are not one of them. You believe in the gods of Rome and Greece. Christians have brought bad luck to the empire. I fear your Christian legion will now bring bad luck to you."

Septimus frowned.

Marciana flung her arms around him. "Do not be angry with me. We must not be cross with one another, now or ever. Our wedding is next week."

The tribune did not respond.

She touched his cheeks and lowered his head until their eyes met. "What did the centurion mean by *arrangements*?"

Septimus averted his eyes from hers.

"You are leaving soon?" she asked.

"Tonight."

"Tonight? What of our wedding?"

Septimus's jaw tightened. "It cannot be helped," he said, just above a whisper. "I have my orders."

"Why must you go to war?" she asked. "There are other officers."

"They are all being recalled to duty."

"Resign," she suggested.

"I cannot do that. Not now."

"Yes, you can. Your father is a Roman senator with connections and influence. Your family is one of the wealthiest in the empire.

You could get out of this war—if you wanted. Buy your way out. We could run off together and live on one of your family's estates in Iberia. Let someone else take your place."

Septimus shook his head. "There is my duty to my legion . . . to myself . . . to what is right. One cannot surrender honor and send another in his place. I must be faithful to my legion." He pulled her close. "If I were to do what you suggest, I would not be the man with whom you fell in love."

Marciana broke away from him. She stepped back. Tears flowed down her cheeks as she sobbed. "I hate you," she said as she fled the library.

Septimus reflected for several moments before hurrying after her. Rushing down the hallway, he encountered Leontius who placed an arm across his path, blocking his pursuit of Marciana.

"I saw her go by in tears," said Leontius. "Whatever she said to you, she does not mean it. She is upset. I will speak to her on your behalf. She loves you. You know that. Do not worry."

"You are a good friend," replied Septimus.

"You saved my life, remember? It is the least I can do."

"Look after her until my return."

"Upon my life, I will do so."

***

Septimus stood outside the now silent and darkened banquet room visualizing the happy moments of the party, although the guests had long since departed. In his mind, he heard the happy strains of the flutes and lyres, and the thumping of drums and the ringing of tambourines. Before him now was not an empty hall but one full of people dancing and laughing, bright sunlight from the terrace illuminating everything. There on the floor, he saw his beautiful Marciana, beckoning to him, waving for him to join her.

"All is ready, Tribune," said Eumaeus, standing beside him with a torch.

The servant had startled Septimus from his happy vision.

The apparition melted away. Gone was the bright dining hall, the music, the guests, and the laughter, and gone too was Marciana, all replaced once again with shadow and silence. From within the hall, the light of the torch reflected off the suit of armor Marciana had given him. It still stood alone in the center of the banquet room.

The tribune lowered his head.

"Your baggage is loaded on the carriage," said Eumaeus. "I have saddled Ulysses."

"Fortunes change as day into night," said Septimus. "Just hours ago, there was music, wine, and laughter. Family. Friends. Marciana. Now, I leave all I know and love behind."

Eumaeus noticed the glint of the armor. "Tribune Marius, my apologies—there is still time to pack this gift of armor for your journey."

"Leave it."

"Leave it?"

"I promised Marciana that I would wear it on her wedding day. I will not wear it before then."

***

Septimus rode Ulysses through the streets of Rome while his dog ran along with them. The servant Eumaeus followed behind in the carriage. Passing through the center of the city, they arrived at the Temple of Venus and Eternal Rome. The temple was, in reality, two temples combined, built back to back. One was dedicated to Eternal Rome and the other to Venus, Bringer of Good Fortune. Across from the temples loomed the Coliseum. The white marble facades of the buildings, bathed in bright torchlight, stood out against the black of night that enveloped all else.

Septimus dismounted at the foot of the steps of the dual temple. "Wait here," he said to Eumaeus. He ascended the steps to the temple.

"Good evening, Tribune," said one of the watchmen, as he stood aside to let Septimus pass inside the temple of Venus. Inside, Septimus stood alone before the giant statue of Venus, gilded in gold, seated upon a throne. The pupils of her eyes, made of large black stones, seemed to follow him.

"Venus, Bringer of Good Fortune, return me safe and whole to Marciana," Septimus prayed, his voice echoing in the empty space.

He made an offering of burnt incense to the goddess and then returned to his horse.

The tribune's eyes widened when he caught sight of Argus. The dog sat at the feet of Ulysses wagging his tail.

"I did not realize you followed me from home," said Septimus. He got down on one knee and patted the dog on the head. "You should not have come along, Argus, faithful friend. I cannot take you with me where I am going."

The dog whimpered.

The tribune smiled, a wistful look on his face. "Not you too! I have already had too many long goodbyes this night. They are the hardest and saddest of goodbyes." The tribune hugged the dog one last time. "Farewell, old friend."

Septimus mounted his horse. He rode several yards then stopped. He glanced back at Argus who had moved to follow him. He held out his hand. "Stay!"

Argus tilted his head to one side.

"Stay," commanded the tribune. The dog laid on the street and placed his head between his paws and watched as the tribune proceeded on his way.

Septimus and Eumaeus came at last to the Porticus Aemilia along the Tiber River. There he found Longinus waiting for him with a hired barge. Crewmen brought the baggage from the cart onto the craft. A mist rose from the river and drifted toward shore. As if rung by an invisible hand, a small bell rang out slow and somber as its clapper swayed back and forth with a soft breeze rolling off the water. *It is as I imagine the Styx might appear,* thought Septimus. He gathered his cloak over his shoulders as a chill entered the air. *It must be an omen of disaster. I am certain of it. An omen of doom.* The fog began to thicken, making it difficult to discern shapes and objects only a few feet away.

"Tribune," called Longinus from the barge. "We must go."

Septimus led Ulysses along the wharf. He turned to Eumaeus. "Take care of my parents while I am gone."

"You have my promise, Tribune."

"Mind Argus. Be sure he gets home."

The servant nodded.

"Farewell, Eumaeus, until my happy return," said Septimus.

THE TWO KINGDOMS

Then, guiding Ulysses up the gangway, he boarded the boat.

Chapter 3

A Wedding

(Constantinople, Late Spring, 351 AD)

Julian leaned against a column of the long colonnade beside the Great Palace. Laughter and the strains of music from the palace's banquet hall echoed along the colonnade. Yet, Julian heard and saw nothing as his thoughts drifted back to his recent encounter with the other world in the Temple of Hecate. Obsessed with what he had witnessed, he was oblivious to his current surroundings. Giant statues of emperors and heroes of the past stood in niches in the wall which lined the way. Lifelike in color and appearance, they seemed to look out with him over the Hippodrome—the large chariot racing stadium just below and beside the palace—and beyond it, the city of Constantinople. Domes of basilicas and roofs of monumental buildings, covered in brass and gold leaf, glittered in the last rays of the setting sun.

"There you are, little brother!" came a voice from behind.

Wakened from his daydreaming, Julian turned to see who it was. There stood a handsome and muscular man in his mid-twenties who wore an ornate armored breastplate with his military uniform. Both the plume of his helmet and his cloak were purple, signifying his high rank.

Julian's face lit up at once. "Gallus!"

Gallus took off his helmet, revealing his curly, yellow hair. He stood beside Julian to take in the vista with him. "Look at it . . . the City of Constantine." Gallus faced one of the statues in a niche across the colonnade. He saluted the figure with a wineskin he carried over his shoulder and took a swig. "Indeed . . . a city of emperors!" He placed his arm around Julian. "We have not had time to chat, little brother. Why are you off by yourself—away from the celebration?"

Gallus offered him a drink.

"I am not one for parties," said Julian as he pushed it away. "But, congratulations on your wedding day. You look happy."

"Ha! I am happy, but not at the thought of being married to that ugly cousin of ours, Constantina."

Julian burst into a laugh but fought to stifle it in case imperial spies might overhear such an indiscretion regarding the Emperor's sister.

"You laugh because you know it to be true—you mock me!" Gallus chuckled. "She has over ten years on me. She is thirty-eight years old, but I swear she looks to be a dozen years older than that."

"Then why marry her?"

"Then you have not heard?"

"Heard what?"

"Our cousin, the Emperor Constantius, has elevated me to the rank of Caesar."

"A Caesar?"

"I am to rule the Eastern Empire while he is away in the West."

"How is this possible? What do you mean, *while he is away in the West?*"

"Have you not kept up with events during your studies in Pergamum?" asked Gallus. "Our uncle Constans was murdered last year in Italy and the throne of the Western Empire usurped by General Magnentius. Our armies gather in Sirmium even now. Constantius will leave in a few days to lead them into the West to regain the lost throne and unite the empire under himself."

Julian ran his thumb and fingers along the sides of his dark beard as he contemplated what he had just heard. "You are to be a Caesar? It seems unbelievable."

Gallus moved to the edge of the colonnade and looked toward the city. "Think of how grim our fortunes once were, Julian. Over a dozen years ago—in the days following the death of Constantine—

36

rioting soldiers murdered our father, brother, and many of our uncles and cousins. Some say Constantius incited the soldiers to kill our kinsmen to secure the throne of the Eastern Empire for himself. You and I were mere children then, fearing for our own lives. Now look at us, little brother—here tonight in the Great Palace—many years later, I stand here before you, a Caesar! Married to the sister of the Emperor."

"Fortune has favored you, brother," said Julian.

"No. Fortune has favored us ... both of us!" said Gallus, as he placed his hands on either side of his brother's pudgy, bearded face. "As my fortunes rise, so do yours." Gallus then led Julian to the center of the colonnade. He fixed his eyes on those of his brother. "But fortune is fickle. Many members of a family may suffer for the indiscretions of only one."

"What do you mean?" asked Julian.

"Be careful of the company you keep."

"The company I keep?"

"Company such as your philosopher friends in Pergamum."

"You mean my instructors?" asked Julian.

Gallus smirked. "Do not play your game with me, little brother. You have convinced Constantius that you study the Greek classics in Pergamum. But I know the truth about you—that your true interest is in the gods of the Greeks and Romans."

"But—"

"I know the reputation of your instructors. You have hidden this from Constantius and his spies, but you cannot hide it from me."

Julian blushed. *What has he learned about me?*

Gallus took another swig of wine. He glared at Julian. "Maximus of Ephesus is one of your friends. He is not an 'instructor' in Greek classics or philosophy, but a practitioner of the dark arts of the Old Religion ... a magician ... a sorcerer."

"I do not know what you are talking about," said Julian, his eyes avoiding contact with those of his brother.

Gallus placed his hand over Julian's mouth to quiet his protests. "You know the law against sorcery and magic. Constantius would have Maximus's head on the point of a spear and yours alongside it—if he discovered the truth about this man."

Julian wiped away beads of sweat from above his manicured eyebrows.

"You are wondering how I know this?" asked Gallus.

"Captain Marcus?"

Gallus nodded. "He is a loyal friend. He has done me and you a favor. You are fortunate the spies of the Emperor were more interested in wine and women than are you."

Gallus placed a hand against Julian's face. "But do not worry, little brother. I have no interest in matters of religion. Catholic. Arian. The gods of Rome and Greece. I have no interest in any of them, whatsoever. Expediency is my 'faith.' Were Constantine still alive, I would profess myself Catholic. Were Diocletian still emperor, a pagan. The present fashion under our cousin Constantius favors the Arians. So, I will be one too, if necessary. Never let faith stand in the way of your rise in this world, little brother. Change what you believe like you do your clothes to suit the weather. Expediency, I say—when doing or saying otherwise might discomfort or prove fatal." Gallus chuckled. "You have chosen the old gods of the Greeks and the Romans. I have chosen mine—me, myself, and I."

Julian took several steps backward, away from his brother. *He has discovered my secret.* His mind raced, and the beat of his heart quickened. *He knows of my apostasy from the Christian faith.* Julian backed into the pedestal of a statue, which startled him. "What is it you ask of me?"

"The secret of your apostasy is safe with me," said Gallus. "But it is not me you need to worry about. You should be concerned with our dear cousin Constantius. He barely tolerates Catholics in his family or in the imperial court. Even less would he tolerate an apostate among his kin—not one who practices the Old Religion and consorts with magicians and sorcerers! Do not be so stupid and foolhardy to imperil this opportunity. Who knows where this path will lead me—one day I might become joint emperor with Constantius. It can happen! Today a Caesar, tomorrow an Augustus. Who is to say? You can be by my side the entire way, little brother."

Gallus placed his helmet back on his head. "But, if Constantius discovers your secret, I cannot save you, nor will I try. Do not jeopardize this opportunity for yourself. I will not allow you to jeopardize it for me." His jaw set firm, he studied his brother. "Do we understand one another?"

I am discovered, found out, trapped, thought Julian. He could feel the blood coursing through his veins. *I have no choice but to trust my brother's discretion. Surely, he will not surrender me to the Emperor. Would he?*

"Do we have an understanding?" repeated Gallus, impatient for an answer.

Julian nodded.

"Good," replied Gallus. He then observed a small crowd of people flanked by palace guards approaching them along the colonnade. "The Emperor comes."

Emperor Constantius, wearing a white toga with a broad purple border, approached the two brothers. A golden diadem, encrusted with jewels, rested atop his head. The Empress, frail in bearing and pale in appearance, walked beside him, seeming to support herself by resting a hand upon her husband's forearm. Behind them followed an entourage which included a dozen or more imperial officials, court bishops, and imperial guards.

"Ah, Gallus, I thought we had lost you," Constantius said. He glanced back at a woman in his entourage. Dressed in a white stola, a garland of flowers sat upon her head. "Your place is with Constantina, your bride."

Gallus bowed. "I would not choose any other place, sire. I went to find my brother." Taking his place beside Constantina, he gave her a peck on the cheek.

The Emperor fixed his dark eyes upon the younger prince and frowned. "Julian, where have you been all day? You should be seen with the rest of the imperial family. It is not often I recall you from your studies to public life, but when I do so, I expect you to be . . . well . . . public."

Always anxious in the presence of the Emperor, Julian remained speechless. He could only lower his head in submission.

The Emperor looked to one of the two court bishops. "Now what were we discussing, Valens?" he asked of a red-bearded bishop.

"Remember, Athanasius," interjected the other court bishop, a heavyset man named Ursacius.

The Emperor grit his teeth at the sound of the name of Athanasius, and his jaw muscles twitched as if fighting against a fit of anger. "Quite right, Ursacius!" he said. He then turned to Gallus. "You will need to keep an eye on Bishop Athanasius of Alexandria while I am away in the west. He has been obstructing my efforts to reconcile the Arians to the Church."

"Obstructing, sire?" asked Gallus.

"Over twenty-five years ago the Council of Nicaea ruled against the Arians, who in their doctrine deny that Christ is God," said Constantius. "In punishment, my late father exiled many of the Arian leaders. But, now, we have many external threats in the east, such as the Parthians. We cannot alienate any part of the population at a time like this. What are Athanasius and his allies thinking? I cannot afford division and controversy within the empire."

"The Emperor, in his beneficence, wishes to reconcile the peoples still attached to the doctrines of Arius," said Valens, his long red beard flowing over his clerical robes. "The Nicene doctrine is too firm and unyielding, teaching that Christ is eternally God. This view does not accommodate the opinions of those whom the Emperor wishes to reconcile. There must be flexibility. There must be mercy for those with contrary opinions."

"We need a creed which all parties can affirm—a compromise formula," said Ursacius. "However, Athanasius insists on the Creed of Nicaea and riles the people against the bishops of the Eastern Empire who might agree to a compromise."

"Arrest Athanasius!" said Gallus.

"Yes!" said the two bishops.

Constantius held up his hand to quiet everyone. "If only it were that simple. We will be at war soon with the West, where a quarter of the population is Christian, and which supports the teaching of Nicaea. I cannot afford Alexandria and the rest of Egypt going over to the enemy's side. No, we must wait." He glanced at the court bishops. "Fear not, your excellencies. I will settle accounts with Athanasius once the war is over. For now, we must leave him be."

A WEDDING

***

Athanasius, Bishop of Alexandria, stood at a stone railing overlooking the city. The setting sun lit the facade of Great Palace which stood high over a wide terrace outside the banquet hall. A few wedding guests strolled about outside enjoying the evening air while most remained within the banquet finishing their dinners. Beside the bishop stood two men dressed in the uniforms of senior military officers.

As he looked out over the city, Athanasius addressed the two men with him. "General Florentius . . . Count Varronius, it is good to see you both again." The two men towered over the shorter Athanasius, who stood a little over five feet high. "Long has it been since I have been to Constantinople—not since the days of Constantine. The city has changed much since those days."

"The empire has changed much in my fifty plus years," said Florentius. "Under Constantine it was one and unified. With his passing, it was divided between his sons. There was at first the hope they might rule together in peace." He shook his head. "But, neither the bonds of blood nor of faith proved strong enough to secure tranquility amongst them. Now, of the three brothers, Constantius alone survives."

Count Varronius, who appeared the same age as Florentius, nodded. "Yes, he survives . . . but with only half of the empire that his father bequeathed to his three sons."

Athanasius followed the terrace rail until he reached the northeast corner. From this new vantage, they overlooked scaffolding surrounding a great basilica under construction just north of the Great Palace. "Back then too, the faith of the city and of the Church was one and unified following the Council of Nicaea." He looked at the construction. "What sort of Church would Constantius build now?"

Florentius leaned against the railing. "Constantius has fallen under the influence of Arian-minded clerics and eunuchs—once banished by his father."

The bishop shook his head. "Constantinople seems fated ever to be a city of religious controversies." He turned his back to the railing and looked toward the entrance to the banquet hall. A slight frown came upon his face. "I had hoped to speak with more friends of old during my visit, but none but yourselves have spoken with me."

"I am sorry to say it, but they keep their distance from you," said Florentius. "Fearing the Arians who have the ear of the Emperor, they do not want to be seen in your company. Grand Chamberlain Eusebius and the court bishops—Valens and Ursacius—are ever at the side of the Emperor saying to him, 'remember Athanasius,' ever hoping to incite him to take action against you once again."

"Then it is dangerous for you to be seen with me," said the bishop. "I pray you to keep your distance. I would not want the Emperor's ill opinion of me to bring his displeasure down upon you."

Count Varronius waved his hand at the thought, dismissing the bishop's concern. "Do not worry about us. We are old soldiers . . . accustomed to danger."

Florentius fixed his eyes on Athanasius. "Do not underestimate the guile or determination of those who surround the Emperor. They will not rest until you are deposed and every one of the Episcopal thrones of the East has Arian-friendly bishops seated upon them."

"You cannot compromise the truth," replied Athanasius. "True peace is not born of lies."

"If they gain the power, they would depose Catholic bishops and faithful from the churches," said Varronius.

"Though they may have the buildings, we will have the faith," replied Athanasius.

Varronius watched as a young officer, hobbling on a cane, came out of the banquet hall onto the terrace and approached them. "Your Excellency, Athanasius, may I present to you my son, Lucius. He is a captain of the cavalry."

Athanasius smiled. "I remember you as an infant, Lucius. How you have grown so. Is your brother Jovian here with you in the city as well?"

"Jovian is with the army in Antioch," replied Lucius, a young man of twenty-two years with thinning hair.

"You are a fine-looking young lad," said Athanasius. "I

42

remember you as a young boy in Alexandria." Athanasius looked at Lucius who supported his left leg with a cane. It appeared thin and weak beneath his military trousers. "What happened to your leg, my son?"

"A riding accident," replied Lucius.

The count grimaced. "It has been many months, but the leg has not mended properly. Lucius will not be able to ride a horse again."

Lucius lowered his head. "At least not well enough to stay in the cavalry."

"I am sorry to hear it," said the bishop.

"Although he cannot serve in the cavalry, Captain Lucius will serve as my chief aide on the army's planning staff," said Florentius. "He will be my right arm."

Lucius bowed his head. "I thank you again for the appointment, General. I could not bear to sit out this war—to see my friends march off and fight while I stay behind, a cripple."

Athanasius turned to Florentius. "I have yet to see any one of your family this evening."

"My sons are at school in Antioch and Caesarea Maritima," said Florentius. "But you shall see my wife Portia, and my daughter—they are both here, somewhere. I lost them in the crowd after the wedding mass." He cast a glance toward the banquet hall. "At the moment, I suspect my wife is otherwise occupied somewhere in the palace. No doubt, she is on the lookout for suitable romantic matches for Melissa, who is attending her first imperial event. There is little hope in distracting Lady Portia from that objective until she has introduced our nineteen-year-old to as many eligible, young officers as possible." He patted Lucius on the shoulder. "You are an eligible man. Prepare yourself! My wife will have you in mind for our daughter."

Lucius smiled. "I hope so, General. I remember Melissa from when I was a toddler. I expect she is quite beautiful now."

***

Melissa straightened the sapphire blue tunic that clung to her voluptuous form. Her long brown hair was set in a bun, from which shoulder-length ringlets hung. Around her neck, she wore a silver necklace. The young beauty looked about with wide eyes as her senses took in her first experience of an imperial celebration. Senators in their official togas, robed clergy, officers with plumed helmets and cloaks, and noble ladies wearing colorful stolas strolled or mingled in groups within the banquet hall. The aromas of roasted meats, sweet fruits, and fine wine filled the air, and as did the songs of musicians playing their lyres and flutes. As the sun disappeared beneath the distant horizon, Melissa and her friends—chaperoned by her mother, the Lady Portia—walked out onto the terrace. Palace slaves hurried to light the torches spaced at regular intervals along the terrace railing and the braziers set upon tripods beside each of the statues along the colonnade.

Melissa turned to one of the several young women with her. "Weddings are wonderful. I would love to hear the story of how the couple met—I love a romantic tale."

Lady Portia, her brunette hair now almost all gray, glanced back at her daughter. She shook her head. "Melissa, you and your tales of romance, again."

"Do not shake your head mother." Melissa turned to the young woman next to her. "Princess Helena, it is your sister who has been married this day to your cousin—tell us their tale."

Helena, a pretty girl who was the same age as Melissa, wore a tiara in her blonde hair. "I think the story of this couple would disappoint you, my dear friend. There is nothing romantic about it."

"A marriage not romantic?"

"It is an official act of state, you might say—arranged for the good of the empire."

"An arranged marriage?"

Helena nodded. "Just as my brother Constantius married a cousin for the good of the empire, today my sister Constantina married our cousin Gallus for the good of the empire. In fact, this is her second such marriage to a cousin. The first had a tragic ending."

Melissa frowned.

Helena giggled. She touched the forearm of her friend. "See! I told you their story would disappoint you. I'm sorry that I have been the one to ruin your dream of a romantic tale."

44

"But how is the good of the empire served by the marriage of your sister to Gallus?" asked Aurelia, one of the other young women who walked with them. However, without the advantages of Melissa's figure or Helena's imperial title, the plumpish Aurelia did not attract as much attention from the men as did Melissa and Helena.

"It has to do with the coming civil war," said Helena. "While my brother, Constantius, is away in the West with the army, Gallus will rule the East. The marriage strengthens the bond of trust between them. Gallus will rule in the stead of Constantius—not only as a cousin but now as a brother."

Melissa shook her head. "I would never accept an arranged marriage."

"Not even if you gained an empire by it?" asked Aurelia. "You would not want to be an empress if you could?"

Melissa leaned against the terrace railing. "Only true love and romance for me," she said as she viewed Constantinople in the fading twilight. The light from lanterns and torches began to appear like stars from windows and along the city's avenues.

"Who is to say love and romance cannot be found in an arranged marriage?" asked Helena, as she straightened the tiara on her head then brushed the sides of her purple and white tunic. "I hope it is possible. As an imperial princess, like my sister, the Emperor will choose my husband for me." The princess grinned. "If so, I hope he is as handsome as Gallus." Her smile dissolved into a frown. "It should have been my place to marry him. Gallus and I are closer in age than are he and Constantina. My sister is a dozen years older than him. He would have been happier with a younger wife . . . rather than with my sister—the old shrew!"

Melissa burst into a laugh, joined by Helena and Aurelia. Nearby along the railing, a group of nobles and their wives, the peace of their quiet conversation disturbed by the laughter, glanced in their direction with scowls upon their faces.

Seeing their reaction, Portia brought a finger to her lips. "Shush, girls! To speak of or laugh at such things in the Great Palace is not wise."

Helena lowered her voice. "Constantius thought he needed a shrew, like my sister—with experience as the wife of a king—to keep a close and watchful eye on Gallus ... the man who will govern his empire while he is gone." She giggled. "Gallus to rule the East. Constantina to rule Gallus!"

"Constantina had been a wife of a king?" asked Melissa.

"She was married to my cousin, Hannibalianus, who my father, Constantine, made a king,"

"What happened to him?"

Portia glanced back at the women. "I do not think we should chat about Constantina's past." Her voice was firm. "The imperial court is full of straining ears and loose mouths. Some topics are best left alone."

Chastened for the moment, the women walked on in silence. After strolling another dozen yards, the princess paused when she saw a male slave passing through the midst of the guests and carrying a platter of wine. Grabbing two cups, Helena leaned close to Melissa as she handed one to her. "Some say my brother had him executed," she whispered.

Melissa gasped, bringing a hand to her mouth.

"It can be a dangerous thing to marry into my family," said Helena. She rolled her eyes upward as if to look at the tiara set in her blonde hair on her head. "It can be dangerous to be in the imperial family."

Portia glanced back at the women and shook her head. "Enough of such tragic tales! Instead, let us speak of happy unions and marriages yet to be. There are many eligible officers and court officials here for you young ladies to meet and gossip about afterward." She fixed her attention on her daughter. "Which reminds me, Melissa—your father appointed a young captain to his staff the other day. His name is Lucius. He is the son of Count Varronius, an old friend of your father from his days in the navy in Alexandria. I understand Lucius is here this evening. You must meet him."

Melissa closed her eyes in frustration. "My parents have wanted to arrange a marriage between Lucius and me, though I haven't seen him since we were small children," she whispered to Helena. "I would never agree to an arranged marriage."

"Do not dismiss the possibility," interjected Portia without turning around to face the girls. "He was handsome when I last saw him."

Helena smiled. "Your mother hears everything!"

Melissa sighed. "Mother, he was a toddler when last you saw him! You cannot know how he has turned out since then. Whether he be handsome or not." She took a long sip from the cup of wine that the princess had given her. *I need this.*

Portia led the young women along the railing, nodding now and again to acknowledge officials and their wives with whom she was acquainted as they passed. "Well . . . it might have been long ago. But a handsome toddler he was—and, I am sure, destined to have become a handsome young man."

Melissa started to reply, then bit her lip. *Best to ignore her and enjoy the evening.* She scanned her surroundings and then inhaled as if to breathe it all in. The terrace of the Great Palace and the colonnade beside the Hippodrome were now teeming with hundreds of the wedding guests who had by now migrated from inside the banquet hall to the outdoors to enjoy the cool of the evening beneath the starlight. The night air itself seemed to be alive as the light from the flaming torches and braziers glimmered and reflected off the breastplates and helmets of the officers and the necklaces and bracelets of the women. Musicians with lyres, harp, and flute, playing softly, wandered here and there in twos or threes among dignitaries. The strains from their instruments echoing along the colonnade. Melissa smiled. *I wish I could hold on to this night and never let it go.*

Melissa's moment of ecstasy was interrupted by the sight of her mother waving to a group of young officers she had spied but thirty feet away. Melissa took another swig of her wine. *Mother, stop!* She turned to the princess. "This is my first formal event at court," she whispered. "Father gave Mother the task of shielding us from young officers—not hurling us at them."

Helena smiled. "I don't mind. Would you rather not meet any officers?"

"There is a happy medium. But mother only treads along the edges of the extremes."

Melissa tapped her mother on the shoulder. "Leave those officers be. I am neither in a rush nor as desperate to meet men as you appear to be for me. Your help is neither wanted nor needed. I am content to let love find me where and when it might and in its good time."

"Ha!" Portia snickered. "There is a word for the woman who wanted to let love 'find' her—"

Annoyed, Melissa averted her eyes from her mother's. *I know, I know. I have heard this many times before.*

"And that word is 'spinster,'" said Portia, as Melissa mouthed the word along with her. "Every daughter can use a mother's help in finding a man." She paused when she observed the Emperor and Empress, followed by their entourage, greeting guests on the terrace. From afar, Portia examined each of the men with the Emperor. She turned to Helena. "Princess, you know everyone in the imperial court."

"Most everyone," replied Helena.

Portia fixed her attention on one man in particular standing with the Emperor. "Who is that? The finely dressed, blonde-haired one, with the red belt and sash."

Melissa took a deep breath. *Here we go, again. I know where this is headed.*

The princess cast a glance at Melissa and fought back a smile. "That is a very important man. He is Eusebius, the Grand Chamberlain . . . one of the closest advisors to my brother."

"He is handsome and not too old for Melissa," said Portia. "Has he a wife?"

Melissa glared at her mother. *Mother. No. Stop.*

"No, he does not," said Helena.

Portia clasped Melissa by the forearm. "There . . . you see . . . a fine potential catch. A mother can sense these things." She adjusted the tunic on Melissa to ensure it showed off her ample figure.

"You need not bother with that one for Melissa," said Helena, fighting back the urge to smile.

"Not bother with a handsome, important, and single man—why not, Princess?"

"Because he is a eunuch."

The young women broke out again in laughter. The officials in the company of the Emperor glanced over at the young women.

Melissa saw that one of the officials next to the Emperor, a senior officer in a black tunic and cloak, and a black plumed

48

helmet, was staring at her. *His eyes are on my body. He is leering at me.* She blushed a deep red. *I don't like it.* She then turned her back to him.

"Helena, who is that officer in black?" Melissa asked. "The tall, slender one."

"That is Arbitio, the Commander of the Imperial Guard," said the princess.

Portia looked over to the officer in black. "Yes, he is handsome enough. I'd say in his thirties. That is not too old for you, Melissa."

"Enough," whispered Melissa to her mother with a hiss. She then turned to see that Arbitio was still watching her. *Never in a million years.*

"Giggle if you want, girls, and dismiss my efforts to find you a husband, Melissa," said Portia. She wagged a finger at the young women. "But, if you do, it is your own folly and to your own nuptial peril. The Emperor soon marches the army into the West. The city will be empty of eligible men from the better families—and all that will be left to keep you company will be the eunuchs, who are ever more common these days. Quite an unnatural thing to do, if you ask me."

"The city will be emptied?" asked Melissa, disappointment in her voice. *But we have only just got here.*

The princess gave a solemn nod, sharing in her friend's gloom. "No more banquets or parties."

"No banquets, no parties, and no eligible men," said Portia. "And who knows how long this war may last."

"A city long emptied and without a social life simply will not do for us," said Helena. She squinted as she thought to herself. After a long silence, she took Melissa by the hand. "I have an idea. Many wives of senior officers and officials, and other ladies of the court, including the Empress, plan to go with their menfolk when the army marches off to campaign in the West. My brother has asked me to come along to keep the Empress company."

"How exciting!" said Melissa. "I wish I could do that."

"But that is my idea," said Helena. "You must come along to keep me company—and your mother as well to chaperone us both and keep us out of mischief."

Melissa's green eyes seemed to sparkle at the suggestion. "That

49

would be wonderful. I have never been farther west than Constantinople. I want to see the lands and cities of the West. Mediolanum. Sirmium. Arelate. Rome!" Her smile melted away, replaced by a frown. She turned to her mother. "But would father let us accompany the court and the army?"

It was now Portia who flagged down a slave with a wine platter. Waiting for her response to Melissa's question, the women watched in silence as she took a cup. Portia leaned back against the marble railing, and slumping against it as if in defeat, she rested her elbow upon it. She looked down over the empty Hippodrome, its track and the statues which ringed the oval top of the stadium well-illuminated for the occasion of the wedding.

"Well?" asked Melissa, impatient. "Would Father let us accompany him?"

Portia sipped her wine. "Your father has been a military man as long as I have known him. Not once has he taken me on a campaign—even though other officers brought their wives along with them. I am sure he would never agree to it now."

Melissa turned to Helena. She pouted. "Mother is right. No one could convince my father to let us go."

A sly smile crept across Helena's face, and there was a twinkle in her brown eyes.

"What is it, Helena?" asked Melissa. *I know that look.* "What are you planning."

"I will ask my brother to convince him," said Helena.

"Convince my father? Not likely."

"You forget. My brother is Emperor—and emperors can be very convincing," said the princess. She pointed across the terrace. "There, I see my brother—even now he approaches your father, Bishop Athanasius and Count Varronius." She winked at Melissa. "Come along and see how I will get my big brother to convince your father."

"Lucius is over there too," said Portia, as she brushed back a lock of Melissa's brown hair which had fallen across her forehead. "He is the new officer on your father's staff that I told you about and wanted you to meet, Melissa. Yes, come along, dear."

***

Melissa followed Helena as she rushed to see her brother. Right behind them were Portia and Aurelia. When they reached the Emperor, they found he was surrounded by a small crowd of hangers-on that the women struggled with difficulty to find their way through. As they pressed their way through the throng of officials and sycophants, Melissa heard her father's voice and then saw him through a gap of bodies.

"Hail, Augustus!" said Florentius as the Emperor, the Empress, and their entourage approached.

Athanasius and Varronius greeted the Emperor with a bow. "Hail, Augustus!"

Emperor Constantius acknowledged their obeisance with a polite nod and a slight wave of his hand. "Bishop Athanasius, may I present to you the bride and groom—my sister Constantina and my cousin Gallus."

Swaying back and forth where he stood, Gallus raised his wineskin to toast the bishop. Julian reached out and grabbed him, preventing the Caesar from tumbling over.

The Emperor rolled his eyes at the sight. He pressed on with the introductions. "And my cousin, Prince Julian. He is a student of . . ."

Constantius paused for a moment. He raised an eyebrow and glanced at Julian. "What is it you are studying?"

"The Greek classics, my lord," replied the prince.

Constantius fixed his attention on Athanasius. "I have elevated Gallus to the rank of Caesar. He will rule in the East while I attend to affairs in the West. I trust Alexandria will not give him any trouble while I am away."

"There will be peace as long I have a say," replied Athanasius.

Bishop Ursacius stepped forward. The rotund cleric dressed in black robes glared as he pointed a finger at Athanasius. "There will peace as long as the bishop of Alexandria watches what he teaches."

Alongside Helena, Melissa emerged from the crowd into the midst of the circle surrounding the Emperor. She was disturbed to have happened upon what seemed a tense standoff between two bishops. The bearded Ursacius towered over the bishop of

51

Alexandria, who she reckoned was no taller than she. *Yet, the taller bishop seems to fear the bishop of Alexandria who in his countenance is friendly, peaceful and confident.*

Constantius lifted his hand and gestured for silence. "Your excellencies, we will not argue theology this evening. It is a wedding feast."

It was at that moment that Princess Helena burst forward and flung her arms around the Emperor. "Constantius! Brother!"

The Emperor smiled as he hugged her in return. "I have not seen you all afternoon, Helena. Have you been hiding from me?"

Helena pointed at Melissa. "Look who I have found—an old friend."

Constantius's gaze fell upon Melissa. He furrowed his brow. "An old friend?" He grinned. "Melissa? Could that be you?" He glanced at Florentius. "General, is this your daughter?"

Florentius nodded.

Melissa curtsied. "Yes, sire."

"How long has it been since I last saw you, Melissa?" asked the Emperor.

"Several years, my lord."

He stepped toward her with the Empress. "I remember you and Helena as little girls playing in the palace halls in Antioch and Caesarea. You were another sister to Helena—and me." He turned to the Empress. "She has grown very beautiful, has she not?"

The Empress looked upon Melissa, her eyes kind and gentle. "Yes, she has." She stepped forward and hugged the young woman. "It is good to see you again. You are now a young woman. Nineteen?"

Melissa bowed. *I remember the Empress, one of Constantius's and Helena's cousins.* "Yes, my lady." *She is so beautiful, but she looks so pale. Is she well?*

The Empress turned to Florentius. "You are looking for a husband for her, yes?"

Florentius stumbled for something to say. "Well—"

"Yes, Empress," interjected Portia.

Melissa bit her lip. *Mother, not now. Not now.*

"There are many fine young men here tonight for whom she would make a lovely wife." The Empress pointed to one of the

52

bodyguards attending them. "Here is Marcus Scudillo—a captain in the Imperial Guard, just returned from Pergamum with our cousin Julian."

Captain Marcus bowed to Melissa. "Pleased to make your acquaintance."

"Or, perhaps someone more advanced in his career and in years," interjected Constantius. He stepped aside, revealing the senior officer who stood behind him.

Melissa's head cocked back in surprise. *It's him. That officer in black who undressed me with his eyes. Arbitio.*

The Emperor gestured to the officer. "How about a Commander of the Imperial Guard?" he said. "Arbitio, you have not yet taken a wife."

"No, sire," said Arbitio.

"Then what say you of the daughter of Florentius?" asked the Emperor.

Arbitio bowed. "Lady Melissa would be a prize for any man, sire . . . young . . . or old. A fine prize."

Melissa blushed and she fidgeted under his gaze. *I want to flee or die if I can't.* She looked to her father as if to plea for help, and then she turned to the princess beside her.

Helena, seeing her friend's great discomfort, put an arm around the waist of Melissa. "Brother, I beg a favor of you."

Constantius kissed his sister on the forehead. "I am fond of your little sister. You know I grant your favors whenever it is within my power to do so. Pray tell—what is the favor?"

"Many ladies of the court will go with their menfolk when you lead the army into the West. You have asked me to come to keep the Empress company. It will be such a marvelous adventure. Would you permit Melissa and her mother to travel with the court? It would be more female companionship for both the Empress and me."

"I do not see why not, it seems a wonderful idea to me," said the Emperor. He then turned to his wife. "But we must ask the Empress herself."

The Empress smiled and nodded. "I would so much love to have both Helena and Melissa as travel companions. Their youthful energy would lift my spirit and be good for my health."

Constantius clapped his hands together. "Then, yes, of course—it is settled! More companionship for the Empress. Marvelous idea! Helena, it will be as you say. Melissa and her mother must come."

The two young women embraced each other. "How exciting," said Helena.

"Thank you," whispered Melissa.

Florentius stood there with his mouth open. He mumbled something. "Melissa to come?"

Constantius raised an eyebrow. "General Florentius, you have no objection to this?" said the Emperor, his tone firm. It was not a question—it was a command. *You will have no objection to this.* "The Empress and the princess want more female companionship on the campaign. You cannot have any objection." The Emperor tilted his head as he glared at Florentius. "Or do you?"

Florentius dropped his shoulders. Protest was impossible. He shook his head. "No, sire. Against the decisions of emperors, wives, and daughters—there is no appeal."

Constantius nodded. "Then it is decided."

Chapter 4

The Encampment

(Late September, 351 AD)

Tribune Gaius Marius Septimus stood atop the walls of a military camp. He held his scarlet cloak about himself against the late September chill. His back to the battlement, he looked out over the interior of the fortified Roman encampment. The camp, laid out in the shape of a large square, sat on a patch of high ground near a right-angle bend in the Drava River. The four walls, constructed of a high wooden palisade atop mounds of earth, were each over a quarter-mile in length and encompassed by a deep trench. Wide avenues beginning at each of the four main gates bisected the camp east to west and north to south. Dozens of smaller streets ran parallel to these avenues. Thousands of tents lined either side of the avenues and streets to quarter the troops, while large corrals held thousands of horses. Along the inside length of the walls was the intervallum, an empty space several dozen yards across, which lay between the defenses and the camp. The Praetorium, the headquarters of the army, was in the center.

Although Septimus observed the camp before him in all its detail, the reality of it faded away in his mind as his thoughts brought him back to Rome. *Marciana.*

"Good morning, Tribune," said Longinus, walking up behind him, his vine staff held beneath his right arm. The sounds of the clanking of armor of legionaries engaged in marching drills, horses moving along the avenues, and the hammers of blacksmiths against anvils filled the air.

Longinus waited for several moments for a response, but none came. Septimus, lost in thought, took no notice of the centurion. "Sir, I have the report of the watch." He paused again to wait for the response. None came. "Good morning, sir. I have the report of the watch. Remember? The Third Italica supplies the sentries this morning along the eastern wall." Longinus cleared his throat. "Tribune Marius!" he said in a loud voice which caused sentries a dozen yards away to turn toward him.

The tribune jerked his head back, startled awake from his daydream. Septimus glanced at the centurion.

"What is it, Tribune . . . something wrong?" asked Longinus.

The tribune looked toward the camp. "Look at it."

"It is just a Roman legionary camp. Perhaps bigger than those you have seen before."

"Just a legionary camp? It is more than that. Regulus. Scipio. Aemilianus. Marius. Sulla. Pompey. Caesar. Octavian. Vespasian. Titus. Trajan. Each in their day experienced these sights and sounds. Thus, it has been for half a millennium. Legions encamped. Waiting. Preparing for a battle."

"You are in a strange mood this morning, Tribune. If you do not mind me saying so."

"And if I minded?"

"You know I would say it anyway. In the army for thirty years, I need no lessons on a Roman camp. Not from a youngling of an officer."

The tribune, still facing the camp, looked at Longinus out of the corner of his eyes. "I do not think I like your tone, Centurion. If I did not know better, I'd say it smacks of insubordination."

The centurion's face, covered with thick stubble of black and gray hair, and deep-wrinkled skin, weathered by years of sun and battle, was unaffected and undeterred by the barb. Several inches taller than Septimus, Longinus looked down at him. "This is not about a history lesson." Longinus squinted as he searched the eyes of the tribune. He tilted his head a little to one side as he studied the officer. "Something is bothering you. Whatever it is . . . pull yourself together, sir."

"If you must know—I was thinking of Rome."

"Oh?"

"It seems so distant. So very long ago."

"It has only been a few months since we left Rome. You have been away from Rome before—at greater distances and for greater lengths of time."

"Measured by calendar or by map, fate has taken me from Rome many times for longer periods of time and to lands more distant than this. Measured by the heart, the time and distance are greater than they have ever been. I fear I shall never see Rome again."

"Nonsense! You are not thinking of Rome, now. You are thinking of a woman!"

Septimus lowered his eyes.

The centurion laughed, the weathered wrinkles on his face seeming to multiply. "Ha! I knew it!" His smile faded, but his eyes grew soft and kind. "Do not worry, sir. You will see Lady Marciana again. This mess will all be over one day soon. You will marry her and settle down on one of your family's country estates. No doubt, there will be many children. "

Septimus and Longinus walked along the battlement. When they reached the Praetorian Gate, Septimus stood beside one of the towers. A city atop higher ground, several miles distant to the East, was visible. "Mursa Major," said the tribune.

Mursa Major, tiny compared to Rome with its population of one million inhabitants, was the largest city in the province of Pannonia. North of the city flowed the Drava, a tributary of the great Danubius. Several miles to the south lay a range of small mountains and ridges covered by thick forests awash in the colors of fall. The countryside around the city, and between the river and mountains, was one of rolling hills dotted with farms and villas. Above it all, the morning sun, set in a clear blue sky, began to warm the September chill.

"An idyllic view," mused Septimus. "It reminds me of one of my father's estates in Iberia." He pursed his lips as he recalled Marciana's words at the engagement party. *Your father is a Roman senator with connections and influence. Your family is one of the wealthiest in the empire. You could get out of this war—if you wanted. Buy your way out.*

We could run off together and live on one of your family's estates in Iberia. Let someone else take your place. "I could have been there by now with Marciana as my bride."

The tribune took in the calming vista for a minute. Then came the loud pounding of a drum and the blare of a horn. The sound of it all seemed to startle the tribune. Beneath them, through the Praetorian Gate, a cohort of infantry paraded out of the camp.

The tribune's gaze shifted reluctantly from the beautiful countryside to the column of soldiers as it marched off along the road to go on patrol. "That idyllic view belies the stark reality. Two opposing Roman armies encamped only miles apart—poised to settle the fate of the empire." He fixed his attention on Longinus. "That reminds me—where is the watch report?" he asked, a hint of impatience in his voice.

Longinus brought the tip of his vine staff to his ear. "Excuse me, sir? What was that?"

"What was that, Centurion?"

"There is an implication in your tone—that my watch report is late."

"I have not yet seen it or heard it."

"I tried to give it to you before, Tribune."

"Before?"

"Yes—before—when I found you in a maudlin stupor . . . pining away for a woman."

"You are fortunate you are the best First Centurion in the army. I overlook your habitual insubordination. Any other legionary commander would have had you flogged and beaten by now as might have I—had I thought sense could be beaten into that hard head of yours."

Longinus brought his hands to his hips. He glared at the tribune.

"The report, Centurion?" asked Septimus. He smiled, amused he had gotten a rise out of Longinus. "If you please."

Longinus pulled a scroll from his gray cloak. "At the ninth hour, an enemy delegation from Emperor Constantius approached the Praetorian Gate under a flag of truce. General Marcellinus, along with Silvanus and a detail of his cavalry, rode out to meet them and escorted them into camp to meet with Emperor Magnentius. The enemy delegation comprised of Arbitio, Commander of the Imperial Guard, and Eusebius—"

"A delegation sent by Constantius?"

Longinus nodded.

The tribune took several steps along the battlement. He placed his hands upon the wall. "The empire might yet be spared a civil war." His eyes brightened. "I might return to Marciana sooner than I dared hope."

"Do not count on it," said the centurion. "There will be a battle tomorrow. I can feel it in the air."

"A premonition or just your insufferable pessimism, Centurion? I prefer to be optimistic. I will have Marciana in my arms soon."

"A premonition? No. I know human nature. That suffices to make a prediction. Magnentius will not surrender his imperial diadem. Constantius will not surrender his desire to reclaim it. Do yourself a favor, Tribune. Save your optimism for another day."

"Tell me, Centurion. You could have retired long ago. Even now you could. You are not fighting for Magnentius. What is this coming battle to you?"

"Constantius is an Arian."

"One who does not believe Jesus Christ is one with God the Father?" asked Septimus.

"Tribune Marius, pagan that you are—you are learning," said Longinus. He pointed the end of his vine staff against the tribune's breastplate and tapped it as he spoke. I will make a Christian of you yet!"

Septimus chuckled. "But is that what this war is to you? That Constantius is a *heretic* to you and your fellow Christians?"

"If it were only that, there would be no bother," said Longinus. "But Constantius persecutes Nicene Christians in the East. He has deposed Catholic bishops and replaced them with Arian-minded ones who will compromise the Faith. If Constantius conquers the West, he would try to bring the pope under his control and turn the whole Church Arian."

"And you can stop him?"

"Weak and compromising bishops may fail to stand up against him," said Longinus. "Yet, the task remains to defend the Faith. I have neither the wits nor eloquence of an Athanasius." He grabbed

59

the hilt of his sword and pulled it part way out of its scabbard. "But I have this."

"One man?"

"If it comes to that. The Lord has often used one man."

"And if one man be not enough?"

"Men may fail God. He will not fail men. He is faithful. Hell will not prevail."

The sound of hoofbeats signaled the approach of a cavalry detachment, coming toward the gate from inside the camp.

"It is General Marcellinus and Tribune Silvanus coming down the Via Praetoria," said Septimus. "They lead the enemy delegation out of camp."

As they neared, Marcellinus separated from the detachment and remained by the gate while Silvanus continued on with it. The tribune looked upon the general from the battlements above. He thought back to the engagement party in Rome, where Marcellinus had been a guest. *He seems to have aged several years over the last few weeks. Haggard and worn.*

The old general looked up and saw Septimus atop the wall. "I will meet the officers of my command in my tent. In two hours." Marcellinus turned and headed back to the center of camp.

"It appears the negotiations are over," said Longinus.

Septimus looked over the parapet. "But to what end?" he asked as he watched the enemy delegation riding away. At a point one hundred yards away from the gate, the escort turned about and headed back to the camp while the enemy delegation continued on toward Mursa Major. Yet, as the two sets of riders parted, Silvanus and one of the Easterners lingered behind together.

"Silvanus is chatting with one of their officers," said Septimus. "One who wears the black of the imperial bodyguards"

"That must be Arbitio," said Longinus.

"Who?"

Longinus took a deep breath and exhaled with a loud sigh. "If you had paid attention to the watch report—which I read to you— you would know Arbitio is the Commander of the Imperial Guard."

"Look," said Septimus. "Silvanus and Arbitio just parted company with a handshake. They parted on friendly terms. Perhaps it is a sign both emperors have reached an agreement."

"Do not count on it."

"You are ever a pessimist, Centurion. I wager there is to be peace. We will be back in Rome before you know it. Silvanus returns. Let us meet him at the gate."

"I am a realist, Tribune!" Longinus called after Septimus, who hurried down the ladder.

"Hail, Silvanus," Septimus called out as Silvanus approached the gate. The tribune hurried across the drawbridge which spanned the trench outside the wall.

Silvanus reined in his horse to a halt as he reached the tribune. He took off his helmet with its alternating plumes of white and black. He wiped the sweat from his brow with a forearm.

Septimus looked up at his friend. "Tell me. What news? What of the negotiations?"

Silvanus smirked. "Negotiations? Constantius sent only an ultimatum to Magnentius. Surrender or war."

Septimus lowered his head. "Then war it is," he whispered to himself in a melancholic voice. His heart and mind drifted back to Rome. *Marciana.*

***

General Marcellinus and his senior officers, a couple dozen men in all, gathered in his large tent for a council of war. Along the inside canvas of the circular tent, a shield from each unit under his command was on display, each bearing its own emblem. In grim silence, the officers, Septimus among them, studied a large map of the surrounding countryside set on a table in the midst of the general's quarters. Dozens of small figurines placed on the map represented the major infantry and cavalry units of the Western and Eastern armies.

Marcellinus looked around the table at the officers, his expression grave. "The rumors you have heard are true. Negotiations between West and East have failed. There is to be war."

His words drew no response. The officers around the table were silent and grim-faced. All eyes were now fixed on the three-dimensional map of the battlefield.

Septimus examined the map, noting to himself the two armies depicted by the figurines were not evenly matched. *We are outnumbered. We are doomed.* Across the table, his eyes met those of Silvanus, who seeming to have read the tribune's thoughts, affirmed them with a nod.

"When can we expect battle?" asked one officer, breaking the tense silence in the tent at last.

"Tribune Claudius Silvanus and I have just come from a council of war chaired by Emperor Magnentius," said the gray-haired Marcellinus "The consensus is that Constantius will order an immediate attack."

Silvanus placed his helmet on the table. "It is not in his temperament to delay. We should expect an attack tomorrow at first light."

"The Easterner army, with its greater numbers, is twice the size of our Western army," said Marcellinus.

As Septimus watched Marcellinus as he spoke, the tribune thought back to earlier in the day when he had seen the general at the Praetorian gate. *He does seem older and tired, perhaps worn out by the campaign and camp life. Or is it he is not confident of the outcome of the coming battle?*

The general gestured toward the map. "The one factor to our advantage is that the field of battle favors us." He handed a pointer stick to Silvanus.

Silvanus took off his helmet and placed it on the table. He swept his long black hair away from his face. "Our battle plan remains as we have long discussed. Our army will take a position on the hills to the west of the valley in a battle line that runs from the river in the north all the way to the forest and ridges to the southwest. With the river protecting our left flank and the forest our right, we channel the enemy into a narrow area—preventing Constantius from taking full advantage of his greater numbers."

"Silvanus's command is responsible for the right wing," said Marcellinus "Victory or defeat rests on his success in preventing Constantius from turning our flank."

"We can always count on Silvanus," said Septimus with a firm nod to his friend.

"Here, here!" shouted the other officers in agreement.

Silvanus raised a hand to silence the cheers. "Your trust in me is humbling, Tribune Septimus Marius. I am honored you deem me worthy of it." He bowed.

General Marcellinus spent the next several minutes reviewing the placement and duties of each legion and cavalry squadron for the coming battle. When he came to Silvanus, he placed a hand on his shoulder. "Tribune Claudius Silvanus, with his infantry and heavy cavalry, take their usual place of honor—the far right of the army." Marcellinus pointed to forested ridges represented on the map along the southern edge of the battlefield. "Silvanus will also have responsibility for the defense of the passes and ravines in the forest. This will prevent any attempt by the enemy to surprise us on the flank. He will also provide several cohorts for the defense of the pontoon bridge across the Drava, should the enemy try to attack our rear from across the river."

Septimus searched the map for where his legion would be stationed. *Where is Third Italica? I do not see it.* He raised his eyes from the table to find Marcellinus looking straight at him.

"I have made one change to the existing plan, Tribune," said Marcellinus. The general picked up the figurine representing Third Italica which had been sitting off of the map. He set it down on the map behind the main body of the right wing. "Third Italica will be held in reserve."

Septimus's posture stiffened at this news.

"That is all," said Marcellinus, dismissing the officers. "You all have your orders and know your assignments. Good luck. May God be with us tomorrow."

While the officers filed out of the tent, Septimus remained where he had stood, his jaw clenched.

On his way out, Silvanus passed Septimus. "Good luck tomorrow, friend. May the end of this battle find us both alive. We shall share a drink when the battle is done."

"Good luck, friend," said Septimus. "Until we meet again."

When the last officer had left the tent, Septimus approached Marcellinus. "General, the original battle plan called for Third Italica to defend the approaches through the forest."

The general sat at his desk. "I am aware of that."

63

"Third Italica was to man the fortifications along the road, passes, and ravines in the forest to protect against a surprise attack. My legion built most of those fortifications. They spent months of labor in the heat of summer—cutting trees . . . digging trenches. My men will take it as an insult . . . to be relegated to the reserves."

"No insult is intended."

"Why the change?"

"A friend of yours recommended it."

"What—who?"

"Silvanus."

Septimus's eyes widened. "Silvanus? Why would he do such a thing?"

Marcellinus walked back to the map table. He pointed at it. "Look at this, Tribune. The only avenue for an enemy surprise attack is through the forest. You, better than anyone, know that terrain. But anyone looking at our defenses along the forest road and the passes through the ravines can see it would be absolute folly to lead legions and cavalry through them. The passes are few. The chokepoints narrow. It is heavily fortified. Thanks to the efforts of you and your men, a few cohorts in these positions could hold off an entire army for days. The enemy has scouted our positions. They know this."

"What are you saying?" said Septimus, shaking his head in protest. *Even if so, why would Silvanus care where my legion is stationed? Why would he do this to a friend?*

Marcellinus picked up the figurine from the table which represented Third Italica. "Third Italica is too good of a legion to waste defending against an attack that will never come. Silvanus knew this. He suggested I redeploy your legion to where it might do good in a historic battle. He thought he was doing a friend a favor."

"And who will man the forest positions, now?" asked the tribune.

"Silvanus offered one of his own legions for the task," said Marcellinus, as he poured two cups of wine and offered one to Septimus. The tribune hesitated to take it. "I forgot you do not drink often," said the general.

"On rare occasions."

The general thrust the cup against his chest. "Take it. Consider it an order."

Septimus accepted with reluctance. *I still don't understand why Silvanus felt the need to get involved in repositioning Third Italica.*

Marcellinus glanced around at the shields lining the inside of the tent. His gaze settled upon one in particular. It was a circular black shield with a large Chi Rho painted in white upon it. He walked over and stood before it. Painted on either side of the intersection of the Greek letters were the words *Pia Fidelis.*

General Marcellinus nodded as he studied it. "The shield of the Third Italica did not always bear the Chi Rho, you know. When Marcus Aurelius founded the legion during the Marcomani Wars, two hundred years ago, the shield bore—"

"Storks," said Septimus. "The legion used to have the stork as its emblem."

"Third Italica served with Constantine at the Battle of the Milvian Bridge. His army was outnumbered, much like we will be tomorrow. Before the battle, Constantine and the army beheld a vision of the Chi Rho in the heavens. Below it appeared the words *In This Sign, Conquer.* By order of Constantine, the whole army placed that symbol on its shields for the coming battle." The general paused for a moment as if reliving the moment. He turned to Septimus. "Did you know I commanded Third Italica at the Milvian Bridge? I was a pagan but converted after seeing that great sign."

The tribune shook his head. "I did not know you were a convert."

"Your legionaries carry the Chi Rho on their shields. Yet, you still bear the emblem of the storks on yours. Why?"

"The legion is a Christian one. I am a pagan. I did not think the men would appreciate it if I, a believer in the Old Religion, bore a symbol of their god upon my shield."

"Nonsense! Your men would be honored if you did so. They trust your leadership. They acclaimed you 'Romanus,' remember?"

Septimus ran his hand over his face. *I am not the brave leader they think.*

"They would consider it an honor if you bore the Chi Rho on your shield," said Marcellinus.

Something caught the tribune's eye across the large tent. Behind the general's own shield, there stood a labarum. Septimus walked over to examine it. The labarum was a military standard as long as a spear. Where the spearhead would be at one end of the shaft, there was instead attached a Chi Rho made of gold. This Chi Rho, in turn, was encircled by a laurel wreath, also made of gold. A bar formed a cross just below the Chi Rho. From the bar hung a square red banner with a border of golden tassels. The banner itself was embroidered with a depiction of a woman holding a baby, the outline and features of each outlined in gold and embroidered with colored gems.

Marcellinus joined the tribune. "I received it from the hands of Pope Julius, Bishop of Rome, before we left the city. A gift to the army. He told me it was patterned on a painting of the Lord's mother, done by St. Luke, the Evangelist. Emperor Magnentius granted my legions the honor to bear it before the entire army in battle tomorrow, just as a labarum was carried at the head of Constantine's army."

The general studied the tribune's face. His mind seemed elsewhere. "What is it, Septimus? I sense something else weighs on you."

"Marciana wanted me to use my father's influence to leave the army."

The general nodded to himself as he pondered the tribune's words. "You could do that. You can do that still. Even now. Your father certainly has influence with Magnentius. The senator is a wealthy man who could equip a few more legions for the Emperor. He will need them before this war is over."

"You think it possible that I could leave," said Septimus. *Dare I hope?*

"What would the resignation of a single officer be in comparison to having a few more legions?" asked Marcellinus. His stare seemed to pierce the tribune's soul. His words seemed to test him. "You must decide what to do soon, don't you think?"

The tribune watched Marcellinus walk back to his chair. *What would the resignation of a single officer be in comparison? Roman nobles have equipped and sent others to war in their own place. My father can send several legions in my place.* "I have wondered something since Rome," said

66

Septimus.

"Yes?"

"Why did you pick me, a pagan, to command Third Italica, a Christian legion? You are a Christian. Nearly a quarter of the army is Christian. Why did you not choose a Christian commander for these men?"

"Since it first came into existence, Third Italica received the honorific title of *Pia Fidelis*—Loyal and Faithful—seven times for its bravery and steadfastness in battle. I was there when Constantine awarded it to the legion for its seventh time at the Milvian Bridge, when it helped turn back the Praetorian Guard and drove it back into the Tiber."

Marcellinus sat. "Constantine had a special fondness for the Third." He looked Septimus in the eyes. "I picked you to command the Third because you remind me of myself as a young officer."

A half-smile appeared on the tribune's face. "You think to convert me too?"

The general laughed. He held his cup up as if toasting Septimus. "I have great hope the Third Italica might make a Christian out of you yet."

"You sound like my Primus Centurion, who—when he is not being insubordinate—hopes the same."

"Longinus is a good centurion—the best in the army—and a good man. But, no . . . I did not choose you to convert you."

Septimus raised his cup. "That I will drink to. But if not to convert me, then why?"

"The Third Italica has always been close to my heart. I wanted it to have the best officer I could give it. That is you." Marcellinus took a sip of wine. "Do not be mad at Silvanus. He convinced me to place your legion elsewhere. I chose where to place it.

"So, why did you place Third Italica in reserve?" asked Septimus.

The general placed his cup down on the table. He leaned back in his chair, his expression and tone somber. "I have a sense of foreboding about tomorrow, Septimus. I cannot say what it is, or even why I do. But I do. I want Third Italica in reserve—fresh and ready for any surprises—like it was forty years ago at the Milvian Bridge."

***

The centurion and Father Paul, the unofficial chaplain of the legion, met Septimus as he returned to his quarters just as the sun touched the horizon. Tents lined either side of the road in both directions, and legionaries prepared their evening meals over campfires. The priest, in his late forties and of average height, had accompanied the Third Italica on its campaigns for a dozen years. Having shared the rigors and hardships of military life, he was in fit condition and could be mistaken for a legionary.

Longinus saluted Septimus as he dismounted. Ulysses lifted his front right leg high off the ground as if to return the centurion's salute. Longinus tilted his head as he observed the horse's movement.

Father Paul chuckled. "Another trick, Tribune?"

Septimus nodded.

The priest patted the horse on the neck. "Well done, Ulysses."

"Thank you, Father," said Septimus.

The centurion, his lips pursed, tapped his vine staff against the side of one of his grieves.

"Is there a problem, Centurion?" asked the tribune.

"That is a warhorse, Tribune—not a puppy dog!" said Longinus. "I hope Ulysses knows something more useful to you in battle than the tricks with which you have flooded his head."

The centurion glared at the priest. "'Well done, Ulysses,' you say?" he said as he shook his head at the priest. "Father, do not encourage the tribune and these . . . horse tricks. Do you know last week he taught his horse to play dead? That animal will get the tribune killed one of these days."

The tribune, ignoring the centurion's jibe, proceeded into his tent. The circular tent, smaller than the general's, was rather spartan. There was a single cot, a couple of trunks, an armor stand, a small table, and several chairs. A dozen men could stand with comfort within it.

"What is it?" asked Septimus, seeing that the centurion and the priest had followed him into the tent.

"You asked us to come by at sunset," said the centurion.

Septimus took off his scarlet-crested helmet and unfastened his armored cuirass. *It has been too long a day already.* He leaned over a bowl and splashed water from it against his face, running his hands and fingers through his hair. "You have heard the news going around the camp. Tomorrow—we fight."

"May I say, I told you so?"

"No, you may not," said Septimus, cutting the centurion short. He picked up a towel draped over the armor stand, revealing a blue shield with two large white storks painted on it. He dried his face, leaving the towel around his shoulders.

"Should I get the men ready to march tonight to take up our positions in the forest fortifications?"

"The battle orders for Third Italica have changed."

"Changed?"

"The legion will be held in reserve."

Longinus frowned. "The reserve line? But—"

"You heard me, Centurion—the reserve line. It is something Claudius Silvanus suggested to the general."

"I never liked Silvanus," muttered Longinus.

"Watch what you say," said Septimus. "He is my good friend, Centurion." He took the towel off his shoulders and threw it onto his cot. "Believe me, it is a sore topic for me as well. I do not care to discuss it. We will hold a council of war for the centurions and decurions of Third Italica, here in my tent, within the hour. See to it. We will go over the details then." The tribune noticed the priest standing behind Longinus. "Yes, Father?"

"You sent for me," said Paul.

"By the gods, I did," said the tribune. He leaned forward with fatigue, bracing himself with one hand against one of the center tent poles for support. "Forgive me, it has been a long day." After a few moments, he stood straight again and faced the priest. "We will need the help of heaven tomorrow whether it comes from your one God or from the many gods of Rome—it does not matter whence it comes. I will worry about the gods of Rome. You see to the welfare of the legionaries of Third Italica—that they gather and praise your God according to your traditions and rites. See they confess their sins according to your beliefs. This seems a wholesome custom. Having confessed, their prayers and

69

supplications might be favorably heard in Heaven and good fortune granted to our legion in battle." Septimus splashed more water on his face. He toweled himself dry. "We will need all the help we can get."

The tribune sank into a chair beside a small table near the center of the tent. He closed his eyes to rest. "That is all for now." He rubbed his hands to his face. After several moments, he opened his eyes to see the centurion and the priest had not made a move to leave. "Is there something else?"

"There is," said the centurion. He called to four legionaries standing outside and invited them into the tent.

Septimus narrowed his lips. He could surely do without more interruptions to have time to think. *The general himself said I could resign. Even now, he said.* The legionaries entered and saluted Septimus. One of them, a legionary named Cornelius, stepped forward. Cradling a sword still within its scabbard, he offered it to the tribune.

"What is this all about?" asked Septimus.

"A gift, sir," replied Cornelius.

"A gift?"

"From Third Italica."

The tribune, with furrowed brow, looked to Longinus and Father Paul. *What is this all about?*

"It is your birthday, Tribune," said the priest.

"Happy birthday, Tribune Marius," said Cornelius, holding out the sword to Septimus. "From the whole legion."

Septimus stood. He took the sword and scabbard from Cornelius. "My birthday?" he muttered as he examined the scabbard, decorated with inlaid silver and gold. A wistful smile came to his face. "I had forgotten." *My thoughts have dwelled on the possibility of war. On Marciana. On leaving. I had been too distracted to even remember my own birthday.*

The metal of the sword rang out as he drew it forth from the scabbard, and the blade glimmered as it caught the rays of the setting sun coming through the open flaps of the tent. Septimus read aloud the gold engraving on the hilt. "Libera Nos A Malo . . . deliver us from evil." He looked to Father Paul and smiled. "From one of your Christian prayers, I believe."

70

The priest nodded.

"Father blessed it," said Longinus. "That its bearer be kept safe by his angel."

Septimus smiled. "My angel?"

"Seeing as you are a hopeless pagan, Father blessed it three times to make sure it stuck," said the centurion with a wink.

"The sword was to be a wedding gift from the legion," said Cornelius. "But, given the circumstances, the men thought it best not to wait. You might have use for it now."

Septimus removed his old sword belt and fastened on the new one. He placed the new sword back into its scabbard. His movement was slow and deliberate as the blade rang out as it slid into place. "Yes, I will have use for it now," he said a firm tone. *I cannot leave my men, not now. Not on the eve of a great battle. I have my duty.* "Pia Fidelis."

"Pia Fidelis!" said the legionaries in reply.

The tribune placed his hands on the shoulders of the young legionary. He then looked at each of the other soldiers in the eyes. "This is a fine gift, men. A fine gift. I doubt that either emperor has a finer sword than this. Convey my thanks and appreciation to the men. I will wear it and carry it with honor, and wherever I am and whatever happens—I will always remember Third Italica with great affection."

Chapter 5

Mursa Major

Melissa stood on a balcony of a third-floor apartment as the sun was disappearing over the horizon. "What are you doing out here, dear?" her mother said as she came outside.

Melissa smiled. "It is such a beautiful view." She rested against the balcony railing. The curled brown locks of her hair that hung down to her shoulders swayed in the gentle breeze. The last rays of the day touched the autumn-colored foliage of the hills and ridges to the south. On her right, to the north of the city, the dwindling light reflected on the Drava. Her gaze then fell upon the camp of the Western Roman army, several miles distant to the northwest. Her smiled faded.

"We are fortunate the Emperor assigned this residence to our family," said Portia. "It belonged to the provincial prefect, you know. But the Emperor wanted us to have it because he wanted you close to Princess Helena and the Empress." She crossed her arms and shivered. "There is a chill in the air. You will catch a cold—come inside. There is enough sickness, fever, and death in the city these days."

"I am fine, mother."

The blare of distant horns interrupted the still of the evening. Startled, Melissa turned in the direction of the sounding horns. She followed the balcony which wrapped around the north side of the apartment. The first ranks of a long column of infantry and cavalry entered the city through the eastern gate. The clattering of warhorses and heavy footfalls of armor-clad infantry marching along stone pavement echoed through the streets and buildings of the city. The sounds grew louder as the leading element of the column drew nearer. Melissa moved close to the railing to watch as legionaries tramped along the avenue below.

"More soldiers have poured into the city, the fortress, and the camps to the south these last few days," said Portia.

"I sense a greater urgency and purpose in them this day," said Melissa.

"You feel it too? I have heard rumors that battle is imminent."

Melissa lowered her head.

"If the battle is tomorrow, this night may be the last one for many of these poor men," said Melissa. She looked up and searched the eyes of her mother. "Did we do wrong in coming?"

"*Wrong?* What do you mean?"

Melissa gestured in succession toward the apartment and outward to the city. "All of this!"

Melissa pinned her arms against her stomach. "Our travels with the imperial court have only been a diversion for us. Seeing new lands. New peoples. Rides and picnics in the countryside. Banquets. It has been the adventure I hoped for that night in Constantinople when Helena first suggested it."

Portia observed tears forming in Melissa's green eyes. She brushed a lock of her brown hair away from her daughter's face. "You have enjoyed it, dear—have you not?"

"I have," said Melissa. "That is why I feel so guilty. It all seems so frivolous, now. This has been entertainment . . . a lark—for me." She glanced down at the soldiers marching by their building. "But, blood and death for them." She paced the balcony. "And father! Poor father! He has much on his mind as it is without the added worry of a wife and daughter—in the midst of all this . . . war . . . and battle."

Portia smiled. "Do not mind your father; he did not complain."

"But that is just it! We did not give him a choice in the matter. Perhaps, we should not have come on this journey."

"Do not say that!" shouted a voice from behind. Princess Helena, her arrival unannounced, stood at the entrance to the balcony. She raised an eyebrow. "What have you two been discussing?"

Melissa greeted her with a hug. "Oh, nothing."

Helena tilted her head. She squinted as she searched the eyes of her friend. "Oh, really? *Nothing* you say? I heard enough to know it was not *nothing*."

Melissa turned red.

The princess frowned. "Do not for a moment doubt coming was a good thing. You and your mother, both, have been great company for me and for the Empress."

"But the war!" said Melissa.

"Whether you were here or not—the war would still be here all the same. We must not reproach ourselves for things beyond our control." The princess's frown faded, replaced by a tender light in her eyes. "It is good for men to have women about them. They become too pompous otherwise. Besides, this war, as horrid as it is, will soon be over according to my brother. You will see. He expects that before too long we may soon see Mediolanum and even Rome."

Helena leaned back against the railing. She glanced down at the legionaries marching along the street below. "If you had not come, I would have been desolate, not knowing what to do with myself. I would have been alone with all the handsome, young officers—and having no one to talk to about them." She looked at Portia. "And without your mother to chaperone me, there would be no one to keep me out of trouble!"

Melissa laughed.

"I am glad you came by now as you did, Princess," said Portia. "You have helped cheer up my daughter."

Melissa studied the princess's face. "Helena, you look tired. There are circles beneath your eyes. You have not told us the purpose of your visit."

"It is my cousin, the Empress. She has been ill since we left Constantinople," said Helena. "The Empress has the fever. The doctors believe she has taken a turn for the worse. I go now to the fortress to bring news of my cousin to my brother and to fetch him back to her."

"I will go with you," said Melissa.

"I hoped you would. The streets are full of men and horses—

74

impassable for a carriage. We must go by foot. It will be much quicker." The princess remembered Portia. "Do you mind if Melissa comes with me? It is not far."

Portia brought her fingers to her chin. "Two pretty women alone? At night? In the dark? With all these men on the streets?"

"No one would dare bother us—I am a princess!" said Helena. "These soldiers owe allegiance to my brother."

Melissa glared at her mother as they locked eyes, as if to say, *We cannot refuse her.*

Portia nodded. "Yes. By all means. Melissa should go with you." As soon as she had spoken, Melissa was hurrying back into the apartment with Helena. "But you must dress in something warm!" she called after them.

***

Darkness had fallen when Melissa and Helena left the palace of the prefect. Wearing hooded cloaks, they headed across the small courtyard toward the main gate. Nearby, several soldiers stood around a campfire.

"What are you doing out on a night like this, Princess?" asked an imperial guardsman standing watch at the gate.

"We are going to the fortress," Helena said.

"You cannot go alone without an escort," said the guardsman. "It will not be safe on the streets for two young ladies."

Helena gathered up her blond hair as she pulled the hood over her head. "We will be fine, thank you."

"Princess, Captain Marcus will have me flogged if I were to let you leave without an escort. Wait here, and I will see if there is a carriage and an escort available." He walked off a short distance to speak with another guardsman.

Helena slipped through the gate. "Come on," she said to Melissa.

Melissa saw the guardsman coming back to the gate, then looked to see Helena hurrying down the sidewalk. She threw the hood over her head, then stepping outside of the gate, she ran after her friend, all the while ignoring the guardsman's shouts of "Come back!"

Melissa ran down the short, empty street until it intersected the main avenue which ran from the eastern to the western gate. There she found Helena. Before them both, the avenue was teeming with men, horses, and wagons, all in motion.

"We will need to cross the avenue," the princess said in a loud voice to be heard over the din of horses and armored men upon the stone pavement.

Melissa shook her head. "But the street is clogged with men and horses! It is impossible. They will never stop for us. We must wait here until there is a gap in the column."

"Nonsense!" said Helena. "We will waste time, waiting. We will follow the street and cross where we can." She grabbed Melissa by the hand. "This way!"

The princess and Melissa hustled along the sidewalk toward the western precincts of the city. They kept their eyes lowered, avoiding the leering eyes of the soldiers marching down the street beside them.

"Come along with us to the camp tonight, girls," one of the soldiers called out.

"We've a tent big enough," shouted another.

"For all of us," added yet another, who, reaching out as he went by, slapped Melissa on the rear. The men surrounding them erupted into raucous laughter.

Recoiling in shock and fright at the touch, Melissa stepped under the arch of a doorway, pulling Helena back toward her. "I am not comfortable with this. The guardsman was right. Even my mother. It is not safe for us to be out. We are getting farther and farther away from the safety of the imperial compound."

"How about a little fun tonight, girls?" came the calls from each new rank of men passing them.

Melissa, her back to the door, clung as close to it as she could. She turned and pounded on the door with desperate knocks, desperate to gain entry. There was no response. She tried the latch, but it was locked.

"Follow me," said Helena as she continued on the way.

Melissa looked down the street after Helena. *Sometimes, I'd swear she is crazy. But I am not staying here alone.* She hurried after the princess.

"Perhaps we should turn back," said Melissa as she caught up to Helena, shouting to be heard over the whistling and lewd catcalls directed at them.

Helena stopped in her tracks. She glared at the legionaries as they marched by with each new rank of men taking up the continuous catcalls, invitations for intimate relations, and whistles as the women came into view. Her face red, she looked at Melissa. "They have insulted my imperial dignity." Helena stepped to the edge of the sidewalk. "I am a princess!" she yelled at the soldiers as they passed. "A princess! My brother will hear of this!"

The shouts came back at her unabated.

"Sure you are, honey."

"I am a prince, too."

"I will be your prince tonight."

The princess scowled at their invitations. "I *am* a princess!"

Melissa grabbed her away by the elbow and pulled her back from the edge of the sidewalk. "A princess you are—but it is not a princess they see!" Something up the avenue attracted Melissa's attention. It was her turn now to tug the princess by the hand. "I see an opening in the column. Come!"

Melissa dragged Helena along, crossing the street through a gap between the last rank of the infantry column and a squadron of cavalry following a couple dozen yards behind it.

"We did it!" said Melissa when they reached the sidewalk on the north side of the avenue. The moment of relief was brief. A couple of legionaries had stepped out of the infantry column. The soldiers headed back up the sidewalk toward the two young women. "Oh, no!" she whispered.

"What now?" asked Helena. She turned to see the legionaries coming their way. "I can imagine what they want."

"Let us not wait to find out!" said Melissa as she pulled Helena down a side street.

The legionaries followed them. "Let's have fun tonight girls!" one of them called out after them.

"Princess, wait for us!" shouted the other.

The women fled down the street. They could hear the echoing footsteps of the legionaries in the shadows behind them.

"They are gaining on us!" said Melissa.

The women came upon an entrance to a narrow alley to their right. Down it, the princess could see the moon low on the horizon. "That way!" said Helena. "There is a way out. I see the sky."

They went fifty feet and came to an abrupt stop. Before them was a low wall, about head high. Melissa brought a hand to her mouth. "It is a dead end."

Helena shook her head. "I did not see the wall in the dark—only the moon beyond it. I thought there a way out." She then linked her hands together, offering to boost Melissa up over the wall. "We can help each other over. You go first." It was too late.

"There you are!" said one the legionaries.

The women spun around. Through the shadows, they saw the outlines of the legionaries at the entrance to the alley. The two men leaned their shields and spears against walls. As they approached the women, they unbuckled and dropped their sword belts. The women backed away but soon bumped against the end of the alley. The two legionaries stood only several feet away, their faces now discernible in the moonlight. One had a patch over an eye, and the other a deep scar down the left side of his face.

"Hello, my lovelies," said the one with the patch.

"How about a kiss?" said the other with the scar.

Helena took one step forward toward them. She stood as straight and as tall as she could. Folding her arms, she turned sideways and tilted her head back to look down her nose at them. "I am not one of your lovelies! I am Princess Helena . . . daughter of Constantine the Great . . . sister of Flavius Julius Constantius Augustus—your Emperor!"

The legionaries glanced at each other. They laughed. "I never kissed a princess before!" said one with the scar.

"And you never will!" came the strong voice of a man from behind the legionaries.

At the head of the alley was the dark outline of a man.

The legionaries spun around. "Who is there?"

The slow metallic scratch of a sword being drawn from a scabbard echoed in the alley.

"Leave the ladies alone," said the stranger, his tone authoritative and confident. "Return to your formation at once." The stranger came within feet of them. He pointed a sword at them. "At once, I say."

The two legionaries reached for their swords at their sides but grabbed nothing but air. They looked at each other with wide eyes.

"Our swords!" one legionary said to the other. "We left them up the alley."

The legionary with the patch nodded. "All right. We'll go. Don't need no trouble."

"Be off with you!" said the stranger. "Be quick."

The stranger stood aside as the legionaries hustled past him. They collected their weapons and hurried away.

Helena and Melissa sighed.

"Thank you, kind sir," said the princess. "They would not have dared utter such vulgarities if they had known I was the sister of the Emperor."

"You are the Emperor's sister?" asked the stranger.

"I am Helena, sister of Constantius. This is my friend Melissa, daughter of General Florentius."

The stranger drew closer. His face became visible by the light of the moon.

Helena turned to Melissa. "He is handsome," she whispered.

The stranger put away his sword. "It is not safe for noblewomen, especially ones as pretty as yourselves, to be out and about the streets after dark without an escort. Unsavory and treacherous men lurk in shadows."

"Who are you, sir, that we might thank you?" asked Melissa.

"Yes, your name, please, so that my brother can you thank you for saving his sister."

"Tribune Claudius Silvanus at your service," he said with a bow.

"Thank God!" Melissa said. "It is an officer."

Silvanus leaned up against one of the walls of the narrow alley. "What errand brings two pretty noblewomen out on a night like this?"

"I must speak to my brother on an urgent matter," said Helena. "We were on our way to see him."

"Our purpose is the same this evening. I, too, must speak with your brother on an urgent matter."

"Does my brother know you?" asked the princess.

"He does not. But I hope to get an audience with him this evening to discuss an important matter concerning the war."

"In view of your kindness to us, I will make sure you meet my brother tonight."

"You are gracious and kind, Princess," said Silvanus as he walked the ladies out of the alley. Emerging from it, they came upon a saddled black horse. Silvanus grabbed its bridle. "I was on my way to the prefect's palace, hoping I might find the Emperor there." He looked down the narrow, darkened street toward where it intersected the main avenue. There, a continual stream of soldiers passed by. "But my way as you see is for the moment blocked."

"My brother is not at the palace this evening. He is at the fortress. It is there we must go."

"If it pleases you both, I will escort you there myself. My horse shall bear you."

The two women smiled. "Yes, thank you!"

***

Silvanus led the women, the princess seated behind Melissa on his horse, through the back streets of the city. After a quarter-hour, they emerged unto a street that ran beside one of the fortress walls within the city.

"The fortress of Mursa Major," said Silvanus as he beheld it. He headed toward the gate.

Melissa explored the fortress walls with her eyes. *For all my time in this city, this is the first time I have seen it.* The light from torches set on the parapet every thirty feet made visible dozens of legionaries patrolling the battlements and towers above.

Silvanus observed Melissa's curiosity. "For hundreds of years, this fortress has served as the base of the Seventh Legion."

"The gate," said Helena, pointing to the entrance which was only a couple hundred feet away.

Outside of the gate, a dozen legionaries stood around a fire. Others stopped and interrogated the drivers of several wagons waiting in line to enter the fortress.

As they drew closer, Melissa smiled. "I think I see Captain Marcus Scudillo by the gate. She pulled back the hood from her head. She waved. "Captain Marcus!"

"Lady Melissa, is that you?" asked Marcus, grabbing a torch from the campfire. He approached the women and smiled. "I did not recognize you at first."

Helena revealed herself as well, as she drew back her hood.

The captain bowed. "Princess Helena? Lady Melissa. Good evening, ladies. What brings you to the fortress—and at this hour?"

"An urgent errand," said Helena. "Where is my brother?"

"In the Praetorium."

"I must speak to him. Could you take us to him, Captain?"

"Yes. But I cannot guarantee he will see you. He is holding a council of war."

The captain noticed Silvanus, who stood on the other side of the horse, for the first time. Marcus stepped around the animal to take a closer look at this stranger. He held the torch forward, casting more light on Silvanus.

"And you are?" asked Marcus.

"He is Tribune Claudius Silvanus," said Melissa. "He saved us from two nasty soldiers who accosted us on our way here in a dark alley."

Marcus stared at the women. "You met him in a dark alley? What were you both doing in such a place? Treacherous and unsavory men lurk in the shadows."

"That is where he rescued us, Captain."

Marcus eyed the stranger. "Tribune Claudius Silvanus is it? I do not know a tribune by that name."

Helena laughed. "Are you always so suspicious, Captain? There are tens of thousands of soldiers in and around the city this evening. You do not know every tribune in the service of my brother!"

"Princess—the captain is right to be suspicious," said Silvanus. A sardonic smile crossed his face. Drawing forth his sword, he pressed its point against the neck of Marcus, where the protection of his leather cuirass ended.

Melissa screamed. She made a sign of the cross. "Marcus!"

Marcus stared down the length of the blade. Helpless, he could do little else but raise his hands in surrender. Several sentries—observing the threat to their commander—rushed forward.

"Stand down!" Marcus shouted at them. "He will run me through."

The sentries froze.

Helena lowered her eyebrows. "What is the meaning of this, Tribune Claudius Silvanus?" she asked, her tone stern and unafraid.

"As I said, Princess, the captain is right to be suspicious," said Silvanus.

"What do you mean?"

"While I am a tribune in the army—I am not one in your brother's army."

Melissa brought her hands to her mouth. She gasped. "You are a . . . Westerner!"

"Yes."

"He lied to us," said Melissa. She turned around to Helena, seated behind her on the horse. She was shocked at the sight that greeted her. "Helena! You are smiling!"

"Are you kidnapping us, Silvanus?" asked Helena, her voice brimming with eagerness and enthusiasm—even hope. "Are we now your hostages?"

"Princess!" gasped Melissa. *Does she actually want to be abducted?*

Silvanus chuckled. "No, Princess, you are not my hostages. And no, Lady Melissa, I never lied to you. I never said I was in the service of Constantius and his army of Easterners."

Helena patted the shoulders of Melissa. "That is true—he never said that." She moved her mouth closer to the ear of Melissa. "Such a handsome man could not be a liar."

"The truth is, as I have told you. I seek an audience with the Emperor."

Marcus smirked. "An audience?"

"Take me to the Emperor," said Silvanus. "I bring a gift for him—one of great value."

"Take you to the Emperor? At the point of a sword?"

Silvanus looked at the sword he held against Marcus. He smiled and then bowed to him. "Of course not." He surrendered it to the captain.

The sentries seized Silvanus and held him by the arms.

Melissa breathed a sigh of relief. *We are safe.*

"Now, take me to the Emperor," said Silvanus.

"A gift for him, you say?" asked Marcus. He glanced at the sentries. "Search him."

A centurion patted Silvanus down from head to foot. He checked inside his cloak. The centurion shook his head. "Nothing, sir."

"There is no gift, Claudius Silvanus—you carry nothing," said Marcus. "You will see the Emperor at your trial after the battle." He turned to the centurion. "To the dungeons with him."

Silvanus struggled against the sentries as they began to carry him off. "Commander Arbitio will vouch for me! He knows who I am. He knows I am coming this night."

"Away with him."

"Wait!" interjected Helena. "Do not remove him yet."

Melissa's mouth dropped. *What are you saying? He is dangerous. Let them take him away!*

The sentries obeyed the princess's order. The froze where they stood.

Helena addressed the captain. "This man, a Westerner, came into the city at great risk to himself."

"He is a spy—an assassin sent to kill the Emperor, perhaps," said Marcus.

"He could have harmed Melissa and me—an imperial princess—this evening, but he did not. Instead, he brought us to the gate of the fortress where he gave himself into your custody. Do you not think that strange? I believe he might have something to say that will interest my brother. Is that not possible?"

The captain thought for a moment. He gave a grudging nod. "It is possible."

"Take him to my brother."

Melissa listened in awe. *I have never seen Helena like this before. She can be silly and at times reckless, but underneath it all, she is truly an imperial princess.*

"Very well, Princess," said Marcus. "It will be so because you ask it. I will bring him to Captain Lucius. He is the officer of the watch in the Praetorium during the council of war. He can decide whether to interrupt the Emperor to deal with this spy."

Chapter 6

The Council of War

Marcus led the women and the prisoner, escorted by several legionaries, into the fortress and across a square to the Praetorium, the central administrative building of the fortress. They entered the building through a pair of wooden doors and followed a short corridor that opened into an internal courtyard bordered on its four sides by colonnades.

Melissa stepped aside and stood at the end of the corridor. She smiled as she took in the sight. Statues of emperors and generals, set in niches, lined the walls of the colonnades, as did doors to offices and quarters. The courtyard echoed with the conversations of several dozen officers, clergymen, and other dignitaries who milled around in small groups or gathered around the several campfires for warmth. "All the years my father has been in the army ... and this is my first time within a Praetorium," she whispered to herself.

Waking from her momentary daydream, she saw Helena and the others making their way through the crowded courtyard. Melissa hurried to catch up, picking and weaving her way around the men until she collided into a large hulking figure of a man who stepped in her way. He wore a chain mail shirt covered by a heavy cloak made of bearskin. Being only five foot three inches, her eyes were only as high as his stomach.

"Excuse ..." Melissa said. She tilted her head to look up, her gaze met by cold, dark eyes. A wide, bearded and fierce face scowled at her. The man was tall and large, dwarfing any legionary she had ever seen in size or strength. He wore an iron helmet topped with high, colorful plumes, which made him appear even taller.

"Barbarian," she whispered to herself. Melissa had never seen one before, but he appeared just as she imagined from the stories she had heard. "Barbarian!" she said again. Intended as a scream, her words came out as a whimper. She stepped back to flee but found her retreat blocked. Four other barbarians, also covered in armor and fur, surrounded her. Not as tall as the first barbarian, they were just as fierce-looking.

The barbarians spoke in a language, harsh and guttural, that she had never heard.

"I do not understand," she said, though she knew from their leers that they were speaking of her. They asked her questions to which she could not respond. "I do not speak your language," she said. They laughed as they shoved her back and forth amongst themselves as if the object of a game. She found herself in the grasp of the tallest one. He gazed into her eyes and snarled. She closed her eyes. She thought she might faint.

"That is enough!" interjected a calm but firm voice. She recognized it.

"Captain Lucius!" she exclaimed. She felt his hand take hold of her forearm. He tried to pull her away from the towering man, but the warrior held her fast by the shoulders.

Lucius glanced up at the barbarian. He placed the end of his walking cane against the giant's chest. "You have had your fun—now let her go."

The barbarian bent down to Melissa's height and stared into her eyes. He growled as if a wild animal. Her eyes widened. She screeched. The other barbarians laughed as he let her go.

Lucius led her away. "Follow me, Lady Melissa."

She sighed. "Those were barbarians," she said, still in shock.

"Yes. Alemanni. From the dark forests of Germania."

"What are such uncivilized men doing here in the city—in the heart of the fortress?"

"Odd as it may seem, they are allies of the Emperor."

They reached the other side of the courtyard. Beneath the

portico was a closed door guarded by a dozen imperial soldiers. She saw the princess, Marcus, and the prisoner standing twenty feet away from it.

The princess rushed up to them. "Melissa, where did you disappear to? I turned around and you were gone." Melissa's face was flushed. Long locks of her brown hair had broken free from her bun and now flowed down about her shoulders. "You look flustered. What on earth happened to you?"

Lucius leaned on his cane. "Lady Melissa just met Gundamar."

"Gundamar?" asked Melissa.

"He is a king of the Alemanni. *Gundamar the Giant* they call him."

Helena hugged Melissa. She grinned. "How exciting! A barbarian king, here! A giant, no less! And you met him!"

Melissa frowned. "Met? I assure you, Princess—it was not a formal introduction!"

"Can I meet him too?"

"Princess, you do not understand—it was not an enjoyable experience!"

Lucius observed the legionaries restraining the prisoner, his hands bound. "Marcus, who is your prisoner?"

"Tribune Claudius Silvanus," said Marcus. "A Western Roman officer. A spy or an assassin. He requests an audience with the Emperor."

"The Emperor is not in the habit of granting audiences to enemy spies and assassins."

"He claims to have brought a gift."

Lucius stood in front of the prisoner. "Oh? What is this gift for the Emperor?"

The prisoner remained silent.

Marcus grabbed Silvanus around the neck by his tunic. "Captain Lucius is the officer of the watch. He is the gatekeeper to the war council this evening. If you want to get in and see the Emperor, I suggest that you cooperate with him and answer his question."

"My message is for the Emperor's ears," said Silvanus.

Marcus shook his head. "That is all we have gotten out of him, Lucius. I say we do not trouble the Emperor with such nonsense. The Emperor can try him for treason later at his leisure and then have him executed." Marcus turned to the prisoner. "You are in no rush to lose your head, are you?"

Silvanus smirked. "It will be your head that rolls, not mine, if you prevent me from seeing the Emperor before the battle." He turned to Lucius. "Arbitio is inside, yes?"

Lucius nodded.

"Send word to him. He can vouch for me."

"Very well," said Lucius. "We will see what Arbitio says."

Lucius walked over to a table and scribbled out a note on a small piece of parchment. He handed it to legionary. "Bring this inside to Commander Arbitio." He fixed his attention on the women. "What are you ladies doing here this evening?"

"I must speak with my brother," said Helena.

"My orders are strict—only urgent military matters are to be brought to the Emperor while he is in the council of war. Those are his orders. You know his temper when these are disregarded."

Helena nodded. "He has a fearful temper."

Melissa frowned. "How much longer will he be?"

"There is no telling," said Lucius. "Is it an important matter?"

"It is," said Melissa. She reached out and touched Lucius on the forearm. "The Empress is sick with the fever. Can you get word to him?"

Lucius drank in Melissa's green eyes. He smiled as he nodded. "I will gladly deliver the note myself."

Melissa stood on her toes and gave him a peck on his cheek. "Thank you, Lucius!"

Lucius blushed. He turned to the table and scribbled out a note regarding the Empress.

The door to the antechamber opened. Out stepped a tall, lanky officer, wearing a black tunic beneath his cuirass and a black cape. It was commander Arbitio holding the note he had received. "Where is the prisoner?"

"Here, Commander," said Marcus. "He claims to be a tribune in the Western army. He wishes to see the Emperor. He says you can vouch for him."

Arbitio nodded at the prisoner. "You said you would come this evening. Now, here you are."

"You know this man?" asked Marcus, surprised.

"I saw him in the enemy camp this morning," said Arbitio. "His name is Claudius Silvanus." The commander was about to say more when something else caught his attention. In the background beside a pillar, he saw Melissa and the princess.

The commander approached the women. "Ladies, it is an unexpected but pleasant surprise to see you both here." Though his words were intended for both women, his dark eyes remained glued to Melissa. "I hope you are both well. Can I be of service to you in any way?"

Melissa squirmed. *I don't like that stare.* "Thank you, Commander—but, no. Captain Lucius is seeing to our request."

"So be it," said Arbitio. "But, if I can ever be of service, you will let me know. Now, if you will excuse me, I must return at once to the Emperor." He bowed and as he did, he leered at Melissa. She shuddered as their eyes met.

"Bring the prisoner along!" said Arbitio as he headed back inside to rejoin the council of war. Lucius and Marcus, with the prisoner, followed behind. The door shut behind them.

Grinning, Helena tapped Melissa's elbow. "Did you see the way he looked at you?"

"I did not like it one bit!" said Melissa. "Was it not awful?"

"Lucius—awful?"

"Why are you speaking of Lucius?"

"Did you not see the admiration for you in his face—I dare say, his affection for you, did you see how he looked into your eyes?" asked the princess. She took a deep breath and fanned herself with her hands.

Melissa shook her head. "Lucius? Heavens no—*not him*! I was speaking of Commander Arbitio! He looked at me that same way at the Great Palace in Constantinople, as if he saw me without my tunic. I did not like it then. I did not like it now."

"Oh, him? Yes. He is a detestable man. Ambitious ... sycophantic ... lecherous. A horrible combination of vices. I do not know why, but my brother trusts him. You must learn to ignore him."

The princess led Melissa to a nearby bench where they sat. "I was speaking before of Captain Lucius."

"What on earth about him?"

THE COUNCIL OF WAR

"I have seen the way he has looked at you these past months, just as he did the night of the wedding celebration for Gallus and Constantina. He looks at you, but not as Arbitio does. Lucius looks at you with true affection befitting a noble man with a pure heart and mind. If I am not mistaken, he loves you, Melissa."

"You can be worse than my mother. She and my father have long hoped to wed me to Lucius. I will not tolerate an arranged marriage. No one will tell me who it is I am to marry. I will do so for love."

"You have no feelings for Lucius?"

"None. I have no romantic interest in him. He is a family friend. A nice man. An honorable man. But that is all he is, can be, or ever will be to me."

***

Gathered around a large map, a dozen generals argued back and forth, each shouting over the other. At the head of the table, Florentius stood next to the Emperor.

"Gentlemen, quiet!" shouted Florentius. The room fell silent at his command. "Let us hear from General Lollianus. Give us your opinion, general. Proceed."

"Sire, I believe I represent the views of many here who have reservations about giving battle tomorrow," said Lollianus, a heavyset soldier in his mid-thirties. He picked up a pointer stick from the table. He looked out over the map which represented the countryside and terrain near and around Mursa Major. Placed across it were dozens of figurines representing units of both the Eastern and Western armies. "Our Eastern army outnumbers the Western army of the Usurper. However, the Westerners have chosen the ground for battle. They have chosen it well. The river and swamps protect their left flank. The forest and ridges, which they have fortified, shield their right. The river prevents an attack on the enemy from behind. The enemy has thrown a single pontoon bridge across the river, but it is defended by several cohorts. Even if we were to overcome that defense, the Westerners will burn the bridge before they let us cross."

Lollianus placed the pointer back onto the table. "Therefore,

89

without the possibility to maneuver, our options have been reduced to one—to attack across the valley which separates us, along a narrow front across which the enemy has placed obstacles to channel our attack. We outnumber the enemy two to one, but we will not be able bring the full weight and advantage of our greater numbers to bear. The outcome of this battle is foreseeable. It will be a bloody battle of attrition. It is unlikely to be decisive—in anything but its cost in the lives of men and horses."

The generals looked to the Emperor. He was frowning.

"What do you suggest as an alternative, General?" asked Florentius.

Lollianus, sensing the Emperor's growing displeasure with the course of the discussion, took a deep breath before continuing. "We should not offer battle on this ground."

"Not tomorrow?"

"On this ground? Not tomorrow. Not ever."

The Emperor pursed his lips. He appeared ready to speak, yet he remained quiet.

"Not tomorrow or ever?" asked Florentius.

"I recommend we wait the Westerners out," said Lollianus. "We should block their line of communication across the Drava. Our barbarian allies led by Gundamar can harass their supply trains. In time, this will force the enemy to attack on ground of our choosing or to withdraw. If they withdraw, we pursue."

"No! No! No!" shouted the Emperor. He pounded the table, striking the table with each *no*—each *no* and thump louder than the one before. Figurines on the table toppled over with the vibrations. "The imperial diadem of my dead brother has rested upon the head of Magnentius the Usurper for far too long. I wait no longer to avenge the blood of my brother. By this time tomorrow, I will have both the diadem of the West, and the head upon which it has rested." He pointed at the map. "Magnentius is here. I am here. The battle is here!" The words came out slow and distinct in a staccato cadence.

Constantius glared at the generals gathered around the table. "There will be no further discussion or debate. Tomorrow we fight—bloody battle of attrition or not. Victory—whatever the cost!"

The room fell silent. It seemed no general even dared to breathe for fear of setting off another imperial tirade. The air was still and tense. The door opened. Lucius and Marcus, with the prisoner in tow, entered the council of war. The attention of all focused on the unexpected sight of a bound prisoner. Yet, even with this interruption, the generals still feared to say a word. Still simmering from his outburst, even the Emperor said nothing.

"The battle need not be one of bloody attrition," said Silvanus, his words shattering the silence. All were astonished that the first one foolhardy enough to utter a word was a prisoner. "My apologies, Lord Constantius, I was not eavesdropping. I could not help but hear the frustration in your voice from without."

Marcus drew his sword and pressed it against the neck of Silvanus. "Quiet—or the next word will be your last!" he whispered through his teeth.

Constantius glared at Lucius. "You are the officer on watch! Why have you interrupted this council of war?"

Lucius saluted the Emperor. He approached and handed him the note. "First, I bear an urgent message from your sister, my lord Augustus—regarding the Empress."

Constantius, his attention fixed on Silvanus, took the note but did not open it. "Who is this man?"

"Claudius Silvanus, my lord," said Lucius. "A Western tribune . . . captured in the city by Captain Marcus."

"You know not to bother me with deserters or spies."

"He claims to have brought you a gift."

"Of what sort?"

"My lord, we searched the prisoner but found nothing on him," said Marcus.

"If he has nothing, then why bother me?" said the Emperor. "He has overheard part of our discussion. Captain, take him out to the courtyard and execute him immediately."

Arbitio stepped forward. "Great Augustus, I believe we should hear him out. This morning I accompanied the delegation you sent to the enemy camp. There, Silvanus confided in secret he would seek an audience with you this evening to present to you a valuable gift for the coming battle."

The Emperor stood before the prisoner. "What is this gift?"

"Victory over Magnentius—tomorrow, sire," said Silvanus.

"Victory?"

"Guaranteed."

"It is a trick!" said Lollianus. "He will tell us nothing but lies. Do not listen to him, sire!"

"General Florentius, what do you say?" asked the Emperor.

"It may be a trick of the enemy," said Florentius. "However, it may sometimes be useful to know what an enemy wants you to believe. It might give us insight into a weakness. I see no harm in it."

Constantius nodded. He turned to Silvanus. "You have your audience. Speak."

The prisoner, his hands bound, lifted them up and brushed the blade away from his neck. He moved toward the table. He picked up the pointer. "Magnentius chose his ground for battle well. A costly frontal assault appears to be your only option."

"You have another option?" asked Florentius.

Silvanus pointed to the forest and ridges beside the right flank of the Western battle line. "Attack the flank of your enemy from the forest."

Florentius smirked. "We have scouted the forest to the south. The enemy fortified the paths through ridges and forest. It is suicide to assault them. How do you propose we bypass them?"

"I do not propose that you bypass them. I propose you march right through them."

Lollianus threw his hands up. "I have heard enough ... the prisoner wastes our time! Is he a magician who can make our legions invisible—that they might march unseen through these fortifications in the forest?"

The generals erupted in laughter.

Silvanus waited for the laughter to die down. He turned to Lollianus. "I am no magician who can make your legions invisible. I know of no secret ways around the enemy defenses."

Florentius shook his head. "The hour grows late. Do not speak in riddles. What do you propose?"

"I command the units covering the far right of the battle line of the Western army," said Silvanus. "The senior officers under my command have agreed to transfer their allegiance from Magnentius to Emperor Constantius."

"This includes the commander of the legion manning the forest defenses?" asked Florentius, as he picked up one figurine. "The Third Italica?"

Silvanus chuckled. "The Third Italica—no. The tribune who commands this legion would never have consented to such a proposal if he had known of it. He is not the practical sort. Therefore, I had him and his unit reassigned. A legion commanded by one loyal to me now mans the forest defenses." He pointed to the pontoon bridge on the map. "The pontoon bridge is also defended by men and officers loyal to me." Silvanus locked eyes with the Emperor. "Great Augustus, not only will my men let your infantry and cavalry pass through the forest and over the bridge, but they will fight for you tomorrow as well."

Constantius stroked his chin with his hand. "What do you propose?"

Silvanus pointed at the forest on the map. "Take advantage of the dark tonight and early in the morning. Moving legions and cavalry into the forest. They can be in place for an attack by late morning." He pointed to the bridge. "The defenses for the bridge are only strong on the left bank. Once I return to my men, I can send word to the officer commanding the cohorts at the river to withdraw. By noon tomorrow, your army could be in position to launch a coordinated attack on the Western army from three sides—front, flank, and rear. You could surround and destroy the entire Western army."

"What is your price for this betrayal of Magnentius?" asked Arbitio.

Silvanus smiled. "Betrayal? No. It is an alteration of allegiance. It is inevitable the Eastern Empire will win this war, whether tomorrow or at some later date. I side with the inevitable. It is futile to oppose it. As for the price—I ask a year's wages for each legionary and three year's wages for each officer under my command once the battle is over."

"And what is your price, Claudius Silvanus?" asked the Emperor.

Silvanus bowed. "Sire, for myself, I leave that to you," he said in an affected, humble tone. "I am content that you, great Augustus,

93

determine the value of the services I will render."

"How do we know you are not leading our legions into an ambush in the forest?" asked Florentius.

"I will lead your units through the forest," said Silvanus. "You have me in your custody. If you detect a trick, kill me on the spot."

"Silvanus, you also say the officer and men guarding the bridge are loyal to you?" asked Florentius.

Silvanus nodded. "Once we pass through the fortifications in the forest, I will send word for him to withdraw from the bridge.

"Take the prisoner outside until I call for him," said the Emperor. "Be sure he cannot hear me should I get *frustrated* again."

Marcus and Lucius took Silvanus out of the room. The Emperor waited several moments until after the door was shut behind them before turning to Florentius. "What is your opinion, General?"

"There is certainly the risk this is a trap," said Florentius. "However, we can take precautions to detect if Silvanus intends to betray us. And, if he does, he can be killed on the spot."

"You are suggesting we take this risk?"

"I am, my lord," said Florentius. "Taking precautions, we can minimize the risk of any traps. At worst we will lose a day or two. However, if Silvanus can do as he says, we may avoid a bloody battle of attrition and gain a decisive victory."

The Emperor looked around the table at the other generals. "Are we in agreement to risk this plan?"

The generals nodded their heads.

"Very well, it is agreed," said Constantius. "We will do as Silvanus suggests." He faced Arbitio. "I want you to command our forces in the forest. Captain Marcus's squadron of cavalry will lead the way. Silvanus will be with him. If Marcus determines the way is safe, he will send word back to the rest to follow. If a trap is detected—kill the prisoner."

On the map, Florentius saw the figurine of an infantry unit across the river from Mursa Major. It gave him an idea. "The barbarian mercenaries of King Gundamar are encamped on the opposite side of the Drava, northeast of Mursa Major," he said. "They have the best chance to arrive at the enemy's bridge by noon. If Gundamar can capture the bridgehead defenses, both he and our river fleet could block the Western army's escape."

The Emperor nodded. "Yes. Use the barbarians. I do not care if they suffer heavy losses. It is time for Gundamar to earn the gold I have been paying him." The Emperor now remembered the note in his hand. He wrinkled his brow as he read it. "Florentius, see to the details of the plan. I must attend to my wife."

***

The moon floated high in the sky, ducking in and out from behind passing clouds. Across the valley, the campfires from the enemy's sentry line dotted the hilltops to the west. To the northwest, even the glow from the Western army's great camp, miles distant, could be seen.

Florentius, together with Lucius alongside, rode along the marching lines of men. "As quiet as you can, lads. All depends on surprising the enemy."

The long column of thousands of Eastern cavalry and infantry marched in the darkness to the southeast of Mursa Major. To conceal their movements from enemy pickets across the valley, the soldiers moved along the road and across the countryside without the use of torches. Soldiers even shrouded the blades of their weapons in cloth lest a reflection of moonlight give them away.

Florentius and Lucius joined Arbitio and Marcus at the head of the column as it came to a halt.

"One hundred yards ahead there lies a path that leads through the thicket, into the forest beyond and to the Western defenses," said Silvanus, his hands bound behind his back.

Arbitio addressed Marcus. "Take a detachment ahead and scout the thicket and tree line."

Marcus saluted. He rode forward with a couple dozen of his men.

Long minutes passed without any sign of Marcus and those under his command.

Florentius's jaw tightened. *This is my fault if something happens to them.*

"Do not worry, General," said Silvanus, seeing the concern on the general's face. "They are fine. No harm will come of them. I am a man who can be trusted."

"Are you?" asked Florentius, sounding unsure. He turned to Lucius. "Wait here." He spurred his horse onward until he was only feet from the path that went through the thicket. The moonlight grew bright and dimmed in succession as clouds passed over. The shadows seemed to move about the thicket, as if alive. There were sounds here and there of rustling leaves. *Woodland animals?* Florentius leaned forward in his saddle, straining to discern the shadows and to listen for signs of Marcus or of an ambush.

"Your daughter is beautiful," said Arbitio as he rode up slowly.

Florentius saw the commander beside him. "I did not hear your approach." He resumed scanning the thicket.

"I said, your daughter is beautiful. A man would be fortunate to have her as his wife."

"As her father, I believe so. But, is this not a strange time for such a conversation?"

"Have you considered her prospects?"

Florentius jerked his head back. "Prospects?"

"Arrangements for her marriage, of course. A girl of her station and beauty deserves a man of prominence for a husband—a powerful man of influence and means. Have you anyone in mind?"

Florentius stifled a chuckle. "Tell me who it is you have in mind. Clearly, you are thinking of someone."

"Do not toy with me, Florentius. You know well I do—my speech has been plain enough. You know of my place in the imperial court. I could well provide for your daughter. Such a marriage would unite our two families—and our interests in the imperial court. We could be beneficial allies to each other."

There came the cracks of snapping twigs and branches along the path before them. Florentius stiffened in his saddle. "Marcus?" he called out in a hushed tone. No response.

After several minutes of silence, Florentius addressed Arbitio. "If I decide anything regarding Melissa's future, it will be to look after her interests—not those of my own. As for my service to the Emperor, I am duty and honor-bound to serve his interests and those of the empire, and not those of my own. I have no need of court alliances—with you or anyone else."

"Florentius, do not despise my offer or discount the necessity of alliances in court. You are one of the last few Catholics left in high office under an Emperor who favors the Arians. Once this war is over, your position will be precarious. Your friendship with Athanasius and allegiance to the pope of Rome are annoyances tolerated by the Emperor for the moment because he finds your services and advice useful—but these will be your undoing once this war is over."

"Do not threaten me, Commander."

Marcus and one other rider emerged out of the thicket along the path. "All is clear. No sign of the enemy," said the captain.

"Very well," said Arbitio. "Captain, order your squadron forward. Send back word if the way is safe." He glared at Florentius. "Remember what I said, Florentius."

With that, the commander spun his horse around and rode back to rejoin the column, passing Lucius, who rode up to join Florentius and Marcus.

Marcus called to one of his riders. "Order the squadron forward. Bring the prisoner."

"Marcus, be quick as you can," said Florentius. "Even if Silvanus is to be trusted, it will be difficult to get this column into position to join the attack by noon, as planned."

"Understood, General," said Marcus.

Florentius watched as Lucius rode up to join him. "Captain, I thought I asked you to stay with the column."

"I was getting worried about you, sir," said Lucius.

"I am all right. The way is clear. You and I can go back to the city."

"General, may I accompany Marcus and his squadron?"

"No," said Florentius, his tone terse. *You are my friend's son and have a crippled leg. A battlefield is no place for you.* "You are to come back to the city with me." He turned his horse about and headed back toward the column.

"I am sorry, Lucius," said Marcus. "I know you want a taste of adventure and battle."

"In the general's mind, he is doing my father a favor by keeping me away from danger," said Lucius, wincing as he shifted in his saddle.

Marcus shook his head as he watched Lucius try to rub the pain away in his injured leg. "It is more than that. With the weakness in your leg, it is difficult to sit astride a horse. Even a peaceful ride along a country road causes you pain. It is not your fault, but you are too weak to ride into combat. You would be a danger to yourself in battle. The general protects you for your own good."

"I can handle the pain," said Lucius, stung by his comrade's words. "You know me; I would be fine."

"I say this as a friend. Not to hurt you. The general is right."

As Lucius was about protest, the rider returned with Silvanus in tow and the rest of the squadron.

Silvanus smiled confidently as Marcus considered him with a cold stare. "I know, I know," said Silvanus, as if reading the captain's thoughts. He spun about in his saddle and called out for the squadron to hear. "At the first sign of trouble, death to the prisoner!" He chuckled as he faced Marcus. "Did I get that right?"

"No need to tell them to kill the prisoner," said Marcus. "I'll do it myself." He then waved the squadron forward. "Follow me!"

Chapter 7

The Battle of Mursa Major

The legionaries of Third Italica stood at ease on low-lying ground between two lines of hills that ran parallel to each other. Each legionary, equipped with a helmet and a chain mail shirt which fell below the middle thigh, wore a long-sleeve, red tunic and military trousers beneath his armor, as well as dark boots and a long gray cloak. The common legionary gripped a long spear and a javelin together in one hand and carried a large black rounded shield bearing a white Chi Rho. The legion also had a detachment of a dozen riders. These, dressed and armed like the infantry, carried smaller round shields with the Chi Rho.

Sitting atop his horse at the head of his legion, Tribune Marius squinted and blocked the sun with his hand as he looked up at the sky. "It is almost noon."

The tribune rode forward a dozen yards, his scarlet cloak caught up in the breeze. He came back to his place beside Centurion Rufius Longinus. Septimus alternated between sitting up straight in the saddle and then sitting back to rest for a few moments, only to repeat the pattern.

"Tribune Marius—you seem impatient, sir," said the centurion.

Septimus pointed to the hill before them. "I see the pennant of General Marcellinus on the high ground. Our battle line is on the opposite slope. This morning before dawn, to the blare of horns, legions of heavy infantry and squadrons of cavalry, ours and theirs, sallied forth from fortified camps. Yet, since the time both armies

99

took up positions after sunrise, nothing. No battle horns . . . no trumpets . . . no clash of men and arms. The battle should have begun hours ago."

"Perhaps Constantius does not intend to give battle this day."

Septimus gathered the reins in his hands. "Stay here."

"Where are you off to now?"

"To have a look for myself," said Septimus as he spurred his horse, Ulysses, forward. The tribune galloped past two legions of reserve infantry positioned at two hundred-yard intervals ahead of Third Italica on the near slope. When he crested the hill, he pulled Ulysses to a halt as he took in the sight. The battle lines of the opposing Roman armies eyed the other across a shallow valley. Men and horses waited in formations of neat squares, armor glittering in the midday sunlight and banners and pennants swaying in the breeze. General Marcellinus and his staff stood a short distance farther down the slope, behind a long line of Western infantry.

Septimus rode up beside Marcellinus. He saw a Chi Rho shield of the Third Italica, the one from the general's quarters, hanging from the side of the horse that Marcellinus sat upon. "Not bearing your own emblem of office today?" asked the tribune.

"I told you I had misgivings about today," said the general. "The enemy has not moved in hours. All is an eerie calm."

"You sound as if you want them to attack."

"I dislike the unexpected. This is unexpected. It worries me."

"Worries?"

"Let us say it puzzles me. We have the advantage of position, but the enemy outnumbers us. Constantius cannot expect us to move forward. He has already wasted many hours of daylight. All very odd."

"What do you make of it, General?"

"Something is afoot, but I do not know what. I fear something has escaped our notice."

The sound of an enemy horn echoed from across the valley, its call taken up by other horns up and down the length of the battle line of the Easterner army. Distant shouts of Eastern centurions barking out orders resounded in his ears. Bright, dazzling rays of light danced across the valley floor and upon the Western lines, reflecting off the armor and weapons of thousands of Eastern legionaries now in motion. Down the opposite slope of the valley, they marched. The clanking of armor and a continuous roll of thunder rumbled through the countryside as each soldier pounded spear against shield as they advanced. After one legion cleared the crest of the hill, another soon appeared behind it and followed it down the slope.

"Finally!" shouted Marcellinus to his staff.

Septimus grinned. "This makes you feel better, General?"

"Better? No. Relieved? Yes." The general watched as the enemy advanced. "This makes sense. This I understand!"

The Eastern legions marched across the valley floor and began their ascent up the slopes toward the lines of the Western army.

Marcellinus raised his arm. "Upon my signal!" he shouted. Upon his word, the Roman artillery, batteries of scorpions along the Western army's line readied for action. They placed the artillery just behind the front ranks on higher ground and upon wagons so that they could fire over the tops of the infantry.

Thirty yards farther down the hill, Septimus observed a line of a dozen scorpions. Two-man crews cranked back the arms of each machine to increase the tension in the spring mechanism, and then each was loaded with an iron-tipped bolt.

The advancing ranks were now two hundred yards away, the echoing sound of their armor and the pounding of their shields growing ever louder.

Marcellinus winked at Septimus. "Like wheat ready for the scythe."

The general dropped his hand, followed at once by a flagman pointing the scorpion banner to the ground. The batteries of scorpions launched a barrage of iron-tipped bolts that flew with high-pitched screams. Each bolt, fired with such speed and force, pierced through shields and armor, even passing through the bodies of several men in its line of flight, tearing gaps in the Eastern ranks.

Septimus clenched his jaw as the fire from the scorpions—each launching four to five bolts a minute—continued to reap a horrifying toll of blood and death as the Easterners drew closer to the Western ranks. *Why did it come to this, Roman killing fellow Roman?*

101

When the Easterners came within range, Western archers rained volleys of arrows down upon them. When the armies were less than fifty feet apart, the opposing legionaries launched a volley of javelins at one another and then, letting out loud war cries, each side surged forward toward the other. The two armies collided. The din of clashing weapons and shields, and the yells and cries of men locked in mortal combat echoed throughout the countryside. The scorpions, atop carts and fortified platforms, continued to fire bolts over the heads of their own infantry and into the dense formation of Eastern legionaries.

The ongoing carnage before them, Marcellinus patted Septimus. "We have the better of the fight."

Septimus gave no response.

"You seem a bit grim, Tribune Marius," said the general above the sounds of battle.

"All things are wretched in civil war," said Septimus.

"Cicero again?" said Marcellinus. "It was Constantius who brought this upon us all. His desire for one empire, and a desire to make the Church Arian and to rule it too."

The general sat up high in his saddle to better view the battle. The Eastern legionaries along the line began to fall back. "The enemy attack has lost momentum!" said Marcellinus. "Their first assault has suffered heavy casualties. See, they are withdrawing for the moment and must bring fresh troops forward." The general nodded in satisfaction. "Our right wing is holding solid. Nowhere does the enemy threaten to break through our line. It seems we have taken the best of what Constantius can throw at us!"

A messenger approached at a gallop. He pulled his horse to a quick stop, its mouth frothing as it snorted. "What is it?" asked Marcellinus, still smiling.

"Barbarian mercenaries, perhaps five thousand strong, march along the left bank of the river," said the messenger, out of breath. "They are marching toward the pontoon bridge!"

"Calm down, son. Do not fret. The bridge is secure. There is a garrison there."

The rider shook his head. "There is no garrison at the bridge."

"Nonsense," said Septimus. "Silvanus has at least six cohorts guarding the bridge."

"I rode first to the bridge to give them the report, but . . ." said the messenger, pausing to catch his breath.

"Come on, man, spit it out," said Septimus, impatient.

"There are no troops guarding it. Not even a cohort. Not a single legionary. The bridge is undefended!"

"Undefended?" asked the general, alarm spreading across his face. "Impossible."

"Silvanus withdrew his cohorts from the bridge?" asked Septimus.

"I gave no such order!" Marcellinus said. The general kicked his heels against the side of his horse, jolting it forward. He spun about and rode off toward the top of the hill.

Septimus grabbed the reins tight. "Come on, Ulysses," he called out as he spurred his horse into action. He raced up the slope after the general at a gallop. Septimus passed by scores of wounded legionaries, their blood staining the ground where they lay as comrades and doctors tended to them. Ahead, Marcellinus had by now reached the top of the height. The general sat as high in the saddle as he could, straining to see into the distance.

Ulysses snorted as Septimus reined him to a halt beside Marcellinus.

"I glimpse the river to the northwest, but I cannot see the bridge," said Marcellinus, as he scanned the countryside for signs of the enemy. "The rider's report cannot be true," he said as if hoping to convince himself.

Septimus held his right hand high to block the glare of the sun. He searched the terrain in the distance. "There, to the north," he said as he pointed. "The glint of steel moving along the opposite bank of the river. The sun reflecting off armor and weapons." He turned, grim-faced, to the general. "It must be the barbarians of which the messenger speaks."

"Then it is true. They make for the bridge."

"The barbarians will reach it within the hour," said Septimus. "General, you must send word to Silvanus at once. He must reinforce the bridge."

Marcellinus grimaced. "I will send word for him to dispatch cavalry to defend the bridge until help arrives, but we do not have time to wait for a reply. Third Italica is closest to the bridge. You must march at once."

"Third Italica is closest, but the bridge is over two miles away. The barbarians will reach it first."

"All the more reason to make haste," said Marcellinus.

From behind them, enemy horns sounded. The two officers turned in their saddles. Across the valley, more enemy lines of infantry than before made their way down the far slope.

"The Easterners attack again, in greater force," said Septimus, sweat lacing his neck. "You may need my legion here."

"We do not know what has befallen the garrison at the river," said the general. He pursed his lips as he observed the forward ranks of enemy legionaries. "We do not know what may befall us. Something strange is afoot." He turned to Septimus. Their eyes met. "The bridge must not fall into the enemy's hands. The whole army would be surrounded ... cut off without possibility of escape." He grabbed the tribune by the forearm. "Make safe the bridge."

"Understood, sir."

"I always considered you like another son, Septimus," said Marcellinus. "May God go with you!"

The tribune saluted. "May your God be with you, sir," he said. He then urged Ulysses on to a gallop as he raced to rejoin Third Italica.

***

Septimus rode at the head of the Third Italica. He kept looking back at the legion and the landscape around them.

"Impatient, sir?" asked Longinus, who rode beside him.

"The general said he would send word to Silvanus," said the tribune. "There has been no sign of his cavalry. Septimus turned about in his saddle. "Faster men! Third Italica must reach the river before the barbarians!"

"Tribune Marius, you cannot wish a legion on any faster than it can go. The men are already marching double-time."

"You are right, Centurion," Septimus said. He pursed his lips in thought. "Decurion!" he said, calling for the officer who commanded the small detachment of a dozen horsemen attached to the legion.

"Sir?" said the decurion as he rode up to Septimus.

"Order your riders forward. They will follow me."

Longinus raised an eyebrow. "What do you think you are doing?"

"We cannot count on cavalry from Silvanus to reach the bridge ahead of us. Centurion, you will continue on with the infantry."

Longinus shook his head. "What do you plan to do now, Tribune?"

"I will go ahead with the cavalry."

Longinus glimpsed the horsemen lined up in pairs behind the decurion. "Cavalry is it? You mean these dozen riders?"

"I do."

"How do you plan to halt several regiments of barbarians from crossing the river with a dozen men?"

"Pliny the Elder, as he set off to rescue a friend from a volcanic eruption near Pompeii, was heard to say, 'Fortune favors the bold.'"

Septimus waved the decurion and his riders forward.

"Wait!" said Longinus, calling after the tribune as he began to ride away.

Septimus turned Ulysses toward Longinus. "Something else, Centurion?"

"What happened to him?"

"To who?"

"To Pliny the Elder, the one who said fortune favors the bold."

"Oh, him? Killed by poisonous vapors from the volcano . . . died an agonizing death." The tribune winked.

"Why do I ever bother to ask?" Longinus muttered to himself as he watched Septimus ride away. The centurion rode along the column of legionaries as they hustled along. "Come on, you storks!" he shouted. He pointed his vine staff toward Septimus riding away over the next hilltop. "As quick as you can, lads! We have our tribune to rescue!"

***

It was three hours past noon when Septimus, emerging through

105

a line of trees, crested a hill that overlooked the pontoon bridge, only a few hundred yards away. Constructed across three dozen boats held in place by anchors and tethers tied to piles hammered into the river bottom, the wood bridge spanned a straightaway between two bends of the river.

Septimus and the decurion surveyed the bridgehead defenses from their vantage point. Across the river, the bridge was shielded by a flooded trench, 200 yards in length. Behind this moat, taking advantage of the bend in the river, there ran a long palisade with battlements from water's edge to water's edge, with a half dozen towers with artillery.

"If Third Italica arrives in time, we can easily hold the far side of the river," said Septimus. He then looked to the near shore where construction of the fortifications had not yet been completed. A long trench had been dug, but not yet flooded. Behind it ran a line of earthenworks upon which only segments of a palisade had been built.

Septimus furrowed his brow as he studied the fortifications. He saw no sign of the defenders. All of it was useless if none manned the defenses.

"At least we beat the barbarians to the bridge," said the decurion.

"No sign of Silvanus or his cavalry," said the tribune. "Let us hope it arrives soon."

The Romans galloped down the slope. Septimus led them over a level plain, only a hundred yards across. As they neared the defenses, he saw that the gate had been left open. Coming to within twenty yards of the gate, he signaled to his men to halt.

Septimus scanned the earthenworks and the battlement over the gate for signs of life. For signs of an ambush. *Nothing. What happened here?*

The tribune led the detachment forward. "Careful, men."

Crossing the drawbridge over the trench, they entered through the gate and rode to the river. Again, Septimus halted his small column of riders.

The tribune looked to his right downriver. Within the confines of the bridgehead loomed a tall tower at the water's edge. On each side of the river, the Western Romans had constructed a tower, three stories high. The towers, equipped with artillery, defended the bridge from any attacks by the enemy's fleet of river galleys.

"Decurion, send a man to the top of the river tower," said Septimus. "Have him sing out if he sees anything on land or water."

The decurion saluted.

Septimus led his men across the pontoon bridge, which spanned two hundred feet, to the left bank.

"We are not alone," said Septimus as they crossed the bridge. Ahead, a few small groups of unarmed men roamed here and there about the camp inside the fortifications. He approached the closest of these, three bearded men sitting by the river.

"Gaius Marius Septimus," said the tribune.

One of them, a man in his late twenties, stood to his feet. "Hail, Tribune Marius."

"Who are you men?"

"Jason is my name."

The two other men stood up beside the first, one shorter than Jason, who was himself of average height. The other, having a huge and muscular build, stood six and a half feet tall.

Jason pointed first to the shorter of the two men. "His name is Drusus. The big one—we do not know his name. We just call him Samson."

"Your accents . . . your appearance—you are not Romans."

"We are not Romans!" said Samson. "Do not insult us!"

Jason patted the big one on the shoulder. "Calm down, friend." He turned to Septimus. "No, we are not Romans. We are Jews."

Septimus raised an eyebrow. "Jews? In the midst of a Roman civil war?"

Jason pointed to the groups of men seated or milling about the camp. "These men you see are fishermen and merchants from Ostia and Rome. We have made common cause with Magnentius, joining his army to fight against Constantius. Our people rebel against him in the East. They struggle now against his cousin, Caesar Gallus."

"You are in the service of Emperor Magnentius?"

"We work as laborers . . . sappers."

The tribune glanced at the decurion and his riders. He pointed

107

to the gate. "Raise the drawbridge. Close the gate. Post a watch on the wall."

Drusus approached the tribune. "We work as laborers and sappers . . . but we volunteered to fight Romans!"

"To fight and kill them!" said Samson.

"You men worked on this bridge?" asked the tribune.

Jason swept back his long black hair from his face. "We did."

"Where did the legionaries defending it go?" asked Septimus.

Jason shrugged. "I only overheard a messenger tell them that Claudius Silvanus ordered them to withdraw from the river."

"Silvanus ordered them to withdraw?" Septimus muttered aloud in disbelief. He rubbed his chin and face. His heart sank as he thought of his friend. *What was Silvanus thinking? All knew the importance of holding the river. What could motivate him to do such a thing?*

"They seemed to be in a great hurry."

"Do you men have a leader?"

"I suppose that would be me," said Jason.

"How many are there of you?"

"Less than two hundred."

"Can they fight?" Septimus asked.

"We joined to kill Romans," interjected Samson.

Septimus looked at Samson. "How about barbarians? Can you kill them?"

"If our lives depended on it," said Drusus.

A battle horn sounded from the forest beyond the wall. The tribune cast a glance in the direction from which the sound came. He then glimpsed the undefended wall. Septimus nodded. "Your lives depend on it. That was an Alemanni battle horn."

"We have no weapons," said Jason.

"Use what you can find," said Septimus. "Shovels, axes, hammers, anything. Get your men to the walls, at once."

Septimus rode to the gate. He hopped off of Ulysses and scrambled up the ladder to the battlements.

A long column of barbarian infantry tramped along the road that came out of the forest and led to the gate. There was no common uniform among the warriors, though most wore armored shirts and helmets and long brown trousers tied tight around the ankles. The barbarians, armed with spears, swords, and battle-axes, carried round shields with emblems of animals upon them.

"I'd say five thousand of them, maybe more, Tribune!" called out a Roman soldier who climbed into the tower above the gate.

The barbarian column came to a halt fifty yards away from the wall. At the head of the barbarian column, on top of a large white warhorse, sat a giant of a man. His armor glimmered in the sun. Upon his head, the tall feathered plumes of his helmet swayed in the breeze.

"Who is that?" asked Jason as he joined Septimus along the battlement.

"Gundamar," said the tribune.

"Gundamar?"

"He is called Gundamar the Giant by his people. One of the nine kings of the Alemanni."

Samson snickered. "He does not appear so giant."

Gundamar, with several of his mounted warriors, trotted forward another twenty yards. "Open the gate!" he called out.

Septimus looked at the decurion. "Spread the word. Disable the scorpions we cannot man. Be prepared to disable the ones we do. Best not to make a gift of them to the barbarians."

"The gate is to be opened to us!" shouted Gundamar. He sat tall in the saddle as he surveyed the wall before him. The barbarian king rode forward a few more yards. "There was an agreement . . . the gate is to be opened to us!"

Septimus climbed on the very top of the palisade. He balanced himself with his right hand against the leg of the tower beside the gate. In full view of the barbarians, his red cloak and the plumes of his helmet fluttered in the breeze. "Greetings, Gundamar!"

Gundamar leaned forward in his saddle, he squinted. "Who is that I hear?" he said. He laughed. "Septimus? Can it be? Septimus Lupus?"

"It is I, Gundamar."

Jason glanced up at the tribune. "Septimus Lupus?"

The tribune shook his head. "It is a long story."

"Septimus, it has been a long time!" shouted Gundamar.

"Yes, a long time, Gundamar," said the tribune.

"You know this barbarian?" whispered Jason.

The tribune nodded. "My blood brother . . . according to a

custom of his people."

Jason smiled at Samson and Drusus. "We are safe. It is his blood brother."

One warrior behind Gundamar raised his bow and let fly an arrow. It struck the leg of the tower, inches from the head of Septimus. The tribune remained still for a moment. Stone-faced, he considered the arrow, and then pulled it from the wood. He hopped down behind the battlement.

"I thought you said he was your blood brother?" asked Jason.

"I did not say we were on good terms," said Septimus. He tossed the arrow over the wall. He signaled to the men in the tower above him. The metallic thud of a scorpion's firing mechanism sounded, followed in quick succession by second. Two bolts whistled through the air. The first of the missiles sailed over Gundamar's head. But two men cried out as the bolt sailed clean through one warrior's neck and into the chest of another behind him. The second missile struck the head of a horse beside Gundamar. The horse toppled over dead, bringing its rider crashing to the ground.

Jason shook his head. "Some family."

"It is a long story," said Septimus.

The barbarian, his leg pinned for a brief moment beneath his dead horse, freed himself. He stood up and took several strides toward the gate. He yelled in defiance, daring them to try again.

"This gate was to be opened to us!" said the barbarian king.

"It will not be opened," said Septimus. "Turn back—while you still can! There is a full legion defending this wall."

Gundamar laughed. "It is no use, Septimus Lupus! You have been betrayed by one of your own! I can see that you are few. You cannot hold the wall against us. There is no hope! Open the gate to us. I promise, my blood brother, you will die a quick, painless death."

"The gate will stay closed!" said the tribune.

Gundamar threw his head back and laughed. "So be it! It is death for you either way!"

The king rode to the column of warriors, yelling orders to them as he went. The lead battalion of the column deployed into a battle line two hundred yards long and ten men deep.

Jason saw doubt on the tribune's face. "We are only two hundred. Most armed with axes, picks, and shovels. We cannot hold out against so great a number."

Tribune Marius stepped toward a scorpion positioned behind the battlement. "Not hold out. Buy time, perhaps."

A chorus of high-pitched battle horns blared along the line of barbarians. The warriors began to march toward the palisade. At first, their pace was slow, each step in line, each movement precise.

Coming to within fifty yards of the water-filled trench, another blast of horns sounded. The warriors let out a terrifying war cry as they rushed the palisade. Bolts from the few scorpions manned by the handful of Romans rang out and flew into the onrushing line, each felling several barbarians at a time. The first wave of the barbarians reached the moat.

Some, diving into the water to swim across, impaled themselves on sharpened poles hidden just below the waterline. Blood and water swirled. Many gathered at the banks fearing to enter lest they drown beneath the weight of their weapons and armor. Still, there were many, who stripping themselves of their armor shirts and helmets, swam across the moat bearing only their swords or clenching knives in their teeth. When they reached the other side, they scrambled up the slope of the earthen mound to the base of the wall. There, forming human ladders, the barbarians began to scale the palisade in various places. All the while, the Romans continued to snipe at the barbarians massed at the edge of the moat with the scorpions.

Helping the Romans, Jason and his Jewish company, armed only with shovels, picks, and other tools, hacked away at the barbarians with whatever tool each had in their possession as the enemy attempted to climb over the battlement. The first attempts to scale the wall were beaten back. Bodies of the dead and wounded tumbled back into the moat which began to turn red with blood. However, unable to man the entire length of the palisade, the defenders could not prevent the warriors from coming over the battlement in increasing numbers. The barbarians attacked along the top of the wall, hoping to gain control of the gate.

A desperate melee raged, attackers and defenders everywhere intermixed. The Romans and Jews fought side-by-side, trying to

111

fend off the barbarians who pressed them back at both ends over the gate. Samson, wielding a heavy sledgehammer, felled barbarians with each swing as they attempted to rush him. Septimus ran his sword through a warrior as he topped the battlement. *Almighty, these brutes are tough.* The weight of his falling body knocked the barbarians beneath him off balance, collapsing the whole human ladder.

Looking over the battlement, Septimus's jaw tightened. Groups of barbarians carried forward fallen trees, long enough to span the width of the trench. Throwing the trees down over the moat as a makeshift bridge, warriors began to cross it in single file.

Septimus saw Jason plant a pick deep into the chest of a barbarian. "Jason," he called, drawing the Jew's attention to the greater number of barbarians crossing the moat and now scaling the wall. "We are in danger of being overwhelmed. Your men have fought bravely. Get them across the river."

Jason nodded and signaled to his men to retreat.

"Fall back!" shouted Septimus. "Fall back!" he urged as he moved along the battlement, stepping over the dead, slaying barbarians as he went, helping to extricate defenders from the melee.

Jason paused as he hurried toward the bridge. Turning around, he searched the top of the wall. There was the red of the tribune's cape and horsehair helmet. Septimus was still on the wall above the gate, locked in hand-to-hand combat with barbarians. "Tribune, save yourself!"

Seeing the last of the surviving defenders running for the bridge, Septimus hurried to the closest ladder. As he reached it, a line of four barbarians rushed toward him. Seeing a scorpion a few feet away, he spun it around and fired at the first of the warriors, right in front of him. The bolt flew through the bodies of three of the onrushers, dropping them at once. The fourth came at the tribune, swinging his battle axe as he did. The blade, missing the Roman, struck deep into the scorpion. Before the warrior could withdraw it, Septimus plunged his sword into the attacker, sending his body falling to the ground below. The tribune descended the ladder and looked to his own escape.

"Ulysses!" the tribune muttered to himself. He surveyed the

interior of the bridgehead. He saw his horse—Ulysses—grazing grass two hundred feet away. Septimus ran toward the animal. He had covered half the distance when he stopped in his tracks. A sound of the grating and clicking of metal gears came from behind him. He glanced toward the gate and saw barbarians turning the winch to lower the drawbridge.

Septimus looked toward his horse. "Ulysses!"

The horse lifted his head, a wad of grass protruding from his mouth. The tribune whistled. He waved and beckoned to the animal to come to him. The horse dithered, seeming to weigh the relative risks of flight or of rescuing his master.

"Ulysses!"

A loud thud echoed as the drawbridge hit the ground. Shouts and a war cry filled the air. Warriors streamed through the gate, bearing down on Septimus. Master and horse locked eyes. With a loud neigh, Ulysses bolted away at a gallop, riderless, back to the bridge and across the river to safety. The tribune ran for the bridge. Dozens of barbarians were in close pursuit.

"Stupid horse," muttered Septimus as he went. Reaching the pontoon bridge, he kept glancing over his shoulders at his pursuers, who were several yards behind him. He could not tell whether the pounding in his heart or of barbarian feet upon the bridge was louder.

When Septimus was halfway across the bridge, he heard a shout from the right bank ahead of him. It was loud and familiar. "Tribune, get down!"

There, at the end of the bridge, sat Longinus on a horse behind a wall of black shields, each bearing a white Chi Rho. Two dozen archers stood behind it, bows at the ready. Tribune Marius dropped to the deck of the bridge.

"Fire!" shouted the centurion.

Volley after volley of arrows whistled over Septimus's head. Bodies splashed into the river and collapsed with thuds on the bridge. The whistling stopped. The pounding of running feet ceased. The tribune rolled to his side and looked back. Dozens of arrow-ridden bodies lay strewn along the bridge, a half dozen more floated downriver.

Tribune Marius stood and surveyed the bridge behind him. He

exhaled in relief. *That was close.* He approached Longinus, seated high upon a horse, at the end of the bridge. More legionaries of Third Italica were streaming into the bridgehead and forming a line of battle facing the river.

Septimus took off his helmet and swept the sweat from his brow with his forearm. He looked up at the centurion. "I told you—fortune favors the bold."

Longinus tapped his vine staff against one of his grieves. "Oh, is that it? I would say, by the looks of it, it would be more exact to say, fortune favors the fleet of foot." He snickered. "Nor does it hurt if fortune comes armed with a squad of archers."

The tribune, a half-smile on his face, nodded.

"By the way, did you lose something?" Longinus asked. He pointed his vine staff toward a legionary standing thirty feet away. The soldier held the reins of a riderless gray horse.

The smile on the tribune's face melted away.

"I had the distinct impression Ulysses ran away from you," said Longinus. "Or, was that just one of the clever tricks you taught him?"

"I do not appreciate your sarcasm, Centurion."

"One day that horse will get you killed."

Septimus stomped over to his horse. He grabbed the reins from the legionary. "A noise startled him," he said as he mounted the animal.

Longinus looked across the river at the mass of barbarians marching through the gate and forming in ranks by the water's edge. On the opposite bank, the barbarian king sat upon his horse. "I see that you have met an old friend."

Septimus observed the king. "Gundamar said we were betrayed."

"Betrayed?" asked Longinus, as he followed Septimus down to the river.

"Gundamar expected the gate to be opened to him . . . that he would be allowed to freely pass over the bridge. He is surprised to find Third Italica blocking his way. I doubt he will now risk forcing his way across a narrow bridge, even with his greater numbers. Whatever the truth of it, we must prevent the barbarians from crossing. Make preparations to set fire to the bridge."

"I advise against that," said Longinus. "A messenger from Marcellinus brought word just as we reached the river." The centurion paused. He grimaced.

"Word of what?"

"The Easterners launched a surprise attack against our right wing from the forest."

"From the forest? How is that possible?"

The centurion shook his head. "I do not know. The messenger's report was that the situation was dire. The army has been outflanked."

The tribune gazed into the river, his thoughts troubled. *What of Silvanus?*

Longinus studied Septimus, seeming to read his thoughts. "The bridge and forest defenses were under the command of Silvanus. And it was Silvanus who convinced Marcellinus to reassign Third Italica. I am sorry, sir. I know he is your friend, but it appears inescapable that Silvanus has a hand in this treachery."

Septimus grimaced. *My friend could do no such thing. Silvanus a traitor?* He ran his hand through his hair as he considered what to do next. "Whether Silvanus is traitor or not, we must first burn the bridge to prevent the barbarians from crossing. Third Italica must then march back to the battlefield. We must do what we can to save Marcellinus and the army."

"We cannot, Tribune! The battle is several miles away, and we are only one legion. Marcellinus ordered Third Italica to hold the bridge at all cost—it is the only escape for the army."

Septimus pursed his lip. He thought back to his last encounter with Marcellinus and the general's command. *Make safe the bridge.*

The tribune surveyed the mass of barbarians filing through the gate to enter within the defensive palisade across the river. "There must be two thousand of them now within the bridgehead. Several thousand more wait outside the wall."

The Alemanni warriors taunted the Romans with shouts and whistles from the safety of the opposite shore.

"They outnumber us over two to one," said Longinus. "But they will not dare try an opposed crossing of the bridge. Still, I will have the men prepare defenses, just in case. We still have a couple dozen scorpions on this side of the river."

The tribune squinted across the river.

The centurion shook his head. "I know that look, Tribune. What are you thinking?"

"What were our orders?" asked Septimus.

"You know well the orders. Hold the bridge."

"Yes, but we don't hold the bridge. We hold only one side of the river."

"And?"

Septimus spurred his gray horse into a trot till he came to where the bridge touched the bank held by the Romans. Longinus rode along behind him.

"In holding one side of the river, we hold nothing," said the tribune. "If it should come to it, the army could not escape across the bridge. We have not made safe the bridge. I have lost it."

Longinus pushed his helmet up off his wrinkled forehead with the tip of his vine staff. He raised an eyebrow. "What are you suggesting?"

"We must recapture the far side."

"An opposed bridge crossing against a numerically superior foe? The odds will be against us, you know."

"We both know the odds," said Septimus, grim-faced. "But we both know the fate of many requires we try." He set his jaw. "Prepare the legion to attack."

A slight grin appeared on the centurion's face. He straightened his helmet and fastened it tight around his chin. "I was afraid you would say that."

The Romans organized into ten cohorts, two hundred men each. Legionaries brought the scorpions down from the earthen rampart and placed them in two batteries near the river. When the preparations were complete, Longinus dismounted his horse. He grabbed his shield and took a position in front of the First Cohort, which was closest to the bridge.

The centurion glanced up at Septimus, seated astride Ulysses. "'Fortune favors the bold,' is it?" he said, his tone gruff and annoyed.

"Fortune punishes the reckless, too," Septimus said with a wry smile.

The centurion nodded with a grin.

Tribune Marius turned toward the legion, arrayed by cohort for battle, to address it. "Third Italica and the whole Western army have been betrayed by one of our own—Claudius Silvanus. The army is in peril. General Marcellinus ordered Third Italica to make safe the bridge. It is the only hope of escape for our comrades . . . and for ourselves."

The tribune took up his round shield emblazoned with two white storks. He drew his sword and held it high. "Pia!" he shouted.

"Fidelis!" came the thunderous reply from the legion.

The centurion shouted out orders to the First Cohort. "Testudo!"

The cohort formed into a narrow column, five men across. Legionaries on the outside of the formation presented their shields outward while those in the interior files held their shields aloft to create a protective covering. The appearance was that of the shell of a giant turtle—from which the formation received its name. Longinus knocked at one of the lead shields. "All right, knuckleheads, let me in. You cannot go anywhere without your centurion."

Gundamar, his back to the river, stood atop the wall that his warriors had stormed less than an hour before. Around him stood several of his chieftains, over whom he towered. Below him, the bodies of dead warriors lay on the banks of the trench and floated in the moat. "To have crossed paths once again with Septimus Lupus. To have him so close and within my grasp." He held his hand open like the claw of a bear. "Only to escape me once again," he said, as he closed it tight into a fist, the knuckles whitening.

"Shall we launch the attack on the Romans across the bridge?" asked one of the chieftains.

Gundamar shook his head. "We would lose one to two thousand warriors trying to force a crossing."

"But what of the Emperor's gold?"

"The Emperor's general, Florentius, assured me there would be no Romans defending either these walls or the bridge; that all had been betrayed into our hands," said Gundamar. He observed the bodies of dead warriors below. "The terms of our deal have changed. Constantius paid us half in advance. We have won this

117

shore, giving him half of this bridge. The enemy cannot escape."

"And what of Septimus Lupus?" asked a chieftain.

Gundamar laughed. "I will not forget him. His blood will stain my sword one day."

"Then it must be this day."

"What do you mean?"

The chieftain pointed toward the river.

"Impossible!" said Gundamar, turning toward the river as the lead Roman cohort marched onto the bridge.

"This Roman is brave but foolhardy," said a chieftain.

Gundamar nodded. "My blood brother is both." A glint of admiration appeared in his eyes but then disappeared. He bared his teeth. "But this day I will have his head on the end of a spear." He pointed toward the bridge. "Go, quickly. Return to your men at once! Stop the Romans at the water's edge."

Gundamar rushed down off the battlement. There his bodyguards awaited him. Mounting his large warhorse, he rode to the front of several companies as his chieftains worked to form them into lines, trying to give them a semblance of organization. Impatient, King Gundamar waved the companies forward. "Meet them at the water's edge!"

At the king's command, the battle horns blared. The barbarians advanced to the river in one large, unorganized mass. Companies of warriors waiting outside of the palisade, eager for battle, crossed the moat and entered through the gate. Coming inside the bridgehead, they rushed toward the river, but only added to the confusion. Thousands of barbarians crowded and pressed toward the water, penned in by the river in front of them, and on the sides by the bend of the meandering river. Each man had little room to spare to either move or to wield his weapon.

Septimus observed the predicament of the barbarians. He smirked as a chieftain lead a band of fifty warriors onto the far end of the bridge. The barbarians, wanting to show off their bravery within sight of their king, waved their weapons and taunted the Romans with shouts.

The tribune turned to the legionaries manning the scorpions along the river, and in the high tower. "Okay, lads. Let them have it. Fire!"

A hail of scorpion bolts flew across the river. The first bolt went through the chest of the chieftain on the bridge, felling him and those behind him at once. Each successive bolt likewise pierced several men at a time. Bodies dropped to the bridge with a thud, others into the water with loud splashes. The Romans poured volley after volley, several each minute, into the mass of barbarians. Ballistae, firing from the high tower, joined the rain of death. The ballistae, larger versions of the scorpion, launched ten-pound stones across the water. Intended to smash the hulls of enemy galleys on the river, the stones pulverized the skulls and bones of those in their line of flight. Unable to move about as death rained down on those around them or to fight back against the whistling terror, warriors pushed toward the rear to escape the scourge. Within moments, the band of foolhardy barbarians had been wiped out, with only a few warriors surviving to scamper off the bridge. Two-thirds of the barbarians by the river retreated back the wall, outside the range of the Roman artillery.

"First Cohort, advance!" shouted Septimus.

Inside the turtle, Longinus blessed himself with the sign of the cross. He glanced around at the legionaries beside and behind him. "Courage, lads!" he shouted. "They can only kill us."

The cohort set out across the bridge. The legionaries took short, shuffling steps in unison to maintain the cohesion of the protective shell of overlapping shields. As the First Cohort passed the halfway point on the bridge, barbarian archers launched a hail of arrows. However, these became either embedded in the shields or glanced off of them.

As the Roman formation reached the end of the bridge, one of the barbarian warriors ran forward and threw his weight into the shields bearing down on him. The weight and momentum of the formation pushed him back. As he raised his axe to strike, a spear thrust through a gap in the shell of shields and plunged deep into his chest. The barbarian collapsed to the ground with a groan. The Romans marched over the fallen body. A legionary within the turtle pierced the body with the end of his spear as he stepped over it to be sure the warrior was dead. The Roman formation plowed into the line of barbarians who remained close to the river. Barbarian warriors tried to hack at the shields with their battle-axes and swords while the Romans thrust their spears outward through openings in the shield wall.

"Form a wedge!" shouted the centurion after the front of the turtle formation had forced its way fifty-feet inland from the river. At the command, the turtle morphed into an arrow-shaped wedge as the Roman wall of shields fanned out. The legionaries pressed into the line of barbarian warriors with their shields, while their comrades added their weight to the push from behind, thrusting their spears over their heads into the enemy. With each barbarian trying to engage in single rather than team combat, the entire line gave way, step by slow step, before their more disciplined adversaries.

The tribune ordered the next wave of legionaries across the bridge. "Second Cohort, advance ... double time!" He led them across, riding Ulysses at a gallop across the bridge. He pointed to the men to reinforce and expand the wedge forming. "Reinforce your comrades! Push them back from the river." Once the Second Cohort was across, Septimus sent word for the next cohort in line to follow and the others to be ready.

***

Gundamar sat on his great white steed, flanked by his mounted bodyguards and chieftains. The King of the Alemanni, stone-faced, seemed unaware or even uncaring of the scorpions striking the men about him. "Only a few hundred warriors engage the Romans in combat." He turned to see a thousand of his men clinging close to the inner wall of the bridgehead. "The rest are afraid to draw close to them. They will not advance and the others outside of the wall cannot enter!"

Beside Gundamar was a red-bearded chieftain named Balen the Red. The chieftain grimaced when a stone from a Roman ballista decapitated a warrior standing only yards away. Scorpion bolts struck into the formations of infantry around them, felling a couple or more men at a time. "They fear the Roman artillery," said Balen.

More Roman cohorts marched across the bridge.

"The Romans will push us back little by little until they have brought their whole legion and their scorpions with them across

120

THE BATTLE OF MURSA MAJOR

the bridge," said Gundamar. "We must drive them back into the river."

Wheeling his horse about, he rode along his line of warriors who hovered back close to the palisade, as far from the river as they could. "Don't let the Romans see you to be cowards!" he yelled in his barbarian tongue. "If death finds you this day, let it be a glorious one—your body found amidst the many Romans you have killed. Do not let him kill you from afar, like a frightened deer. Draw near to your enemy. They cannot use their artillery if are close to their legionaries."

"See, great king, they hearken to your words!" said Balen, watching as a few dozen of the warriors ran forward to join the battle.

Gundamar shook his head. "It is not enough." He again rode along the line of his warriors. "I declare a bounty on each Roman head. Ten gold pieces for the head of a legionary. One hundred for a centurion. A thousand if you bring me the head of Septimus Lupus!"

A great cheer went up amongst the warriors as the entire mass of barbarians swept toward the river and joined the melee. They flung themselves into the fray, engaging Romans in combat or pushing against the backs of their comrades.

Gundamar waved to his detachment of bodyguards. "I see a weakness in the enemy line. To the fight! Follow me!"

***

Septimus observed the wave of barbarians surge toward his men. "They will drive us back into the river." He turned to a centurion beside him. "Persius, quick, send word for the next two cohorts to cross the river."

"Sir!" said the decurion, mounted on his own horse beside the tribune. He pointed beyond the enemy infantry. A line of several dozen barbarians on horseback galloped to the right of the battle. The armor of the lead rider gleamed in the fading sunlight. The tall feathers stood high atop his helmet.

Septimus gritted his teeth. "Gundamar." He watched the barbarian king and his detachment of bodyguards. "He is up to something." He shifted his focus to see where they were heading. He noticed something toward the end of the Roman flank. He grimaced. "There is a gap between our right and the river. Gundamar intends to turn our flank."

Gundamar led his horsemen wide of the Roman right. They plunged their horses into the shallows. They turned to their right and rode back along the shoreline, the horses kicking up water, mud, and rocks. The sun reflected brightly off their scale armor and weapons, as they waved their swords and battle-axes above their heads. The riders let out a high-pitched war cry as they galloped forward.

"Our right is in danger!" said the tribune. Seeing Persius arriving with a fresh cohort, Septimus waved to him and the decurion with his riders. "Follow me!"

Septimus galloped along the rear of the Roman line, his red cape fluttering in the air as he went, until he and his riders encountered the barbarian charge head-on in the shallows of the river. "Gundamar!" he shouted, seeing him only yards away. As Septimus headed toward him, one of the king's bodyguards intercepted him. The bodyguard rammed his own horse into Ulysses, who wobbled from the impact. The warrior swung a battle-axe at the tribune. Septimus raised his shield. The force of the blow shattered his shield in half. He shouted in pain as his left arm went numb. As the warrior lifted his ax again, Septimus swung his sword against the head of the warrior, inflicting a long gash down his face. The warrior, writhing in agony and grasping at his bloody wound, fell off his horse into the river.

"Brother!" came a shout.

Septimus turned to his right toward the voice. "Gundamar!"

The king slammed his shield against Septimus. Unable to steady himself, with his deadened left arm, Septimus fell off of Ulysses. Losing his sword and helmet as he tumbled, he landed face down in the shallows of the river. Struggling to his knees, he saw Gundamar towering above him on his white horse. The King of the Alemanni snarled at him like a wild animal, a crazed look in his eyes.

Septimus gritted his teeth. His head and eyes darted about as he searched the water for his sword. He saw a reflection. It was the clear, golden glint of the engraving from his sword, a foot beneath the surface. The words were legible. "Libera nos a malo," he whispered to himself. He reached for the weapon, but it was beyond his grasp.

"You are done for, Septimus Lupus!" yelled Gundamar. He raised his long broadsword high.

Tribune Marius glanced up, resigned to his doom.

As the barbarian king began to bring the sword down, a scorpion bolt pierced the neck of his horse. Recoiling from the impact and trauma of the wound, the animal reared up, causing Gundamar to swing his sword wide of the tribune. Blood gushed from the animal's wound, turning the river red around the creature. The creature took a few halting, wobbling steps toward the shore. It collapsed into the shallows with a great splash, carrying the King of the Alemanni with it.

Grabbing his sword, Septimus raced the several yards over to where Gundamar had fallen. The tribune placed his knee on the chest of the barbarian king and pressed the sword against his neck. Seeing the tribune's sword at Gundamar's neck, the barbarians and Romans nearest to them shouted to their own comrades, leading to a pause in the fighting around them. Warrior and legionary alike waited to see what would happen to the King of the Alemanni. Word was shouted from man to man through both armies. This strange, unspoken truce continued to spread across the battlefield like fire until the din of battle had faded away. All was silent except for the trickle of the river.

Gundamar locked eyes with the tribune. He laughed. "I am not afraid to die, Septimus Lupus."

The tribune pressed the sword against the king's neck. A line of blood oozed from where the weapon met the flesh. The laughing stopped. "And I am not afraid to kill you, Gundamar, King of the Alemanni."

"Kill me, blood brother. I would have killed you. You know that. Why do you hesitate?"

The tribune lifted his head and looked around. Roman and barbarian eyes were upon him and Gundamar. He glanced down at the king. "Withdraw your men!" he said. Septimus yelled out to the barbarians in their own tongue. "I spare the life of my blood brother this day. Your king fought bravely and nobly against his brother—but he must now withdraw."

Septimus stood, his left arm bruised and bloody. He placed his sword back in its scabbard. He picked up Gundamar's sword and offered it back to him.

The king looked at the sword. A devious smile crossed his face as if he thought to grab it and strike Septimus dead. Gundamar saw his warriors watching him as he took back his weapon. He returned the sword to its scabbard. He glared at the tribune. "Until we meet again, blood brother."

To the great surprise of the outnumbered Roman legionaries, Gundamar ordered his warriors to withdraw. The battle was over.

***

The tribune stood upon the broad earthen rampart of the bridgehead on the right bank of the river. To his right, the sun was about to set. Hours before he had been beside Marcellinus as the battle of Mursa Major had begun. Now, before him, a stream of survivors of that great battle to the east made their way toward the bridgehead and the river. One soldier with an arrow deep in his leg limped along using a spear as a crutch. Septimus lowered his head. Earlier in the day there had been disciplined ranks of thousands upon thousands of finely arrayed legionaries. Now, an intermittent line of wearied and disorganized bands of legionaries, several or a dozen men each, stumbled along, helping the worst of the wounded among them. Bruised and bloodied faces and bodies, tattered tunics, and gore-drenched armor passed before Septimus. Some of the survivors carried their weapons, while many others did not, having cast them aside in their flight to escape. There were a few riders and, now and then, a riderless horse, which plodded along. Entering the gate, they all continued to cross the pontoon bridge to the safety of the opposite bank of the Drava.

"The exhaustion of both armies and darkness have brought an end to the battle for today," said Septimus. "Another hour of daylight would have brought the complete destruction of the army." He glanced at Longinus, who stood beside him shaking his head. "Something on your mind, Centurion?"

"What were you thinking?" said Longinus. "That was quite a chance you took with Gundamar, Tribune. Is that an Alemanni custom of which I am unaware?"

"I spared his life. He is in my debt until he spares mine. He could not do otherwise without losing face in the eyes of his chieftains and warriors."

"Gundamar is a treacherous sort. How could you be so sure he would honor the tradition of his people?"

A faint smile appeared on the tribune's face. "I was not sure."

"Tribune Marius, sometimes, I fear you are more reckless than bold."

"Gundamar is treacherous, yet there is some honor in him. But I believe there was also a calculation behind his willingness to withdraw."

"Calculation?"

"Gundamar was paid to take a bridge that he thought was unguarded," said Septimus. "Running into Third Italica changed his thinking."

"How so?"

"The barbarian kingdoms of the North benefit from a weakened empire—one divided by civil war. If Gundamar had taken or destroyed the bridge, he would have ensured the destruction of the Western army and the end of the war. But then he would face Constantius, ruler of a unified empire, as his new enemy. By leaving us the bridge, Gundamar prolongs the civil war—and further weakens the empire."

The tribune put his hand to his bloodied and bandaged left forearm. He winced.

"How is your arm?" asked the centurion.

Tribune Marius bent his elbow and worked his shoulder to test its range of motion. He opened and closed his hand. "Sore. But I have recovered feeling and use in both hand and arm." Something caught his attention outside of the defenses. A hundred yards away, a group of about twenty riders galloped toward the gate. Above them, a red pennant emblazoned with a golden eagle flew. "It's Magnentius. He will have news of the battle and Marcellinus!" Septimus ran to the gate. He waited at the end of the lowered drawbridge across the trench with Longinus.

The lead rider, wearing a purple-crested helmet, raised his hand as they neared the gate. The column came to a halt. The rider wore a white cape that was torn, frayed, and stained with blood and gore. Splashes of blood covered his cuirass and grieves as well. His bay horse, snorting and out of breath, bore several slash wounds.

The tribune saluted. "Hail, Magnentius!"

"Tribune Marius, it is good to see you and your legion here," said the Western Emperor, his pudgy face drenched in sweat. "We did not know what we'd find at the bridge. I feared it had fallen into the hands of the Constantius or his barbarian mercenaries."

"The barbarians came close to taking it," said Septimus. "But Third Italica holds it."

"Well done."

"What of the battle?" asked the tribune.

The Emperor watched one haggard-looking legionary, his shield embedded with several arrows, shuffle across the drawbridge on his way to the river. Another soldier with a bloody leg limped past, supported by a man whose arm hung limp from injury. "A disaster as you can see," said Magnentius. "The battle went well for us until about the noon hour. Then there came desperate reports that the Easterners in great numbers had appeared through the forest behind our right flank. It is not clear how the enemy caught us by surprise."

The tribune gripped the bridle of the Emperor's horse. "But what of Marcellinus?"

The Emperor took off his helmet. "I received a report that his position on the hilltop was surrounded by several legions and then overrun by a squadron of cataphracts bearing the emblem of an eagle." Magnentius wiped the sweat from his brow. "I am sorry, Tribune. I know that you and the general were friends."

"The Eagle squadron was one of the cavalry units under the command of Silvanus," said Longinus in disgust.

"What are you saying?" asked Magnentius.

"Silvanus withdrew his units from the bridge this morning," said Septimus. "It was unguarded when Third Italica arrived. You say the Easterners surprised us on the flank. It too was guarded by Silvanus. Now it appears his cataphracts attacked Marcellinus." The tribune released the horse's bridle. His hands fell to his sides.

"There can be little doubt, now. Silvanus betrayed Marcellinus. He betrayed us all."

The Emperor stared blankly at Septimus in shock and disbelief as he considered his words. He leaned back in the saddle. "Silvanus, a traitor? But, why?"

"If I may be so bold to say, sire, that is a question for another day."

"If we live that long," muttered the centurion.

Septimus squinted at the horizon. "There is a red glow to the southeast."

The Emperor turned in his saddle to see. "The battle continued into the camp, most of what remains of the army retreated into it. Parts of it are in flames. But we hold the camp for now." He faced Septimus. "What orders did Marcellinus give you?"

Septimus began to massage the wound to his arm again. "Hold the bridge. Keep it safe. Those were Marcellinus's last orders for Third Italica."

"Keep to his orders," said Magnentius as he donned his helmet. "We must save as much of the army as can be. Send word to the camp the bridge is open. The bridge must be held for as long as possible. Then burn it. Constantius must not be allowed to have it."

"Yes, my lord," replied Septimus with a salute. "And you?"

"I make camp on the other side of the river. There I will rally the army to carry on the fight another day." Magnentius waved his arm forward as he led his column of riders on through the gate, down to the river and across the bridge to the safety of the other bank. Septimus and Longinus reentered the gate. To one side, Father Paul cared for some of the wounded. The priest, unarmed, wore an armored cuirass, with a crucifix hanging down over his chest.

"Father Paul," said Septimus. "Can't these men walk? We cannot care for the wounded here. There is no safety to be had on this side of the river."

The priest shook his head. "These men can make it no farther on their own."

"You there!" shouted the centurion to several legionaries warming themselves by a fire. "Help get these wounded to the other side of the river."

The legionaries jumped up and rushed over to help the priest.

"Father Paul, remain here by the gate," said Septimus as the wounded were carried off. "I will have need of you shortly. I have a special task for you, if you are up for it." He squinted toward the horizon to the south, in the direction of the battle of Mursa Major.

The priest nodded. "Of course, Tribune. I understand."

Septimus and Longinus observed the other side of the river. Torches lined the bridge and campfires burned on the far shore. Guards stood watch on the battlement.

"The Emperor camps tonight on the opposite shore—safe," grumbled the centurion.

Septimus shook his head. "I venture he will not sleep well, wondering what news daylight will bring about the extent of the disaster that has befallen the army." He then saw something next to the storehouse a hundred feet from the gate. Near it, a couple dozen legionaries guarded well over a hundred men, seated on the ground with their hands tied.

Approaching the storehouse, Septimus recognized Jason, who sprang up at once seeing the tribune.

"Tribune Marius—we captured these saboteurs when the legion arrived at the river this afternoon," said Longinus. "They escaped across the river ahead of you. I had them kept here for safe-keeping until you could decide what to do with them. Forgot about them in the excitement of the battle."

"Saboteurs?" shouted Jason, overhearing his comment.

"This man claims to be their leader," said Longinus. He waved to two of the legionaries to bring Jason forward. "They protested all along they were hired by Magnentius. One of them claims to know you."

"I am no saboteur!" said Jason, his hands bound before him.

"Tribune Marius will decide that," said Longinus.

Septimus smiled. "Release him."

"Release him?" asked Longinus, his eyebrow raised.

"He is no saboteur. He and his men are Jews in the service of Magnentius."

"Jews serving in a Roman army? Unheard of."

"They serve as sappers," said Septimus. "They have made

128

common cause with us against Constantius and Gallus. He and his men fought alongside us when we first arrived at the river this afternoon. He helped us delay Gundamar. Untie and release him. Release them all."

Once freed, Samson and Drusus rushed over Jason's side.

The giant Samson straightened his posture, and his large biceps grew tight. He glared at Longinus who stood across from him, as if ready to strike out at him.

The much smaller Drusus grabbed a hold of Samson by his tunic. "Steady old friend. We are free now."

Jason stepped between Samson and Longinus. "He will do you no harm, Centurion."

As sturdy a man as Longinus was, Samson had a hundred pounds on him, all of it muscle. The centurion pushed back his helmet from his forehead with the tip of his vine staff. He stared back at Samson. "You can be sure he will do no harm to me."

"Do not worry, Centurion," said Jason. "We want no trouble." Standing between Samson and Drusus, he placed his hands on their shoulders. "When I left to join Magnentius in his war against the East, my father asked my two older comrades, Samson and Drusus, to stay by my side and keep me safe. They are protective of me. Samson especially."

Septimus took off his helmet. He ran a hand through his light brown hair, sweat-filled and matted from the day's battle. "You say you want no trouble. The Easterners will try to take the bridge at first light. You and your men are now free to go." He pointed to the opposite bank. "Get across the river. There you will find safety for now."

Jason shook his head. "We are still in the service of Magnentius."

"It is your choice. Go or stay and fight."

Longinus shook his head. He pointed the end of the vine staff against Jason's chest. "Tribune, you cannot be serious. Are you giving this man and his men an option to stay and fight?"

Jason glowered at the centurion. He brushed away the staff with his arm. "We will fight, Tribune."

"Tribune, these men are not soldiers," said the centurion, insistent.

"We can use every man we can muster to defend the bridgehead until the army crosses to safety," said Septimus.

Samson brushed past Jason to stand toe to toe with Longinus. "We want to kill Romans!"

Longinus glared at the large Ostian, who was taller than even he by a few inches. "*Eastern* Romans. You want to kill *Easterners*. We are the *Westerners*. We are the good guys. *Easterners*—bad guys. Remember that." Longinus turned to Drusus and pointed his thumb at Samson. "Make sure this one understands that, and we will get along."

Septimus addressed the three Jews before him. "The enemy will try to capture the bridge in the morning. Arm yourselves and your comrades as best you can. There are weapons among the dead, barbarian and Roman."

Longinus glanced at the defenses. "These defenses are unfinished. Two hundred yards of earthen rampart behind a trench. A partial palisade and a few towers. We cannot hold out against a full-scale assault by a couple of legions. They will drive us into the river."

"We must hold out as long as possible," said Septimus. The red glow in the sky flickered in the distance. "They may think the camp a safe refuge tonight. Tomorrow it will be their prison." He walked toward the gate, the others following behind him. "Send messengers to the camp. "Tell all within it they must evacuate at once. Everyone must cross the bridge before first light."

"Understood, sir," said Longinus.

"Keep the survivors moving. None are to rest until they have crossed the river." Septimus now fixed his attention on Jason. "You said you and your men helped build this pontoon bridge?"

Jason nodded.

"Can you destroy one?" asked Septimus. "Quickly?"

"Quick enough," said Jason. "There is plenty of pitch in the storehouses here to set several bridges ablaze."

Septimus led the group to the gate, giving instructions to Longinus and Jason as they went. When they reached the drawbridge, Father Paul met them.

The priest blessed himself. He gave a nod. "I am ready to go, Tribune."

"Ready to go?" said Longinus. He tilted his head as he eyed Septimus. He stood arms akimbo. "And where do you think you are going now, Tribune? Another adventure like this afternoon?"

The tribune looked toward the hills to the south. "Marcellinus is out there, somewhere."

"Most likely dead."

"I cannot leave him lying on the cold, bloody ground, his remains to be picked at by birds and rats."

"The battlefield is crawling with the enemy."

"The fighting is over for now. No one will be able to distinguish friend from foe in the darkness, and I doubt any will bother to do so. Any man on the field of battle this night seeks to find and comfort fallen comrades, not to continue the fight. Septimus winked. "Besides, no one will think a Westerner reckless enough to return to the field of a lost battle."

"Reckless is more like it. I will go with you."

The tribune shook his head. "No, Centurion. I have given you and Jason instructions. See to them. They must be completed by first light."

"You must take someone with you," said the Longinus. He sounded annoyed.

"I am. Father Paul is coming with me."

Longinus struck his vine staff against the side of one of his grieves. "Bringing a priest along is not what I had in mind."

"I'll go with the tribune!" said a legionary standing watch by the gate. It was Cornelius, the young legionary who, the night before, had presented the tribune his birthday gift.

"Come along, lad," the tribune said. Septimus gave Longinus one final command as he departed. "If I am not back when the enemy is sighted in the morning, get the legion across the river and set fire to the bridge."

Chapter 8

Night in the City

Icons of Jesus Christ, His mother, and the apostles covered the walls of the antechamber. An aroma of incense lingered in the air, as did the soft, feminine echoes of nuns chanting prayers from an adjoining chapel. Lady Portia, along with a dozen other women of the court—the wives of officials and senior officers—sat, heads bowed, in silent meditation. Melissa, Helena, and their friend Aurelia sat together on a cushioned bench in prayer.

Melissa turned to Helena, who sat between her and Aurelia. "Do you think the Empress will live?" she whispered.

"I fear her fever is beyond the ability of the doctors to treat," said Helena. "I believe that is why my brother had the Empress moved here, to this Church and convent—to be close to the prayers of the holy nuns."

Aurelia leaned toward Helena. "If she does not live, do you think your brother would marry again?"

"Aurelia Eusebia!" said Melissa. Although she meant to whisper, her voice sounded like a sudden shout in the quiet antechamber.

All the women looked up from their prayers to stare at Melissa. From across the room, Portia glared at her daughter. "Shush!"

Melissa blushed in one part in embarrassment, the other in anger. *I can't believe Aurelia could say such a thing, especially at a moment like this. Or maybe I can. It is just like her.* She lowered her head. She waited for the other women to take their eyes off her and return to their prayers. She turned to Aurelia. "This is not the time to discuss such a thing," whispered Melissa. "In fact, there is *no* time to discuss such a thing—and definitely not while the Empress still

132

lives!"

Aurelia shrugged. "I meant no harm by it."

A servant entered the antechamber and lit the candles and lanterns. Melissa lifted her head as the room grew brighter. "I have lost all track of time. How long has it been since the Empress was brought here? Is it night again already?"

"We came here late last night, but it feels forever ago," said Helena, as the two conversed in hushed voices. "Our little adventure in the city last night now seems so long ago." Her eyes sparkled as she seemed to recall a memory.

A hint of amusement crossed Melissa's face. "You are thinking of Claudius Silvanus, aren't you?"

"I hope we might see him again."

"*We?*"

"Yes, *we.*"

"I think you mean you hope *you* see him again."

Helena primped her blonde hair as if preparing to see Silvanus. "Yes, you are right. I thought him very handsome."

"I think the feeling was mutual. His eyes were on you most of the time."

"Do you think so?"

Melissa nodded. *Helena is as innocent as she is reckless. I hope it doesn't get her in trouble one day.* "I do. But, do not get your hopes up, Princess—he is an enemy prisoner after all."

"Given the grave news about the Empress, I did not dare ask my brother what became of Claudius Silvanus," said the princess. She held Melissa's hand. "Thank you for being here. It is a great comfort having you here. You, your mother, and the other women of the court."

"I would not think of being anywhere else."

Melissa stood. She walked to a shuttered window and opened it wide. Helena and Aurelia came to her side. A short wall, shoulder height, surrounded the building. A couple of legionaries patrolled the garden just outside the window.

"The sun has already gone down," said the princess.

Melissa tilted her head to the side, turning an ear toward the window. She stood still for several moments. "There are no sounds of a distant battle. I heard them throughout the day—but, now, I can no longer hear the echoes of battle."

Helena stepped closer. "I cannot hear the sounds of battle

either. The battle must be over."

Melissa clasped her hands together. Her knuckles whitened. *What has become of father?*

The princess placed an arm around her friend. "I worry for your father, too." She glanced about at the others in the room. "For your father . . . and the husbands of these women . . . and for our friends—like Lucius and Marcus." Her eyes welled with tears. "I know it must be difficult for you, Melissa, and these women to wonder about the fate of their loved ones on the battlefield. Yet, even with your own worries, you found time to be here and to include the cause of my cousin, the Empress, in your prayers. Thank you."

A door opened behind them. The Emperor stepped out from the bedchamber where the Empress was being attended. His face had grown sullen and pale, dark rings beneath his eyes. The Grand Chamberlain and the court bishops Valens and Ursacius followed him out. Melissa glimpsed inside to see the Empress lying on a bed, nuns attending to her as physicians discussed what to try next. Seeing Helena, Constantius approached the three young women.

"How is the Empress?" asked the princess.

Constantius grimaced. "Hot with fever. The nuns prepare her now for another bath to cool her." He saw the open window. "Is it night already?" He lowered his head. "I could not lead my army into battle today. I was too consumed with worry for the Empress."

"You were right to leave the battle to your generals," said Helena as she took her brother's hand in her own. "Here, in this church, you could pray for both the Empress and for victory."

The Emperor gave a weak nod in reply. He now took notice of the other women. "And thank you for being here and for your prayers. Please, sit. You must be tired. You have not slept since last night." Melissa and Helena sat back down on the bench. The Emperor offered Aurelia the empty place on the bench. "Do you care to sit?"

"No, my lord," she said as she took a half step toward him. "I am not tired at all. I am strong and healthy and do not mind standing at all."

Melissa pursed her lips as she observed Aurelia. *Aurelia already wondered aloud if the Emperor would marry again. What now? Is she wanting to show the Emperor how young and healthy she is, even while his wife still lives? Good grief.*

"Very well, Aurelia Eusebia—then you are stronger than I," said Constantius as he sat on the bench between Helena and Melissa, leaving no space for Aurelia.

Melissa squinted at Aurelia. *You thought you'd be able to stand beside him. Ha. Serves you right!*

"Melissa worries about her father—is there any word of the battle?" asked the princess.

"What I know is that we surprised the enemy as we had hoped," said the Emperor. "That officer you met last night—"

"Claudius Silvanus?" interjected Helena.

"Yes. Information he provided helped us take the enemy by complete surprise. The battle was going well for us at midday. But I have not received an update in the last few hours. No messenger has come since then."

Melissa lowered her head. Tears began to form in her eyes. She brought a hand to her face to wipe them away.

The Emperor patted her hand. "I last saw your father late in the morning before I returned to the church. Try not to worry. I am sure he is fine." He reached out and took the hands of the princess and Melissa into his own. "I remember you both as children. Helena was my father's favorite child of all his own sons and daughters."

"You think so?" asked Helena.

"I do," he said. "Your sisters were always so moody and serious, while you were always lively and adventurous." The Emperor turned to Melissa. "And of all the friends of his own children, I think you were his favorite. Do you know how your father came to serve my father?"

Melissa shook her head.

"Your father was a naval officer during the civil war against Licinius," said Constantius. "Florentius came to the attention of my father during the time of the Battle of the Hellespont and the Battle of Chrysopolis. After these victories, the Emperor brought him on as an advisor. Because your father was at the court so often, he brought you to the palace as a toddler, where you and Helena befriended each other." He smiled. "You and Helena would play in the halls and rooms of the palace in Antioch and in Caesarea Maritima."

"Hide and seek!" said Helena. Her eyes lit up. "I remember!"

The Emperor leaned his head back against the wall. His diadem shifted forward toward his forehead. He closed his eyes, in part to search his memories, but also to shut out the world for a moment. "You would command whoever you could to join the game to seek and find you both in the palace. "Slaves ... eunuchs ... palace guards."

"Sometimes I would beg you to look for us! And, being a good brother, you would sometimes play."

Constantius peaked at his sister with one eye. "Sometimes I *pretended* to look."

The princess nudged her elbow into her brother's side.

"Father enjoyed the two of you, even if you might have interrupted a meeting or two with your play," said Constantius. "I recall that when I was a young man of eighteen or nineteen years, there was a meeting with father, Florentius, and other generals, and I was there. The two of you had been hiding from servants when Father discovered you both in the room. You both must have been five or six years of age. Florentius was quite unhappy that his daughter had interrupted an important meeting. But Father laughed."

"I remember that!" said Helena.

"As do I," said Melissa, holding a hand to her face in embarrassment.

The Emperor smiled. "After the death of father—when the Eastern Empire came to me—I resolved to keep my dear sister Helena happy and to keep echoes of laughter in the dreary hallways of the palace. So, I insisted that Florentius let the two of you be educated together by the palace tutors."

"Yes, that made me very happy. But then you sent Melissa away when she was seventeen!" said Helena, feigning a pout.

The Emperor shook his head. "I did not *send her away*. I gave her father an assignment in Caesarea Maritima. It was a question of imperial business. An emperor cannot be so cruel as to separate a father and a mother from their daughter. Besides, although I may not have seen our Melissa from that moment until Gallus and Constantina were wed in Constantinople—dear sister, you took trips to Caesarea Maritima and saw her occasionally."

"That is true, Princess," said Melissa. "You cannot blame the Emperor."

Constantius winked at Melissa. "Thank you, for your support."

The door leading to the bedchamber opened. One of the physicians stood at the entrance, his face somber. "My lord Augustus—come quick!"

The Emperor jumped from the bench and rushed inside the room. Several nuns knelt in prayer at the foot of the bed on which the Empress lay. Constantius looked down at his wife. Her face was without color. Her body still. He looked at the physician next to him.

"She has passed, my lord," said the physician.

Constantius fell to his knees beside the bed. He lifted the Empress's hand to his lips. "My love." Tears filled his eyes as he pressed her hand against his cheek. "It is my fault. You were weak. I should not have let you come. I should have ignored your pleas to come. Forgive me." He buried his face into his wife's shoulder. The crowded room remained silent and still save for the whispered prayers of the nuns and the sobbing of the Emperor. When at last after several minutes he lifted his head, he placed a gentle hand to her cheek, then ran his fingers through her hair. "Be at peace, my love. Be with God."

The Emperor stood and shuffled to the doorway where he was met by Helena and Melissa. Looking at them both, his eyes full of tears, he lowered his head. "She is dead. The Empress is dead. My wife—"

The princess threw her arms around her brother. "My dear brother. I am so sorry."

"She was too young to die."

"May I see her?"

He nodded.

Helena left his side to pray beside the body of the Empress for the repose of her soul.

Melissa stood with her hands folded beneath her chin. Tears welled in her eyes.

"Melissa, I cannot believe she is dead," said the Emperor, as he held out a hand to her. She took it. He hugged her.

Melissa put her arms around him. "My lord Augustus, I am so sorry."

"*Lord Augustus* you call me?" he asked. "Have I not just spoken of you as being like a sister, Melissa—to Helena and me both? There is no need for formalities when mourning." He pressed her head against his chest. "It is not an *empress* who is dead—but my

137

wife and dearest companion, who I will never again be able to embrace with love and affection in this life."

Captain Marcus Scudillo entered the antechamber from the outer hallway. The clanking of his full suit of armor announced his arrival. He raised his brow at the sight of Melissa in the arms of the Emperor and her head resting against his chest.

"Marcus!" she said, seeing his armor and cloak splattered with blood. "Are you hurt?"

Marcus looked at the blood on himself. "Excuse my appearance, Lady Melissa. I have come straight from the battle."

"The Empress has passed away—just now," said Melissa.

"O Emperor, I am saddened at the news of your great loss," said Marcus.

Constantius lifted his teary eyes toward Marcus. "What news of the battle?"

"A victory, my lord!"

"And Magnentius?" asked the Emperor. "Did he fall in battle? Did we capture him?"

"He fled toward the river and the pontoon bridge."

"Then he has fallen into the hands of Gundamar, perhaps."

"Perhaps, my lord."

"Casualties?"

"We caught the Westerners by surprise, but they fought with tenacity. Casualties were high for both sides. There is no certain count as yet. Most of what remains of the Western army fled back into their camp. They are trapped."

The Emperor nodded. "Thank the generals for their efforts. I will address them later. I remain in seclusion for the night to grieve the loss of Lady Augusta."

"As you say, great Augustus."

Marcus turned to leave but paused when Melissa called after him. "Captain Marcus—what of my father? Any news of him? Is he safe?"

"I understand that he went to scout the river."

"My father—by himself?" she asked. *What was he thinking? He is no longer a fighting soldier. He is too old for that.*

"Captain Lucius is with him."

"Yes, but . . . Lucius is a cripple!" said Melissa. *He can't help my father if there is trouble.*

"Captain Scudillo, go search for General Florentius," interjected

138

the Emperor, still holding Melissa. "It is my wish you find him and make sure he is safe. Ride at once."

"My lord, I will do as you command. But first I must find a fresh horse. Mine is exhausted from battle and will collapse if I ride him another hundred yards."

The Emperor nodded. "I understand." He thought for a moment. "Take my horse. It will be the freshest one you will find for miles around Mursa Major after this day's fighting. My attendant is in the courtyard. Take the horse. Find Florentius. Bring word to me and the Lady Melissa of his whereabouts."

Marcus saluted. "Yes, my lord."

After the captain left, Melissa—still in the arms of the Emperor—looked up at Constantius. "Thank you, my lord."

Constantius released Melissa from his embrace. "Do not worry. Marcus will find your father." He then returned to the side of the bed to kneel and pray with Helena as Bishop Valens recited prayers over the body.

As Melissa watched from the doorway, Aurelia came to stand beside her.

Aurelia wagged her head. "Well *that* did not take you long," she whispered.

"What do you mean?"

"To move in on the Emperor. To pursue him as you are."

Melissa glared at Aurelia. "How could you say such a thing? How could you think such a thing at a time like this?"

Melissa tightened a hand into a fist at her side, about to raise it. She paused, checking the impulse. *A lady doesn't strike another lady.* The sobbing from the room reached her ears. *Certainly, not at a time like this. Even though she deserves it. Aurelia doesn't understand. The Emperor and I are like brother and sister. He said so himself.* She relaxed her fist.

"I saw you in his arms. A short while ago you berated me for wondering if the Emperor would marry again. It seems we both are thinking the same thing—only you are a bit quicker than I. At least I planned to wait until he buried her."

"Aurelia Eusebia—" Melissa began to reply. She closed her eyes and took a deep breath. She shook her head. "Never mind." She then went and knelt beside Helena at the bedside and joined in the prayers for the soul of the Empress.

Chapter 9

The Search Party

Septimus, Father Paul, and Cornelius set off on foot toward the hills to the south, carrying torches to light their way. They passed stragglers, trudging and limping along, heading for the river. Signs of battle became evident the further they went, grim carnage everywhere.

"Clusters and heaps of the dead, by the hundreds," said Septimus as he surveyed the bodies of the fallen. "Cut down by enemy cavalry as they fled toward the river." He scanned the surrounding terrain in the darkness. "Third Italica was here earlier today." Septimus pointed to the long slope of a hill. "There. I last saw Marcellinus on the other side of that hill."

Septimus led them up the slope, stepping over body after body. "A desperate battle raged here," he said grim-faced.

"Thousands of men and horses dead," said Cornelius, his voice trembling. He looked at his feet in the darkness. "Rain has muddied the ground."

"It is not water that muddied it," said the tribune. He lowered his torch to the ground. His boots and grieves were red and wet. "It is blood." Septimus observed where the heaps of bodies were positioned, hoping to reconstruct the flow of the battle in his mind. "See how the bodies lay, Easterners and Westerners," he continued. "Our right wing was encircled. Pushed back. They made a last stand on this hill."

Cornelius wandered among the bodies, his stomach queasy. He

came upon a legionary, his head cleaved in half. He averted his eyes. Cornelius had seen the aftermath of battles before, but not at this level of carnage. "There are more Eastern than Western dead."

"Our fallen comrades gave a good account of themselves."

As they neared the crest of the hill, the air of the black night took on a red hue on the other side. Reaching the top, the three of them looked down on the valley. From the forest to the river, almost three miles, the ground over which much of the battle had been fought was ablaze with dozens of large pyres heaped with bodies. The lights from hundreds of torches moved along the slopes and floor of the valley for miles as the living looked to the wounded and carried away the dead. The glow of the pyres, the torches, and moonlight reflected off of the weapons and armor of the fallen, numbering in the tens of thousands, and cast strange shadows across the landscape. The plaintive moans, cries, and pleas of the wounded and dying echoed throughout the hills and valley. The smell of death and burning flesh hung heavy in the air.

The tribune surveyed the valley. "Behold, Hades. Let no man tell you it does not exist—for you have seen it."

Father Paul blessed himself. "God save us—may we never see the real one," he whispered.

Cornelius, likewise, blessed himself. "Amen."

There came the sound of a horse, letting out a neigh. The soft thud of hooves approaching at a slow pace followed.

"Douse your torches," said Septimus in a whisper. "Get down."

The three men ducked to the ground, hiding on the ground among the many dead.

Atop the horse, a single rider attired in cataphract armor guided the animal through the chaotic mess. He picked his way with care to avoid tripping his horse on the dead. He paused just feet from the tribune, towering above him in the saddle.

The rider held the torch aloft. "Florentius?" he called out. "Was that you? General?"

Septimus reached his hand down to his sword.

"Lucius?" the rider called out in the dark. "It's me, Marcus."

The tribune gripped the handle. He began to draw it out, inch by slow inch. He tensed his body, preparing to leap up at the cataphract. Just as the tribune was about to do so, the rider spurred

141

his horse forward and continued on his way.

"All clear," said Septimus after the rider disappeared over the crest of the hill.

Among a heap of bodies near them, Septimus spied a shield that caught his eye. It lay beside the carcass of a horse. He lifted it. He considered the emblem with a cold stare. "The Eagle Squadron," he muttered.

"Tribune Marius?" asked the priest.

"This is where the last of the right wing was cut down. Here they were overrun by Silvanus and his cavalry." The tribune cast the shield aside. "Marcellinus must be near."

The three searched among the hundreds of bodies lying about the hilltop. As they did, they happened here and there upon the dying, who called out to Father Paul, "Baptize me, priest," or "Absolve me of my sins, father." Hearing their cries, the priest would run to them to minister to their spiritual needs.

Septimus looked to the sky across the valley. "The king star rises in the eastern sky," he whispered to himself.

"Did you say something, Tribune?" asked Father Paul.

Before Septimus could answer, Cornelius called out from a short distance away. "I found him, Tribune. The general!"

The tribune and the priest ran to Cornelius. There they found Marcellinus, his back against the carcass of his horse, his chest bloodied. Bodies of Eastern legionaries and cataphracts strewn about him, the general clenched the Labarum, the standard with the Chi Rho set atop it. The severed hand of one who had tried to take it from him still grasped the bottom of the pole.

Father Paul knelt beside him. "He still has a life in him!" He then administered the last rites to the general. When he had finished, the priest held a flask of water to the general's lips.

The general turned his head away, refusing to take a sip. He grimaced and gasped with each breath. "Save what water you have left for your baptisms this night, Father. It will do more good for the souls of others than it can do me for my body. I am done for." He saw the tribune standing over him. "Septimus?"

The tribune crouched down beside him. "Here, General!"

"The battle?"

Septimus shook his head, reluctant to speak the word. "Lost."

"And Third Italica?" asked the general. "The bridge?"

Septimus placed his hand upon the bloody chest of the general. "Third Italica holds the bridge. Just as you ordered. It took convincing—but Gundamar relented." Septimus winked.

A smile crossed the pained face of Marcellinus.

"Even now, the army withdraws across it to safety," said the tribune.

Marcellinus gripped the hand of the tribune with his own bloodied one. "Pia fidelis!" he declared and then breathed his last.

Septimus lowered his head.

"God rest his soul," said Father Paul.

The tribune brought his hand to the general's forehead. He swept the eyes closed. He stood to his feet. At that moment, the light of the moon, until now obscured by passing clouds, illuminated the Chi Rho of the black shield the general had carried that day. The words written upon the shield, *Pia Fidelis*, became visible.

Tears welled in the tribune's eyes. "Pia fidelis," he said. "The faith and hope of Marcellinus was to see his God, face-to-face. May his God reward that hope."

The tribune picked up the Labarum and handed it to Cornelius. He reached down for the shield and flung it over his own back. Septimus lifted the body of Marcellinus and put it over his shoulder.

"You do not intend to carry him back the whole long way to the river, do you, Tribune?" asked Cornelius.

"I will not leave him out here," said Septimus. "Not for the wolves and vultures."

***

General Florentius and Captain Lucius stood on a rocky outcrop on the long hilltop that overlooked the pontoon bridge over the Drava. Campfires lit the inside of the bridgehead fortifications. Men on foot, horseback, and in carts loaded with the wounded entered the bridgehead in a long procession winding its way back along the bank of the river to the camp to the southeast.

Lucius smiled. "The tattered remnants of the Western Roman

143

army." He glanced at Florentius. "We won a great, historic victory—one to be remembered in the annals of the Roman Empire."

"Remembered as a victory?" said Florentius. He pulled his cloak around himself. "May the Lord save us from another such victory!"

"Sir?"

"It will be remembered as the disaster it is for the empire."

"I do not understand, General."

"Barbarians and Parthians threaten the empire from all sides. This day the empire—East and West together—lost tens of thousands of legionaries in a useless civil war. The empire may never recover from the loss of so many good legions. In winning this battle, our army alone lost half its number. It is a Pyrrhic victory. We have gained nothing. The enemy escapes."

The hoofbeats of an approaching horse sounded out of the darkness.

"Captain Marcus, what are you doing here?" the general said to the rider as he emerged from the shadows.

"Good morning, General." He dismounted and led his horse to a line of trees part way down the slope. There he tied his horse near theirs.

"What news of the Empress?" asked Lucius.

Marcus shook his head. "She passed away earlier this evening."

Florentius lowered his head. He blessed himself and whispered a prayer. When he had finished it, he looked to Marcus. "Where is the Emperor?"

"He mourns with his sister. The ladies Portia and Melissa are with them."

Marcus walked to the edge of the outcropping. "I see the enemy runs away."

"You must bring word to the Emperor at once that the enemy is escaping across the bridge," said Florentius. "Constantius must send as many legions and cavalry squadrons as can be mustered. The bridge must be taken intact, and the enemy pursued and destroyed before he gets away."

"Shush!" Lucius whispered. "Be still. I hear something." Lucius limped toward the sound. He crouched behind a large boulder. He spotted a man leading a horse up the hill from the tree line. The moon emerged from behind the clouds, the light revealing a horse with the body of a man thrown over it.

"Halt!" shouted Lucius. He drew his sword and placed the point of it against the chest of the man leading the horse.

It was Septimus. The tribune froze.

Hearing the shout, Florentius and Marcus rushed to Lucius.

Marcus slapped Lucius on the back. "Well done, Captain! Your first encounter with the enemy and you captured a tribune single-handed."

A blade suddenly slipped close to Florentius's throat. "And I have captured a general!" came the voice of Cornelius. He had come up and caught Florentius unaware.

Marcus drew his sword.

Cornelius stared at Marcus. "Do not try it! The head of your general will roll down the hill before you take another step."

"If you harm the general, it will be the death of your tribune," said Lucius.

Suddenly, Father Paul came walking out of the darkness to find himself in the midst of the standoff. He glanced around at the men holding swords toward one another. "I missed something—didn't I?"

A tense silence followed for what seemed minutes but was only a few moments.

"There will be no prisoners tonight," said Septimus. The tribune addressed at Cornelius. "Put your sword away. Release the general. Get back to the bridgehead."

Cornelius cocked his head back in puzzlement. "Sir? A general would be worth a fine ransom."

"Do it! And take Father Paul with you."

"We cannot leave you here," said Father Paul. "What will become of you?"

"I will be all right, Father," said the tribune. "Go!"

The priest and the legionary began to leave with hesitant steps at first. They glanced back over their shoulders, doubting the wisdom of the order. A cold stare from the tribune told them not to dare disobey him and to move on. A few moments later, they disappeared over the hilltop and headed down the slope.

Marcus turned to Lucius. "Run him through with your sword!"

"Put your sword away," said the general.

"Lucius, this is your chance for a taste of battle,"

"There has been enough death and gore this day," said Florentius. "Release the tribune. Let him go."

Lucius, torn as to what to do, glanced at the body across the horse. "Was he a friend?"

The tribune nodded. "He was. A dear one."

Lucius lowered his sword. He placed it back in its scabbard. "You may pass."

Septimus proceeded on his way, giving a nod toward Lucius as he did.

Florentius, Marcus, and Lucius followed him at a distance to the top of the hill. They watched as the tribune, leading the horse carrying the body of his friend, made his way down the slope toward the river. He disappeared into the darkness.

"Captain Marcus, you must ride back to the Emperor at once. He must hear what I told you."

Marcus opened his eyes wide. He turned around and looked toward the tree line. His shoulders slumped. "The Emperor will not be pleased that you let the tribune go."

"He need not know about it."

"He must."

"Why must he?"

"That was his horse."

***

Longinus stood outside the gate, at the end of the drawbridge. A long, thin line of soldiers made its way past him into the bridgehead and across the pontoon bridge.

The centurion spied Cornelius and the priest approaching the gate. Other legionaries on watch, seeing Cornelius with the Labarum, rushed forward.

"Marcellinus?" asked Longinus.

Father Paul shook his head. "Dead."

The centurion peered into the darkness. "And Tribune Marius? Where is he?"

"We encountered Easterners on the hill," said Cornelius. "One held the tribune at sword point."

The centurion pulled out his sword. "Come on you storks, we have a tribune to rescue," he said to the dozen legionaries standing by the gate. As they gathered around Longinus, Septimus came out of the darkness leading a horse.

The centurion breathed a sigh. "Welcome back, Tribune. We thought we had lost you."

Septimus handed the reins of the horse to a legionary. He pointed to the body of Marcellinus. "Form an honor guard for him."

The legionaries lifted the body of Marcellinus aloft on their shields while others formed in ranks in front and behind the body. Father Paul and Cornelius, who carried the Labarum, led the legionaries bearing the general back inside the gate. Activity within the bridgehead came to a standstill as legionaries of Third Italica lined the way of the procession down to the pontoon bridge. The legionaries stood at attention as their general passed them by, as if in review, for the last time. Then they raised their spears with a shout. "Pia Fidelis!"

Chapter 10

The Bridge over the Drava

As the sun peeked over the horizon, Constantius, accompanied by a retinue of officers and a squadron of cataphracts guided by Marcus, came upon Florentius and Lucius standing on the crest of the hill overlooking the pontoon bridge.

Florentius saluted. "Hail, Augustus!"

The Emperor appeared pale and dark-eyed.

"My condolences, my lord, on the passing of the Empress," said Florentius. "She was a great lady."

Constantius, his jaw clenched, acknowledged the greeting with a single nod.

"My lord, my apologies for pressing this matter during your time of grief, but the urgency of the moment dictated I not delay," said Florentius. The general pointed to the pontoon bridge. "You see before you the last of the Western army hurrying to cross the river. Western legionaries, cavalry and wagons wait their turn to pass over the bridge or to ride the ferry across the river. The stream of survivors flowing into the bridgehead, heavy in the early hours of the morning, is now only a trickle. Thousands have crossed to safety since midnight. The last of the Western army will soon cross."

A slight smile appeared on the Emperor's face. "Two days ago, Magnentius the Usurper haughtily refused to surrender. Now, three-quarters of his men lay dead in the fields of Mursa Major. Look at him run."

148

"It is a great victory for you, Lord Augustus," Arbitio said. "Let us erect a triumphal arch in Constantinople in commemoration of it!"

The officers along the hilltop let out a great cheer of approval.

The Emperor raised his hand to acknowledge the adulation. His smile broadened at first, but then he observed Florentius. "General, you do not share the happiness of the others? You appear somber."

"Great Augustus, I cannot celebrate a victory we have not yet achieved," said Florentius.

The Emperor cocked his head. "Florentius, reveal your thoughts to us."

"Sire, you have won a battle, but you have not yet won the war. You have saved a city, but not won an empire. King Gundamar failed to either take or destroy the pontoon bridge. If he had done either, you would have captured the entire Western army and won both a victory and an empire."

"Gundamar is not worth the gold I paid him and his horde." The Emperor's words came out as grinding rocks. "I look forward to destroying him and his people when this war is over."

Florentius pointed to the bridge. "My lord, the Western army is wounded and weak. We must pursue and destroy it before it escapes back into Italy or Gaul and regroups. This will prolong the war for years."

Constantius nodded. "This why I value your counsel—you do not shrink from telling me what I must hear." The Emperor focused his attention on the river and the bridgehead. "What is the strength of the defenses?"

"A single legion—Third Italica—remains as the rear guard."

The Emperor turned to one of his generals. "Lollianus, how long until your infantry arrives?"

The young general removed his helmet, his black hair fell to his shoulders. "Within the quarter hour."

"Since we must wait, let us see if the enemy commander might surrender to us," said the Emperor. "Third Italica fought for my father at the Milvian Bridge. With such a history, perhaps they might yield to a son of Constantine." He beckoned to Marcus. "Captain, choose a flagbearer. Parley with the commander of the bridge defenses. Offer leniency ... pardon ... riches ... the friendship of Caesar ... anything. Whatever is necessary in my name. In exchange, he must hand over the bridge, whole and intact."

"As you command, Lord Augustus," replied Marcus. He rode over to Lucius. "How would you like a small adventure? Care to be my flagbearer?"

Lucius grinned. "Thank you, Marcus."

"It is not the combat you have longed for, but perhaps one day you can tell your children and grandchildren how you received the surrender that reunified the empire."

The Emperor turned in the saddle, his purple cape fluttered in the breeze. "Claudius Silvanus, do you know the enemy commander? The commander of Third Italica?"

"I do, my lord," said Silvanus. "Tribune Gaius Marius Septimus. A friend of old from campaigns along the frontiers of Gaul."

"Is he the sort who might surrender the bridge for a price?"

"Unlikely, sire. He can be a rather obstinate, old-fashioned sort."

"Still, go along with Captain Marcus and see if you can help convince the tribune to hand the bridge over to us."

"As you wish, sire," said Silvanus.

***

Septimus and Longinus stood on the earthen rampart. A cool autumn breeze out of the north blew at their backs. In the distance, two dozen riders were positioned along the hilltop across the field.

The tribune squinted at the sight. "They bear imperial banners. Emperor Constantius himself pays us a visit."

"That's trouble—sure enough," said Longinus. He placed his vine staff between his upper arm and side as he tied the chin strap of his transverse-crested helmet.

"Three riders approaching under a flag of truce!" shouted a sentry above the gate. The men on horses rode down the hill to their south. They came to a halt about one hundred yards from the gate.

"I will ride out and hear what the Emperor offers," said

150

Septimus. He surveyed the line of rag-tag men still entering through the gate. The line snaked along the river to the east. "The column goes on for another couple hundred yards. Get the last of the men, horses, and carts within the bridgehead as quick as you can. We do not have long before the Easterners attack."

"Understood, sir."

Septimus exited the gate astride his horse. Along the inside of the trench, Jason and his men labored, toting large buckets. "Is all ready with the bridge?" asked the tribune.

Drusus leaned his head back, glancing up at Septimus on the drawbridge above. "It will go up in flames if you so much as belch upon it."

Septimus smiled. "Very well, but have a torch ready all the same."

The tribune took a deep breath as he gripped the reins tight. *Is there any honorable way out of this with our lives intact?* He kicked his heels into the sides of the horse. "Let's go, Ulysses." Septimus rode across the field and to the delegation a hundred yards away from the trench, halfway between the bridgehead and the top of the hill from where the Emperor watched them. He saluted Marcus and Lucius. "Good morning, Captains . . . Gaius Marius Septimus at your service. We meet again. I suspect our meeting today will not end as amicably as our first."

"I am Captain Marcus Scudillo," said Marcus introducing himself and the officers with him. "Next to me is Captain Lucius and beside him is Tribune—"

"Claudius Silvanus," interrupted Septimus. His back stiffened as he stared with cold eyes at Silvanus. He gripped the hilt of his sword, seeming to debate within himself whether to draw it forth and strike the traitor dead. "There is no need to introduce us. Silvanus and I know each other well."

Silvanus smiled. "We are old friends. Are we not, Septimus? And, speaking of old friends, I understand that you may have met another old acquaintance of yours yesterday—Gundamar the Giant. He was supposed to take or destroy this bridge. But I see the bridge is still there. Gundamar was always the treacherous and unreliable sort, as you know, Tribune. Still, my compliments to you and Third Italica. Bravely done."

"Treacherous and unreliable? Those words describe you, Silvanus." The tribune now turned his attention back to Marcus. "I see the Emperor has risen early. I hope his sleep was not disturbed on our account."

"The Emperor sends his compliments to you and your men, Tribune Gaius Marius Septimus," said Marcus. "The matter at hand is one of urgency for him." The blare of horns sounded from the hills behind him. He paused for a moment to listen. "You hear the approach of several legions. Your defenses are weak. A mound of dirt, a trench, and an incomplete palisade. Our attack will be pressed without quarter. You and your men will be killed where they stand or driven into the river and drowned. However, my orders from the Emperor, who watches us even now, are to bid you to surrender yourself, your legion and the bridge—intact—and without delay. In return, our gracious and beneficent Augustus, Constantius, will manifest his mercy toward you and your men by granting pardons and bestowing generous gifts to every man. You will be named a *Friend of Caesar*."

Septimus's shoulders slumped forward. He lowered his head, the sun reflecting off his crested helmet. He sat still and quiet. Those observing him could not discern whether his reaction was one of disappointment with the offer or an inner admission of defeat and surrender.

Marcus smirked as he observed his enemy.

There was a pained expression of pity on Lucius's face. Though the tribune was the enemy, Lucius admired his bravery in leaving the safety of his lines to find a fallen comrade. It would be a shame that such an honorable man should die such a wasted death for a lost cause.

"Consider this generous offer, Septimus," said Silvanus. "For the sake of friendship."

Tribune Marius patted the neck of his gray horse. He sneered. "For the sake of friendship? Was it for friendship you betrayed your comrades? What of Marcellinus, your friend and mine? Was it for friendship that your cataphracts overran his men and killed him?"

Silvanus pursed his lips as he gave a shallow, almost

imperceptible, nod. "His death is regrettable. But, neither of our actions, yours or mine, could ever have altered the inevitable course of this war. Magnentius cannot win this war. Each must look to his own interests in this world—as best he can. I saw an opportunity to make a bargain and took it. I shall not apologize for it or worry about your opinion of me. You would have done so too had you been smart about it and thought of it as I had. But there is still a chance for you, even now, to come around to this reality. Bow to the inevitable. Consider and accept the offer of the Emperor. You would become a Friend of Caesar, receiving his goodwill, treasure, and position. Think of your love for the beautiful Lady Marciana, who awaits you in the Eternal City. You will not survive this war to return to her unless you surrender this bridge."

"And what of loyalty and faithfulness? Do they not have a part in this world of yours?"

"Pia et Fidelis?" asked Silvanus with a snicker. "I was loyal and faithful to Magnentius. Now, I am loyal and faithful to Constantius. Come, Septimus . . . consider what this world offers as have I. Embrace it. Accept the Emperor's offer."

Tribune Marius leaned his head back. The sky was blue and cloudless. A flock of birds flew overhead. *How I wish I had such freedom.* He faced Marcus. "I have considered the offer of the Emperor."

Lucius leaned forward in his saddle in anticipation of the answer, hoping battle might yet be avoided.

Marcus sat back, relaxed and cocky, sure of a surrender. "And your answer?"

Septimus straightened himself atop Ulysses. His back was now stiff, his shoulders square and back. "Your Emperor may keep his mercy, pardon, and gifts—and bestow them on others, less steadfast of heart. This bridge he cannot have for any price."

Marcus's smirk disappeared. He glowered at his enemy. "Such impertinence!"

The tribune glanced over his shoulder toward the river and then back at Marcus. "I like this bridge and am using it at the moment," said Septimus with a sardonic smile. He wet a finger with his tongue and held it high in the air. "And, when I am done with it—

there being a nice strong breeze from the north this morning—your emperor will breathe its smoke and ashes. That is all of the bridge he will ever have."

Marcus kicked his heels hard against the sides of his horse, which jumped into a brief trot. He pulled his mount alongside Ulysses. He squinted at the tribune with menacing eyes. "How dare you speak of the Emperor in such a way!" He reached his hand to the hilt of his sword.

"Marcus, we meet under a flag of truce!" said Lucius, cautioning his friend. "Do not draw your sword."

Silvanus laughed. "And who are you, Septimus Romanus? Are you the great Horatio—returned to us from ancient times—who will hold the bridge against impossible odds?"

"General Marcellinus ordered this legion to hold the bridge until the army has crossed to safety," said Septimus. "Third Italica, loyal and faithful to this order, awaits your emperor should he wish to try to take it."

Silvanus grabbed the white flag away from Lucius. He threw it down to the ground at Ulysses's feet. "Insolent fool! So be it."

Marcus and Lucius headed back up the hill. The tribune and Silvanus remained on the field alone.

"Silvanus, you will pay one day for what you have done," said the tribune. "For all those you betrayed—especially for Marcellinus."

"You are a fool, Septimus." Silvanus reared his horse back. "This very day, you could be on your way back to Rome and to Lady Marciana. You needed only to have stood aside." He turned and rode away. "Farewell, Tribune!"

Septimus grimaced. The traitor's words stung. *This very day, you could be on your way back to Rome and to Lady Marciana.* "This very day," he muttered to himself.

***

Longinus and Jason stood at the end of the drawbridge across the trench, watching as Septimus returned. The last of the retreating Western army had just jammed inside the gate, a squad of legionaries from Third Italica shepherding them along into the bridgehead.

The centurion tilted his head back at Septimus, who pulled Ulysses to halt before him. "Well?" asked Longinus.

"Silvanus was with them," said the tribune, spitting out the name with contempt.

"Then our fears were true. Silvanus betrayed us."

Tribune Marius stared at the eastern sky, seeming to see a distant point not visible to the other men. "Last night I saw the King Star in the eastern sky. It seemed a sign or omen that Constantius will be triumphant over the West. Silvanus said I should bow to the inevitable and surrender the bridge . . . to think of saving our lives and of returning to Lady Marciana. If I did so, he said I would become a Friend of Caesar—obtaining his goodwill and treasure."

The centurion grinned. "You told him to stuff it?"

Septimus nodded. "Pia fidelis . . . to whatever end."

Longinus pointed in the direction whence Septimus had come. The lead cohorts of an Eastern legion had crested the hill and now marched down the slope toward them. "Well, that *end* is coming to call on us."

The three entered the bridgehead. The gate shut behind them and the drawbridge raised.

Septimus saw a throng of soldiers, horses, and carts pushing toward the bridge and ferry. "It will take another hour or more to get them all across."

"If we can hold out that long," said the centurion.

"The Emperor thought we might be willing to surrender to Silvanus."

"Constantius does not know this legion," said Longinus, his tone gruff.

"Nor does he know of my men from Ostia," said Jason.

"Then let us give him a lesson," said Septimus with a wink. He spurred Ulysses up the slope of the earthen rampart. The rampart stood four feet high above the ground inside the bridgehead and its level top was ten feet across. The other side of the rampart sloped down into the deep trench. At the foot of the rampart on the inside, Third Italica's legionaries lined up for battle. They fell to their knees as Father Paul ascended the slope before them. Standing beside Cornelius who held high the Labarum that Marcellinus had saved from the enemy, the priest blessed the legionaries and gave them general absolution for their sins, finishing by saying "And I absolve you from your sins in the name of the Father, and of the Son, and of the Holy Spirit."

When the priest had finished, the legionaries made a sign of the cross and replied with a loud "Amen" and then stood to their feet.

To his own surprise, the tribune found he had lowered his head as the priest conducted his ritual. *By Zeus why did I do that? I am not a Christian. I hope the centurion didn't see that. I'd never hear the end of it.* He then rode along the top of the rampart as he addressed the entire legion in a loud voice. "The enemy advances even now, under the watchful eyes of their emperor—eager to come to grips with us, each of them wanting to perform acts of valor within sight of Constantius, hoping to be awarded with laurels and treasure. You fight within the sight of the remains of the Western army, whose safety, now depends upon you, and you alone. You fight under the eyes of our general, Marcellinus, who now lives, as you believe by your Faith, with your Christian God. It was Marcellinus who ordered us to hold this bridge. Legionaries of Third Italica, stand true to that command! Let no one think of flight, or the security of the far shore for himself alone, for there will be no security for any should we fail. Remember, he who remains steadfast in battle is more likely to preserve his life whilst he who flees puts not only the lives of his comrades in peril but his own life as well. The one who prefers life to honor will keep neither—whether in this world or the one to come."

Septimus put the Chi Rho shield of Marcellinus on his left arm. He pulled forth the sword the legion had presented to him as a gift only two days before. Brandishing it above his head, the legionaries cheered as he rode past them on Ulysses.

"C'mon you storks, to the ramparts!" shouted the centurion.

The first three ranks of legionaries ran up the inner slope of the earthenworks and lined the length of the rampart not protected by a palisade. Stationed behind the line and in the several towers crouched squads of archers.

"Well said, Tribune," said Jason, as Septimus approached.

"Inspiring words."

"It is a paraphrase," said Septimus.

"The words of a great general from ancient times?"

Longinus glared at Jason and shook his head. "Do not encourage the tribune. You must learn not to ask him about quotes or history."

"Pay no mind to him, Jason," said Septimus. "It was a paraphrase of Agamemnon's speech to his men outside the walls of Troy."

Over the shoulders of the legionaries standing ahead of him, Jason saw the enemy legion lining up for battle across the field. He took a deep breath. "Agamemnon's men were victorious—yes?"

"The Trojans drove them back to the sea, to the water's edge."

Jason took a quick glance at the river, only fifty yards behind them. He swallowed. "To the water's edge?"

The centurion rolled his eyes at the Jew. "I told you not to ask the tribune. There is always a twist . . . always."

The trumpets of the Eastern legion sounded. In unison, the disciplined ranks moved forward. The metallic rustling of their armor and the barked orders of the centurions echoed as they marched.

Samson lifted the much shorter Drusus several feet off the ground so that he could see all that was happening for himself. Spears bristled from the square formations of the Eastern Romans, each unit behind its own standard. Drusus observed the sight in a combination of awe and fear. "And I thought the attack of the barbarians was a frightful sight to behold," he said.

When the Eastern legionaries drew to within fifty yards of the trench, a war cry arose from among them. They quickened their pace across the narrow field. The Western archers launched several volleys of arrows while the scorpions fired away into the oncoming ranks. Gaps in the ranks appeared as legionaries fell to the rain of arrows and bolts, the spaces filled by those next in the file.

Septimus held his sword high. "Third Italica!" he shouted.

The front ranks stepped forward to the edge of the rampart. The men of the Third Italica responded. "Ready!"

"Pia!" shouted the centurion.

On cue, the front rank of legionaries interlocked their shields with their companions next to them, and their spears and those of their comrades behind them bristled outward from behind the wall of shields.

"Fidelis!" came the shouted response from the legionaries.

The front ranks of Eastern infantry descended into the trench that ran the length of the rampart. Enemy legionaries scrambled over piled logs and branches placed in the ditch as obstacles by Jason's men to encumber the attackers. Cornelius stood behind a legionary at the front of the Third Italica line, holding the Labarum high. It seemed to him the main thrust of the Eastern assault centered on him and the Labarum. Each enemy legionary within view was intent on wresting the standard from him, a grave dishonor to the Third Italica should any one of them succeed in doing so.

Cornelius gripped the shaft of the Labarum tightly. "You shall not take this from me," he muttered to himself as a burly centurion led Eastern legionaries up the slope of the earthen rampart toward him. Cornelius leaned forward, bracing himself for the collision.

The Eastern legionaries attacking up the slope crashed into a wall of black shields and gleaming spears in front of Cornelius. The first several enemy legionaries rushing toward Cornelius were pierced by spears to their sides and necks as they tried with their shields to swipe away the spears that faced them.

Cornelius screamed as he felt a sharp pain in his calf. He glanced down to see the tip of an enemy spear had pierced him just behind the grieve on his left leg. It was then he realized that Eastern legionaries coming up the slope were jabbing their spears at the feet and legs of Third Italica legionaries, trying to drive the defenders, who held the advantage of the high ground, back from the edge of the rampart. Eastern legionaries in increasing numbers succeeded in climbing the slope, gaining a foothold atop the rampart. A general melee ensued along the entire line. The clash of spear against shield and sword against sword, mixed with the shouts and cries of men in brutal combat reverberated across the battlefield.

Cornelius felt his comrades to his front being pushed back by the weight of the attack, as more of the enemy gained a foothold on the level ground before him. "Rally to the Labarum, men!" Cornelius shouted, as several of the legionaries assigned to protect him and Labarum were cut down around him. Holding the Labarum aloft with his left hand and pinned beneath his left arm, Cornelius drew his sword. He hacked away at the enemy, trying to fend off the Eastern legionaries who surrounded him. Stabbing one soldier deep in the gut, he lost his sword as the mortally wounded man wrenched it from his hand as he fell.

Cornelius felt a pull on the shaft of the Labarum.

"I'll take that!" came a deep voice, filled with rage and hate. It was the burly centurion he had seen leading the enemy charge toward him. The enemy centurion gripped the Labarum with his shield hand and pulled hard, trying to take it away.

Cornelius saw the centurion raise his sword to strike him. Fearing for the loss of the Labarum over his own life, he closed his eyes to the oncoming blow, wanting to die grasping tight to the Labarum if he must. "Save the Labarum!"

"No, you don't!" came a more familiar shout. There followed a cry of pain and then a loud gasp of a man in agony. The tug of war for the Labarum came to a sudden end.

"You can't fight with your eyes closed," came the same voice, now annoyed.

Cornelius opened his eyes.

Longinus stood beside him with his sword planted deep in the chest of the enemy centurion. "Forward, lads!" said Longinus, who had led fresh reinforcements into the battle. Western legionaries rushed forward and slew the enemy soldiers around Cornelius.

"Thank you, Centurion," said Cornelius.

"Where's your sword?" asked Longinus.

"Lost it, sir."

Longinus pointed his sword toward the ground. "Use that one." There on the ground lay the muscular arm and hand of the centurion who had just tried to take the Labarum. The hand still gripped the sword. "He no longer has need of it."

The tribune rode along the rampart, ordering squads up from below to reinforce the line wherever he saw gaps developing in the line. Seeing a hole, he rode Ulysses into the midst of several

Eastern legionaries as they reached the level ground. The collision with the horse sent them tumbling back down into the trench. "Jason!" he shouted, seeing him nearby.

Jason and his two comrades joined in the struggle to plug the gap. Samson rushed forward, and wielding his large sledgehammer to crush opponents, repelled the Easterners, yelling "I hate Romans" as he hit each one.

The Easterners' assault, thinned by high casualties and a lack of fresh reinforcements, wavered. The enemy legionaries began to fall back.

"After them!" said Longinus, leading legionaries down the outer slope of the earthworks.

Not yet having his fill of taking the fight to the Romans, Samson also chased retreating stragglers into the trench, slaying them as he caught up to them.

A great cheer arose from the legionaries of Third Italica at the sight of their fleeing foes.

Septimus nodded to himself in quiet satisfaction, but happiness dissolved away in a moment and his stomach plummeted. Another Eastern legion appeared over the hill, followed by another. "Sound the recall!" the tribune ordered.

A horn blared, calling the Western legionaries to return to the rampart.

"Back to your positions—reform your ranks!" shouted Longinus.

The other centurions of Third Italica took up the call along the battle line, ordering men back to their positions.

Longinus approached Septimus as he inspected the line. The centurion watched as the larger Eastern force now converged on the bridgehead. "Two legions. Against the weight of these numbers, we can neither hold the rampart nor withdraw across the river in good order."

Septimus turned toward the river. The remains of the Western army were still crossing the Drava, and more men and carts waited their turn to escape to safety. "We must find a way."

The decurion kicking his horse onward, galloped to the top of the rampart. "Tribune, enemy galleys sighted approaching from downriver."

"Wonderful," said Longinus.

The tribune's jaw tightened. "How long till they are here?"

"Maybe a half-hour," said the decurion.

"Very well. Direct the artillery in the river tower to target the galleys when they arrive."

The decurion saluted.

The Eastern horn blared. The enemy legions surged forward.

Longinus stepped through ranks of legionaries until he stood at the front. Eager to fight, Samson and Drusus followed him. The centurion tapped a finger against Drusus's chest. "Make sure your friend Samson knows who the good Romans are."

"There will be no problem," said Drusus. "Don't worry."

"Jason," said Septimus calling after him as he moved to join his friends. "You stay close to me."

The Jew nodded. "Understood."

The tribune drew his sword. "Third Italica. Pia!"

The legionaries responded with "Fidelis!" The legionaries in the front of the line interlocked shields and presented their spears forward.

As before, the Eastern legionaries rushed into the trench, and over the obstacles of logs and branches piled into it, and then up the outer slope of the rampart.

The first of the enemy reached Longinus and was chopped down by him. "Hold the line!" yelled the centurion as the enemy assault collided with Third Italica's wall of shields. A confused melee ensued.

Drusus and Samson battled in the midst of the struggle for control of the rampart, fighting alongside legionaries of Third Italica. Samson, having broken his sledgehammer across the helmet of an enemy centurion, picked up Eastern legionaries as they came at him one at a time and, holding them high above his head, yelling "Romans!" tossed them back down onto enemy legionaries scrambling up the slope from the trench.

Seeing Samson lift another legionary, Longinus grabbed him by the shoulder just as the Ostian was about to hurl him. "Careful with that one!" shouted the centurion. "He is one of ours!"

Drusus rushed over. "Put him down, Samson!"

The giant looked overhead at the legionary—his arms and legs flailing about. "One of ours?"

Drusus nodded. "Yes. Nice Roman. One of ours."

Samson placed the legionary down on his feet. He picked up the legionary's helmet. He patted him on the head and replaced the helmet. "Sorry," he said sheepishly.

Drusus breathed a sigh of relief.

The centurion glared at Drusus. He pointed his thumb at Samson. "Make sure you keep that one pointed in the right direction!"

The section of the Third Italica line defended by Longinus, the main focus of the enemy attack, was weakened by casualties and exhaustion. Here, the Eastern assault gained strength. Increasing numbers of the enemy swarmed to the top of the earthen rampart.

Septimus rode Ulysses into the midst of the melee leading a fresh company of legionaries, coming to the aid of the centurion. Swinging and hacking at Easterners within his reach, the tribune encouraged the men forward.

After slaying a legionary, Septimus high atop Ulysses observed a senior Eastern officer across the trench. The officer waved fresh reinforcements forward, pointing them to attack across the trench in front of Septimus. Hundreds of Eastern reinforcements poured into the trench below and were soon upon the tribune and his legionaries.

Longinus strode through the midst of the swarm of attackers, felling Easterners one after the other. Yet, they were too many for the defenders. "Tribune, if they break the line here, all is lost!" he shouted above the din of battle.

Septimus wheeled Ulysses around. "Jason, we are losing the rampart. Now's the time!"

At once, Jason ran to the inner edge of the rampart. He waved his hands above his head to several of his men from Ostia who were stoking a campfire below the inside of the rampart. One of them lifted a red pennant on a long pole and waved it. At this signal, dozens of his Ostians, assigned to wait by campfires along the earthenworks, grabbed lit torches. They scrambled up the rampart and hurled the torches over the heads of the combatants. Likewise, archers on the towers launched flaming arrows.

The flaming torches and arrows landed in the trench causing fires to erupt. In a matter of seconds, a loud *whoosh* accompanied the fire as it spread. Flames, rising high, raced along the whole length of the trench until it was all ablaze. The loud popping and crackling of the raging conflagration echoed through the nearby hills. In a moment, the assault disintegrated into confusion. The weight and momentum of the dense formation of Eastern troops, twenty men deep, carried the forward ranks closest to the trench into it. Those legionaries pushed forward fell onto those trying to escape, only to perish together with them in the flames.

The flames roared above the centurion's head. Longinus raised his shield, to block the intense heat from his face. The rising smoke swirled and billowed around them. The centurion and the legionaries stepped away from the conflagration. He found himself beside Jason. "What is all this?"

"A little surprise the tribune thought up," said Jason. "We placed the wood stockpiled for construction of the palisade into the trench as an obstacle. Last night we smothered it all with pitch, oil, and resin."

Septimus, seeing the confusion of the enemy, waved his men on. "Third Italica, forward!" he shouted, calling to the rest of his reserves. "Push them back into the trench!"

The legionaries along the front line of the Third Italica, leaning into their shields, pushed into the foes in front them, while their comrades in the ranks behind pushed those ahead of them forward.

Longinus strode along the rampart. "Push them back, push them, you storks!"

The ranks of Third Italica pressed against the line of desperate Eastern legionaries, driving them backward foot by foot, either to tumble off the rampart into the flames or to be killed by the sword. Once again, Third Italica controlled the rampart.

Longinus glanced at the bridge and the far shore. "Tribune, the last of the wagons carrying the wounded are crossing the river."

Septimus turned about in his saddle to see for himself. "The army has safely crossed the river." He nodded. "Third Italica has done its duty. Centurion, prepare the legion to withdraw."

THE TWO KINGDOMS

***

From his position on the hill, Constantius blanched as hundreds of his legionaries were pushed into the fiery trench. The Emperor clenched his jaw. He gripped the reins tight. *Damn Third Italica.* Hundreds of men ran about the field below in all directions, attempting to extinguish the flames that engulfed them. Two full legions turned in retreat. Smoke billowed from the trench making it difficult to see beyond the flames to the bridge and river. The Emperor's face turned red. "Damn Third Italica!" he shouted.

Helpless, Constantius and his officers watched as the blaze in the trench prevented the resumption of the assault. After a half-hour, Constantius sat higher in the saddle and leaned forward to get a better view. "The rear guard is pulling back across the river, under cover of the flames and smoke. They will set fire to the bridge once they have crossed, and I will lose the opportunity to destroy Magnentius and end this war here, and now." Constantius beckoned to Marcus. "They are withdrawing. This is their one chance to save themselves. They are running. Take your squadron of cataphracts. Rally what infantry you can—but, get me that bridge before they destroy it!"

"But the flames, sire!" said Florentius.

"Damn the flames!" said Constantius. "Go, Captain!"

"As you command sire," said Marcus, who at once signaled for his squadron of cataphracts to follow him down the hill. The cataphracts wore full body suits of linked armor, a helmet, and visor, while their horses were covered in scaled armored which flowed down around the animals' chests and flanks like a skirt down to their knees.

As Marcus led his cavalry down the slope, he came upon hundreds of legionaries resting from the fight. "Come on men, the Emperor is watching you!" he shouted to them. "The enemy is taking flight! There is no one on the rampart. The Emperor demands we save that bridge. We will find a place where the flames are weakest and cross. Follow me!"

The Eastern legionaries looked up the hill and saw Constantius glowering down at them. They stood to their feet. "Forward men!" urged their own officers. "Better the flames than the wrath of the

Emperor!"

***

His face, armor, tunic, and cloak darkened by ash and smoke, Septimus sat mounted upon Ulysses near the bridge, watching as units of the Third Italica streamed across it to the safety of the opposite bank. Beside him stood Jason, holding a lit torch.

Longinus rode his horse up alongside the tribune. He pointed downriver. Several long boats, fifteen oars to a side, were making their way around the bend in the river at best speed. "River galleys heading our way. They'll be here in minutes."

Septimus watched as the last squad of infantry stepped onto the bridge to cross. "Hurry across, lads, as quick as you can." He squinted down river at the approaching galleys. "They'll try to save the bridge." Septimus dismounted and grabbed the torch from Jason. He walked onto the first segment of the bridge. Taking the torch, he ran it along the pools of pitch prepared by Jason and his Ostians.

"What are you doing?" asked Jason, as the flames began to rise.

Septimus handed him back the torch. "Here. Have your men get to work. Torch the rest of it."

"What about you and the centurion? You still have men in the high tower."

"Go now," the tribune said. Reluctant, Jason turned and joined the first team of his men, who then set about destroying the next segment of bridge.

Longinus cocked his head. "Yes, what about *us*, Tribune?"

"We will follow when we can."

The centurion pointed his vine staff at the growing flames. "Then should we not have waited to cross the bridge before setting it aflame? That would have been the customary thing to do."

"Ordinarily."

"That's the problem with you, Tribune. Nothing is ordinary with you. Do you have a death wish?"

Septimus shook his head. "Me? No. There's a woman in Rome to whom I plan to return. I intend to survive this war."

"Good. I just wanted to make sure. You do a fine impression of someone trying to get himself killed at times."

Septimus lowered his brow. "Thank you?"

"You can thank me later," said the centurion. "What is your plan now? I assume you have one."

"If this bridge doesn't burn, all would have been for naught," said Septimus. "We must help buy as much time as we can for Jason and his Ostians. Get to the high tower. Direct the artillery against the galleys best you can for as long as you can. Then torch the tower. I would not want to make a gift of it to the enemy."

"You?"

"I'll stand watch on the rampart."

"And after that?"

"We'll escape on the ferry, said Septimus. "Satisfied with the plan?"

The centurion tied the chin strap of his helmet. "It sounds like one of your plans. But it will have to do." He prompted his horse forward. "Can't wait to see what goes wrong with this one," he muttered beneath his breath.

***

Jason and his men set about destroying each segment of the bridge. He had positioned his comrades at intervals along the length of the bridge. As Jason made his way across the bridge, one of the men in each team started the fires, while others, led by Samson, wielded axes to hack at the ropes that kept the pontoons connected and anchored in place.

They were a third of the way across the bridge when a high-pitched whistling noise was heard. Jason turned toward the sound. It was the high tower by the river launching flaming projectiles at the Eastern galleys as they came within range. Already, the artillery found targets with deadly effect. Fire raged on a couple of the galleys, while ten-pound stones launched by the ballistae shattered planks of the long boats as they struck.

Jason's heart sank. Two other galleys made it past the high tower unscathed. The first of the boats neared the bridge. A row of round shields lined the sides of each long boat.

The shouts of one of the ship's captain could be heard. "Ship oars! Prepare to come alongside." The crew pulled the oars aboard as the steersman turned the galley to bring it gliding alongside of the bridge. "Arm yourselves!" The crewmen grabbed their shields from the side of the boat and drew their swords, ready to leap into battle. "Save the bridge!"

The Eastern galley's crewmen threw grappling hooks and then leapt onto the decks of the pontoons closest to them.

The first of the Easterners were met by Samson, who swung his axe at him. Though the blow was met by a shield, the Easterner was knocked off balance and fell into the river. Drusus and the other sappers rushed forward to join the melee as the second galley came along and moored itself to the first. As the Eastern crew armed itself, a barrage of scorpion bolts began to strike in and around the second galley. Several of the crew fell dead.

Jason gestured to the other teams along the bridge. "Torch it all, now!" he ordered, as he began to light fire to the segment of the bridge on which he and his men stood as they battled the Easterners. The rest of Ostians did the same, even though it meant their comrades would now need to swim to their safety.

As Jason torched the bridge, an Easterner pushed into him with his shield, knocking Jason back into a sitting position. Stunned for the moment from the blow, he just sat there, helpless. The sailor raised his sword. As Jason flinched to receive the blow, the sailor fell over onto him, dead. There stood the short Drusus, retrieving his axe which was embedded in the back of the sailor.

Drusus helped his friend to his feet. "Come on, we have work to do."

Flames were all around, even as the battle continued. Most conspicuous of all in this fight was Samson, who now wielding an axe in each hand, battled several Romans at the same time.

Jason pointed to the ropes linking their segment of the bridge to the next. "Cut the ropes."

Drusus severed the ropes as commanded. At once, the bridge shifted and buckled beneath their feet.

"Get the men into the water," said Jason, as he grabbed a bucket and a torch. He leapt into the galley. The boat's hull alongside the bridge was now engulfed by the fire. The steersman came at him with a sword, which Jason fended off with the torch, then pushed the sailor into the water. Seeing his own men jumping into the river to escape, Jason tossed the bucket into the second galley, its flammable mixture spilling on the deck. He climbed into the galley and tossed his torch to the deck, lighting a new blaze. As another sailor came at him, Jason dove into the river.

As the Ostians jumped in the water and swam toward the left bank, the Easterners tried to save their galleys from the flames, but it was now too late.

"Abandon ship!" ordered the captain of the first galley, seeing that both his ship and the one moored to it were now caught up in the general conflagration.

***

Septimus stood watch on the earthenworks. Through the smoke and flame, he glimpsed Eastern cataphracts and infantry approaching the trench. Behind him, the whole pontoon bridge was now in flames. From the river tower, fire began to appear on its several levels. *Longinus has done all he can.*

The artillery crews scrambled down the ladder, followed by Longinus, who was the last to touch earth. "Tribune, come on!" he yelled.

Septimus acknowledged the centurion with a wave of his arm. "Make for the ferry!" he called back. No sooner had he said this then Eastern legionaries in single file began to brave a narrow break in the flames in the trench below. In a matter of moments, a half dozen of the enemy rushed up the hill. "Ulysses," said Septimus, urging the horse forward into the midst of the Easterners. Wheeling about, the horse knocked over and trampled several of them. The tribune fended off the thrust of spears with his shield, then leaned toward one of his attackers and stabbed him in the neck.

"The gate!" shouted a mounted Eastern officer from across the flames. "Let down the draw bridge!"

The last of the legionaries battling Septimus broke off contact. Leaving the tribune behind, he ran off along the rampart to the gate. Septimus wheeled his horse about. Many other enemy soldiers appeared here and there through the flames, a dozen of these converged on the tribune. He patted the horse on the neck. "Time to make our own escape." Spurring Ulysses on, Septimus rode broke through the midst of the legionaries now surrounding him, swinging his sword at them as he went. He headed down the slope of the earthenworks and headed for the pier where the ferry was moored.

There came the clanking of chains from behind. Septimus pulled the reins back on Ulysses, bringing the animal to an abrupt halt. *The drawbridge.* Turning around in his saddle, he saw it lowering.

"Tribune!" shouted Longinus from where the pier touched the bank. The centurion moved to one side to avoid the thrust of an enemy spear. Grabbing it, he pulled the enemy close and then drove his sword into the soldier's side. "Hurry, Tribune!"

Septimus placed himself and Ulysses halfway between the gate and the pier which were about one hundred yards apart. "Do not wait for me!" said the tribune above the roar of the fire and the crackling of burning wood. "Ring the bell! I will catch up!"

"You heard him!" the centurion shouted to the artillerymen waiting on the flat vessel. "Ring the bell!" he ordered. The soldier rang a bell on board the vessel. At this signal, legionaries from Third Italica positioned on the opposite bank began yanking on the ropes to pull the ferry across the river.

"'I'll catch up,' he says," muttered Longinus as he ran to the end of the pier and jumped onto the ferry which was already pulling away from the pier. He placed his sword back into its scabbard. He stood hands akimbo as he faced the shore. "I want to see how *this* plan works out," he said with disgust.

The drawbridge struck the ground with a thud, followed by the clatter of hoofbeats. Through the heavy smoke which engulfed the gate, an enemy cataphract with his sword drawn charged through the gate and headed for Septimus. Pulling his horse alongside Ulysses, the cataphract swung his sword at Septimus, who blocked it with his shield. The tribune struck back in a like fashion, but the blow was deflected by the cataphract's shield.

The cataphract drew his horse back several feet. He threw back the visor on his helmet. It was Marcus. "You escaped the sword last night—you shall not be so fortunate now!" Marcus declared.

The tribune glanced toward the river. The ferry was moving away from the pier. He faced Marcus. "Convey my compliments to the Emperor. I am now finished with the bridge. He may have what remains of it. Fire and smoke."

"I will see you dead or in chains," said Marcus.

"It will not be this day," said the tribune. He then spun Ulysses around and headed away at a gallop just as the squadron of cataphracts thundered through the gate.

"After him!" shouted Marcus.

The cataphracts in close pursuit were only a few yards behind as the tribune approached the river. Ulysses thundered onto the pier and galloped along it toward the ferry, which was now five yards distant from the end of the pier, the gap growing with each tug of the rope from the opposite bank.

"I think he means to jump," said one of the legionaries on the ferry, as Ulysses barreled toward them.

"Saints Peter and Paul!" Longinus shouted. "Move back!" he said, pushing a couple of the legionaries toward the opposite end of the ferry as the clatter of several horses rattled the deck of the pier.

"He's going to make it!" shouted one of the legionaries. "He's going to make it!"

Reaching the end of the pier in full stride, Ulysses launched himself with all his might into the air. It was a great, beautiful, and graceful arc of flight toward the deck of the ferry. A tremendous splash of water bathed Longinus and the legionaries. The horse had fallen short.

Two of the pursuing cataphracts, unable to stop at the end of the pier, tumbled horses and all into the river.

The centurion wiped the water away from his face. He shook his head. "That's about how I thought the tribune's plan might end." He threw a line of rope to Septimus, who slipped the loop around the neck of Ulysses. Pulled along with the ferry toward the other side of the river, the tribune held onto the mane of the gray horse.

Reaching the safety of the other bank of the river, Septimus emerged from the water, leading Ulysses by the reins. Now ashore, he took off his helmet to empty water from it.

Father Paul, who had observed all that had transpired, approached Septimus. "I was praying for you, Tribune. A marvelous escape—at least until the landing. Landing on the deck of the ferry would have been more impressive."

Tribune Marius patted a firm hand down on the priest's shoulder. He locked eyes with him. "You might have prayed harder to your God for a drier landing."

The priest smiled. "I will try harder next time."

Septimus stood on the bank of the river, taking in the view before him. The whole bridge was engulfed in a raging inferno, as was the high tower. Several river galleys burned. Thick columns of smoke billowed into the air. A segment of the bridge collapsed into the river. Others, which had been cut loose, drifted in the slow current.

The tribune thought of Marcellinus. *Third Italica has done its duty. The remains of the army are safely across the river, General.*

***

Across the Drava, Emperor Constantius, red-faced, looked out over the bridgehead and river from his position on the hill. The bridge, in flames, broke apart. Burning galleys drifted downriver. He gripped the horse's reins until his knuckles were white. Their eyes on Constantius, the officers in the Emperor's retinue sat still on their horses, each fearing to say a word or make the slightest noise that might interrupt the dreadful silence as his frustration and anger simmered.

A dense cloud of smoke from the conflagrations below wafted toward the Emperor and engulfed him as it drifted by. Constantius coughed as it surrounded him. "Damn Third Italica!"

Chapter 11

The Pope and the Prefect

(Rome, Spring, 353 AD)

Leontius and Claudius Silvanus followed a minor court official through the great halls of the imperial palace on the Palatine hill. The vaulted ceiling of the corridor, with its coffered panels, soared above floors of marble and mosaics depicting scenes from Roman and Greek mythology. Statues, pilasters, and columns of marble and porphyry lined their way as they went.

Leontius marveled at their surroundings as they went. "I never imagined being invited to the Imperial Palace as a guest of the Emperor. You have kept me in suspense long enough as to the purpose of my presence here. I know only that the Emperor wishes to speak with us."

"You will discover why soon enough when you meet the Emperor," said Silvanus.

"I am a soldier. I dislike surprises."

Silvanus kept an eye on their guide who walked thirty feet ahead of them to be sure he was not listening. "I will tell you, but you must act surprised when you learn of it from the Emperor himself."

"Yes, yes. I will act very surprised. But tell me now."

"It has been two years since the battle of Mursa Major. In this time, I have gained the Emperor's trust. I learned that Constantius wishes to appoint a new Prefect of Rome."

"You are to be Prefect? Congratulations!"

Silvanus shook his head. "No. I spoke with the Emperor and recommended you for the post. That is why you are here today. The Emperor will appoint you the new Prefect."

Leontius stopped in his tracks. "I am to be named Prefect? You did this for me?" he asked, running his hand over his balding head as he tried to fathom his good fortune.

Silvanus nodded. "You are an old friend, are you not?"

"I do not know what to say! I am honored beyond belief! It is an important post. How can I ever repay you for this favor?"

"The Prefecture of Rome is a lucrative office. You will be in a position to profit from those willing to pay for official favors. The Grand Chamberlain would have extracted a great sum of money from you in return, had he helped you to win this post."

"Yes, of course—I will pay whatever you ask!"

Silvanus waved off the suggestion with his hand as the two began to proceed down the corridor again. "No. I am not greedy like the Grand Chamberlain or Arbitio. A modest annual payment will suffice. You choose the figure. There is no purpose served in quibbling over an amount. It is more important to have happy and trustworthy friends and allies in imperial posts as I rise."

Leontius paused again, standing before a statue of Julius Caesar, which towered over them atop its pedestal. "You are too generous, Silvanus."

"Yes. Just remember what I have done for you."

"Always!" said Leontius. "But tell me—if you have the trust of the Emperor, why did you not seek the prefecture for yourself?"

Silvanus listened as he admired the statue of Caesar. "I have my sight on other, higher imperial posts," he said.

"I see," said Leontius, observing his friend's eyes upon the statue.

"Now, tell me, what is the latest news of Lady Marciana?" asked Silvanus as the two continued on, their steps on the marble floor echoing in the corridor. "Has she married?"

"Ah, I see we share an interest in her," said Leontius. "If so, I shall step aside in deference to you. You have been quite generous to me. Besides, I could never have competed with you for her affections. You cut a more dashing figure—you have better looks

173

and more hair than I."

Silvanus chuckled. "Marciana is beautiful, yes. But, again, my sight is set on higher posts. There is another woman who might help me on my rise."

"Princess Helena?" asked Leontius in a whisper so that their guide would not hear.

Silvanus responded with a coy smile. "So, I leave Lady Marciana to you. You have always had an eye for her."

"Yes, but she still pines for Septimus."

"Tribune Marius and Third Italica by all reports are in the Alps near Mons Seleucus. In a few months, Constantius will take the army over the mountains and destroy the remnant of the Western army. Septimus will be destroyed with it. You will not have to compete with him much longer for the affections of Lady Marciana."

"But if Septimus survives the war?" asked Leontius as their guide led them to a double door outside of which stood several imperial guards. Above the door was a mosaic of the sun. On the doors themselves, as well as the walls on either side of them, a lush, green scene of the outdoors had been painted. In one depiction, nymphs danced in the background amidst a pool and garden as the god Pan played his flute. The official disappeared through the doors to announce them.

"Heed my advice," said Silvanus. "Speak with Marciana's mother, Lady Tertia. She knows the fate of those who supported Magnentius against Constantius. If Septimus survives the war, he will be executed or sent into exile. Even if he avoids this fate, he will be a criminal . . . a fugitive. Lady Tertia will understand the benefit of her daughter marrying the Prefect of Rome. Trust me, old friend, the mother will be your ally in winning the hand of Marciana."

Leontius nodded. "Yes, I see your point. I will speak to Lady Tertia after I am named Prefect."

The doors opened again. The official reappeared and gestured to Leontius and Silvanus. "This way."

The official led them through the double door into the open air of a large peristyle. The columns of the surrounding portico, the pathways through the garden, walls, and fountains, like the rest of the palace interior, were made of colored marbles and porphyry. In the center of the courtyard sat Emperor Constantius, attired in purple robes and wearing a laurel wreath of gold about his head. On either side of him sat Eusebius and Arbitio, and the court bishops Ursacius and Valens. Constantius smiled as the official led the guests toward him.

"Great Augustus, may I present to you Commander Leontius," said Silvanus. "Leontius is an old friend of mine."

"Ah, Leontius, you have come well recommended to us by Silvanus," said Constantius, standing to greet him. "He has spoken highly of you."

Leontius bowed. "Thank you, my lord."

The Emperor took several steps along one of the paths. "Come walk with us, Leontius."

Leontius walked beside the Emperor, while Silvanus and the others followed. Constantius led them beneath the high portico. Maps of the empire and its many provinces, their boundaries made of inlaid marble, covered the walls.

The Emperor pointed at a map of the empire. "Two years ago, after my victory at Mursa Major, Magnentius the Usurper fled with his army back into northern Italy." Constantius placed his finger to the marble map beginning at the city of Mursa Major and traced a path with it as he narrated the course of events. "We pursued the Usurper into Italy where we fought several skirmishes and battles, which forced him to retreat into the Alps." He pointed at a city amidst the mountains. "Much of what remains of the Usurper's army is here, near Mons Seleucus, guarding the pass into Gaul." He then placed his finger on the city Mediolanum. "Our army wintered in the north of Italy and has spent the spring preparing for the final push against Magnentius to end this war once and for all. Now, the fleet has arrived in Portus and will move on Arelate. While my generals prepare the army, I have taken the opportunity of this time to dispatch imperial agents throughout Italy to root out all vestiges of support for Magnentius—to depose and arrest officials and leading citizens who had once supported the Usurper."

Constantius squinted at Leontius. "Eusebius tells me you supported the Usurper." He gave a quick glance to his Grand Chamberlain. "Is this not so, Eusebius?"

175

The blond-haired Eusebius straightened the sash hanging about his waist as he nodded. "So I have been informed, my lord."

"Is this true, Leontius?" asked the Emperor.

Leontius's head cocked back. His eyes darted nervously about as he took a moment to think. "In outward appearances only, sire," Leontius said with a slight tremble in his voice. "My heart was always with your family—looking only for the proper opportunity to manifest my support for your cause."

Silvanus glared at the eunuch, Eusebius. "Now I see that Eusebius disagrees with my nomination of Leontius for imperial office. Perhaps the Grand Chamberlain—or his informers—are unaware that Leontius, using his authority as commander of the garrison of Rome, secured the city for the Emperor long before his army had even entered Italy following the battle of Mursa Major."

Silvanus addressed the Emperor. "My lord, it was Leontius who led the mob in toppling the statues of Magnentius throughout the city. Leontius, at the head of the garrison, ensured that the populace of Rome accepted a change of the imperial government in your favor. As you know, there was no opposition and gates flung open to you upon your arrival to Rome. All this owing to the efforts of my friend, Leontius."

"I can think of others who are qualified for the high office," interjected Eusebius. "Men who have *always* supported the cause of the Emperor." His words seemed targeted as much at Silvanus as they were against Leontius. "Such men can more readily be trusted."

Silvanus, resting his hand on the handle of his sword as if he might draw it forth, approached Eusebius. Their faces but a foot apart, Silvanus stared menacingly at the shorter, thin-framed eunuch, who seemed to shrink in stature before him.

Arbitio came to the rescue of his court ally. He stood beside Eusebius, placing his hand upon his own sword as well. "The Grand Chamberlain is bound to give the Emperor his honest opinion and advice. Do you have a problem with that, Silvanus?"

"Enough of this," said Constantius, annoyed. "I have considered the advice of Eusebius, who has indeed presented a fine candidate for imperial office."

"Thank you, my lord," said the eunuch, bowing his head. "I will

176

inform him immediately of your decision."

Constantius raised his hand to silence Eusebius. "However, I am aware of the great service rendered by Leontius. In recognition of this service, and in no small part due to the fact the suggestion came from Silvanus himself, I have decided to appoint Leontius the Prefect of Rome."

Leontius fell to a knee and kissed the Emperor's ring. "Thank you, sire!"

Eusebius's head tilted back. "My lord, is this not a precipitous choice? Should you not first review the nominee I suggested to you in more detail?"

Constantius shook his head. "There is no need. I am content with the nominee presented by Silvanus." His attention turned to Leontius. "Look around you. The beautiful statues and fountains that adorn the peristyle. This Imperial Palace stands as a reminder of this city's historical importance but—more starkly—a reminder of its current irrelevance in the government of the empire." He faced again the map of the empire. Hairline cracks through the map suggested an age dating back to the first emperors. He pointed to Rome, marked at the center of the map. "Rome has stood for over eleven hundred years," Constantius said as he examined the map. He ran his fingers across the city's name. "It has grown from its humble beginning as a settlement along the Tiber to the largest city of the empire, with over a million inhabitants. The city has served as the capital of the republic and of the empire for half a millennium."

"A great city that has stood against time without falter," Leontius agreed.

The Emperor bit his lip in thought. "Yes. Rome sent forth its legions from here to conquer Iberia, Gaul, Britannia, Africa, and the East. Its outposts along the Rhine and Danubius have long held back the barbarians. However, since the time of Diocletian, the constant perils and catastrophes that have befallen the empire have required the personal attention and presence of the emperors elsewhere, closer to the frontiers. My father transferred his capital to Constantinople. The dangers of this age have thus led to a decline in the city's political importance. While Rome boasts of the presence of the Senate, it has become rare, almost unheard of, for an emperor to visit the city. So rare is it, that my presence in Rome might be regarded as something of a prodigy."

"Your presence is always a wonderful prodigy," interjected Eusebius at his obsequious best.

"Indeed, sire," said Arbitio. "Rome is fortunate to have you."

"Truly," added the court bishops in their turn.

The Emperor headed back toward his seat. "Still, while the political authority of Rome has been eclipsed, it now boasts something more potent. It claims a spiritual authority. An authority derived from the line of its bishops, who are the successors of Peter, the prince of the Apostles. The bearer of the keys of the kingdom."

The Emperor took Leontius by the elbow. "We must make certain the bishop of Rome remembers where ultimate authority rests in this world."

Constantius sat. He invited Leontius and Silvanus to take the places beside him. "So, from time to time, we must remind the Bishop of Rome that even his authority, and the authority of all bishops, must yield to the greater authority of the civil government, and the Emperor as its head."

The Emperor beckoned to a court official by the door. "Send him in."

The door swung open. In came Captain Marcus Scudillo with several imperial guardsmen who escorted a bishop with a gray beard.

Constantius rose from his seat and stepped forward to embrace the bishop. "Pope Liberius! Thank you for accepting my invitation to come and visit me this morning."

Liberius raised an eyebrow. He glanced from left to right at the guards who flanked him. "How could I refuse?" he said.

"I wanted you to meet someone. This is Leontius, who I have just named the new Prefect of Rome."

The pope bowed politely toward the prefect.

The Emperor returned to his seat. "The war will soon end. I have sent magistrates throughout Italy to put men into office loyal to me." He stared with cold eyes at the pope. "I will not allow any who oppose my will to stay in a position of authority." He placed a hand on Leontius's shoulder. "The new Prefect will have full

178

authority to enforce my will in Rome."

"My lord, remember Athanasius," urged Ursacius.

"Speak, Bishop Ursacius," said Constantius.

Ursacius approached the pope. "There is the matter of the Nicene creed."

"What of it?" said Liberius. "The Council of Nicaea, approved by my predecessors, taught Jesus Christ is consubstantial with God the Father. This is the teaching of the Church. Christ is of the same substance as the Father."

Ursacius, his face radiating annoyance, began to pace back and forth before Liberius. "But the Arians reject this. They are equally convinced that Christ is *not* of the same substance as the Father. They demand the Church adopts their view."

"Men must hold to what the Church teaches and professes."

"Your excellency, Pope Liberius, if I may interrupt," interjected Bishop Valens, as he stroked his long red beard. "The Emperor desires peace between religious factions in the empire. Mercy suggests we find an accommodation between factions, a common creed—one that all can affirm. Being too firm on certain points, such as claiming the consubstantiality of the Son and Father, as the Council of Nicaea and its creed affirmed, can only result in continued division. While there is need to find a common formula, Bishop Athanasius of Alexandria continues to preach against any compromise."

Liberius shook his head. "There can be no compromise when it comes to the truth."

"All in the Church will follow the bishop of Rome," said Valens. "If the Pope of Rome accepts compromise, the rest will follow."

The pope observed the Emperor's eyes sternly fixed upon him. Liberius swallowed as he began to perspire.

Bishop Valens's eyes now seemed to plead with Liberius. His voice took on a softer, friendlier tone. "The Nicene creed says 'of the *same* substance' while the Arians deny this. Cannot common ground be found with the Arians? Perhaps, it might be agreed that while the Father and the Son are not 'of the same substance' we might in compromise agree to say the Father and Son are 'of a *similar* substance.' Not of the same, but of *similar* substance."

Valens waited for the pope's response. In the background, the gurgling of the fountain echoed within the peristyle.

The pope felt the Emperor's gaze upon him. "This is not possible to say," he said, his voice trembling. "*Similar* is not the *same*," he added. "I do not see where there can be compromise. There is no middle point between truth and falsehood. If you surrender a part of the truth, you surrender the whole of it."

Valens tightened his jaw as he clenched his hands into a fist. "You and Athanasius must compromise!" he shouted, his body shaking in an angry fit. "You are too rigid. Most bishops of the East, including the episcopal sees of Constantinople and Antioch, have accepted compromise. Of all the great sees of the East, only Alexandria under Athanasius opposes reconciliation. Now that Emperor Constantius will soon rule over all East and West, it is only fitting that all bishops, especially the Bishop of Rome, share in this common view and show willingness to compromise to remove the cause of division with the Church."

The Grand Chamberlain rose to his feet. "The will of the Emperor is the law of the empire, of which both cleric and layman are subjects," declared Eusebius. "No bishop, not even a pope, can resist it."

The pope glimpsed the guards close by his side. He looked down at his feet, seeming to regret his momentary display of courage. His shoulders slumped forward. "I am against division in the Church," he said, his voice quivering again. "Perhaps there can be another council to consider the matter."

Constantius sprang to his feet. "Excellent! I am glad we had this opportunity for a discussion." He placed his hand upon the shoulder of the pontiff. "Consider what you have heard here, today. Now you know what I, your Emperor, expect of you and of all bishops within the empire. We will discuss these matters again once the war is over. Perhaps we will even have a council of bishops or two as you suggest, your excellency." He turned to Marcus. "Return the pope to his residence."

Valens watched as Liberius was led away. Once he was gone, he addressed the Emperor. "My lord, why did you let the pope go?"

"Is now not the time to move against him?" asked Ursacius. "He is within your power!"

The Emperor smiled. "Your excellencies, I have not forgotten

180

Athanasius. Nor have I forgotten all those who have supported him, like the Pope of Rome. But I dare not move against Liberius yet, lest it causes unrest in Rome. I do not want to do anything that might create sympathy or support for Magnentius when he is on the verge of defeat. I must leave Athanasius and Liberius alone for now. Once the Usurper is defeated, I will be free to deal with both. But you have seen for yourself. Liberius is a weak man. With a little pressure, he will bend and submit to my will."

The Emperor strolled over to the map of the empire upon the wall. Fixing his attention on the spot that marked the city of Rome, he addressed Leontius. "In the meantime, as my new Prefect in Rome, you must keep a close watch on Liberius. The Bishop of Rome and I may one day disagree. I need a prefect who will side with his emperor, and not with the people of Rome, who are fond of their bishop. I need a prefect who will do whatever is necessary or requested of him. Is that understood?"

"My only purpose is to see that your will be done, my lord Augustus," replied Leontius. "I am your servant."

The Emperor smiled. "I will host a banquet in your honor in the palace, showing the people and Senate of Rome that you are now a Friend of Caesar. Bring along what family or friends you will to celebrate your good fortune."

Leontius knelt before the Emperor. "Thank you, sire!"

***

"I remember in Mursa Major, you once said you regretted having traveled with the court into the West," said Princess Helena. She looked out over the center of Rome from a terrace of the imperial palace on the Palatine Hill. The roofs of the great buildings of the fora and city, covered in bronze plates, reflected the afternoon sun. Melissa sat in the sun working on a sketch of the fora, while Portia and Aurelia sat in the shade.

Melissa looked up from her sketch of the Roman Fora, which she intended to paint later as a keepsake. "Did you say something?"

Helena smiled. "You know well what I said."

"I said that almost two years ago," said Melissa.

"That does not answer my question. Do you also regret

traveling with my brother and me through Italy and now seeing Rome?"

Melissa shrugged. "Rome is marvelous. But—"

"But? How can there be a *but*?" Helena asked. She grabbed Melissa by the hand and brought her to the railing. "Look at it! What could be wrong with Rome?"

The two breathed in the vista of the city before them. The architectural grandeur of it all testified to the glorious history of Rome. To their right stood the Flavian Amphitheater, known as the Coliseum, owing to the large statue of Nero standing near it. Constructed during the time of Vespasian and Titus, it still drew tens of thousands of spectators to the gladiatorial games and spectacles. Across from it stood the dual Temple of Venus and Roma, the largest of the temples of Rome. Beyond the Coliseum stood the Baths of Titus, and of Trajan.

"It's magnificent," Helena whispered.

She pointed below and to their left at the Roman Fora, dominated by Trajan's Forum, with its huge golden statue of that emperor seated upon a horse, and a towering column commemorating his victory over the Dacians two hundred and fifty years earlier.

Melissa laughed as she brushed away a long strand of her brown hair that a breeze had blown across her face. "There is nothing wrong with Rome, or your company! I only meant to say I miss my father. I have not seen him in the several months since we left Mediolanum."

"Melissa, do not trouble yourself about being separated from your father, my dear," said Portia. "He has been busy working on the military campaign these past months. You would not have seen much of him had we stayed in Mediolanum."

"There is to be a banquet tomorrow evening in honor of the new Prefect of Rome!" said Aurelia, her cherubic face red from the sun. "There will be music, foods, and wines!"

Helena winked. "And many young officers and Roman noblemen."

The young women laughed.

Portia shook her head. "Do not forget, girls, I will be there watching you."

"Princess, with whom will Constantius sit at the banquet?" asked Aurelia.

Melissa glared at Aurelia. She shook her head. *Aurelia has been throwing herself at Constantius since the moment the Empress died.*

Aurelia observed Melissa's green eyes upon her. "What? Why do you look at me so? He is a widower."

"Why, do you think of my brother as eligible?" asked Helena with a wry smile. "Aurelia Eusebia, are you interested in him?"

Aurelia blushed. "No, no . . . I am not saying that. It is only that his wife has been dead these past two years. He must be very lonely. That is all."

The princess winked at Melissa as the two exchanged a knowing glance. Melissa bit her tongue. *We are on to you, Aurelia. Of course, you are after the Emperor! Must you be so obvious about it?*

Aurelia lifted her eyes to Helena. "Do you think he will ever marry again?"

Helena shrugged her shoulders. "I do not think he could ever find someone he could love again."

"Marriage need not be about love," said Portia. "Love or not—an emperor needs an heir." She smiled to herself. "But I wager the Emperor will find a woman to love and bear him children."

"What are you smiling about, mother?" asked Melissa. *No doubt she has heard idle gossip among the other ladies of the court. She knows something, or more like it—as is usual for my mother—she thinks she does.*

A loud knock echoed from inside the apartment.

Portia jumped up from her seat. She brushed the wrinkles from her light-gray stola. "Someone is at the door. I will see who. You girls keep up with your art." She hurried inside and down the hall just as a servant opened the door. There in the hall stood two men in military attire.

Portia brought her hands to her mouth as the more senior officer removed his white-plumed helmet. "Florentius!" she said as she embraced him. "It is so good to see you again, my love. It has been so long." She cupped his cheeks. "I did not know you were coming. Why did you not write me to let me know? What brings you to Rome?"

"The Emperor summoned me," said Florentius.

"On military matters?"

Florentius furrowed his brow. "I assume so. But it is odd—the Emperor gave neither explanation nor purpose for the summons. There is no agenda. That is unlike him. All very mysterious."

Portia squinted and rolled her eyes to one side as she thought for a moment. "Aha!" she muttered.

Florentius tilted his head. "Aha? What do you mean, *aha*?"

"Oh . . . nothing," said Portia, as she straightened her graying hair, which was tied in a bun atop her head. She saw Lucius beside her husband. "I hope you have been well, Captain. It is so good to see you."

"Thank you, Lady Portia," said Lucius. He removed his helmet, uncovering his balding head.

Florentius eyed Portia, studying her face. "What did you mean by *aha*?"

"Dear, do not interrupt, I am speaking with Lucius," Portia said. She turned again to Lucius. "Your father is in Rome. He arrived this week with the fleet. It is anchored in Ostia and Portus."

Lucius's face brightened. "Yes, I heard."

Florentius glared at his wife. "Portia—"

She waved him off. "How long has it been since you have seen your father, Lucius?"

"Over a year," said Lucius. "Near Pavia."

Portia grabbed the young captain by the hand. "There is a banquet tomorrow night, in honor of the new Prefect of Rome. You and your father must join us at our table."

"Portia," muttered Florentius.

"Lucius, let us go out to the terrace so you can greet Melissa and her friends."

"Portia!" said Florentius in a firm voice as if issuing an order to legionary.

She blushed. "Yes, dear?"

Florentius turned to Lucius. "You go out to the terrace. Tell Melissa we will be along in a few minutes." He then stared at Portia. "My wife and I must speak first."

"Melissa is outside?" said Lucius. He ran a hand back and forth over his thinning hair to make it appear fuller. He saluted Florentius and walked off down the hallway toward the terrace, his cane tapping on the marble floor as he went.

Florentius led Portia by the hand into the master bedchamber. He closed the door.

Portia embraced her husband. "I have missed you so."

Florentius stared into her eyes. "In the hallway, just now, you suggested you knew why I was summoned by the Emperor."

"Did I?"

Florentius lowered his head as he kept his eyes fixed on hers. "We have been married thirty-five years. I know your moods and manners. You cannot keep a secret. If you know why the Emperor summoned me—tell me."

Portia sighed. "Very well." A bright light sparkled in her eyes. "It was only an intuition at first, which came to me the night the Empress died and stayed with me these past two years. It has grown stronger these last few weeks as we have traveled with the Emperor. But now that you say you were called to Rome, and in such an odd, mysterious manner—I think I might be right. I am sure I am right."

Florentius exhaled. "Woman, stop speaking in riddles. I love you my dear, but you are always roundabout to the point of things—if you ever get to them at all. Please, get to the point."

She looked around the room with a furtive expression.

Florentius shook his head. "We are alone, my dear."

"They say the palace is honeycombed with secret passages which allow spies to listen at the walls," Portia whispered. She led her husband away from the closest wall to the center of the room. She leaned close to him. "They say the emperors of old would roam the cavities in the walls and listen to their guests."

Florentius rolled his eyes. "For heaven's sake, my love—get to the point."

"I have wonderful news to tell you about Melissa."

"Melissa? How does my trip to Rome concern her?"

"We have had a marvelous six months traveling through Italy with the Emperor, Princess Helena, and his entourage. Melissa has seen so many wonderful cities and sites that she might not have ever seen. We went to Capri—"

"The point, dear . . . the point . . . please."

"I have one of my intuitions," she said.

Florentius threw up his hands. "I give up." He turned to walk

185

out.

"An intuition about the Emperor's attentions toward Melissa."

He stopped and turned back to face her. "The Emperor's 'attentions' toward our daughter?" he asked with a hint of alarm. His normal, general bemusement with his wife's muddle-headedness had evaporated. "What do you mean by 'attentions'?"

Portia giggled with giddiness, unable to answer.

Florentius grabbed her by the shoulders. "Good heavens, woman! Tell me of the Emperor's attentions to our daughter."

"That is the wonderful thing I want to tell you about, if you but quit interrupting me."

Florentius pursed his lips.

"During our travels around Italy these last several months, we have had many opportunities with Princess Helena to be close to the Emperor. Over time, I have sensed and seen in his manner of behavior toward Melissa—"

"Sensed and seen what?"

"That his fondness for her has grown. You should see how the Emperor looks at her now."

"Why did you not write me of this? Why did you not warn me?"

"You have always told me to use discretion in letters—that your rivals in court might intercept them and use them for their own purposes."

Florentius closed his eyes and nodded. "Yes. I have told you that."

"But, as I said, only in the last few weeks have I felt more certain of the Emperor's affections for Melissa," said Portia. "And, now, when you said you were summoned by the Emperor without an explanation, my mind thought this might have something to do with Melissa. Perhaps he summoned you so that he can ask your permission to marry her!"

Florentius snickered. "Oh, that is quite the stretch, Portia." He kissed her on the forehead and then sat down in a nearby chair. Leaning back, he chuckled to himself. "My dear, you have an overactive mind and heart." As he sat there, his chuckle and smile faded away. Leaning forward, Florentius rested his elbows on his knees. He placed his face into his hands. His brow wrinkled with concern.

186

Portia tilted her head at the sight of the change in his countenance. "What is wrong, dear? You look worried."

Florentius rubbed a hand across his face. "You have an overactive mind, but . . . then again . . . you might be right."

She rushed over and knelt beside him. She flung her arms around him. "Do not worry. I know nothing is certain, and it may not come to pass. The Emperor and his family tend to marry their cousins. The Emperor's first wife was a cousin. Helena's sister Constantina has had two husbands—both cousins. Who knows, there might still be hope. Do not worry!"

Florentius lowered his hands from his face. He locked eyes with Portia. "Good heavens, woman," he said with displeasure, stifling a shout. "Do you think that is what worries me—that the Emperor might prefer one of his cousins to Melissa?"

Portia jerked her head back. "What else then could disturb you?"

Florentius stood. "You know we have long had other hopes for Melissa. Have you given up on Lucius? It is clear he has grown fond of her the last couple of years."

"There is no arrangement between our families for them to marry," she said. "Plus, she does not love him."

"She can learn to love him," said Florentius. He paced about the room. He stopped beside Portia, who still knelt beside the chair. "Has she taken note of the Emperor's attentions or interest? Does she have feelings for him? Does she love him?"

Portia shook her head. "Melissa is young and innocent. She has not spoken of it. She may not have noticed."

Florentius heaved a sigh of relief. "Good."

Portia's head recoiled. "You intend to reject the Emperor if he asks for her hand!"

"I do."

"But why?"

"Constantius is an Arian."

Portia raised her hands to her cheeks. "If you refuse him, the Emperor might have your head."

"He may have my head. He will not have my daughter."

"What will you say to him?"

Florentius resumed pacing about the room. "I do not know yet.

I must think of something." He stopped and turned to Portia. "You said Lucius's father, Varronius, is in Rome. I will speak to him about Lucius and Melissa, right away . . . as soon as possible. Before the banquet."

Portia dropped her arms to her side. Her shoulders slumped. "You are not suggesting—"

Florentius nodded. "Lucius can provide for her. He is a good man . . . a fine, smart officer. He is of a noble and wealthy family. He will make her a good husband."

Portia burst out in crazed laughter. "Lucius is all of those things, but . . . Constantius is an *emperor*!"

"Constantius is an Arian! I will not give my daughter in marriage to a heretic—no matter how high his station in this life."

"Perhaps she would convert him?"

Florentius shook his head. "Constantius would turn the whole empire Arian. Do you think he would suffer his wife remaining a Catholic? I will not take that chance."

"But—"

"That is my final word."

Portia sat down in the chair. Her shoulders slumped forward, and with her elbows on her knees, she placed her face into her hands. "My daughter might have been an empress."

***

Out on the terrace, Melissa, Helena, and Aurelia continued to chat about the upcoming banquet. Leaning against the railing, the princess saw Lucius come to the doorway. "Look who is here! Melissa, it is Lucius."

Lucius blushed when his eyes fell upon Melissa. "Good afternoon, Lady Melissa . . . Princess Helena . . . Lady Aurelia Eusebia."

Helena and Aurelia rushed over to greet and embrace him. Melissa remained seated.

"It is so good to see you again, Captain," said Helena. She glared at Melissa and beckoned to her. "See Melissa, it is Lucius. Come give him a hug."

Melissa stood and gave Lucius a quick hug. "I hope you have

been well, Captain."

"Much better, now I have seen you again, Melissa," Lucius said. He blushed. He cleared his throat. "I mean, much better now I have seen you all of you ladies, again."

The princess's face beamed at the sight of the young captain. "What brings you to Rome?"

"The Emperor summoned General Florentius to Rome," he said.

Melissa grinned. "My father is here?" she asked. She got up to peer through the door. "Where is he?"

"He and your mother are speaking in private—he will join us in a moment."

Lucius walked over to the railing and looked out upon the great city. "Lady Melissa, have you enjoyed your travels with the Emperor?"

"Very much so," said Melissa. She stood near Lucius and held out her arms as if about to embrace the city. "Of all the cities and sights we have seen, Rome surpasses them all." She turned to him. "Is this not a beautiful sight?"

Lucius gazed into her green eyes and became lost in them. "Very beautiful."

Melissa's cheeks burned pink. *I think he means me, not the city. But I do not care to have his affection. He is just a friend. He can be nothing more.*

A breeze fluttered, rustling the parchments upon which the women had sketched the city.

"I see you are sketching," said Lucius, coming somewhat to his senses. "Please, do not stand on my account. Continue with your art."

The women returned to their seats while Lucius inspected their work.

"Your sketches are so true to the reality," he said. "You all are talented."

"Melissa is the most talented," said Helena. She gave a secret wink to Melissa.

Melissa rolled her eyes.

"Sit, Lucius," said Helena. "You have had a long journey. Relax. I believe there is an open seat—there on the bench next to Melissa."

Lucius approached the bench. "May I?"

Melissa slid over to make room for him. "Of course, Captain." As he sat down, she leaned back and glared at Helena. *Princess, please do not play matchmaker!* Once Lucius was seated, Melissa inched away from him as nonchalantly as she could, drawing a nasty glance from the princess. Melissa shrugged off Helena's disappointment in her. *Well, that's what you get if you try to play matchmaker for me.*

The clack of footsteps notified everyone of Florentius and Portia's arrival onto the terrace. The general saw Lucius seated next to Melissa. He nodded to himself with satisfaction at the sight. "I am sorry to interrupt you two."

Melissa stood from her seat. She straightened her tunic. "No . . . father . . . really . . . you interrupted nothing." *There is absolutely nothing between Lucius and me to interrupt.* She ran to her father and pressed her head against his chest. "I missed you so much!"

He kissed the top of her head. "And I missed you, my honeybee."

"I have had such a wonderful time these past months traveling with the Princess and the Emperor," said Melissa. Her father's smile melted away. *Father appears troubled by something.* "Is there something wrong, father?"

Florentius addressed Lucius, now sounding very serious. "Captain, find your father at once."

The young captain stood. He stole a quick glance at Melissa. "Now, sir?" he asked with a tinge of disappointment.

"He is here in the palace," said Florentius. "I must speak with him at once about a matter of the utmost urgency."

"Yes, General—at once," said Lucius. He said his goodbyes and took his leave.

"That sounded rather serious, Father," said Melissa.

He hugged her. "Nothing for my little honeybee to worry about."

Chapter 12

The Imperial Palace

Members of the imperial court, senators, and representatives of the leading families of Rome gathered the great palace hall. Laughter and the strains of music from lyres and flutes sounded through the halls, mingling with the forgotten echoes of ghosts from ancient times. One half of the vaulted ceiling, which soared high above the floor, depicted a bright-blue sky with painted clouds, birds made of colorful gems, and a large sun—several feet across—made of gold. The other half of the ceiling depicted a night sky with moon, stars, and constellations fashioned from diamonds and glass, which reflected the light. Mosaics and frescos, depicting mythological and historical moments of Rome since its founding by Romulus and Remus, covered the walls. Gilded columns lined the walls while lifelike statues of Roman gods and goddesses stood within niches.

"Here is our table for the banquet," said Princess Helena as she led Melissa and her parents and Aurelia through the crowd to their seats.

Florentius glimpsed Melissa's attire. Her long brown hair was woven into a bun atop her head, held in place by a silver headband. Around her exposed neck she wore a choker necklace of silver, which, like the headband, was studded with green gems. She wore a deep-green, low-cut, form-fitting tunic. The coloring made Melissa's green eyes sparkle.

Melissa felt her father's eyes upon her. "Mother selected this for me," she said as she spun about to display her outfit.

Portia nodded.

Florentius pursed his lips. His jaw tightened.

"Is something wrong, father?" asked Melissa. *Is father displeased with my appearance?*

"Nothing is wrong," he said as he reached out to hug her. "You look so beautiful tonight, my honeybee." He frowned over Melissa's shoulder at Portia. "*Too* beautiful."

"My brother's table is just over there," interjected Helena. She pointed to a table a dozen yards away. "The new Prefect and his guests will dine with him, but my brother said he wanted to be sure we were close to him tonight."

"We?" asked Portia.

"Melissa and I."

"And me too!" added Aurelia, her cheeks red with sunburn from the day on the terrace.

"Oh, he wanted you and Melissa close by?" said Portia. She glowered at her husband. "How nice."

The group took places at the table, lounging on their couches.

"Princess, where is your brother?" said Aurelia, as she plumped down in her place beside Melissa.

Melissa lifted a cup to her lips to take a long sip of wine, but it was empty. *Good grief. We just arrived and Aurelia is already talking about the Emperor. And where is the wine? I need one already!*

Helena sighed. "My brother is late as usual. The banquet cannot start, and they cannot pour the wine until he arrives."

Across the table, Melissa saw that her father's eyes darted about the room. *Father seems tense this evening.* "Are you looking for someone, Father?"

"Ah, there's Lucius now, with his father, Varronius," said Florentius. He elbowed Portia, which made her jump in surprise. She caught at the sight of the two men and huffed.

"Oh—there is Lucius and his father!" said Portia with enthusiasm that appeared put on. She called out and beckoned to them until they approached the table.

Melissa turned to Helena by her side. "Father and mother have been acting very strange the last day."

Helena shrugged. "I hadn't noticed."

Melissa squinted as she observed her parents. *What are they up to?*

192

"Good evening!" said Varronius in his deep, booming voice, as he approached the table.

"We have saved seats for you both," said Portia as she popped up from her couch. Lucius went to sit beside his father, but Portia grabbed him by the forearm and led him to the other end of the table. "You sit here, with the other young people, Lucius." She tapped Aurelia on the shoulder. "Do you mind? Could you let Lucius sit here between you and Melissa?"

Aurelia scooted to one side of the couch. "Not at all."

Melissa managed a polite but muted smile when Lucius sat down beside her. *Now I see what they are up to!* She turned to Helena who reclined on her other side. "See . . . my mother never ceases!" she whispered. "She will not relent—throwing me together with Lucius."

Helena smiled. "It is cute."

"Where is the wine?" Melissa asked as she fiddled with her empty cup. "My mother will make a drunk of me."

"I don't know what is taking my brother so long," mused Helena. "There will be no wine served until he arrives."

***

The princess stood to her feet as a fanfare of trumpets echoed throughout the banquet hall. Along with everyone else, she turned to observe Constantius as he entered the great hall to the cheers and applause of the assembled guests. His usual retinue of advisors and hangers-on followed as he made his way toward the head table.

"Brother, you are late!" said the princess, as Constantius approached her table. Ignoring Helena's greeting, he fixed his attention on Melissa. Helena quirked her lips as she raised an eyebrow. *That is interesting—I never noticed that before.* She studied her brother as he gazed upon Melissa, oblivious to all else around him. *For once in his life, Constantius is dumbstruck and silent. I kind of like that. Is he romantically interested in Melissa?* Helena smiled. The princess kissed her brother on the cheek and lingered to whisper into his ear. "Brother, do not stare so at Melissa! Greet your other guests!"

Chastened by his sister, Constantius snapped back to reality. He turned to the others at the table. "General Florentius . . . Count

Varronius, Lady Portia, Lady Aurelia Eusebia . . . and Lady Melissa . . . thank you for joining me this evening to honor the new Prefect of Rome." He gestured to his entourage in tow. "May I introduce Leontius, who I have just appointed Prefect of Rome. Beside him is his guest, Lady Marciana Quarta, who is here tonight with her brother, Cyprian, and sister, Domitia of the Vestal Virgins—and her mother, Lady Marciana Tertia." The Emperor pointed to one of the senior officers with him. "Helena, I believe you and Melissa know Tribune Claudius Silvanus."

Helena batted her eyes at Silvanus. "I could not forget meeting the tribune."

"Nor I, you," said Silvanus with a bow.

"Pardon my tardiness, sister," said the Emperor.

Helena feigned a pout. "Brother, you have kept your guests waiting for over an hour. I thought you might have forgotten us!"

Constantius chuckled. "I may be late to a party on occasion, but—I would never forget one! Tell me, sister—do you greet me with a smile because you missed me, or is it only that my arrival signals that the food and wine may now be served?"

Helena gave her brother a playful punch in the arm. The Emperor laughed. "I have never seen him laugh before," a few guests whispered to those beside them.

The Emperor turned to Melissa. "And, what say you about Helena's reproach of my tardiness? I hope you do not think as poorly of me as she does."

Tongue-tied in the presence of the Emperor, Melissa only managed to curtsy.

"Please—speak Melissa," said Constantius, his tone kind and gentle. "Think not of me as your Emperor. You are like a sister."

Helena tilted her head in amused disbelief as she observed Constantius. *Brother, are you flirting with my friend?* Out of the corner of her eyes, Helena saw Aurelia glaring with envy at Melissa. *It seems Aurelia thinks so!* The princess pursed her lips and placed a few fingers to her mouth to contain a chuckle.

Melissa curtsied again. "The presence of an emperor makes an imperial banquet—*imperial*. It cannot be so otherwise. Therefore, an emperor can never be said to have arrived late."

Constantius laughed. "A wise girl you are!" He took her hand in

194

his and kissed it. As his lips parted from her hand, he gazed into her green eyes. "A lucky man is he who wins your hand and heart," he whispered to her.

Melissa's cheeks glowed red.

The princess nodded to herself. *Yes, there can be no doubt. He is flirting with her.*

Constantius turned to Florentius. "I am glad you have come to Rome, General. I hope you had a pleasant journey. There is an urgent matter I would like to discuss with you. Let us find time to chat later this evening."

Florentius bowed. "I am ever at your service."

The Emperor and his entourage continued on their way to the head table.

***

With the arrival of the Emperor, servants now flooded the banquet hall. Several attended to each table, pouring wine and serving selections of meat and fruit. Small groups of musicians playing flutes and lyres roamed from table to table playing to and serenading the guests.

"I am so glad you are here," Florentius said to Varronius who was seated beside him. "We had little time to chat in Pavia last year. There is much to catch up on." Florentius cleared his throat, signaling to all at the table that he had something to say.

Melissa's attention was drawn to her father, as the separate conversations around the table quieted to hear what Florentius might say. *What's this about then?*

Florentius spoke in a loud voice to be heard above the musicians who were playing for the next table over. "I must tell you, Count, your son has been of great service on the imperial staff these past two years. He is a fine young man of noble character . . . honest . . . hardworking. Lucius is also a sincere and devout Christian. Diligent and attentive to the study of scriptures and the fathers. He has also impressed me with his knowledge of literature, the sciences, and philosophy. Once we were discussing the *Iliad* . . ."

Melissa turned to Helena as her father droned on and on about

195

Lucius. She lifted her wine cup as if to drink but used it instead to hide her mouth as she whispered to her friend. "Before it was only my mother, now it is my father too. He parades before me the merits of Lucius as a man and potential husband."

Florentius cleared his throat again, trying to gain Melissa's full attention. She glowered at him as she set her cup down quickly, wine spilling over the rim when it thumped on the table.

Ignoring his daughter's reaction, Florentius continued with his story. "And that reminds me, Varronius—have I ever told you of Lucius's adventures during the battle of Mursa Major?"

"Adventures?" asked Varronius.

Lucius quirked an eyebrow. "My adventures? I have no idea."

Florentius frowned at the musicians and waved them away as they prepared to play for their table. As the musicians moved on to a more welcoming table, Florentius returned to his tale. "Lucius is only being modest. One night near Mursa Major, we approached a large fortress to gain intelligence on the strength of the enemy. Thousands of the enemy roamed about—but there were only three of us! We were in constant peril of being discovered. Suddenly, an enemy tribune appeared, with several of his men. Lucius, through amazing swordplay, single-handedly disarmed and captured the tribune. But, while Lucius was busy with this tribune, I was captured—a sword held to my neck! Blessed with quick wits, Lucius traded the tribune to his comrades for my release. He saved my life."

"Oh my, God," said Portia, fanning herself. "You have never told me of this. How frightening. Melissa, did you hear? Lucius saved your father!"

The princess applauded. "Bravely done, Lucius."

Varronius nodded. "A tribune for a general—an excellent trade. Well done, son."

Lucius rested his face in his hands, hiding in embarrassment. He groaned as he shook his head.

"And, that is not all, Varronius," said Florentius. "The very next day Lucius led a dangerous mission to the enemy fortifications by the river to demand the surrender of the forces holding the bridge over the Drava. And who was he to meet, but the same tribune from the night before . . ."

All around the table applauded. All, that is, except for Melissa who did not bother to conceal her annoyance.

"Melissa, applaud," said Helena whispering out of the corner of her mouth.

Melissa, urged on by her friend and now a tinge of guilt, clapped her hands. *I know. I know. It is not Lucius's fault my father is putting on this show for me. I should not blame him.* She took a deep breath. As she exhaled, the tension in her face dissipated and was replaced by a sweet countenance. She smiled at Lucius. "Thank you for saving my father."

"Your father is far too generous in describing any role I had in anything that happened at Mursa Major," he said. "There was nothing heroic about any of my actions on this campaign. Owing to my bad leg, I never had the opportunity. Your father would never let me close to any real danger."

"There was no dangerous mission?" asked Melissa.

Lucius shook his head. "As much as I would like to impress you, I am afraid I must disappoint you. I carried a flag of truce. There was no real danger."

Helena leaned across Melissa. "And the dangerous enemy tribune?"

Lucius chuckled. "He was conducting the body of a fallen comrade back to his lines in the darkness. He could not have reached for his sword had he wanted. Besides, the general ordered me to let him go."

Helena turned to Melissa and leaned close to her ear. "Lucius is as good and honest a man as you will find in the court. Some men sing their own false praise while others accept it without correction. A good man does not allow an opinion of him to be shaped by undeserved praise."

"If so, why does Lucius not deny these stories in front of all?" Melissa whispered back.

"He does not want to embarrass your father," said Helena. Besides, your true opinion of him is what matters most to Lucius. I think he loves you." The princess looked past Melissa to Lucius. "Captain, you are too modest about your adventures. I remember one pretty, noblewoman rescued from Gundamar the Giant—the barbarian king."

Lucius laughed. "Princess, that was hardly a *rescue!*"

Helena elbowed Melissa in the side. "Remember that, Melissa?"

Melissa trembled at the mention of the barbarian's name. "Yes, I remember." She grabbed her wine and took a quaff of it. "I still have nightmares about that giant. I pray never to see him again, ever."

***

Constantius reclined at the head table with his guests and members of his retinue. Several feet behind him stood Captain Marcus, serving as his bodyguard for the evening. The Emperor listened as musicians wandering nearby played a lively tune, tapping his fingers to the beat against his cup of wine. Prefect Leontius, Lady Marciana Quarta, and Claudius Silvanus sat closest to him on his right. Eusebius and Arbitio and his court bishops closest to him on his left. Others seated at the table include Marciana's mother, brother, and sister.

The Emperor glanced at Marciana, attired in the same golden tunic she had worn to the party celebrating her engagement to Septimus two years before. Constantius leaned toward the prefect. "Lady Marciana is quite beautiful," he said in a low voice. "Do you plan to make her your wife?"

Leontius looked to his right to be sure Marciana was not listening. Seeing her occupied with Silvanus, the prefect replied to Constantius. "I can have no secret from you, my lord. Lady Marciana and I have known each other as friends for several years. The truth be said, my feelings for her, as long as I have known her, have been stronger than those of a mere friend—though I have never revealed this to her because she harbored affections for another. But this other man is now out of the way. I hope to ask for her hand soon."

Constantius placed a hand on the prefect's shoulder. "Do not tarry, Leontius. She is very beautiful."

"Thank you, sire."

"Let us drink a toast between us," said the Emperor in a hushed voice, taking care that even Captain Marcus who stood watch behind him would not hear. He lifted his cup toward Leontius.

"Good luck to us both in romance—for I too hope to be wed soon." Constantius looked to the next table over. There he glimpsed Melissa. He smiled as he watched her chatting and laughing with those around her.

Arbitio, observing the happy countenance of the Emperor, whispered to Eusebius who was seated to his right. "The Emperor is in a good mood this evening. I have never seen him this way. It is not like him."

"His thoughts are of the daughter of Florentius," said the eunuch, fiddling with the ring that pierced one of his ears.

"Lady Melissa?"

"Yes, that is her name."

Arbitio followed the line of the Emperor's gaze. It led to Melissa at the next table. Arbitio wiped away a spot of wine from his dark leather cuirass, which he wore over a black tunic. "This is unhappy news."

"I did not realize, Commander, that you have an interest in Melissa."

"I have had my eyes on her."

"To wed her or bed her?"

"To possess her," said Arbitio. He drank from his cup. "But if what you say is true—one must yield to an emperor."

"Perhaps nothing will come of it," said Eusebius.

The commander nodded. "Let us hope not. It would not go well for us if the Emperor took her for a bride and made her empress. Florentius would be related by marriage to Constantius, and I do not think he cares for either of us. He might use his relationship with the Emperor against us."

The eunuch and Arbitio now observed the eyes of the Emperor upon themselves, bringing their quiet conversation to an abrupt end.

The Emperor reached for his wine and took several long sips. He turned again to observe Melissa. "She has a lovely figure," he said to himself. He quaffed his wine. Fidgeting in his seat, he slammed his cup down on the table. He cleared his throat as he glared at Arbitio and Eusebius. "This is a happy occasion, meant to honor my new prefect. There will be no talk of government or war this evening, or whatever you two are discussing."

199

"Sir?" asked Eusebius.

Constantius glanced round the table. "There is only the Lady Marciana at our end of the table. Her mother and sister are at the other end. I do not want us to bore Marciana with such dry talk. Our conversation needs other feminine perspectives. Indeed, we need more female company at this table." Constantius glared at his Grand Chamberlain. "Do you not agree, Eusebius?"

The Grand Chamberlain shrugged, clueless as to the Emperor's point. "Ah . . . yes . . . I mean . . . well said, sire?" he said. "Female companionship is good."

Silvanus laughed from across the table. "'As if you, a eunuch, know anything of the company of women!"

Constantius joined in the laughter. "Silvanus is right!" he said as he thumped the table with the palm of his hand. "That settles it!"

The Emperor called to Marcus, who stood close by as his bodyguard for the evening. "Captain, inform Princess Helena and Lady Melissa that the Emperor requests their company at his table."

"Right away, sire," said Marcus as he headed off on his errand.

The Emperor addressed the Grand Chamberlain. "Eusebius, give up your seat at once."

"My lord?"

"You heard me. At once," said Constantius. "And that goes for you too, Arbitio. You can keep Eusebius company."

Eusebius and Arbitio stood up from their places. Their stoic façades could not veil the embarrassment on their faces. Before they had gotten more than a few feet away from their seats, attendants had cleared away their plates and cups and were setting out new ones.

Silvanus chuckled and made light of their embarrassment, pointing to a table in the distance. "I believe there are empty seats at that table over there. The one in the far corner of the hall!"

Arbitio flashed a cold and evil squint at Silvanus.

Once Eusebius and Arbitio found space at another table, they grumbled to one another. "Silvanus took great delight in the indignity we suffered," said Eusebius. "He is too free and comfortable in his manner with the Emperor while being disrespectful of his betters."

200

Arbitio tilted his chin. "The upstart does not know his place." Several musicians approached the two and began to dance beside their couches, playing a loud, happy tune. Seething as he thought of Silvanus, he glared at the musicians. "Away with you, before I see you all thrown to the dogs," he snapped. At once the music stopped, and the players scurried off to find a more welcoming table.

"The Emperor has taken to quite a liking of him," said Eusebius. "He relies on his opinions and advice. He may be only a tribune now, but he is very ambitious."

"I fear his future advancement might come at our expense if we are not careful."

"This has already happened."

Arbitio paused as he lifted his drink. "Oh?"

"I had arranged for another candidate to become the Prefect of Rome," said Eusebius. "This candidate had offered me a handsome sum of gold up front, and a hefty annual sum—if I could convince the Emperor to select him for the position. Somehow Silvanus got to the Emperor and changed his mind. He won the appointment for Leontius. The interference and influence of Silvanus cost me a fortune."

"I thought you appeared quite displeased the other day when the Emperor appointed Leontius."

The Grand Chamberlain stroked his chin. "With the civil war nearing an end, the Emperor will need to appoint a military commander over Gaul. I intend to nominate you when the time is right—if you are interested."

Arbitio smiled, crooked and sly. "Such a position would, of course, profit us both."

"I thought it might interest you."

"But Silvanus will have his eyes on that prize as well."

"Did you notice, the princess seemed partial to Silvanus," said Eusebius.

"First, you bring me news of Melissa and the Emperor, and now news of Helena and Silvanus," said Arbitio. A slight smile crossed his face. "For a eunuch, you are very perceptive of dealings between the sexes."

The eunuch eyed Silvanus across the hall. "You joke. But we

must watch Silvanus, Commander. The Emperor listens to him. One day we may need to do something about him."

***

Marcus approached the table where Melissa and Helena sat.

The captain saluted Florentius and Varronius. "Pardon the interruption, sirs. The Emperor requests the presence of Princess Helena and Lady Melissa at his table."

Florentius coughed at the invitation as his wine went down his windpipe. He gagged.

Helena sprang up from her seat. "Oh, how fun!" she said. She pulled her Melissa to her feet.

Melissa looked at her father. "May I?"

"Yes, of course," said Florentius as he cleared his throat. "You must. It is a request from the Emperor."

The two women left the table, skirts flurrying around them.

Aurelia frowned as her friends walked away. She looked across the table at Florentius and Portia. "You don't suppose the Emperor meant to invite me as well?" she asked. Without waiting for a response, she stood up and hurried after them.

Florentius, his face grim, leaned toward his wife. "I fear you are right about the Emperor. It is clear he is smitten with our daughter." He rubbed his face with his hand. He then turned to Varronius on his other side. "The Emperor will ask for her hand tonight," he muttered in a low voice. "Do I have your agreement that we will arrange the marriage of Melissa to Lucius, as we discussed earlier today?"

"I have seen for myself this evening that the Emperor has taken a liking to Melissa," said Varronius. "But are you sure this is what you want? An arranged marriage between Lucius and Melissa?"

Florentius nodded. "You know my reasons."

"If that is what you want. Melissa is a wonderful young woman. I am sure Lucius will be quite pleased to marry her. I will speak with him tomorrow."

"No, that will be too late," said Florentius, his grip on his cup tightening. "I fear Constantius intends to speak with me tonight to request her hand in marriage. All must be arranged before he does."

"If you believe it necessary, we can speak with Lucius now."
Florentius nodded.

The two men stood from the table and approached Lucius.

"Son, come with us, we would like to discuss something with you in private," said Varronius.

***

Melissa and Helena approached the Emperor's table. Melissa spied a statue of Pan which stood atop a pedestal in a niche in the wall behind Constantius. The horned figure made her shiver.

The Emperor jumped to his feet upon seeing the two women. "Please sit and join us."

Respecting Helena's rank, Melissa insisted the princess take the seat left open beside her brother. Melissa took a moment to breathe in her surroundings. As she stood there, she tilted her head back. Above in the vaulted ceiling covered in mosaic tiles, the large sun made of gold seemed to dance in a blue sky and the silver stars set in the night sky sparkled as each reflected the light from the banquet hall below. *I must be dreaming. To sit at the table of an Emperor in the imperial palace in Rome. So much history.* As she prepared to sit, Aurelia, seeming to appear from nowhere, nudged her way past Melissa to take the seat next to the princess. Knocked off balance, Melissa squinted at Aurelia, her knuckles whitening as she clenched her fingers. Out of the corner of her eye, she observed Helena, who shook her head in sympathy for her.

The Emperor introduced the new arrivals to the other guests at the table, including Prefect Leontius, Marciana, and her mother and brother.

"Oh, we know Silvanus," said the princess when the Emperor began to introduce him.

"That's right; I forget," said Constantius. "Earlier this evening you mentioned you had met. Where was that again?"

"Melissa and I met him in Mursa Major," said Helena. She reached for her wine. As she drank, she winked at Silvanus across the table. "It is a pleasure for us to see him again. Is it not, Melissa?"

"Indeed," said Melissa, tilting her head and staring at Helena as if to warn her. *Don't be so obvious with your flirting. You're a princess. Remember yourself!*

"I exiled Eusebius and Arbitio to another table!" said Constantius with a chuckle, as he waved to a servant to refill his cup. "They are poor conversationalists if it does not concern war or the affairs of government. Tonight is for celebration. We needed additional female company to enliven the discussion."

"It is a delight to share this table with such beautiful company," said Silvanus. "To have in our presence the sister of our Emperor, Princess Helena." He bowed his head toward the princess.

Melissa watched as his eyes met her friend's. She took a sip of wine to hide a smile. *Now he is flirting with her.*

"But we must not forget the other beauties at our table tonight," said the Emperor. "Lady Tertia and her daughter Marciana, Lady Aurelia, and the Lady Melissa."

Melissa, her cup still at her lips, glimpsed the Emperor looking in her direction. She turned to find his eyes locked on hers. She felt her cheeks grow warm. *Is the Emperor flirting with me?*

Their gaze lingered for a few awkward moments only to be broken by Leontius. "And, of course, we must not overlook the beauty of Marciana's sister, Domitia of the Vestal Virgins." He held his wine cup out, pointing with it toward the far end of the table where sat Domitia beside her brother Cyprian. The palla of her priesthood about her neck, she wore a frown that seemed chiseled into her face as if it were stone. Seeming to be disinterested in all around her, there she sat, drinking heavily.

Marciana, embarrassed by her sister's grim countenance, called out to the Emperor. "My lord Augustus, I have never traveled to the East. How does Rome compare to the great cities of the East?"

"Lady Marciana, Rome surpasses all the great cities of the East—Antioch, Alexandria, and Constantinople—in size, beauty, and architecture," said Constantius. "This is my first visit to Rome. I am speechless."

"I agree!" Aurelia blurted out. She leaned forward a bit, blocking the line of sight between the Emperor and Melissa.

Melissa frowned. *Aurelia did that on purpose! She's jealous.*

Smiling, the Emperor shifted his position on his couch to see

204

around Aurelia. He addressed Melissa. "Prefect Leontius and Lady Marciana are Romans—the city is not new to them. This is your first visit. Tell me, of all you have seen, what has been for you the most magnificent sight?"

"Well, I—" Melissa began to say.

Aurelia leaned forward even more, again obstructing the Emperor's view of Melissa. "Well, for me . . . I would say the Circus Maximus. For one thing, it is much larger than the Hippodrome in Constantinople!"

Constantius shifted his position in his seat to better see Melissa on the other side of Aurelia. "Lady Melissa, what in your opinion is the most spectacular sight in all of Rome?"

"If I must venture to say, I would say the Forum of Trajan," said Melissa. "The golden equestrian statue of the Emperor . . . the great column of Trajan rising a hundred feet above the ground."

Constantius slapped the table with his hands. "Yes! I agree! It is the most spectacular sight. You and I are of one mind, Melissa."

"Did I say the Circus Maximus?" asked Aurelia.

"Yes, you did, Aurelia," said the princess with a smirk.

"Well, I meant to say the Forum of Trajan," said Aurelia. She turned to Constantius. "Emperor, you and I are of the same mind, too."

Melissa rolled her eyes. *Aurelia is definitely determined to be an empress!*

Helena turned to Silvanus. "And what about you, Tribune? I understand you are of Frankish descent. Have you been to Rome before?"

"Once before, Princess," said Silvanus.

"Only once?" asked Helena.

"A wedding."

Helena grew somber. "Yours?"

"Princess, I have no wife."

"Whose then?" she asked, the sparkle returning to her face. When he hesitated to respond, she pressed further. "Is it a secret?"

Silvanus paused as if debating whether he should say more or not. He glanced at Marciana. The color left her face.

"Lady Marciana, does Silvanus speak of your wedding?" asked Helena.

Tears welled in Marciana's eyes. She lowered her head. "Yes, Princess."

Helena brought her hands to her mouth. "Oh . . . I am sorry! My prying has caused you pain. I have brought to mind a sad memory."

"Princess, do not blame yourself—you could not have known," said Marciana. She turned to Constantius as she stood from the table. "Excuse me, my lord. I will be but a moment." She hurried away.

Seeing her daughter flee the hall, Tertia, her mother, stood. "Sire, excuse me. My son, Cyprian, and I will see to my daughter." She pulled Cyprian along after her as she went in search of Marciana, leaving Domitia sitting alone at the other end of the table, quiet and glum. The Vestal Virgin, continuing to sip from her cup of wine, did not seem to notice the excitement.

Helena, red-faced, looked to Silvanus. "I am so sorry. I have hurt her. I have touched upon a sad story?"

"Princess, the fault is mine," said Silvanus. "The wedding never happened—postponed with the coming of the civil war. The Western officer she was to marry left for Mursa Major days before they were to be married."

Helena lowered her head, clasping her hands upon her lap. "And I have upset her by speaking of it."

"How sad," said Melissa.

"No, not sad!" said the Emperor. "It was fortuitous for her that the marriage was not consummated. The officer chose the wrong side in the war. He chose the side of Magnentius the Usurper. Now another fine man will have a go at her!" Constantius turned to Leontius and winked.

The princess slapped her brother on the shoulder with a playful tap. "Have a go at her? Brother, we speak of a sad memory of a love lost."

"Was he killed at Mursa Major?" asked Melissa.

Silvanus shook his head. "No. He was the last Westerner to retreat across the Drava. Or, I should say, the last one to swim across it."

The Emperor held his hand to his chin, as he paused to think. "Do you speak of the commander of Third Italica? The one who swam across the river on his horse? That is who Lady Marciana was to marry?"

"Yes, my lord," said Silvanus.

"The tribune who burned the bridge over the Drava?" asked the Emperor, his mouth agape.

Silvanus nodded. "The same, sire."

"Constantius, you know this man—the one Lady Marciana was to marry?" asked Helena.

The Emperor chuckled. "Not personally, sister. However, he upset me, greatly. He burned a bridge I very much wanted intact. He disrupted my plan to end the war."

"Well, it serves you right, brother," said Helena with a wry smile, a hint of mischievousness in her voice. "It seems a fair exchange. You disrupted his wedding. He disrupted your war."

Constantius laughed. He leaned over and kissed Helena on the head. "Ha—only a female would think that a fair exchange." His smile dissipated as a realization seemed to dawn on him. He looked over his shoulder toward Marcus. "Captain, was he not also the one who stole my horse?"

Marcus winced. "Yes, my lord. He is the one who stole your horse from me."

"The one you loaned Marcus to find my father?" asked Melissa, both the silver and the green gems of her headband and choker glistening in the light.

"Yes, that is the one," said the Emperor, frowning. "If he is ever brought before me, he will pay for his crimes." It was then he noticed that Florentius was no longer seated in the hall. Constantius stood. "That reminds me. I must speak with Florentius on a question of great importance." The guests at the table rose to their feet when the Emperor stood. "I must go and find General Florentius. Please stay here and enjoy your food and drink. I will return."

As he left the table, he paused beside Melissa. "Your presence on our travels these last two years has made my sister happy," he said in a low voice. "It has brought me happiness as well. You have been a breath of fresh air. If there is ever any favor, you would wish—ask and I will grant it."

Melissa curtsied. "You are too kind, my lord."

207

As Constantius left the hall, the members of his entourage scrambled to follow in his wake as he passed, as if connected to him by invisible tethers.

***

Marciana sat on a bench in the hallway outside of the banquet hall. She sat beneath a niche where stood a statue of Odysseus within it. Her mother and brother sat on either side, trying to console her.

Tertia placed an arm around her daughter. "Your father, if he had not died in the recent plague, would have been so proud to see you here ... tonight ... in this great palace ... dining in the company of great men. Do not let your thoughts linger on memories of Gaius Marius Septimus, who is best forgotten. Memories of old love, like a shrouded mist, obscure the path to happiness. See the world the way it is, and you will see the path to contentment."

Tears trickled down Marciana's face. Her chin rested on her chest. "And what is that path?" she asked.

"To be a wife of a prefect," her mother said.

"A wife of a prefect?"

Tertia grew silent for a moment as several senators in their white togas strolled past. "I speak of Prefect Leontius," said Tertia when the senators were beyond earshot. "He is interested in you. Why do you think he invited you here tonight to share this great moment with him?"

"Leontius invited us because our families are close friends."

Her mother shook her head. "My sweet, you have no clue at all, do you? Leontius did not even invite his own relatives to the Emperor's table. He invited our family to which he has no blood relation. Think, dear! Why would he do such a thing? Leontius honored us because he fancies you."

Marciana's eyes opened wide. "Oh."

"Yes, dear. But you must encourage his affections."

"What of Septimus?"

Her mother rolled her eyes. "What of him?" she asked. She glared at her son, Cyprian, who sat quietly, watching. "Cyprian, you

208

and your sister have always been close to one another. Talk sense into her."

Cyprian placed a finger beneath Marciana's chin. He lifted it gently to look into her eyes. "Sister, the time has come to stop thinking of him. If Septimus survives the war, he will not survive the peace. He will suffer the same fate that many of our friends have who supported Magnentius. The agents of the Emperor will arrest him. We have escaped this fate only through friendship with Leontius—who was smart enough to switch his loyalties before it was too late."

"That is true," said Tertia, brushing loose strands of hair from her face.

Cyprian got down on a knee before Marciana, his expression pleading. "Even if Septimus should escape arrest and you two were married—you would be the wife of a penniless rebel, pursued by imperial agents for the rest of your lives. I cannot bear the thought that this could be your fate."

"And were you to run off with Septimus . . . what of your brother, and mother?" asked Tertia. "What might the Emperor do to us? Or do you expect your mother, in her old age, to go on the run, or into hiding as well?"

Marciana clutched her hands together, against her chest. *They are right. What they say makes sense. What of my love for Septimus? Can I just set him aside?*

Tertia hugged her. "But my dear, beautiful daughter, Leontius is now a *Friend of Caesar*, a friend of the Emperor. He can take care of you—and us. We can live a life of comfort and security."

***

"What is this all about, that you need to speak with me out here all alone?" asked Lucius, a slight tremble in his voice as Florentius and his father led him onto a small terrace that overlooked the fora. The distant strains of music and sounds of laughter echoed from within the palace.

Florentius cleared his throat. "Captain Lucius, I will come straight to the point."

Lucius raised his eyebrows. "This sounds ominous. What is it?

209

You intend to replace me? You have appointed someone else in my place?" He lifted his cane in the air. "It is because of my leg."

"Not at all, Lucius."

"What then?"

"It concerns my daughter, Melissa, and yourself."

"What about us?"

Varronius stepped forward and leaned a hand on the terrace railing. "We—the general and I—have reached an arrangement. Provided it meets with your approval. It is something both of our families have wished for since both you and Melissa were youngsters."

Lucius tilted his head in puzzlement. "Which is?"

"You and Melissa are to be married to one another."

"Married?"

Florentius nodded. "On behalf of Melissa, as her father, I have decided to give her hand to you."

Lucius placed a hand to his forehead, the words gradually sinking in. "Melissa and I are to be married?"

The captain leaned against a column as he thought. Across from him, a small fountain built into the wall gurgled softly. A hint of a smile dawned on Lucius's face, which then brightened into a broad grin. He brushed his fingers through his thinning hair.

"That is right, son," said Varronius, slapping his son on the back. "You and Melissa!"

"Does that meet with your approval, Lucius?" asked Florentius.

"Why, yes—yes of course!" said Lucius, moving away from the column to stand on his own. "I must admit that I love your daughter, General."

Florentius sighed in relief. "Excellent!" he said. He reached out and shook Lucius's hand. "Then it is settled . . . congratulations, son. I can call you *son* now."

"Of course!" said the captain. Lucius turned and started off toward the palace interior.

"Where are you going?" asked Florentius.

"I must speak with Melissa at once."

Florentius shook his head. "No, no! I will speak to her first about this."

"She does not know of this?" asked Lucius.

"Not yet," said Florentius. "I will break the news to her once she returns to Mediolanum. In the meantime, there are delicate matters in play. Should anyone ask you about this engagement, you are to respond by saying it was agreed to long ago between your father and me. Is that understood, Captain?"

Lucius squinted as he thought. He limped to the edge of the terrace and viewed the city of Rome below, illuminated in part by the moon and lights from homes and buildings. "Why . . . yes . . . I suppose. I cannot imagine why that would matter."

"Trust me," said Florentius.

"When will the wedding be?" asked Lucius.

"As soon as the war has ended."

"Wait—but what of Melissa's feelings toward me?"

Varronius gripped the collar of his cuirass, letting his arms hang as he did so. "She is fond of you, I am sure."

Lucius frowned. "Fond? What of love?"

"Do not worry about her love," said Florentius.

"But—"

"Ah, there you are Florentius—at last!" exclaimed Constantius with a grin. The Emperor hurried out onto the terrace, followed by his retinue, which included Marcus, Eusebius, Arbitio, his court bishops, other minor officials, and several guardsmen. "I have been looking all over the palace for you. If I am not interrupting, I thought now might be a time for us to have our private chat. I am sure Varronius and Lucius will not mind if I speak with you alone."

"Of course not, my lord," said Varronius as he and his son took their leave and returned to the banquet.

***

When the father and son had gone inside, the Emperor smiled at Florentius. "I have been looking forward to this opportunity to speak alone with you for several weeks."

"A *private* chat between the two of us, my lord?" asked Florentius, his eyes on the entourage which stood close behind the Emperor. *How can this be a private chat with so many present?*

"Are we not alone?" said Constantius. The Emperor turned to see his retinue standing within earshot. He chuckled. "I often

211

forget they are there. They become second nature once one becomes an emperor." He then banished his entourage, except Marcus, to the far corner of the terrace. Marcus remained a few yards back in the shadows.

Now alone by imperial standards, Constantius cleared his throat. "Has all been well in Mediolanum?"

Florentius nodded. "The army is ready. It is prepared to march into the Alps in pursuit of Magnentius on your command."

The Emperor straightened the diadem on his head. "There are matters I must attend to in Rome. I will return to Mediolanum within the month." Constantius took Florentius by the arm and led him to the edge of the terrace which overlooked the city. "I am pleased to hear all is in order with the army in Mediolanum. But that is not why I summoned you to Rome."

Constantius squinted at Florentius. "Do you suspect why I have summoned you?"

"No, sire. I thought you wanted news about the preparations of the army."

Constantius cocked his head back in surprise. He placed a finger to his chin as he thought. "That is *all* you suspected? Nothing more? No news perhaps of . . . Rome . . . perhaps from Lady Portia . . . or Lady Melissa?"

Florentius shook his head.

The Emperor frowned. "Oh? I see." He took hold of the hems of his purple cloak and began to pace back and forth on the terrace.

"Should there have been something more?"

Constantius shrugged. "I thought you might have received certain reports by now."

"Reports?" Florentius asked. "What do you mean, my lord?"

The Emperor paced the terrace, his golden sandals clicking against the marble. "Florentius, I have known you since the days of my father. You served him well, and you have served me well."

"Thank you, my lord."

"Your daughter, Melissa, has been great company to my sister these past couple of years since we left Constantinople. In these past months away from Mediolanum, as I have settled affairs throughout Italy, I found her company to be a breath of fresh air. I have told her so myself."

"I am glad to hear that you think so, sire," Florentius said. He smiled. "My wife, her brothers and I think of her the same way."

The Emperor turned an ear to listen to the music echoing from inside the palace. "You and your wife have enjoyed the banquet, I hope."

"Yes, sire. Very much."

"Melissa too, I hope."

"I am sure of it, my Emperor."

"Excellent," said Constantius. He began to pace again, his chin down against his chest and his hands together behind his back. "I have said before I have thought of Melissa as a sister. I remember Melissa and Helena, when they were little, playing together in the palace halls and peristyles in Antioch and Caesarea Maritima. She was like another little sister. Now, Melissa has matured and grown into a beautiful woman." The Emperor quit pacing. He tilted his head to Florentius. "How old is she now?"

"Twenty-one, sire," said Florentius.

Constantius resumed his place at the railing beside the general. "Since the death of my cousin—my late wife—I have been alone and without female companionship."

Florentius bowed his head. "Her death was a great loss."

The Emperor locked eyes with Florentius. "My fondness for your daughter has grown these past months," he said. Constantius cleared his throat. "I must now declare that the nature of my feelings toward Melissa has changed of late. Before, I spoke of her as being like a sister, I must say now that I have come to feel of her less of a sister . . . and more of a . . . as of a—" The Emperor paused as he struggled to find the right word. "A cousin."

"A cousin?" asked Florentius.

Constantius squinted. "Yes, perhaps a strange way to put it, I suppose. But it has been a recent custom for imperial marriages to be contracted between cousins . . . and I wanted only to express I now think of your daughter as more than a sister, as I once had. A poor way to put it. My apologies, Florentius. But I am accustomed as Emperor to commanding, not asking. This has all been a roundabout way of telling you I seek your consent, as Melissa's father, for me to have her hand in marriage. I want to make Melissa my wife and empress."

Florentius bowed to the Emperor. "My lord, I am honored beyond measure, both at the expressions of your fondness for Melissa and the respect you pay your servant by asking for my consent to a marriage."

Constantius grinned and nodded smugly as he awaited the formality of the affirmative answer he undoubtedly expected. Marcus, who had remained only a couple of yards away from the Emperor throughout the conversation as his bodyguard, turned his head to hear the general's answer. Even the Emperor's entourage had inched forward by now to eavesdrop on the conversation.

Florentius's jaw tightened. *What do I say? How do I say it?*

Still smiling, the Emperor raised his eyebrows as the moments passed. He clasped his hands and rubbed them together with confidence. "And, your reply?"

The general cleared his throat. His voice trembled as he spoke. "Unfortunately, my lord, I am not able to give my consent."

Constantius turned his ear toward Florentius. "What was that?"

"I am not able to give my consent."

The Emperor's smile dissolved. "Not able to give your consent? Why not? I have the means to support your daughter! I am an Emperor!"

"My daughter is betrothed to another."

"Melissa, betrothed? I was not aware of this."

"It was a betrothal arranged long ago, sire."

Constantius frowned. "May I be so bold to ask . . . to whom is she betrothed?"

"She is to marry Captain Lucius."

"Captain Lucius, the son of Varronius? The cripple on your staff?"

Florentius, his jaw clenched, nodded. "The same, sire. The marriage was agreed to when they were in their infancies. The formal engagement will be announced after their return to Mediolanum. They will marry after the war."

The Emperor straightened his back as he pulled his shoulders back. Constantius glared at Florentius as he mulled over a response to this unexpected turn of events.

"Very well," the Emperor said, his voice brusque and sour. He brushed past Marcus and pushed angrily through the midst of his advisers almost knocking a few of them to the ground as he did so.

Florentius rubbed his face, then looked out over the city. He exhaled.

While Marcus and the rest of the Emperor's retinue had followed Constantius inside, Arbitio lingered behind in the shadows.

"I guess I did not know you as well as I thought," Arbitio said as he approached Florentius. "Your daughter could have been an empress over all you see before you. Your grandchildren might have been Augusti."

Florentius turned to leave. "There are more important things to leave to one's children than the things of this world."

Chapter 13

An Unwelcomed Surprise

(Mediolanum, Late Spring, 353 AD)

Melissa stood on the terrace of the villa where she, her father, and mother stayed in Mediolanum. On the street below, children played as passersby hurried home with fresh fruit and meat from the market for their evening meal.

"There you are, my dear!" said Portia, exasperated. "I have been searching all over the house for you. What are you doing up here?"

"You know I love to watch the city," said Melissa. "It is a beautiful evening."

"Evening indeed," said Portia. She took the wrap from her own shoulders and placed it around Melissa. "You will catch a cold."

Melissa shook her head. "Mother, no matter what weather it is, you say 'You will catch a cold!' It is still summer, you know. I am not a child anymore."

Portia hugged Melissa. "No, you are not a little child anymore," she said, a wistful smile on her face. "You are a beautiful young woman now—the most beautiful of all the young ladies of the imperial court."

"Now you sound just like father. He has been acting strange since our time in Rome."

Portia stiffened. "Oh? I am sure I have not noticed."

Melissa raised an eyebrow. "Come to think of it . . . you both have been acting odd since Rome . . . a whole month. Are you two up to something?"

"Up to something?"

"Yes, I can tell when you are—whenever you answer a question with a question. You can never hide a secret."

"Hiding a secret? I do not know what you mean by that."

"Yes, the more I think of it—"

"Since when?"

"Since Rome, mother!" said Melissa with a huff. "I noticed that the servants have set two extra places for dinner this evening." She searched her mother's eyes. Portia turned her head away. "Who have you invited to dinner—and for what purpose?"

Her mother fumbled with her hands.

"Have you been matchmaking—again?"

Portia pursed her lips. She moved to the railing. Her eyes darted about without lingering long on any one thing. She glanced upward into the sky at a cloud, to a bird flying overhead, then down to the street below at a child hiding from his playmates behind a fruit cart. "Your father is late this evening—he must have stayed late at the palace working on final preparations. The army is to leave Mediolanum soon."

Melissa squinted at her mother. "Do not change the subject. Tell me. What have you done?"

Her mother brought her hands to her face, cupping them over her mouth. "I am awful at keeping secrets," she blurted out. "How do you and your father see through me?" Portia glanced down the other end of the street. She made a fist and tapped it gently atop the railing in seeming frustration. "It is the fault of your father. He was supposed to be here for this moment."

"What secret? What moment?"

"I will tell you—but you must not let your father know I did so. Promise?"

Glaring at her mother, Melissa nodded.

Her mother walked a few paces across the mosaic-tiled terrace. She entered a gazebo and sat down upon a bench. "You are right," said Portia. "We have invited dinner guests this evening. Captain Lucius and Count Varronius."

"It is not out of the ordinary for Lucius to visit and have dinner with us—he is father's aide," said Melissa. She thought a moment.

"However, the fleet is at Portus. What is the Count doing in Mediolanum?"

Portia covered her mouth again, but she could no longer contain herself. "While in Rome, your father and the Count decided and agreed you and Lucius should marry one another."

Melissa's mouth fell open. *That's impossible!*

Portia raced to Melissa's side, placing an arm around her. "I know it is not what you wanted, dear."

"Married to Lucius? How could Father do this?"

Portia fumbled for something to say.

"I do not love Lucius!" said Melissa, her eyes welling with tears. "You both know how I feel about an arranged marriage."

"You are disappointed because this is new to you," said Portia. "There is nothing so horrible about arranged marriages. Your father and I had an arranged marriage, as did our parents before us, and theirs before them. Such marriages are the norm rather than the exception among the nobility. It was neither logical nor practical for you to object to one. And, besides, you are twenty-one. You should be married by now!"

Melissa's head spun and she leaned against the railing. She sobbed.

"Hush, and do not cry, my darling child!" said Portia. She stroked Melissa's brown hair. "All will turn out well for you and Lucius. He is from a fine family. A fine Christian man."

The clattering of hooves and wheels along the stone-paved street echoed loudly from below. There were shouts as servants rushed to open the gates. A carriage entered the grounds of the villa and came to a rest by a fountain in the center of a small courtyard. Out stepped Florentius, followed by Varronius and Lucius.

Portia rushed to the side of the terrace which overlooked the courtyard, dragging her daughter by the hand. In a daze from the secret just revealed to her, Melissa offered no resistance. "Oh, no. It is not only your father as I had expected. Lucius and Varronius are with him! I wanted your father to speak to you before they arrived."

Portia waved. "Hello there. Welcome, Lucius!"

"Thank you for the invitation, Lady Portia," Lucius called out, as he waved back. "Hello, Lady Melissa!"

Portia elbowed her daughter. "Wave to him—wave to Lucius."

Melissa, quiet and sullen, refused to raise a finger. *How could my parents do this to me? How could father? I thought he understood.*

"And smile, Melissa!" Portia whispered. "Men like their women to smile. And tonight, at dinner, be sure to laugh at his jokes. Men like that. That is an important rule for a woman—do not forget it. Men are rarely as funny as they believe themselves to be, but you must laugh all the same." Portia hurried off to greet the guests. Before disappearing inside, she shouted back to her daughter. "Come along, Melissa!"

Bewildered, Melissa wandered back to the side of the terrace which overlooked the street. She stood there staring blankly into the distance, lost in her thoughts. Oblivious to all around her, she did not hear the approach of her father. He put an arm around her. Melissa nestled her head against his chest.

Florentius placed a finger beneath her chin and tilted her head back with a soft touch. "Tears in your eyes? What is this about, my honeybee?"

She placed her head back against his chest.

He pursed his lips. "You have been speaking with your mother."

Melissa nodded.

"She told you about Lucius?"

She nodded again.

"Then, you know why he is here?"

"Yes, father," she said, her voice muffled as her face pressed against his chest.

Florentius closed his eyes. He took a deep breath. "Secrets and your mother do not go together. One would have greater success holding water in a sieve than your mother keeping a secret."

Melissa, managing a faint smile, looked up at her father's face.

"I much prefer your smiles," said Florentius.

"Why did you do it?" asked Melissa.

"I hoped to be the first one to tell you about the marriage."

"I hoped to be the first one to know," Melissa said, coldly. She pulled away from him. "Father, I do not want to be *told* of my marital plans. I should be the first to know—both as to when and to whom it will be." She glared at her father. "Mother might not have appreciated that. In her mind, she has married me off many times by now. But you, father—I thought you understood how I felt. You promised me long ago you would never demand this of me."

Florentius reached out his arms to try to hug her.

Melissa backed away from her father.

Florentius grimaced. "Do not hold this against me. I meant that promise to you when I first gave it. I did. But events often develop beyond our expectations. Things may happen which are beyond our control. Sometimes, promises made in earnest are not always promises best kept. Events developed in Rome which required me to reconsider what was best for you."

"Rome?" she asked. "Mother said that is where you and the Count came to this agreement." She looked into her father's eyes. "What happened in Rome to cause you to break your promise?"

"Perhaps, one day I may tell you more of what transpired there—and of my reasons for my decision. Now is not that day. Trust me. It is for the best."

Her mouth twisted into a sour knot. "I cannot fathom how forcing me to marry Lucius is for the best." Her knees weakening, she placed her arms about one of the marble columns that supported the roof of the gazebo. She rested her cheek against the cool stone and the tears flowed down her face.

Florentius stepped toward Melissa. He hugged her. "I know it is hard to fathom. But it is for the best. Lucius is a good man. He is an honorable man. A Christian man. He will take good care of you."

"I do not doubt that Lucius is all those things—but I do not love him, father!"

Florentius placed his hands on her shoulders. He fixed his eyes on hers. "I must ask you to trust me in this matter," he said. "I am resolved that it be so. You will trust and respect the will of your father in this matter, yes?"

Melissa lowered her chin. Her shoulders sank. "Yes, father," she said, her words almost inaudible.

Florentius brushed away tears from her cheeks. "Tonight, your betrothal becomes official. I expect the war to be over soon after which the imperial court will transfer to Arelate. There, you and

220

Lucius will be married."

Florentius put an arm around Melissa as they looked at the stars which appeared over the horizon. "However distant or obscure the day may seem to you now, you will look back on this moment and smile, my dear."

***

It had been three weeks since the night General Florentius broke the news to Melissa of her arranged marriage. Now, he and Lucius stood in a large chamber of the imperial palace in Mediolanum, providing Emperor Constantius with a final briefing of the army's imminent campaign.

"My lord, beginning tomorrow morning, the army will march west from Mediolanum into the Alps," Lucius said, tracing a pointer stick along a large map which he'd propped up on a table. "To block our descent into Gaul, the Western army of Magnentius has fortified the mountain passes. We will force our way into Gaul here—a mountain pass near the town of Mons Seleucus."

The Emperor listened as he sat on a heavy wooden chair that rested atop an elevated marble platform. Around him stood a dozen advisors, among whom were Eusebius the Grand Chamberlain, Commander Arbitio, the court bishops, and Marcus. Behind Constantius, a paned window, fifteen feet across and over ten feet high, was framed by a stone arch built into the wall. The decorative glass depicted a Roman eagle, on either side of which were the fasces. Beneath them all were the letters "SPQR."

"And after we force our way through the defenses, what resistance should we expect once we are in Gaul?" asked Constantius.

Florentius approached the map. "Reports indicate the Western army was unable to rebuild its strength following Mursa Major and the battles since. Desertions are rampant. Recruitment has not kept pace. Large raids by the Alemanni and other barbarian tribes into Gaul occupy what few reserves Magnentius has. There is also word that cities in the Gallic provinces have begun to declare their allegiance to you. These cities have barred their gates to the Usurper's legions. They deny him material support."

Constantius thumped the table with his fist. "Excellent!" he said. "If we force the pass at Mons Seleucus, support for Magnentius will collapse throughout Gaul and Iberia. For the first time since the death of my father, the empire will be unified." The advisors applauded as the briefing ended. The Emperor stood. "Thank you, General, I will see you in the morning when we march."

Smiling, the heavyset Bishop Ursacius, taking each step with care, descended the platform to the floor. "Once you rule both East and West, you can deal with all who stand in the way of compromise with the Arians."

"Yes, remember Athanasius," said Bishop Valens, fluffing his long, red beard. "He came between you and your late brother Constans. He disturbs the peace of the empire and the Church."

Florentius crammed his notes and maps into a satchel. Listening to the bishops, his back stiffened. He cleared his throat as he stepped toward Constantius. "O Emperor, may I be permitted to speak?"

Constantius nodded. "Go ahead."

"Great Augustus, you know I am acquainted with the matter of Athanasius and have long been his friend," said Florentius. "Years ago, there was a disagreement between you and him. He fled to the West where your brother, Constans, protected him. When you sought to make peace with Athanasius, knowing of my friendship with him, you entreated me to write to Athanasius on your behalf—to convince him of your sincerity, truthfulness, and faithfulness to your promise to allow him to return to the East and safely resume his place in the See of Alexandria. These things I did at your request. Athanasius returned."

Ursacius smirked. "Those were different times, General."

Florentius pointed at the bishops. "Now, these men, these—these bishops—by their words and intrigues hope to make you forget that you once made peace with Athanasius and greeted him again as a Friend of Caesar."

"You are impertinent, General!" said Ursacius. He rested his folded hands on his large belly. "'Intrigues,' you say? How dare you speak to us in such a manner!"

The bishops looked at the Emperor, appealing to him for

support.

Florentius addressed the Emperor. "These men have long sought to turn your heart and mind against Athanasius. In your wisdom, you once turned aside such counsel. Stray not from that course."

Lucius, still holding the map, let it drop to the table. "Amen!" he blurted out.

Florentius spun around quickly to face Lucius. He glared at the captain. *What are you doing?* Florentius mouthed the word *quiet*, but it was too late.

Constantius, red-faced, sprung to his feet. "Enough!" he shouted. He strode over to Lucius. He stood before him, his face inches from the captain's. "A young officer should not speak in the presence of an emperor unless given leave to do so!" The Emperor then fixed his attention on Florentius, who lowered his head. "While those given such leave must not do so beyond their competence. General, you are a military man. You presume much to speak in a rude fashion to these holy and learned bishops on matters of which they are experts. Never speak the name of Athanasius again in my presence, nor do so on matters of the Faith. Is that understood?"

Florentius averting his eyes from the Emperor, kept them fixed on the floor. "Yes, sire."

Constantius glared at both officers. "Leave me!" He looked around at his other advisors and bodyguards. "And the rest of you, as well—get out." All present in the hall quickly departed.

Once outside in the courtyard, Florentius grabbed Lucius by the shoulders and threw him hard against a column. "Son, you cannot behave in such a manner in the Emperor's presence," he said. "You must control your tongue, lad."

Lucius's face became ashen.

The general's anger dissipated. He relaxed his firm grip which had pinned Lucius against the stone. In place of the deep scowl on the general's face, a faint smile appeared. "Look at me. I am a fine example of holding one's tongue!" He let go of Lucius, his eyes now warm with kindness. "You are betrothed to Melissa. You are to be my son, Lucius! Husband to my daughter. Father to my grandchildren. You must be more careful."

"I am sorry, General," said Lucius.

"No harm this time. We still have our heads."

Lucius smiled.

"We march with the army in the morning," said Florentius. "We each must return to our quarters to finish packing for the journey. If you can, stop by later and say goodbye to Melissa."

"I understood she has not been well and is not receiving visitors, or so she has told me," said Lucius. He lowered his head. "I have not seen her in over a week."

Florentius frowned. *Melissa is being cruel and stubborn.* "A week? That is too long for a young couple not to see one another. I will speak to my wife and arrange something. You must see her before you leave."

"Thank you, sir."

The two parted.

***

Lucius's cane clicked upon the stones as he walked beneath the portico that ran alongside the officers' barracks. In the parade ground to his right, a company of legionaries drilled under the command of a centurion. The clanking of the armor and shouted commands of the centurion reverberated among the surrounding barracks.

Marcus ran across the parade ground to intercept his friend. "Lucius, I must speak with you for a moment," he said. "You know I respect Florentius. I do not intend to sound critical of him, but I must warn you."

"Warn me of what?" asked Lucius, his step faltering.

"I saw what just happened between you both and Constantius. Difficult times are ahead for those who oppose the Emperor's policies toward the Church. Florentius must watch what he says about the Arians and their friends in court. They will be his undoing."

"What are you suggesting, Marcus?"

"You must convince Florentius to keep his opinions to himself at all costs. Better still—convince him it is wiser and safer to conform his views of religion to those of the Emperor. If nothing

224

else, he must at least pretend to do so."

"You cannot be serious!" said Lucius. "You want him to lie?"

Marcus grabbed Lucius by the forearm. "Listen. Almost all the bishops of the East accept the Arians. As soon as the war is over, the Emperor will enforce his view upon the bishops of the West. You must make Florentius see that a point will come when further disagreement is futile—and deadly. One must relent in the face of the inevitable."

"I hope that you are not as cynical as that. There must be some things worth fighting for, no matter what. A grim world it would be if faith and all principle could be so easily compromised or surrendered and there was nothing to hold fast to, even against all visible hope."

Marcus took off his helmet. For a moment it seemed as if he might throw it. He ran his fingers back through his wavy, black hair in frustration. "I will not argue philosophy with you—I have warned you as a friend. I add but only this . . . the Emperor holds grudges and is vengeful. Florentius must tread lightly. This is not the first time he has displeased the Emperor."

"What do you mean this is not the first time? What else has Florentius done that has displeased the Emperor?"

Marcus hesitated. He pursed his lips, regretting that he might have revealed too much.

The two men remained silent as several junior officers came toward them along the portico. Once these officers had passed beyond earshot, Lucius glared at Marcus. "You have said much already, do not hesitate now," said Lucius. "We are friends. Tell me—how else has the general displeased the Emperor? He is to be my father. You must tell me if I am to help him."

"Very well," said Marcus with a grudging nod. "Florentius rejected the Emperor's request for the hand of Melissa in marriage."

Lucius furrowed his brow. "What?" he asked. It seemed he might collapse. Lucius placed a hand against one of the portico's pillars and leaned against it for support. On the parade ground before him, the legionaries were being hounded by their centurion for mistakes in their drill. But Lucius, blank-faced, seemed to stare through it all, trying to comprehend all that he had just heard.

"You knew of this already, did you not?"

Lucius shook his head. "I swear, I did not. When was this? How did you learn of this proposal?"

"It was in Rome on the night of the banquet. The night Constantius found Florentius on the terrace with you and your father. Remember?"

"I remember that night well. You were there too with the Emperor—on duty as his bodyguard."

"After you and your father left the terrace, Constantius asked the general for Melissa's hand," said Marcus.

Lucius lowered his head.

"Florentius has never spoken to you of the Emperor's interest in Melissa?" asked Marcus.

"No, he has not," said Lucius. He looked at Marcus. "It was that same night . . . on that same terrace that my father and Florentius first told me of the betrothal—minutes before the Emperor arrived on the terrace."

Marcus chuckled. "Even with your bad leg, you beat the Emperor to the finish line. Truly, the winner is not always the quickest. You are a lucky man."

"Lucky?"

"Yes—lucky! You will marry the prettiest woman in the court."

"The timing is all odd. There is too much of a coincidence."

"What do you mean?"

"I am not sure," said Lucius. He stroked his hand across his face. "Melissa traveled with Constantius and Princess Helena for months. Florentius was surprised the Emperor summoned him to Rome without saying why. Is it possible Florentius divined the Emperor's intent to ask for her hand?"

Marcus laughed. "You are suggesting Florentius chose you to marry his daughter to thwart the Emperor's proposal of marriage? No offense, Lucius . . . but what father or mother would choose a captain over an Emperor to be husband of their daughter. You cannot be serious."

"Yes, I am serious," said Lucius. His jaw tightened. "Unfortunately."

"I was joking. Why would Florentius not want his daughter to marry the Emperor?"

"You know the answer, Marcus," said Lucius, his tone terse. "You witnessed it in court in the general's speech against the bishops. Florentius would not want his daughter to marry an Arian or an Arian sympathizer. With his daughter betrothed already, he could refuse the Emperor."

Marcus cocked his head back. "What are you suggesting?"

"The general arranged my betrothal to Melissa to forestall the Emperor's wish to marry her," said Lucius. "I was merely handy for this purpose. An act of desperation—not one of a hope for Melissa's happiness. I suspect she has no clue about what happened. But what if she does know, or if she were to one day learn the truth? She might have been an empress."

Marcus placed his helmet down on a waist-high wall which lined the way between two pillars. He ran his hand over the top of the helmet's black plume. "Even if you have guessed the truth behind the betrothal, you must not think Florentius would act without regard to Melissa's future happiness. He knows you to be a good and honorable man. Melissa is fortunate that she will have you as her husband."

Lucius winced. "I wish I could believe that. I have barely seen her these past several weeks since our betrothal. She avoids me, pleading illness."

"She is anxious. The betrothal is still new to her. That is all. She will come to see the wisdom of it."

Lucius locked eyes with his friend. "Marcus, you must not speak of these matters to anyone ever. It would be fatal to Florentius if the Emperor discovered the general lied to him to avoid his marriage proposal. Promise me you will remain silent."

"I promise."

***

Melissa sat alone beside a table in a peristyle as the declining sun disappeared behind the roof of the portico. Lost in thought, she stared at the fountain as its gurgling stream of water echoed within the enclosed garden.

The princess came to the entrance of the peristyle. "Melissa, I am so glad to find you outside today."

227

Stirred from her daydreaming, Melissa stood to greet her friend with a faint smile.

"You have not been good company of late," said Helena. "You make me come in search of you. I have not seen much of you over the last few weeks."

They sat down by the table together.

"And, I understand poor Lucius has seen far less of his bride-to-be than have I," said the princess.

Melissa brought a hand to her forehead. "I have not been well."

"The army marches off to the war tomorrow. Your father leaves with it—Lucius too."

Melissa stared at the fountain.

Helena shook her head. "You cannot put off seeing Lucius before he goes. You must see him and say goodbye." She looked on the table. There was the wooden panel on which Melissa had sketched the center of Rome as seen from the terrace of her apartment in the Imperial Palace. Beside the panel sat unused jars of paint. "I see you intend to paint it—at last."

Melissa shrugged. "Mother brought it out, thinking to occupy my time."

Helena examined the sketch. "We had a marvelous time in Rome. Did we not?"

"We did," said Melissa in morose voice, just above a whisper.

Helena giggled. "Remember Aurelia in Rome? On the terrace? And her behavior at the banquet?"

Melissa nodded weakly.

"I think she wants to be an empress," said the princess. "But, could you imagine if it ever happened? She as my sister?"

"No."

"It may sound silly, but the night of the banquet in Rome, I had formed the impression that my brother had fallen in love with you," Helena said.

Melissa's eyes widened. *So, perhaps I wasn't crazy. The Emperor was flirting with me that night.* "You thought that?"

Helena giggled. "I did! It would not surprise me. He has an eye for pretty women. Could you imagine me calling you Empress Melissa!"

Melissa quirked a smile. "Empress Melissa? I could not imagine that." Her smile faded away. *But now that I am betrothed to Lucius, it is impossible. What might have been?*

Helena placed a hand on her friend's knee. "But it is all for the best that things did not turn out that way. It was only in my imagination. Although you would have made a marvelous sister, I am happy you are not marrying my brother! It is very dangerous to marry into my family. You are much more fortunate to be marrying Lucius instead. For one, he does not have the temper of my brother."

"So fortunate," Melissa said. She burst into tears. "The happiness I felt during the days of our travels is gone—as if they had never happened. All of my hopes and dreams ... overshadowed by an arranged marriage. Not only was it done against my wishes, but worse still, it was done with no regard for them at all. My heart is broken. I am sick at the thought of marrying Lucius."

"But why?" asked Helena, startled. "He is a good man. I know he cares for you. You must pray. Love will come."

"Everyone tells me he is a good man—my father and mother. It is not his fault. He has always been friendly and kind. I have prayed about what to do. I have tried and tried to convince myself that true love might come. Lucius is a man of faith. Caring. Intelligent. Loving. Everything a woman dreams and prays to have. It seems that God blessed me with all of this in Lucius. Yet . . . "

"Yet?"

"I cannot make myself love him," said Melissa. "I have no romantic feelings for the poor man. These last few weeks, I have questioned everything about what God wants of me. I have begged Him to show me a way out." Melissa lowered her head.

Helena got down to her knees in front of Melissa. "You must not let Lucius ever see you like this, and never let him know you feel this way, ever. You will break his heart. Your father loves you and would only do what is best for you." Helena placed her hands beneath Melissa's chin. She lifted it until their eyes met. The princess smiled. "You will make me sad with how you talk about an arranged marriage. Such a fate awaits me as an imperial princess. I just hope I get a man as handsome as my sister Constantina did when she married my cousin Gallus. With my luck, Constantius will marry me off to an old man—a fat potentate of a strange, faraway, forsaken land—all in exchange for a trade route. So, you see, dear friend, your lot is not so terrible as mine. Lucius is neither fat nor ugly. He is, in fact, pleasant to look at. He has a friendly countenance and disposition. I would trade my fate for yours if my brother would allow it. Then it would be you living with an ugly husband in a faraway land. But, because I love you as a friend, I will spare you such a fate. I will marry the fat potentate, and you will marry Lucius and be exceedingly happy."

Melissa smiled.

"Dear Melissa, you must set your heart to love Lucius and his good qualities," said Helena. "You do not see it as possible, because you dwell now on your sadness. Underneath it all, love is of the heart . . . of the will. It is not a feeling or a sentiment, apt to be fickle and change like the weather or the seasons. The heart must rule your sentiments. Choose to love your husband—because he is your husband. Be loving in your actions toward him and love there will be. You will see."

Helena stood. She cleared her throat. "You will see Lucius before he leaves tomorrow?" she asked, but her tone was that of a command.

"Yes, I will see him."

"Thank God!" came Portia's voice from just inside the door to the peristyle where she had been eavesdropping. No sooner had she revealed her presence than she disappeared back inside.

Melissa glanced up at Helena. "My mother sent for you on behalf of Lucius?"

"No one *sent* for me. I bumped into Lucius as we were both on our way to visit you. We chatted about things. That is all."

"Look who has come to visit," Portia yelled from inside the villa. "It is Captain Lucius."

Melissa's back stiffened. *I do not want to see anyone, least of all Lucius.* "He is here now?"

Helena squinted at Melissa. "The army marches in the morning. You cannot put him off." She handed Melissa a cloth from the table. "Now, quick . . . wipe away your tears. Do not let Lucius see you have been crying."

Several moments later, Portia came outside, accompanied by

two servants who set about lighting the lanterns in the peristyle, which was now enveloped in shadow as the sun neared the horizon.

"You can do with some light, my dear," said Portia as she stood beside her daughter, her voice quivering with uncertainty. She gestured to the servants, their task completed, to depart. "You are sitting in shadow, Melissa. You will not be able to continue with your sketching and painting."

Melissa glared at Portia, who fumbled nervously with her hands. *You know I do not want to see Lucius.* The only sound to be heard was the soft gurgling of the fountain.

"It is good to see you up and about, my love," said Lucius, who now stood at the entrance to the peristyle, his breastplate reflecting the light from the lanterns. Holding his plumed helmet beneath one arm, he entered the garden. Walking with the support of his cane, he paused before Helena. "Good afternoon, Princess." He gave her a wink. She smiled and did so in return.

Melissa stood reluctantly to greet him. "Good evening, Captain."

Lucius embraced her. Yet, while he wrapped his arms around her, Melissa let her own hands stay limp at her sides. He moved forward to kiss her, but his lips only met her cheek when she turned her head away.

The princess winced at Melissa's coldness. She coughed to get her friend's attention. "I will take my leave. Far be it from me to interfere with the farewells of lovers."

Melissa pulled away from Lucius. She glared at the princess. "There is no reason to leave yet, Helena."

The princess hugged Melissa. Helena placed her lips to her friend's ear. "Be kind to him. Be loving and love there will be."

With that, the princess and Portia went back inside the villa, leaving the couple alone together.

Melissa went back to her chair and sat.

"I have intruded?" said Lucius.

Melissa shrugged.

Lucius walked around and stood behind her to examine her sketch. "An excellent likeness of the city."

"It is nothing."

"You are too hard on yourself," he said. "You are talented. Once the war is over, we should have a portrait done of us together."

Her back still to him, she rolled her eyes.

Lucius cleared his throat. "As I have mentioned, tomorrow I march with the army into the Alps."

"My father says he expects this battle to end the war," said Melissa.

"You almost sound sad when you say it. The end of the war is a happy occasion. Doubly so for us, is it not? For we wed when the war is over."

Lucius rested a hand tenderly on her shoulder. She flinched at his touch. The captain's jaw tightened as he removed his hand. "There are two reasons for my visit this afternoon, Melissa," he said. "First, I came to say farewell to you before my departure in the morning."

He walked around to the other side of the table, his cane clicking on the travertine. He stood across the table from where Melissa sat. She ignored his eye contact, pretending to take interest in the sketch of Rome.

He placed the end of his cane down on the tabletop. The rapping of it made Melissa look up at him. "The second reason I have come regards our wedding plans." He paced about the peristyle. "I am crippled Melissa—not blind. You have avoided me these past several weeks, ever since our betrothal."

"I have not been well."

"I loved you from the first moment I saw you in Constantinople. That love has only grown deeper since that moment. It pains me to say it, but I know you do not love me in return. At least not yet. I also can see that you do not want this marriage. I do not fault you for any of this."

Melissa glanced down at her hands, now clasped together on her lap. "My father has pledged me to you," she said, the words stumbling out. "I will live up to the bargain made between our fathers."

Lucius shook his head. "I desire that your hand be placed in mine by *you*—not by your father against your will. I would not have you think that I would knowingly benefit from a forced union or

232

that I would accept any bargain by which I gain my happiness at the price of yours. I will not be a party to such an agreement. Do not think so poorly of me, Melissa."

Melissa watched as he headed toward the door to the villa. Reaching it, he paused there. He turned around to face her.

"I imagine I am not what you had hoped for," said Lucius, leaning on his cane. "I leave tomorrow for the Alps. I will try to prove myself worthy of your love if I can. But, if deeds and prayers to heaven kindle no desire within you for me, I will release you from the bargain made by our fathers upon my return. That is what I came to say."

Melissa sprung up from her chair. "Wait!" she said as she hurried to him. "What do you mean by proving yourself worthy?"

"I am not half so cruel as you may think of me, to take what I have not earned—to take the hand of a bride who does not believe she could ever love me. When I return . . . if you cannot look me in the eye and say you want this marriage, I will release you from this bargain and take the blame upon myself in the eyes of our two families. That is my promise. Your mind and heart can now be at peace."

Lucius took her hand to his lips and kissed it. "Farewell."

She stood there as he disappeared inside. "Lucius," she whispered to herself.

Chapter 14

The Eve of Battle

(Mons Seleucus, Summer, 353 AD)

It was late afternoon as Septimus walked with Longinus through an army encampment in the mountain pass near Mons Seleucus. The two were prepared for battle, attired in helmets and armored breastplates and grieves. Steep alpine mountain slopes bordered the camp to the north and south. A hundred yards from the camp, the Western army had erected a strong palisade behind a deep trench across the width of the pass, hundreds of yards across, running east to west.

The two officers stopped and visited with legionaries as they stood outside their tents or cooked their meals at the campfires. The warmth of the day was giving way to a chill as evening approached.

Septimus pulled his scarlet cloak about himself as he looked down the lane of tents through which they had just passed. "Long ago, Third Italica once numbered over four thousand men. After years of campaigning in Gaul, the Battle of Rome, Mursa Major, and the battles since, the legion is less than half of that number."

The centurion, his vine staff cropped beneath an arm, looked up the pass to the east. The lines on his face deepened as he squinted. A large camp, bustling with activity and glowing campfires, was visible two miles away. "And we are not done yet, Tribune. Since the first of the Easterners encamped last week, there has been a continual stream of men, horses, and baggage coming down the pass. Scouts say the last of the column entered the camp this afternoon. The Easterners are now at full force. The imperial banner of Constantius was seen."

Septimus's jaws tightened at the report. "Then we can expect an attack any day."

The two men headed towards the palisade. As they went, they heard someone calling after them. "Tribune Marius! Centurion!"

They turned to see three bearded men chasing after them. It was Jason, accompanied by Drusus and Samson.

"I would like to have a word with you, Tribune," said Jason, as he caught up with them, somewhat out of breath. "If I may."

Septimus frowned at the Ostian, then continued on his way toward the wall. "I have heard news that Caesar Gallus has put down the Jewish rebellion in the East."

Jason grimaced. He hustled after the tribune. "We have heard this too."

"Then what are you and your men doing in camp? The war is over for you. There are no more bridges for you to build."

"The war is not over for us," said Jason, trying to keep pace with the tribune. When they were fifty feet from the wall, he stumbled as he stepped into a shallow drainage ditch that carried away the runoff from the mountain. The Roman caught Jason by the arm before he fell.

Septimus helped him regain his balance. He gripped Jason at the shoulders. "The war is not over for you? How does this concern me?"

"There will be no more bridges or palisades to build—but only if this battle is lost."

"You have not answered my question. How does this concern me?"

Jason grinned at Longinus. "I petitioned Magnentius to allow my men to fight in the lines against the Easterners."

Longinus tapped his vine staff against Jason's chest. "Ha! Petitioned Magnentius to fight?"

Jason nodded. "He granted our request to fight ... with your legion."

The tribune quirked a frown. He quickly scaled the ladder to the top of the palisade as if trying to escape Jason. Septimus glared down at him from the battlement. "Take your men and go. Return to your families and friends while you have the chance."

"We want to fight!" Drusus shouted.

"We want to kill Romans!" said Samson.

Longinus glowered at Samson. "*Eastern* Romans," he muttered, correcting him. He now tapped the vine staff against Samson's chest. "*Eastern* Romans."

Jason climbed the ladder and joined Septimus at the battlement. "Drusus and Samson speak for the rest of my men."

The tribune pointed up the pass at the Eastern Roman camp. "There is the Eastern army of Constantius. Thirty thousand men strong. The Western army numbers only seven thousand. We are outnumbered. Four or five to one. The odds are worse now than they were at Mursa Major."

Jason peered over the top of the battlement. He scanned the surrounding terrain and defenses. A steep mountainside bordered the Western Roman army's defensive line on its left flank to the northwest. From its base, a wide and deep trench had been dug, which ran down the slope of the hill, cutting across the pass, until it ended on the right flank to the southeast, near a stream at the base of a wooded mountain slope. The excavated earth had been piled and packed into a high mound which paralleled the trench. The sturdy palisade and fortified towers stood atop the mound. A forest of obstacles, sharpened stakes and spikes, protruded from the slope of the earthenworks and the bottom of the trench.

Seeing all this, Jason turned to Septimus. "What of these defenses?"

Tribune Marius smirked. "We hide behind a wooden palisade behind a trench. A couple dozen towers for archers and scorpions. Behind the wall . . . several dozen catapults and ballistae."

"This counts for something," said Jason. "Does it not?"

Septimus pointed at the high, snow-topped mountains to the east, beyond the Eastern army's camp. "The enemy has crossed the Alps. If the formidable obstacles of nature could not deter him, do you think these defenses, puny and meager in comparison, will resist his efforts?"

The tribune walked along the battlement with Jason and Longinus. "We have surrendered mobility, initiative, and surprise, for the illusion of safety behind several dozen yards of trenches, obstacles and a palisade." He stopped and gripped Jason's shoulder. "It is not with animus I say this to you, Jason. We fought once before together, at Mursa Major. I am doing you and your men a favor. Go! Leave here tonight. Before it is too late."

"Tribune!" interjected Longinus. The centurion pointed with his eyes to the sentries on the battlement, reminding Septimus there were others listening to their discussion.

Septimus saw his raised voice had attracted the attention of the legionaries standing watch nearby. Seeing the concern in their faces, the normally clean-shaven tribune rubbed a hand across his mouth and cheeks, dark with several days of growth. Septimus lowered his voice as he addressed Jason. "There is little hope."

"Little hope?" asked Jason. "Then why do you fight?"

Septimus squinted at the enemy camp in the distance. "Because Constantius and his army stand between me and Rome. And it is to Rome I must return." *I must return to Marciana.*

"Then there is no difference between us. The enemy is no less an obstacle for me or for my men. While we still can fight, there is yet hope for my people and of victory over the Romans."

"*Eastern* Romans," muttered Longinus.

Jason smiled at the centurion. "Yes, *Eastern Romans.*" He locked eyes with Septimus. "My men have fought beside yours before. If this is to be our last fight, my men wish to fight alongside you and your legionaries."

Septimus looked to Longinus as if to ask his opinion. The centurion replied with a single nod.

"Your men will follow my orders?" asked the tribune.

"Yes, of course," said Jason.

"Very well, if this is what you want. Your men will fight with Third Italica. Send them to the quartermaster. Equip yourselves as best you can."

***

237

That evening, the tribune gathered the Third Italica's half-dozen surviving centurions in his quarters, along with Jason and Father Paul. They stood around a table in the center of the room. Atop it, a long parchment bore a simple sketch of the Western army's defenses of the mountain pass.

Septimus saw each of their grim faces in the flickering light of a couple of lanterns. "We all know what we are up against. There is not much to say. So, I will be brief." He placed his finger down on the parchment at the spot marking the gate. "Longinus, with the First Cohort, you will command the center of our position along the wall, which includes the gate.

"Understood," said Longinus.

The tribune then pointed in succession to the sketch on either side of the position marked out for the First Cohort. "Centurions Aetius and Petronius, your cohorts will be on the left and right of Longinus. Sergius, your archers will be stationed in the two towers along our sector of the wall. Your cohort will also supply the crews for the artillery, both the scorpions in the towers as well as the catapults and ballistae behind the walls."

"And the rest of the cohorts. Tribune Marius?" asked one of the other centurions.

Septimus pointed to a position well behind the palisade. "The rest of the legion, half of its men, are to be held in reserve behind the wall."

"Tribune Marius, what of my men?" asked Jason. "Where should they be along the wall?"

Septimus shook his head. "No, Jason—not along the wall. Your men will stay back with the reserve line."

Jason frowned. "The reserve line? But—"

The tribune raised an eyebrow as he stared at the Ostian.

Jason nodded reluctantly. "I said my men would follow your orders. The reserve line it is."

Somber-faced, Septimus looked around at the men assembled in his tent. "If the enemy breaches the wall at any point, we are done for. There will be no escape for anyone. Good luck to you and your men. Good luck to us all. Dismissed."

The officers filtered out of the tent, but Longinus, Father Paul, and Jason remained behind.

THE EVE OF BATTLE

"Father Paul, look after the needs of the Christians," said Septimus. "Jason, see to the Jews under your command."

Longinus slapped his vine staff against the table with a sneer. "The pagan you are—who will see after you?"

"If you must know, I went to the reading of the entrails earlier today, which Magnentius read with the help of the augurs," said Septimus. "It matters not to two Christians and a Jew to hear the report, but the omens were said to be *favorable for battle.*"

"Pagan nonsense," scoffed the centurion.

"Idolatry," said the priest, shaking his head.

"Amen to that," said Jason.

"No offense meant, sir," said Longinus gruffly with a smirk.

"None taken, First Centurion," said Septimus, a corner of his mouth curling up to smile. "I am well accustomed to your insults regarding all matters related to the Old Religion. If I were not sure that you were concerned for the betterment and salvation of my soul, I would have had you flogged long ago. But I take quiet consolation knowing that while your sect is growing, we pagans still outnumber you Christians in both the army and the empire three to one."

Septimus took off his scarlet-crested helmet and placed it upon the table. He unbuckled his sword belt and undid his breast and back plates and set them aside. "But I must agree with you that the reading entrails is rubbish," he said. "I cannot recall a single instance these past few years where the portents accurately foretold the disasters which followed." He sat down on his cot to remove the grieves from his legs. "Contrary to the augurs, it appears that God does not intend that we should clearly or so easily know the plans of His Providence, which governs all things. It is inscrutable."

"Tribune Marius, there is a hint of pessimism about tomorrow in your tone," said Father Paul, his face wrinkled with concern. "It will go badly for the Church if Constantius is victorious."

Septimus shook his head. "Pessimism? No. Realism. The Western army is a shadow of what it once was. Outnumbered; the odds are long."

"A just cause is not daunted by long odds," said the priest. "There is always hope."

"Tribune, if tomorrow is to be the end of all things for us, what better time for you to be baptized," said the centurion with a wink.

Septimus laughed. He held up his hand, gesturing to Longinus to stop. "Always trying to convert me, even 'til the end."

"Knowing how obstinate you are, I thought you might say that," said the centurion. He pulled a wineskin out from beneath his cloak. "So, if you will not be baptized, I thought we might drink a couple cups together, one last time, before the end."

Longinus poured out several cups, offering them to all within the tent. He handed the last of the cups to Septimus, who hesitated at first to take it. Longinus pressed the cup into his hand. They raised their cups together in a toast.

"We are an odd, motley lot . . . two Christians—one of whom is a priest—a pagan and a Jew," said Jason. "To what do we drink?"

"That we may all survive this doom," said Septimus. A wistful smile crossed his face. "To the inscrutable plan of God—may we yet have a part to play in it."

"A part to play in it, beyond tomorrow!" said Jason.

"Amen," said Father Paul.

Longinus gulped down the wine from his cup. "His will be done."

"Yes, a part to play in it beyond tomorrow," Septimus muttered to himself before drinking from his cup. The four sat down as the centurion topped off their cups.

"We are a somber bunch," said Jason. "Let us lighten the mood if possible. Each of us must tell what he will do after this war. Father, you go first."

"Return to Rome to be a simple priest and pastor," said Father Paul.

"After this war?" said Longinus. "Fight the next one, of course." He looked at Jason. "And you—what will you do?"

"After this war?" asked Jason. "Fight more Romans, of course."

Longinus burst out in a loud laugh. He slapped Jason on the back.

Septimus lay back on his cot and placed his forearm across his eyes to block the light from the lanterns. "I will return home and marry Lady Marciana—as I should have done before this infernal mess."

"How long has it been since you have seen her, Tribune?" asked Jason, as he used his forearm to wipe away drops of wine that clung to his beard.

"I have neither seen nor heard from her since I left Rome for Mursa Major," said Septimus. He closed his eyes. "Two years in all." He thought back to the engagement party at the senator's villa in Rome, remembering how he had broken the news to Marciana of his imminent departure. His memories and regrets melted away as drowsiness hung over him, and he fell off into sleep.

***

Emperor Constantius paced about his quarters in the Eastern Roman camp as Eusebius, the only advisor present, watched. Having many comforts found in an imperial palace, the large imperial tent could accommodate fifty men. Partitioned into separate rooms by curtains, the finest rugs, chairs, sofas, tables, and bed furnished the tent. Busts of emperors and heroes resting on short pillars, shields, and banners lined the inner canvas.

Constantius paused to stand before a map of the East and West. "Think of it, Eusebius. This time tomorrow. Once again there will be one empire—one Emperor. "However, while a victory over Magnentius tomorrow will end the civil war, it will not bring peace to Gaul which is threatened by brigands and barbarians. Subduing this province will not be as easily accomplished as it had been in Italy."

Crossing his skinny arms, Eusebius lifted a delicate hand and rested his bearded chin upon his knuckles as he examined the map. "The empire is troubled by many threats. Parthians in the East. Brigands and barbarians in the West. You cannot be everywhere at once to enforce your will. There may be need to appoint someone to help restore and keep imperial control over Gaul while you attend to threats elsewhere in the empire."

"I have thought of this as well," said the Emperor. "However, the government of Gaul and the West is a question for another day." He walked over to a table covered in scrolls, dispatches from around the empire. He picked up one in particular and glanced at it.

"At this moment, we must attend to urgent matters in the East. Have you sent for Arbitio?"

"Yes, my lord. He should arrive at any moment. Commander Arbitio is very capable and resourceful. Should he carry out the task you will ask of him, this would make him a strong candidate for the position to govern Gaul."

"Yes, possibly. But I will not think of that now."

A sentry announced the arrival of Arbitio. The tall and slender Arbitio dipped his head beneath the flap of the tent as he entered the imperial quarters. Wearing an armored cuirass over a black tunic, the commander saluted the Emperor. "Hail, Augustus," he said as he took off his black-plumed helmet and held it beneath one arm.

"Good evening, Commander," said Constantius. "Years ago, as a younger officer, you were of some assistance with certain, let us say, *family matters*, when I endeavored to secure the throne in Constantinople after the death of my father."

"I try to be of assistance wherever I can," said Arbitio, a sly smile appearing in one corner of his mouth.

"I need your sort of *assistance*, again," said Constantius. He gestured toward the Grand Chamberlain. "Eusebius, brief the commander on our problem in the East. I get too worked up when I speak of it."

"As you wish, my lord," said Eusebius. He then addressed Arbitio. "In recent months, the Emperor has received several disturbing reports from the East. Gallus, chosen by the Emperor to rule the East as Caesar in his absence, appears to have exceeded his authority. He has deposed various government officials appointed to their posts by the Emperor himself. Some of these, Gallus put on trial on false charges. Some he even put to death. Having emptied these posts of their rightful occupants, Gallus filled them with his own appointments—whose first loyalty will be to him, not the Emperor."

Constantius, red-faced, sprang to his feet. He held high a sheaf of parchments in his hand, waving them back and forth. "A report has reached me that crowds in the Hippodrome have hailed Gallus as *Augustus*. Gallus has even dared to crown the winners of races!" He flung the papers into the air. "These are all titles and privileges reserved to an emperor alone!"

In his fit of anger, Constantius became tongue-tied. He gestured to the eunuch to continue with the briefing.

"The Emperor fears that Gallus—having enjoyed the trappings of imperial power and the acclamations of the people for the last two years—might not relinquish his office as Caesar now that the war in the West is ending. The fear is that Gallus might even declare himself Emperor and Augustus in the East."

The Emperor stood before the map, his hands clenched into fists. "I am on the verge of winning a civil war in the West. I do not care to fight another in the East. However, if I move overtly against Gallus, this might force him into action." He stared into the commander's dark, cold eyes. "Therefore, we must handle this problem in a more delicate, subtle, and indirect manner—one which avoids the possibility of another civil war. Whatever is done, and whenever we do it, it must be done quickly before Gallus suspects, so that he does not have time to rally support of the army in the East. Do you understand my meaning, Commander?"

Arbitio gripped the handle of his sword. "Perfectly."

"I want you to draw up a plan for me to consider," said Constantius. "When Magnentius is defeated for good, we will discuss it. No option is precluded. Do whatever you must in this matter. But, as he is my cousin and the husband of my sister, whatever you do, it must have the semblance of a legal process. I want you to investigate his activities. Interrogate him. Learn the names of all conspirators." The Emperor picked up one of the reports and glanced at it. He then raised his eyes until they met Arbitio's. "Of course, there must be a suitable punishment."

"As you command, sire," said Arbitio.

***

Arbitio poured a wine for Eusebius, who reclined on a couch in the commander's quarters. While Arbitio's tent had a few comforts, such as cushioned chairs and a bed, it was nowhere near as large or as lavish as the Emperor's quarters. In a corner of the tent stood the standards of the Imperial Guard units.

243

"This mission might turn out very well for you," said the Grand Chamberlain. "I have begun to lay the groundwork with Constantius. If you are successful in this mission, higher positions such as the command of Gaul, are bound to be yours."

Arbitio unbuckled his sword belt and prepared to hang it on the stand holding his armor. "Needless to say, as I profit from higher positions obtained through your help, so will you."

The eunuch toasted Arbitio. "I trust you will be generous should the Emperor appoint you Caesar in Gaul. However, we must not forget Claudius Silvanus. He is an ambitious man. I am sure he plans to attain higher office."

The commander drew the sword part way from its scabbard as he held it. "Do not worry. I have not forgotten Silvanus. We will see to him one day, soon enough." He then slid the sword back into the scabbard with one quick thrust.

A sentry keeping watch outside entered the tent. "Commander, Captain Lucius requests an opportunity to speak with you."

"Florentius's aide?" said Eusebius. "An odd hour, isn't it?"

The Commander placed his sword down and picked up a large flask of wine. "Indeed, it is odd. But let us learn what errand Florentius has sent him on." Arbitio addressed the guard. "Very well, send him in."

Moments later, the captain entered without the use of his walking cane. In fact, he did not have it with him at all.

"Thank you for seeing me at this late hour, Commander," said Lucius, as he saluted.

Arbitio poured himself a wine. "Yes, of course, Captain." He then refilled Eusebius's cup. "You know the Grand Chamberlain, of course."

Lucius bowed toward the Emperor's adviser. "I do, sir."

"Could I offer you a wine?"

"No, thank you."

Arbitio took a drink from his cup. "Captain, I have been meaning to congratulate you on your betrothal to the Lady Melissa. You are a fortunate man."

"Thank you, Commander."

"Lucius, what brings you to my tent at this hour? An errand for Florentius? Perhaps a change to the battle plan for tomorrow?"

"No, sir. I am here on my own errand . . . to request a favor for tomorrow."

"A favor?"

"You command the cavalry in tomorrow's battle," said Lucius. He paused as the clicking of armor and heavy footfalls could be heard as a company of legionaries marched down the lane and passed by the tent. "I would like to serve in one of your squadrons."

Arbitio raised an eyebrow. "To serve in my cavalry?"

Lucius nodded. "If we are victorious tomorrow, the war ends. I fear I will lose the chance to experience battle firsthand in this war."

The commander sipped his wine. "Not content with being a staff officer, are you?"

"No, sir," said Lucius.

"I like that—a man not content with his position. But what does Florentius say of this request?"

Lucius hesitated, pressing his lips tight together.

The commander snickered. "Florentius does not know, does he?"

"He does not."

Arbitio glanced at Eusebius. He called to the sentry outside.

"Yes, Commander?" said the sentry, entering the tent.

"Send for Captain Marcus."

The sentry departed as commanded.

Arbitio took another sip of wine. With his dark, soulless eyes he studied Lucius's face. "Why would you not ask Florentius?"

"Because he would say no," interjected Eusebius, who by now had gotten up from the couch. The eunuch stood by the standards of the Imperial Guard and, with a meticulous eye, straightened one that tilted to the side in its stand. "Is that not right, Captain?"

"Yes," said Lucius.

Arbitio moved to within a couple feet of the captain, his slender frame stood several inches above Lucius. "You want my help," said Arbitio. "But why a combat position now? Once the civil war ends, there will be other battles to come against the barbarians in Gaul."

"Yes, but I marry—" Lucius began to say, but he stopped

himself.

"Go on," said Arbitio.

Lucius lowered his shoulders. "I will marry Lady Melissa after this war."

"What does one have to do with the other?"

"I think I understand, Commander," said Eusebius, his face lighting up as some idea dawned on him. Evidently pleased with himself, he grinned. "Lucius wants to prove himself in combat—to prove himself worthy of his bride before they wed."

Arbitio tossed his head back in laughter. "Eusebius, you continue to impress me. For a eunuch, your powers to discern both the existence and intricacies of romance never cease to amaze me." He turned to Lucius. "The Grand Chamberlain is right, isn't he?"

"The Commander may conclude what he may," said Lucius. "But, with all due respect, sir, my reasons are my own."

Arbitio saw Lucius wince in pain as he stood on his bad leg. "What of your leg? I know you have trouble on a horse. Can you ride in battle?"

"The risk is mine, sir."

"True," said Arbitio with a smirk. "You know Florentius and I have not seen eye-to-eye on matters."

"Then you will not help me?"

"I did not say I would not."

At that moment, Captain Marcus Scudillo entered the tent. He saluted. "You sent for me, Commander." Seeing Lucius, a puzzled expression flashed across Marcus's face, which seemed to say, *What are you doing here?*

"Marcus, you are commanding the Imperial Guard's cataphract squadron tomorrow," said Arbitio. "Does the squadron have its full complement of officers?"

"It does," said Marcus.

"What of Silvanus's squadrons?"

"I am aware that the Eagle Squadron is missing several officers due to sickness."

"Excellent," said the commander, finishing his cup of wine. He proceeded to a desk where he scribbled out a note. He handed it to Lucius. "Go now and see Silvanus. I am ordering him to appoint you as officer to his squadron on a provisional basis. He'll see to it that you are given a proper horse and armor."

Marcus glared at Lucius. "What is this about? You—in the cavalry tomorrow? What about your leg? You can barely handle a horse on a casual ride cross-country, how will you manage one in the heat of battle?"

"My leg has been feeling better," said Lucius. He walked over to the standards of the Imperial Guard in the corner of the quarters and back again. Mustering his concentration, he fought to contain any outward sign of pain. "See. It is much improved."

Marcus studied Lucius. "Nonsense. You are stifling the pain. Does General Florentius know about this?"

"No."

"You must let him know at once," said Marcus.

"Quiet, Marcus—that is enough!" interjected Arbitio. He strolled over to the table. Lifting the flask, he topped off his cup. "One takes a fellow officer at his word. If Lucius says his leg is fine, it is fine. Regardless . . . the risk is his." Arbitio turned to Marcus. "Lucius will serve in the Eagle Squadron tomorrow."

Marcus's jaws tightened. "Commander, if I may *respectfully* point out. It is not within your authority to grant such a transfer if Florentius opposes it."

"Do not worry about Florentius," said Arbitio. "I will speak to the Emperor about this." He smiled. "I am confident the Emperor will approve. That is all. Good night, gentlemen."

Eusebius approached Arbitio after the officers had left the tent. He lifted the flask and topped off his wine. "That was nice of you, Commander," he said with a smirk. "I would say, *uncharacteristic*."

"Florentius once spurned my request for the hand of his daughter," Arbitio said. He squinted, his dark eyes and mind seemed fixed on a past encounter. "He laughed at me."

"Ah, revenge is it?"

"You might call it that. If nothing else, I will take pleasure knowing Florentius will be in dread all day wondering what might become of poor Lucius."

The eunuch snickered. He poured another wine for Arbitio. "Or, you might get lucky. Something drastic might happen to the poor captain. He might become Uriah to your David. That would make Lady Melissa—"

The commander raised his cup. "My Bathsheba."

***

Leaving Arbitio's tent, Lucius started off down the camp lane which was bordered by tents on either side. Torches set on high posts every fifty feet lit the way. Even at this late hour when most of the camp slept, legionaries hurried here and there on urgent matters. Following him out, Marcus watched Lucius limp away without his cane. He pulled his black cloak around himself for warmth against the night chill. Out of the corner of his eye, Marcus caught sight of a walking cane leaning against a tent post just outside of Arbitio's quarters. Grabbing it, he hurried after his friend.

"Forget something, Captain?" said Marcus. He held out the cane as he came up alongside his friend. "What was that all about in Arbitio's tent? You in combat? You know Florentius would object to this nonsense."

Lucius took the cane. "That is why he must not know."

Marcus grabbed his friend by the arm. "Your leg was shattered in an accident and never healed properly. You are not fit to ride a horse in battle."

"I will be fine. Arbitio must think so. We'll see what the Emperor says."

"This is about Melissa, isn't it?" asked Marcus. Before him, the lane pointed toward the mountains. A bright, full moon sat above the highest snow-topped peak in the distance. "You think Arbitio or the Emperor will grant your wish out of a kindness? No. Both Arbitio and the Emperor hold a grudge against the general. Each desired Melissa, but it is you who will soon have her hand in marriage."

Lucius tried to break free from his friend's grip but could not. "I have the promise of her hand, but I desire to have her heart, too. I resolved not to take the one without the other. Her husband might have been an emperor. I will not force her to have a cripple."

"Well and good if that is your resolution, but what has that to do with riding with the cataphracts?" asked Marcus. "Do you think great deeds in battle will sway her heart? Repent of this rash decision before it is too late."

"I do not know whether courageous deeds will win her heart," said Lucius. "But I told you in Mediolanum, there are things worth fighting for. Melissa's love is one of those things. I must know I was worthy of it."

Marcus released his grip on Lucius.

"You have been a true friend, Marcus," said Lucius. "I trust you will not breathe a word of this to Florentius."

Marcus hesitated.

"Promise!" said Lucius.

Marcus lowered his eyes. He nodded. "I promise it."

***

The Eastern Roman camp stirred to life an hour before sunrise. Florentius emerged from his tent. A servant stood there holding the reins of the general's saddled horse. The great black stallion pawed at the ground, snorting out cold air.

"Laurentius, have you seen Captain Lucius yet this morning?" asked Florentius as he took the reins from the servant. "It has been the custom for me and Lucius to share a morning meal together. It is not like him to miss it."

"I have not seen the captain this morning," said the servant.

"If you see him, tell him I will wait for him at the assembly area," said Florentius. The general mounted his horse and rode to the Praetorium at the center of the camp. There he saw Lucius near the tent of the Emperor wearing the heavy armor of a cataphract, mounted on an armored-clad horse.

Florentius brought his horse alongside Lucius. "What is the meaning of this?" he said, seeing his aide suited in armor head to toe.

"He is attached to my command for the duration of this battle," said Silvanus as he and Commander Arbitio emerged from the Emperor's tent.

"By whose authority, Silvanus?" asked Florentius with a raised voice. "I was not notified of this!"

Silvanus mounted his horse. He gave no response.

Florentius glared at Arbitio. "You command the cavalry today. This could not be done without your consent."

"The Emperor approved it, just now," said Arbitio.

"How could the Emperor consent to this?" asked Florentius. "I must speak with him!"

Lucius rested his hand on Florentius's forearm as the horses jostled. "It is all right, sir. This is what I wanted. It was my request."

"This is madness, Lucius," said the general. "Your leg."

"I will be fine," said Lucius. "But, if something were to happen, please tell Lady Melissa that I loved her." He saluted the general, then rode off to join his squadron.

Chapter 15

The Battle of Mons Seleucus

Dark clouds filled the early morning sky above the pass and the mountains to the east. Septimus stood at the battlement above the gate, the red crest atop his helmet and his scarlet cloak fluttering in a light breeze. On either side of him, legionaries lined the length of the palisade, two to three men deep. To the blare of horns, the Eastern Roman army of Constantius marched forth from its camp. The Easterners, line after line, advanced to the pounding of drums, the echoes reverberating throughout the pass and mountains like thunder. The Western Legionaries watched, silent and anxious, as thirty thousand enemy soldiers came down the pass like a slow-moving avalanche, passing around small clusters of trees and boulders as it moved.

Longinus walked behind the legionaries at the battlement as the drums grew ever louder. "Courage men," shouted the centurion. "Be of good cheer. They can only kill us."

Septimus observed out of the corner of his eye that Jason, Drusus, and Samson stood behind him. Each of the Ostians wore whatever armor and helmet they could find in the armory for the coming battle. The chainmail shirts were ill-fitting, either too big as in the case of the short Drusus or too small in the case of Samson. The tribune could not help but quirk a smile at the sight. Remembering the orders he had given the night before, Septimus scolded Jason. "Your company is supposed to be with the legionaries held in reserve."

251

"My men are," said Jason, tucking locks of his long dark hair back beneath his loose-fitting helmet.

The tribune raised an eyebrow.

"But you said nothing of me," said Jason said, wearing a mischievous smile.

"Or me," said Drusus.

"Or me," said Samson, as he tried without success to stretch his tight mail shirt down to his waist.

Septimus frowned. "Very well," he muttered as the centurion joined them.

Longinus locked eyes with Drusus. He pointed his thumb at Samson. "Make sure you keep him pointed in the right direction." The centurion glared at Samson. "*Eastern* Romans ... bad guys. *Western* Romans ... good guys. Understand? Remember that."

Samson replied with a single nod and a wink.

Septimus surveyed the deep formations of Eastern infantry, packed together across the breadth of the pass. "This reminds me of the tale of King Leonides at the pass at Thermopylae." The tribune turned to Longinus. "Would you not agree, Centurion?"

The centurion shook his head. He mumbled gruffly under his breath. He ignored the tribune.

Jason nudged the centurion. "Why will you not answer him?"

"I told you before—best not to encourage him," said Longinus. He tied the chin strap of his transverse-crested helmet.

Disregarding the advice, Jason stepped next to the tribune. "What happened to Leonides at Thermopylae?"

Septimus watched the advancing enemy legions. "Herodotus tells us of how Leonides and his three hundred Spartans faced the whole Persian army of King Xerxes at the narrow pass at Thermopylae."

"Their situation sounds like ours. What happened to them?"

There came a shout from a tower. "Riders under a white flag approach!"

Four Eastern Roman officers, with a protective escort of a dozen riders, approached the fortifications. They came to a halt opposite the gate, fifty yards from the edge of the trench.

A messenger came to Septimus. "Tribune Marius, Emperor Magnentius wants you to ride out and meet the enemy delegation."

"There are over a dozen in their delegation," said Septimus. "Does the Emperor wish anyone else to ride out with me?"

"Just you," replied the messenger.

Longinus gave a quick wink to the tribune. "The Emperor can ill afford to send more than one. There are too few of us left."

The messenger handed Septimus a small scroll.

"What is this?" asked the tribune.

"You are to read this to the Eastern delegation," the messenger replied.

Septimus glanced again at the pass filled across its breadth with enemy infantry. He grabbed the note from the messenger. He stared at it, hesitant to open it. *I fear what it might say. I fear what it will not.*

The legionaries standing close by watched him with anticipation as he unrolled it, hoping that battle might be avoided even at this late hour. When Septimus had finished reading the note, the muscles of his jaw grew tight. He lifted his eyes from the note. At once Longinus understood its meaning.

The centurion pushed the eavesdropping legionaries away. "All right, you storks, back to your positions along the battlement!"

"Bring Ulysses to the gate," muttered Septimus.

Septimus descended from the wall, followed by Longinus.

"Lower the drawbridge!" shouted the centurion.

A half dozen legionaries on each side of the gate turned the winches which raised and lowered the bridge. Wide enough for a half a dozen horses to ride across abreast, the heavy drawbridge struck the ground on the other side of the trench with a heavy thud.

A legionary approached and handed the reins of Ulysses to the tribune. The horse's hooves clattered on the thick, wooden planks as Septimus led the gray warhorse over the trench. Longinus accompanied them to the far side.

Septimus placed the scroll within his cloak. He then grabbed hold of the saddle as he prepared to mount. A couple hundred yards away to the right of the gate, he saw the imperial banner atop the wall fluttering in the wind, indicating the spot where Magnentius stood. "The note listed our Emperor's demands for there to be peace," said the tribune.

Longinus shook his head. "Demands? I don't think he is in a position to be making them."

The tribune mounted his horse. "Apparently, Magnentius has calculated on battle being his only chance of personal survival."

The centurion tapped his vine staff against one of his greaves. "Then the die is cast."

"And, unfortunately, *we* are the die."

Longinus brought the vine staff to his forehead in a salute. "Good luck, sir."

Tribune Marius spurred Ulysses forward to a gallop, his scarlet cloak flew high in the air behind him as he raced toward the Eastern delegation which awaited him. When he reached the delegation, the tribune reined in his horse to a quick stop, kicking up clumps of dirt and grass as it came to a halt. A couple hundred yards behind the delegation, the front ranks of the Eastern army stood at the ready, legionary and unit standards raised above the infantry packed into the pass. In the distance up the pass, lightning flashed above the mountaintops.

At once Septimus recognized Florentius and Marcus, who he had encountered at Mursa Major. Seeing Silvanus with them, he squinted with contempt at his one-time friend.

Marcus threw his head back with a mocking laugh. "Tribune Gaius Marius, the last time I saw you, you and your horse had turned tail and run. How was your swim across the Drava?"

"The swim was cooling and refreshing in the heat of the flames," said Septimus. "I hope your Emperor did not choke on the smoke and ashes."

Marcus drew his sword. "How dare you mock the Emperor."

"Captain Scudillo, put away your sword!" said Florentius. "We are under a flag of truce."

Marcus did as ordered. "Tribune, I promise you will be either dead or in chains before this day is done."

Septimus ignored the captain's threat. "Aside from Marcus, I see other faces I remember." He fixed a cold stare on Silvanus. "And, one face I will not allow myself to forget."

Silvanus chuckled. "Septimus Romanus, old friend, are you still holding a grudge against me? Forget what has passed between us. Let bygones be bygones."

"I will not forget you until the death of Marcellinus and the deaths of many Romans are avenged by your blood."

Silvanus smiled. "This will be your last day to attempt your revenge." He studied the wall in the distance behind Septimus. "You cannot like your chances behind a ditch and a palisade."

Florentius cleared his throat. "Allow me to get straight to the point, Tribune Marius. You are a reasonable man. Enough Roman blood has been shed these past two years of civil war. The empire is beset by threats, on all sides. The need, now, is for unity. The Western legions have fought nobly, but they are outnumbered. The course of this war, and its conclusion, can no longer be considered in doubt. Legionaries, of both sides, who might die here this day are needed elsewhere to protect the frontiers of the empire from our common enemies. For the sake of all within the empire, both East and West . . . let us have peace. Urge your emperor to give up his throne and to surrender his diadem. Constantius pledges to treat Magnentius, his officers and the legionaries serving in his army with leniency."

Taking the note given to him by Magnentius, Septimus read it one more time to himself, as if hoping it might now say something different. *Why could Magnentius not offer peace? Allowing us all to go home. Allowing me to go home. To Marciana.* He sat up straight in his saddle, his back stiff. "Emperor Magnentius authorizes me to present these terms to your emperor. Cross back over the Alps whence you came. In the interest of peace, Magnentius will cede Italy to Constantius, while keeping Gaul, Iberia, Britain for himself."

Marcus laughed. "You jest! Magnentius bargains with what is not his to give. Italy already belongs to Constantius."

Florentius lowered his head. "Is that all you have to say, Tribune Marius?"

"Magnentius does not take my counsel," said Septimus. "Alas, the destiny of empires is to suffer from their emperors."

Florentius lifted his head. He saluted Septimus. "So be it. War to the end."

The tribune returned the salute. "Farewell."

Septimus turned and galloped along the outside of the wall toward Emperor Magnentius, who watched from the battlement, to deliver the response of the Eastern delegation. If Magnentius had harbored any expectations that Constantius would accept any terms from him other than surrender, they were soon dashed. Pausing near the trench, across from Magnentius, Septimus pulled the note which bore his emperor's conditions from his cloak. In view of everyone along the wall, he crumpled up the paper and tossed it into the trench. He saluted and rode back across the drawbridge which closed behind him.

Septimus returned to his place on the battlement above the gate. He stared at the mountains that loomed high beyond the deep enemy formations. He longed to cross over them into Italy and to return to Rome. *Marciana.* A blare of enemy horns echoed throughout the mountain pass, recalling Septimus from his momentary daydream. The thunder of drums began again, pounding in unison at a slow and steady pace. Before him, a line of Eastern infantry cohorts marching abreast began to move toward the trench and wall.

Longinus placed his vine staff away in his belt. He drew his sword. "Tribune Marius, I take it negotiations did not go well."

Jason looked out on the wave of infantry coming toward them. He took in a deep, nervous breath and exhaled. "Tribune, you never finished your story. What happened to the three hundred Spartans at the pass at Thermopylae?"

The tribune placed a hand on the Jew's shoulder as if to comfort him. "Killed to the man."

The color drained away from Jason's face.

The centurion shook his head at Jason. "I told you to leave it alone."

Septimus took his shield from a legionary who had brought it to him. He looked to artillery crews behind the palisade who stood at the ready by catapults and ballistae, much larger versions of the scorpion. The large catapults were loaded with hundred-pound stones or piles of hand-sized stones, while the ballistae were loaded with large stones or long bolts. The tribune drew his sword as the enemy cohorts came within four hundred yards of the trench, the drums growing ever louder. Raising the sword high above his head, he brought it down as a signal. "Fire!"

At once, there was the loud groaning of wood and the twang of rope as each piece of artillery in quick succession flung its projectile with a swoosh into a high arc over the palisade. Septimus followed the flight of one of the stones as it flew overhead. It sailed through the air and came crashing down in the midst of an Eastern cohort, killing and maiming infantrymen as it landed and rolled for a couple dozen more feet. The scene was repeated, as other large and hand-sized stones from the first salvo fell upon the densely packed Easterners, inflicting a great number of casualties as the hail of stone rained down upon them.

Still, undeterred, the Easterners kept coming.

"Reload!" shouted Septimus. The artillery crews scrambled to reset their war machines and place into them the heavy ammunition. "Fire at will!"

The artillery fired another salvo but without the same devastating effect as the first. He clenched his teeth. The stones either fell on the last few lines of the infantry or landed without harm behind them as the cohorts sped the pace of their advance to the quickening beat of the drums.

"The enemy is now too close for the catapults and ballistae to safely fire at them over the palisade," advised Longinus.

"Cease fire!" Septimus shouted down to the catapults and ballistae. Seeing the Easterners were now within a couple hundred yards of the palisade, he called out to each of the two towers on either side of the gate. "Scorpions, fire!"

The scorpions launched a salvo of bolts that whistled through the air. Each of the iron-tipped projectiles ripped into the enemy ranks, felling several legionaries at a time who had had the misfortune to be in its line of flight.

"Scorpions, fire at will! Archers, fire at will!" shouted Septimus, as the Easterners drew closer.

Easterners dropped dead or wounded as arrows and scorpion bolts continued to fly into them.

"Still they come," said Jason to Drusus and Samson beside him.

"You did not think we'd get off so easy, did you?" said Longinus, as the front lines of a cohort reached the edge of the trench below them. "Draw your swords. You'll need them, soon enough."

A great war cry went up among the Easterners as they descended into the trench, and then clambered up the opposite bank. As they clawed their way up the incline, they had to contend with sharpened stakes that protruded from the slope. Legionaries who lost their footing or who fell risked being impaled.

Jason, Drusus, and Samson joined their legionary comrades in hurling down rocks and stones upon the enemy from the battlement.

"Push them away from the wall!" shouted Septimus as Easterners brought forward scaling ladders and threw them up against the palisade. He hacked away at an enemy legionary as he came over the top of the battlement. The soldier fell back, plummeting into the trench below. "Do not let them over the walls, lads!"

The tribune glanced to either side to take stock of the situation. *We're keeping them off the walls for now.* His satisfaction melted away. Volley after volley of arrows now flew all around as enemy archers came up to support their infantry by directing their fire at the defenders along the wall. Septimus ducked behind the safety of a parapet. However, several of his legionaries on either side were struck down.

The volleys had the intended effect of keeping the defenders' heads down, giving the enemy precious moments to climb over the battlement in certain places. The tribune heard a heavy thunk on the wooden planks near him. He lifted his head to see the grieves of a legionary facing him. The tribune sprung back to his feet to confront the Easterner. Striking down his foe with an upward thrust to his neck, Septimus then saw that he and the few Western legionaries with him were about to be overwhelmed by the many Easterners who had come over the top of the parapets above the gate. A fierce melee erupted. Perceiving their desperate situation, he called out for help. "Centurion!"

"Whoever dwells in the shelter of the Most High will rest in the shadow of the Almighty," Longinus said in his gruff voice as he dispatched one enemy legionary after the other as he attempted to come to the tribune's aid.

Jason smiled as he heard the centurion over the din of battle. "Psalms?"

The centurion nodded.

"He is my refuge and my fortress, my God, in whom I trust,"

said Jason.

"His faithfulness will be your shield and rampart," said Longinus. An arrow struck the support leg of the tower next to which he stood, just missing his head. The centurion sneered at the missile. "You will not fear the terror of night, nor the arrow that flies by day."

Alongside Jason, Samson and Drusus also threw themselves with gusto into the fight. Samson, who wielded the great sledgehammer he used at Mursa Major, set it down on occasion to pick up and toss enemy legionaries back over the wall, crying aloud, "I hate Romans," while Drusus would correct him: "*Eastern* Romans!"

Septimus saw that a half dozen of the Eastern legionaries who had made it over the battlements near him had jumped to the ground below just inside the gate as more followed them over the wall.

"They are trying to open the gate," shouted Septimus. He leapt down from the battlement into the midst of the Eastern legionaries, heart pounding in his chest. He scrambled to his feet to find himself beset by the enemy legionaries. These tried to get past Septimus to disable the winch that held the drawbridge closed. The tribune fought them off, one after the other, as he guarded the mechanism. However, several more Easterners leapt down from the battlement to reinforce their comrades. A dozen Easterners now stood sneering at Septimus, ready to fall upon him.

There came a loud thud behind the Easterners, who turned around to behold the sight of Samson, having jumped from the wall, wielding his sledgehammer. He charged into them. Shields were shattered and helmets crushed as he swung it back and forth. Other legionaries from Third Italica rushed to the aid of Septimus and Samson. After a brief melee, the winch was once again safe.

Septimus tilted his head back to look up at Samson. "Thanks."

"Like I said, I hate Romans," said Samson with a sneer. A slight trace of a smile appeared on his face. "*Eastern* Romans."

There arose a loud cheer from the battlements above and along the entire wall. Septimus rushed up the ladder to find the battlement controlled by his legionaries. He looked out at the mountain pass. Faced with continual volleys of missiles and the resolve of the defenders along the wall, the Eastern assault had faltered. Enemy trumpets sounded the recall. Another great cheer arose among the Westerners as they watched the Eastern legionaries retreat.

Jason wiped sweat and blood from his brow as he stood beside the tribune. "That went well for us, Tribune," he said, wearing a slight grin. "Perhaps our chances are better than you first suspected. Perhaps you were too pessimistic!"

The tribune paid no mind to Jason, his attention fixed on something in the mountain pass.

"Tribune, what is wrong?" asked the Ostian.

Septimus turned and lunged at him. "Get down!" he shouted as he knocked Jason to the deck of the battlement.

There came a loud thwack and the cracking and splitting of wood, followed by a great whoosh of erupting of flames which shot up ten feet into the air above them. A long missile from an Eastern ballista, wrapped in cloth soaked in a flammable mix, had struck and pierced through the palisade, its iron point penetrating the battlement where Jason had been standing. A fire now raged where it contacted the wall.

Jason scrambled to his feet. Seeing the iron point that would have killed him, he nodded to Septimus. "Thanks."

Stepping away from the flames, Jason glimpsed what the tribune had seen. Several dozen enemy catapults and ballistae sat in a line across the pass about two hundred yards from the trench.

The tribune grimaced. "Under the cover of the first assault, Constantius has brought up his own artillery."

A hundred-pound stone from an Eastern catapult passed over the wall near where they stood. Shaving off the top of the wall, it pulverized the legionary who stood behind the parapet in a mist of blood. Other stones followed.

"Look out!" shouted Septimus to Longinus who stood on the battlement below the tower to the right of the gate.

A giant stone smashed into the tower, sending the whole thing toppling over and its occupants flying through the air. A roar of approval rose from the Eastern army at the lucky shot.

Septimus looked for Longinus, but both he and the portion of the battlement where he had stood were gone. Septimus felt as if a sword had pierced him. "Centurion!" he shouted. Below, there was a heap of broken and shattered timber which had once been the tower and the upper half of the palisade.

The tribune climbed down the ladder, leaping the last several rungs to rush over to the jumbled heap. He began to assist other legionaries of Third Italica who were already at work, lifting away timber and sifting through the rubble, searching for survivors. Even as they worked, stones and flaming projectiles continued to strike the palisade and sail over it. Flames began to rise from the remaining portion of the palisade beside the debris of the tower.

"Centurion!" Septimus called out as he desperately pulled away at the timber.

A dozen legionaries were pulled from the pile, among them the dead and the wounded.

The tribune lowered his head. *He's dead.*

"I found him," said Samson, several yards away as he lifted and threw aside several heavy planks of wood. Grabbing an outstretched arm covered in blood, he helped the centurion to his feet.

Longinus took off his helmet, which sat crooked on his head. He traced a dent in the top of it with his fingers. He picked out a couple of long splinters caught in his transverse crest. The centurion put on the helmet and fastened it about his chin. Samson stood nearby, seeming to expect something from him. Longinus glared at him. "Well, don't expect me to thank you."

"You're alive," said the Septimus with a sigh of relief.

"You miss me already, Tribune?" said Longinus. "Don't get weepy on me."

Septimus picked up the centurion's vine staff which lay on the ground. He handed it to Longinus. "Miss a legionary as insubordinate as you? It's just that a good First Centurion is hard to find these days." He observed the centurion's bloody forearm. "Are you all right?

Longinus looked at this arm and the blood trickling down it. "This? Just a scratch."

Father Paul hurried over from another wounded legionary and began to wrap the centurion's arm in a bandage. The priest nodded to Septimus. "He will be fine, Tribune."

Another portion of the wall ten yards away caved inward as it was struck by a flaming projectile. A few of the storehouse buildings behind the palisade were ablaze.

"We must wait out the barrage," said Septimus. "Centurion, have the men fall back."

"Fall back!" shouted Longinus. "Get the men off the walls!"

The call was taken up by the other centurions of the legion. "Fall back!"

***

The tribune stood grim-faced with Longinus. He watched the dead and wounded carried away. Father Paul moved from one to another as they were set down out of harm's way, giving absolution and blessings as he went.

"What do you figure our causalities to be?" asked Septimus.

"Perhaps a quarter of our strength at the wall," said Longinus. "One hundred and fifty men. Half of them dead."

The tribune faced the inside of the wall. Large fires raged at various points along the entire length of the wall. The bombardment of stone and fire, still underway, had made several breaches in the palisade in Third Italica's sector.

"They've been at it with the catapults for half an hour," said Septimus.

Longinus observed the damage to the walls. "They will resume the attack as soon as they lift the barrage."

Septimus replied with a grim nod. "Or advance under cover of it." He ran toward the wall, dodging falling debris and projectiles as he did.

Longinus shook his head. The centurion followed the tribune, catching up to him as he reached the ladder to the battlement. "What do you think you are doing?"

"I need to see what is happening," said Septimus as he scaled the ladder to the battlement. Once on top, he placed his cloak over his mouth as he tried not to breathe in the billowing smoke. He squinted along the length of the wall, both to his right and left as Longinus joined him. The flames and smoke made it difficult to discern much beyond fifty yards in either direction. "It appears all of the towers are destroyed or in flames."

Tribune Marius peered over the parapet. Two enemy cohorts, one behind the other, neared the trench in front of him. "As I feared. They advanced under cover of the barrage." He turned to Longinus. "Centurion, go and order the men back forward."

Longinus hurried down the ladder and ran back to the legionaries waiting a hundred feet behind the palisade. He was gone but a few moments when the barrage from the catapults and ballistae lifted.

Septimus stood and waved to his men. "To the walls!"

A horn sounded in the distance to signal the enemy attack. A war cry rose from the Easterners.

The tribune watched, helpless, as Eastern legionaries charged into the trench below him. Engineers and sappers also piled fascines into it, building makeshift bridges of planks. Once across the trench, Eastern legionaries again used scaling ladders to climb to the top of the palisade.

Septimus drew his sword. He cut down the first Easterner who came over the top of the parapet. The enemy legionaries following him up the ladder were knocked off as the body fell back into the trench. The tribune rushed to another spot yards away where more Easterners succeeded in topping the parapet. He charged into them. Pushing one off the battlement with his shield, he sliced another across the neck. But, just as Septimus was surrounded on all sides, Jason, Drusus, and Samson along with a dozen legionaries came to his aid.

Samson cleared the way to Septimus with his hammer, then with the end of it, pushed a ladder away from the parapet. Easterners tried to jump to safety as it fell back, but several of them were impaled on the stakes below as they landed.

"Thanks again," said Septimus with a nod as his men regained control of the battlement. However, down below, the tribune at once saw a different story. Flames and smoke were all around. A thin line of legionaries from Third Italica was engaged in a desperate melee to contain the tide of Easterners coming through narrow breaches in the wall. "Stay at the parapets," Septimus ordered.

"Of course," said Jason, as he ran his sword through a foe. "But where are you going?" he asked, but no sooner had he spoken then the tribune leapt off the battlement into the melee below. The Ostian looked below as Septimus landed on top of a packed mass of Easterners coming through a gap in the wall, bringing them all to the ground.

"Okay, I'll stay here then," muttered the Ostian to himself. "At the parapets."

The tribune scrambled to his feet, smiting any of the enemy who came within his reach. "Hold fast, men!" he called out to his legionaries. Though the defenders slew many of the Easterners, the enemy kept coming through the breaches in the wall.

"We can't hold them, Tribune!" said the centurion named Petronius.

Septimus glanced about. Westerners and Easterners all mixed in a chaotic battle. His men outnumbered. *He's right. It is hopeless.* Then, he glimpsed the flashing glint of gold bathed in sunlight, the reflected rays piercing through the smoke.

"The labarum!" shouted a Third Italica legionary near to the tribune.

Then Septimus saw the Chi Rho of the labarum, carried by Cornelius. The banner bearing the image of the infant Jesus and his Mother billowed in the swirling breeze. Beside it was the standard of the Third Italica. *Longinus and the reserves!*

A cheer went up from the sorely pressed legionaries around Septimus. This was followed by a blare of a horn and loud war cry as Longinus and the reserve force of several hundred men crashed into the Easterners. Surprised by the unexpected appearance of reinforcements, the Easterners panicked and began to fall back, but were cut down as they attempted to flee back through the breaches.

The tribune met the centurion in the midst of the fighting.

"Well done, Centurion!" said Septimus. "You brought up the reserves just in time."

"We've beaten them—for now," said Longinus. "They will return."

The enemy was no match for the fresh and seasoned reinforcements of the Third Italica, which drove them back against the inside of the palisade and slaughtered them nearly to the man.

Septimus coughed. He covered his mouth again with part of his cloak. The din of battle and roar of flames sounded all around as thick clouds of smoke drifted past. "I cannot see how the fight goes elsewhere." He glanced up at the battlement and saw things were well in hand there. One of the last of the Easterners stood at a parapet waving his legion's standard in frantic desperation, signaling for reinforcements. However, Samson seized the standard with one hand, and the enemy legionary in the other, and threw both to the ground far below.

Longinus ran to the gate. "Tribune, come see!"

Septimus followed the sound of the centurion's voice through a bank of smoke. He found Longinus standing before an open gate. The drawbridge was down, laying across the trench.

"Raise it at once!" ordered the tribune.

Longinus held a length of frayed rope. "Don't bother. It cannot be raised." He watched as a couple dozen of the surviving Easterners retreated, scattering across the field. "They cut it down to escape."

Septimus turned to see the winch was broken beyond repair—destroyed by the last of the Easterners—causing the drawbridge to fall across the trench.

The centurion threw the rope to the ground. "It would take a full day to repair this."

The tribune grimaced. "A day which we do not have." Septimus strode across the drawbridge, joined by Longinus and Jason, each covering their mouths from the thick smoke with their cloaks. The tribune tried but could not see the enemy lines in the distance. "With all this smoke, the enemy has not yet seen the gate is open wide to them."

***

Wearing a helmet and cuirass of gold over a purple tunic, Constantius observed the battle mounted upon a white warhorse. To his left were Florentius and Marcus, and to his right Arbitio and Silvanus. A red banner with the imperial eagle flew over their heads. Two squadrons of cataphracts stood at the ready on either side of Constantius. Behind them, over twenty thousand infantrymen formed in squares by cohort and legion.

265

Florentius, the blue plume of his helmet swaying in the wind, beheld the scene five hundred yards in front of them. Flames and smoke rose both from and behind most of the palisade which blocked the mountain pass. Through the banks of smoke, Eastern cohorts could be seen pressing the attack across the trench at both ends of the wall. "It is just a matter of time before the infantry assault overwhelms them," said Florentius.

"They do not have the numbers to long resist," said Silvanus. "We will break through soon enough."

"When we break through, we can run them down with the cavalry and slaughter the lot," said the Emperor, clapping his hands together in satisfaction. "I do not want any to escape. The war ends today."

"The infantry appears to be making headway on each flank," said Florentius.

Constantius leaned forward in his saddle, squinting. "Yes, but what of the attack in the middle? On the gate? I can't make out much in the haze of smoke."

"I saw the infantry enter through the breaches," said Marcus. "But I see no sign of them now."

"Sire, we should send forward another legion," said Florentius.

A rider galloped up to the Emperor. "Sire, the gate is open, and the drawbridge is down! One of our legionary standards was seen waving atop the battlement above the gate."

"Excellent!" said Constantius, wearing a wide grin. "Then we have broken through. We must have them on the run. Send in a squadron of cataphracts."

"My lord, isn't that premature?" asked Florentius. "Should we not first send in a legion?"

"Not at all, general," said Constantius. "You are too timid at times. The gate is down. The infantry has signaled to us. The enemy must be fleeing." He twisted in his saddle to face Silvanus. "Silvanus, send in one of your squadrons. They finished the job at Mursa Major. Sound the charge."

"As you command, O Emperor," said Silvanus, who rode off to the squadron closest to his right. "Eagle Squadron! Advance through the gate. Cut down the enemy as they flee! Sound the charge."

"The Eagle Squadron?" muttered Florentius to himself. A knot formed in his stomach. *Lucius is attached to that squadron.* He glanced at Marcus.

"Don't worry," whispered Marcus. "Lucius will be fine."

***

Septimus stood with Longinus and Jason at the end of the drawbridge. Their armor smeared with blood, their faces covered in sweat and darkened by ash. "It is just a matter of time before they see the gate open."

Jason held his hand to the air. "The wind is changing." The air about them began to clear. He pointed toward the enemy lines up the mountain pass. There was a glint of armor from the rays of the sun poking through the clouds. "Look! More infantry coming our way. Five hundred yards."

Longinus shook his head. "It is moving too fast to be infantry."

"No, not infantry," said the tribune. "Cataphracts."

The centurion spit. "Wonderful."

The tribune squinted. "They bear the colors of the Eagle Squadron." He looked at the centurion. "The squadron that killed Marcellinus at Mursa Major."

"That will inspire the lads at least!" said Longinus.

Septimus and Longinus ran back across the drawbridge, the tribune issuing orders to the centurion as they did. Septimus paused at the gate as Longinus continued onward to rally the Third Italica for the impending attack. The tribune looked back to see Jason standing at the end of the bridge as if in a trance, watching the cataphracts as they drew closer. "Get him!" he shouted to Drusus and Samson.

The two Ostians ran across the trench and each grabbed him beneath the arm. "Jason, come on!" said Drusus and Samson. They carried him back and let him down beside Septimus, who then hustled off to join his legionaries.

"Tribune, where do you want my company?" asked Jason, as he hurried along next to Septimus.

"Your men are not equipped to take on cataphracts," said Septimus. "Get behind my men."

"We want to fight," said Drusus.

"These are cataphracts! Rider and horse covered head to foot in armor! Do not be foolish! Form up behind my men."

"No more behind the lines," said Samson, who, towering over the tribune, glared down at him.

With no time to argue, Septimus locked eyes with Jason. "You want a place in this battle?"

Jason nodded.

"It is dangerous."

"We will do it," replied Drusus.

"Come along then," said the tribune, explaining his idea to Jason as they ran along together.

The Eastern cataphracts, advancing 'til now at a slow trot, were but a hundred yards from the gate. Inside the wall, Third Italica had formed a crescent formation, several ranks deep, a hundred feet behind the gate.

"Steady, lads—they can only kill us!" shouted the centurion, as the echo of hoofbeats and the click of rattling armor grew louder. Glimpses of shining armor were seen through breaks in the smoke.

Septimus pulled forth his sword and held it high above his head. "For Marcellinus!"

"Marcellinus!" shouted the legionaries among whom word had spread like lightning that they faced the Eagle Squadron, responsible for the death of their beloved general at Mursa Major.

The squadron of mounted cataphracts, two hundred men strong, riding five abreast sped to a full gallop. The clattering of the horses upon the drawbridge reverberated like thunder as they crossed it.

"Third Italica!" shouted Septimus.

"Ready!" responded the formation as they interlocked shields.

The cataphracts emerged through the gate. They leveled their spears, ready to smash into and through the thin ranks of legionaries.

"Pia!" yelled Longinus.

"Fidelis!" came the thundered reply. Legionaries leveled their spears at the charging cataphracts. On that same signal, the center of the front rank of legionaries moved aside, revealing a giant ballista pointed into the formation of onrushing men and horses.

"Fire!" commanded the tribune.

The giant bolt leapt forward through the air with a loud, terrifying whoosh. It smashed into the column of cataphracts, ripping through armor, flesh, and bone—of man or horse—which was in its path, one behind the other. Riders and horses struck by the missile toppled over while others collided with and toppled over the fallen. Several dozen riders and their horses collapsed to the ground in a heap. Carried on by its momentum, the column continued on into the line of shields and spears. The legionary line buckled but held firm, absorbing the shock of the charge.

"Attack!" shouted the tribune. The Third Italica's battle horn blared. The wings of the crescent line closed in on both of the flanks of the cataphracts. A company of legionaries hidden just inside of the wall attacked the enemy from the rear. To the horror of the cataphracts, the greatest surprise came from beneath them. Jason's men had taken up positions lying flat in the network of shallow drainage ditches behind the wall. They had covered themselves with the shields of the fallen to protect themselves from being trampled by the horses during the charge. At the sound of the horn, they sprang up from beneath the cataphracts and their mounts. Jason's men stabbed and slashed away at the exposed underbellies of the horses which were unprotected by the armor covering only the neck, back, and flanks of the animals. Tormented by their wounds, many of the horses fell over with their riders or bucked them in their agony.

Attacked from all sides and below, the cataphract casualties mounted. The legionaries jabbed at riders with their spears while others grabbed at them and pulled them down off their horses. Riders, toppled off their mounts, were surrounded and hacked to death. Shouts of "Marcellinus!" and "Mursa!" were heard through the din of the melee, as the legionaries took their revenge. A blood-soaked mass of armor and flesh, men and horses mixed, lay in heaps. Not a man of the cataphracts survived. A few dozen riderless horses were all that remained of the once mighty cataphract squadron. The aquilifer raised the standard of the legion up high. The legionaries rallied at once around it with cheers and shouts of victory.

Septimus walked through the midst of his men. "Marcellinus

would be proud of you." He found Jason, covered with blood and gore, watching Drusus tend to a wounded Samson.

"You all right?" Septimus asked.

Samson nodded.

Tribune Marius patted Samson on his shoulder. "You got your chance to fight Romans."

Samson glared at the tribune. "More horses than Romans."

Septimus smiled. "Yes, but they were *Roman* horses were they not?"

Samson laughed. "That they were, Tribune—that they were."

"Tribune Marius, come see this!" shouted Longinus from the battlement. Septimus scaled the ladder to join him. "The enemy has breached the wall in several places," said the centurion, a grave expression on his face.

Septimus surveyed the situation across the smoke-filled landscape. "While Third Italica has been engaged in a desperate fight here, the Easterners have overrun other sections of the wall. The army has been routed."

The two watched as Eastern infantry and cavalry, pouring through the wall about a couple hundred yards from where they stood, pursued Western legionaries who had fled.

Longinus pointed to flames and columns of smoke rising from the Western camp to the rear. "The enemy has entered the camp," he said matter-of-factly. His line-filled face betrayed no emotion. "For the moment they are more concerned with taking their share of the booty from the camp than with us."

"The pass behind us is now blocked," said Septimus. He looked over the battlement toward the east. A large column of soldiers, several hundred yards distant, marched toward the gate. "There is neither hope for relief nor the possibility of escape for Third Italica."

The two men climbed down from the wall. As Septimus walked amidst the carnage, he came upon one of his legionaries about to finish off a wounded cataphract discovered alive. The tribune grabbed hold of the legionary's forearm. "Stay that sword!" he commanded. He took the sword from him and dropped it to the ground. "There has been enough killing for today."

Septimus knelt beside the cataphract, his chest and side bloodied

270

by grievous wounds. He took off the soldier's helmet. The tribune's head jerked back.

"You know him, sir?" said Longinus.

Septimus nodded. "His name is Lucius. He could have run me through with his sword the night I brought the body of Marcellinus back to the river. He let me go."

"His wound is mortal."

The centurion handed a flask of water to Septimus. As the tribune held it to the lips of the wounded man, he observed Lucius fixated on a point beyond him. Septimus turned to see the aquilifer standing several yards away with the Labarum.

"He sees the Chi Rho and the banner," the tribune muttered to himself. "He is a Christian." He lifted his head and looked among his legionaries. "Father Paul!" he shouted.

The priest came at once and knelt beside the dying cataphract, Septimus only hearing parts of the whispered prayer. "May God give you pardon and peace. I absolve you from your sins in the name of the Father and of the Son and Holy Spirit."

When Father Paul had finished with his blessing, Lucius coughed up blood. Grabbing Septimus by his cloak, the dying man pulled the tribune closer to him with what little strength he had left. "Promise. Rescue her."

"Who?" asked Septimus.

Longinus shook his head. "He is delirious, Tribune."

The wounded man grasped Septimus's hand with his own bloodied one. "Promise! You will rescue her."

Septimus nodded to Lucius to ease his mind. "Yes. I promise. I will rescue her."

"God bless . . ." said Lucius, but his voice trailed off as he breathed his last.

"He's dead, Tribune," said Father Paul. The priest placed his hands over the cataphract's face and closed his eyes. He said a silent prayer and blessed Lucius once again.

Septimus removed the bloodied hand from his cloak. He stood and waved to his attendant to bring forth Ulysses. "The battle is over. The war too." He unbuckled his sword belt and handed it to Longinus. "I will not be needing this." Grabbing the legionary standard of the Third Italica away from the aquilifer, he mounted

271

his horse.

The centurion furrowed his brow. He grabbed the bridle of the horse. "And where do you think you are going?"

"These men have done all I have ever asked of them from the first day I took command of them. I can ask no more of them. I intend now to save them if I can."

"What are you suggesting?"

"I mean to surrender."

The centurion scowled. "Do you think Constantius will show any mercy?"

"Constantius may not spare Third Italica for the sake of mercy. He will spare them because he needs legionaries. Good ones. The Emperor has fewer of them today than when this war started. He will need as many good soldiers as he can find to defend his one empire now."

"And what of your fate?"

"It is beyond a hope of retrieving."

"There is always hope," said Father Paul.

"Not for me . . . not now," said Septimus. "Surrender is the only way to save the men now."

Longinus saluted the tribune and extended his hand toward him.

Septimus shook the centurion's hand. The tribune winked. "But who knows, Longinus, perhaps in God's inscrutable design, He may yet have use for me."

"His will be done," said Father Paul as he made a sign of the cross in the air, blessing the tribune.

"Amen," muttered Longinus under his breath.

The tribune turned Ulysses around to face the legionaries of Third Italica who had now gathered near him. "Legionaries of Third Italica, you have fought gallantly this day. But neither duty, nor honor, nor affection requires more of you. You have done all that has been asked of you. Hold your heads high. You have done all that is within your power to do—no more can be asked of any man. Here is my last command to you. Obey it with the loyalty and faithfulness befitting a legionary of Third Italica." The tribune surveyed the sweat-, blood-, and ash-covered faces of the legionaries around him. "Lay down your arms."

The legionaries made no move. Not one dropped a weapon.

Instead, there were shouts of "We will not lay down our arms," and "We will fight with you 'til the death." The legionaries grew silent as Septimus looked out upon them.

Longinus slapped his vine-staff against the side of one of his grieves, breaking the silence. "All right, you storks, you heard your tribune!" he shouted, his tone gruff and firm. He strode through the midst of the legionaries pulling swords and spears from their hands as he went. "Lay down your weapons as you were ordered! The tribune is watching!"

Urged on by Longinus and the other centurions, the legionaries complied with the order and dropped their weapons and shields.

The tribune sat straight in this saddle. He gave a parting salute.

"Pia!" yelled one of the legionaries.

"Fidelis!" the rest shouted.

***

"Victory!" said Constantius as he surveyed the sight before him. His legionaries poured through the breaches in the palisade. Smoke rose from the enemy camp beyond the wall. A half-hour before, he had watched as a squadron of his cataphracts galloped through the gate. Now, at the head of a great column of infantry and cavalry, the Emperor and his officers approached the drawbridge. His generals congratulated the Emperor on his victory as they went.

"My lord, look!" said Marcus.

Constantius raised his hand, bringing the column to a halt.

Fifty yards ahead, a solitary rider emerged through the smoke that drifted over the gate and drawbridge. He pulled along a second horse with a lifeless body lying across it. Carrying the legionary standard of the Third Italica, he stopped before the Emperor and his entourage.

The rider, his face and uniform covered in soot and blood, saluted. "Hail, Constantius, Augustus et Imperator. Tribune Gaius Marius Septimus at your service."

Constantius responded with a single nod. He frowned at the sight of the legionary standard of Third Italica.

"Lord Emperor and Augustus, congratulations on your victory this day," Septimus said. "While most defenders have fled, yielding

273

the field of battle to you, great Augustus, the Third Italica stood its ground. But now, seeing that victory is beyond reasonable hope of retrieval and that further combat is futile, the legionaries of the Third Italica have laid down their arms and hereby surrender themselves voluntarily into your custody and to your mercy." He leaned forward on his horse and planted Third Italica's legionary standard into the ground.

Silvanus, who rode beside the Emperor, chuckled. "Septimus Romanus, you say you surrender voluntarily? I expect my Eagle Squadron had something to do with it."

Septimus squinted at Silvanus. "They are all dead."

"Impossible."

The tribune produced the crumpled, bloodied pennant of the squadron. He threw it to the ground at the feet of Silvanus's horse. "Consider it partial payment for the death of Marcellinus."

Florentius, seeing the body across the horse behind the tribune, gasped. "Lucius!" he shouted. He dismounted and ran to inspect the body.

Septimus turned around to Florentius. He grimaced at the sight of the general resting his head against the body. "He fought bravely. If it be of comfort to you, he died in peace—attended by a Christian priest."

Constantius looked at the bloodied pennant on the ground. His face grew red. "A whole squadron of cataphracts, lost!" he shouted. "Take the standard from him!"

Silvanus rode up beside the tribune and pulled the standard from the ground. He glared at Septimus. "I told you, did I not, this would be your last day to collect full payment," he said. Silvanus struck the tribune across the side of the head with the hilt of his sword and his armored glove. Septimus tumbled off of Ulysses. He lay sprawled out on the ground, motionless.

Marcus dismounted. He strode over to where Septimus lay. Seeing the corpse of Lucius, he kicked the tribune and spat upon him. "Surrender accepted!"

Chapter 16

The Road to Arelate

In the early morning darkness, Septimus led Ulysses across the gangway from the quay to a barge where a crewman took the reins of the horse. A thick mist rose over the riverbank, its wispy tendrils creeping across the deck. The tribune wrapped his cloak about himself. Urgent hoofbeats and the roll of carriage wheels against the pavement sounded from the street above. They came to a halt, replaced by the soft tap of feet running down the steps, and then toward the gangway.

A woman's voice pierced the mist. "Septimus!"

"Marciana!" the tribune called out. He stepped toward the gangway to go ashore, but a hand grabbed hold of him by the forearm.

"The pilot is impatient to get underway," said the centurion Longinus. "We cannot delay long."

Septimus pulled his arm free and crossed back to the quay where he fell into the arms of Marciana. "My love, what are you doing here?" he asked. The two shared a long kiss. He pulled his head back to gaze into her eyes. "We agreed to say our final farewells last night."

Marciana nodded. "I know. I am sorry. But I had to see you once more."

He pulled her close. He listened for a moment to the peaceful sound of the river lapping up against the shore. "Now our parting will be more difficult." He kissed her once more. "But all the more special."

"Blame me if an agreement between two lovers was broken," came a male voice out of the mist, a few yards behind Marciana. The man stepped forward.

Septimus smiled. "Leontius!"

"It was I who brought Marciana," said Leontius. "She was inconsolable last night when you parted. A promise to bring her this morning was all I could do to bring a smile to her face."

The tribune reached out his arm and placed a hand on his friend's shoulder. "There is no one to blame, old friend. It strengthens my heart so see her one more time. Thank you."

"Tribune Marius—we must get underway!" called out Longinus, unseen from the barge.

Marciana held Septimus close. She pressed the side of her head against his chest. "Marry me before you leave!"

"There is no time," said Septimus.

The clanking of an iron chain echoed in the darkness as the crew raised the anchor. "Ready to cast off!" came a shout from the pilot.

"Tribune—we must go!" shouted Longinus.

Septimus kissed Marciana. He wiped the tears from her eyes. "You will be wed the day I return to Rome. I promise."

"Tribune!" came the shout again from the barge.

Marciana embraced Septimus as if she would never let him go. The mist enveloped them both, and all became darkness. The tribune could see nothing. He could only hear the urgent, repeated call of "Tribune . . . Tribune . . . Tribune!"

The mist and darkness dissolved slowly. First, there came a dim, blurry light. It grew into the brightness of a clear day, lit by a midafternoon sun.

"Tribune!"

Septimus opened his eyes, only able to manage a narrow squint. He grimaced in pain. His head pounded as he felt his physical surroundings rattling and vibrating around him.

"Tribune Marius, wake up."

Septimus rolled his head toward the voice. It was Father Paul beside him, tending to a wound on the tribune's temple. The light hurt the tribune's eyes. "It was only a dream?" Septimus muttered in despair, rolling his head to the side. "I thought I had seen her again. Spoken to her. Touched her." His shoulders sagged. "You have been unconscious for quite a long time," said Father Paul as he cleaned the gash in the tribune's scalp.

Septimus groaned. *I have lost her again.* He was not on a barge at all but instead inside a large prison wagon filled with a dozen other wounded men. On the road behind it, long lines of prisoners chained together, tired and ragged, shuffled along. Eastern legionaries kept watchful eyes on the prisoners, whipping and beating those who lagged or fell to the ground.

The tribune winced with every bump the wheels went over, which shook and rattled the cage. He sat up and leaned back against the bars. Across from him sat Jason, his tunic in tatters and covered with ash and blood. "My head hurts."

The Ostian smiled. "We thought you were a dead man."

Septimus flinched as the wagon went over another bump. "I am not sure I am not."

Jason managed a slight grin. "You took quite a blow to your head."

"It is good to hear you speak again," said Father Paul. "Do you remember anything? What are your last memories?"

Septimus paused as he tried to remember. "I am not sure. Bits and pieces. A battle. Smoke. Cataphracts." The tribune's eyes widened. "Silvanus!" he said. Septimus turned toward the priest. "The traitor of Mursa Major. He is the last one I remember seeing. After that . . . darkness."

Septimus tried to raise a hand to his head, but his arm felt weighed down. He glanced down at his hands. Heavy iron manacles were fixed around his wrists and linked together by a chain. Weak and in pain, he raised both hands and felt where Silvanus had struck him. He grimaced as he touched the black bruise. He touched around his left eye, which was almost swollen shut.

The priest pressed a blood-soaked rag to the tribune's head. "He nearly killed you."

"How long have I been out?" asked Septimus.

"Several days," said Father Paul.

277

Septimus looked at Jason. "The battle? Lost?"

Jason nodded.

"Yes, it is coming back to me now," said Septimus. "What of Magnentius?"

"They say he ended up taking his own life, along with his brother."

Septimus shook his head. "He left his men behind to their fate. Deserted by the one for whose cause they had fought and sacrificed all." The tribune watched the countryside as the wagon rolled along. A thinned-out forest lay on his left and rolling hills of cultivated land with scattered villas lay on his right. "So that is it, then. The war is over. All was in vain." He glanced back at the Alps receding in the distance behind the wagon. His shoulders slumped. *I will never see Marciana again.* "All is lost." He turned to the priest. "What of Longinus and the Third Italica?"

Father Paul shrugged. "Captured—that is all we know. They were alive when we last saw them back at Mons Seleucus. As for us, I believe they mean to put us all on trial."

Septimus coughed as he tried to laugh. "What is your crime, Father? Being a priest?"

Paul nodded. "A Catholic priest. A Nicene priest. If I were an Arian, Constantius would set me free."

The tribune's smile melted away. "Tell them you are one—an Arian. Gain your freedom. Do not suffer the fate that awaits me."

Father Paul folded his hands together. "Pia Fidelis, Tribune . . . remember? Loyalty and fidelity. The Christian must be faithful to the truth."

The tribune turned to Jason. "What is your crime?"

"I am a leader of Jews who revolted against Constantius and Gallus," said Jason.

"And your company of men—where are they? Samson? Drusus?"

Jason pointed at the long lines of prisoners trudging along the road behind them. "Back there. Somewhere. In chains and shackles."

The tribune lowered his head. "I am sorry."

"Sorry for what?" asked Jason.

"I should have forced you to leave on the eve of battle. You and

278

your men would be safe if I had. They would be free."

"Nonsense, Tribune! Do not reproach yourself. Remember? Pia Fidelis. As the priest said. Loyalty and fidelity. There are no guarantees of a happy life or ending in this world. My men and I did what we had to do—just like you, the priest, the First Centurion, and your legionaries did. We all could have run on the eve of battle. If we had, we might have been safe, but never really free. We would forever wear the invisible shackles of our shame, cowardice, and faithlessness." Jason held up his wrists, gripping the chains of his shackles to show them to Septimus. He rattled them. "I would not exchange these real shackles for such invisible ones— they would have been a heavier burden."

A half-smile appeared on the tribune's pained face. "Pia Fidelis."

Jason nodded. "Yes. Pia Fidelis."

"Where will they take us, Tribune?" asked the priest.

Septimus surveyed the countryside, with its villas and fields rolling past, the mountains in the distance behind them, and the shadows of the sun. "We are heading southwest. They are taking us to Arelate."

Chapter 17

The Gates of Hell

(Caesarea Philippi)

"This way, my prince," said Maximus from beneath the hood of his scarlet cloak. "We are close. It is but a short distance from Caesarea Philippi." It was after midnight, well into the third watch, as Julian made his way along a pathway alongside Maximus and Priscus. Julian could see little of the world around them. The only light for them on their darkened way was a torch carried by Priscus. Above them, brooding storm clouds hid the heavenly bodies from sight.

A flash of lightning illuminated the landscape, revealing they were a few hundred feet from the base of a cliff. The enormous rock was over a hundred feet high and a couple hundred yards across. Three temples of white marble abutted the rock face.

"Behold the great Sanctuary of Pan!" said Maximus. "Long ago, the Greeks called the nearby city at the foot of Mount Hermon *Paneas* after the god of the shrine." He led them up a short flight of travertine steps to a terrace level upon which the three temples sat. He took them toward the structure on their right. "There is the Temple of Pan." The building loomed as a tall, vague shape in the darkness, beyond the reach of the light. Between it and them lay a small courtyard behind a crumbled wall. In its center stood a life-sized statue of Pan playing a flute and, beside it, another statue of a dancing goat. Pillars, here and there, lay across the terrace, felled by earthquakes long ago. Grasses grew through cracks in paving

280

stones and vines, wild and unkempt, crept up the side of the walls.

Julian pulled his dark cape about his shoulders. "No one has been here for years," he whispered. The snap of a branch came from the tree line, drawing his attention. His heart raced. Julian gripped the dagger on his belt. *Have we been followed?*

"Man has neglected the gods," said the gray-robed Priscus, sweeping the torch before them, revealing the debris strewn all around.

Maximus guided Julian and Priscus away from the courtyard, keeping the cliff face to their right.

Julian paused as they drew near the middle of the three temples. "What is this temple?"

Maximus pulled the scarlet hood back from his head. "The Temple of Pan and Zeus."

The prince took a few steps for a closer look. He fiddled with the point of his beard. *Is this the temple we are to enter?* He felt a hand on his forearm. It was Maximus.

The philosopher gestured to their left. "This way."

The three proceeded to the western end of the sanctuary. The flickering light of the torch revealed niches carved into the rock. Statues of various gods had once been placed into these, but several now stood empty—shattered stone on the ground beneath the niches being all that remained of them. Maximus, Priscus, and Julian came to a white marble temple, fifty feet long and thirty feet wide at its base, that appeared built into the rock behind it. A short flight of steps led to a portico with four columns.

"The Augusteum—the Temple of Caesar Augustus," said Maximus as they climbed the steps. "Built in the days of Phillip the Tetrarch."

When they reached the top, a shadow emerged from behind a column. Julian gasped. He reached for his dagger as the shadow moved closer.

Priscus grabbed the prince's wrist to keep him from drawing forth the weapon. "It is the watchman."

After exchanging whispered words with Maximus, the watchman opened the bronze doors of the temple to them. The doors creaked and groaned like mournful spirits from the underworld.

The men stood within the entrance. Before them, in the apse of the temple, stood a life-sized statue of Augustus. A brazier on a tripod stood on each side of the statue, their flames lighting it. The figure of Augustus once painted to appear lifelike, now, after the passage of centuries and lack of upkeep, appeared a pale ghost beneath the faded and ragged purple robes draped around him.

As Maximus guided them forward, Julian looked to the side altars dedicated to deities of the Old Religion. Though the light from the torch did not penetrate the shadows to reveal the statues, it reflected off of their eyes, which followed Julian as he passed— or so it seemed to him.

They came upon a door behind the statue of Augustus. Maximus pushed it open. "Priscus, you stay here. Keep watch." Going through the door, he beckoned to Julian to follow.

Peering inside, Julian froze. By the light of the torch, he saw a descending flight of steps carved out of the jagged rock wall on the left, while on the right a void of darkness billowed out. He stepped back. "Where does it lead?"

"Down."

The Prince took a step back. *Down?*

"We must go in," said Maximus. "It is the Cave of Pan, known to the Greeks of old as the *Gates of Hades*. It lies below. You wanted to consult the gods face to face. It is here you will find them."

"The Gates of Hades? A gospel of the Christians speaks of this place. The Galilean spoke to his apostles near this place."

Maximus gripped Julian by the arm. "Fear not the words of the Galilean, Prince Julian. Through such places as this, the gods travel to and from the underworld. Be steadfast and tonight you will commune with the gods." He stared into the prince's eyes. "That is what you want, yes?"

Julian took a deep breath and gritted his teeth. "Yes."

The two made their way down the steep steps hewn from the rock. Fifty feet below the temple they at last alighted on the cave floor.

The prince pushed back the cape from his shoulders. "It is warm here."

"Wait here, Prince Julian," said Maximus. He walked along the walls of the cave and lit the dozen torches set into the stone. In the improved lighting, the extent of the cave now became visible to Julian. The semicircular cave, in the shape of a crude apse, reached sixty feet across at its widest point with statues of the gods spaced at regular intervals along the walls. Opposite the apse and above them stood the back wall of the Augusteum. The ceiling towered a hundred feet over them. Inlaid mosaics of Pan depicted in various settings decorated the marble floor, which bore the scars of many large and lengthy cracks.

The prince's attention soon focused on the circular hole, ten yards wide, in the center of the floor. He tilted his head to the side. *Do I hear whispers from it?* His heart began to race again. His fascination overcoming his fear, Julian inched closer until he stood at the edge of the opening. Below lay a still pool of water. He gazed into the abyss. "How deep is it?"

Maximus held the torch over the gap in the floor. "No length of rope has ever sounded the bottom."

"A bottomless pit?"

"Pools such as this one reach into the underworld itself. Through this abyss, the spirits both enter our world and return to theirs."

Maximus produced a chain from within his scarlet cloak. From the chain hung a golden medallion in the form of a triangle within which was set an eye. He placed it around his neck. Maximus, as he had done at the temple in Pergamum, recited incantations in a language that Julian could not comprehend. After several minutes, the prince observed he could now see his own breath. He shivered. "It grows colder."

Maximus placed his hand to Julian's chest to silence him. He gazed into the pit. "It comes."

A strong gust of warm, noxious air blew into the cave from the pit. The wind extinguished the torch carried by Maximus and several of the others along the cave wall in an instant.

Julian's mouth dropped open as he stared into the pool. Rising inch by inch, a horned head emerged from the water followed by the rest of a shadowy figure, manlike in form and size. Yet, as it rose, there was no commotion or ripples on the surface of the pool. The prince stepped back a couple of feet. His heart pounded within his breast. The horned specter continued to rise until it came to hover several feet above the middle of the pit. Julian felt the temperature in the cave drop again. His whole body became numb from fright. Only fifteen feet from Julian, two fiery red eyes fixed on the prince. Julian gasped.

The prince then heard a voice, calm and peaceful, in his mind, one he was sure was not his own. *You should not be here. Pray!* At once, he fell to his knees. His gaze still fixed on the apparition, he felt strength leaving his body. *What should I do?* He lifted his right hand and blessed himself with the sign of the cross. The specter let out a high-pitched screech and began to sink back into the pit.

Frantic, the prince stumbled to his feet and fled. He tripped and fell in his haste as he reached the stairs. He climbed them quickly using both hands and feet. Heavy footfalls pounded close behind. *It is after me!* He screamed.

Reaching the level of the Augusteum, he hurried through the door and brushed past Priscus.

"Prince, what happened?" shouted Priscus. "Where are you going?"

Julian stopped when he reached the open air of the portico. He clutched his chest as he caught his breath. Within moments, Maximus and Priscus were at his side.

"What happened down there?" asked Priscus.

Maximus stared into Julian's eyes. "What did you do?" he asked, his tone harsh.

"Nothing!" said Julian.

"You must have done something to make the daemon retreat."

"I did nothing."

"A prayer? A gesture? Something. You must have!"

Julian thought for a moment. He nodded. "Yes. I remember. When the daemon looked at me, I made a sign of the cross."

"A sign of the cross? You are no longer a believer in the Galilean. Why would you do such a thing?"

The prince shook his head. He sat down upon the steps. He placed his hands over his face. "I do not know," he said, his voice trembling as he rocked himself back and forth. He glanced up at Maximus. "A reflex from my youth, perhaps? I was afraid. I panicked. Forgive me, master."

"My prince, you must never resort to the prayers or signs of the

Christians in the presence of the gods. Above all, you must never say the name of the Galilean."

Julian raised his eyebrows. "The gods fear these signs—and the name of the Galilean?"

Priscus too looked at Maximus with a puzzled expression.

Maximus glanced from one to the other. He furrowed his brow as he thought of an answer. "No, my prince," he said with a sardonic smile. "The daemons are neither afraid of you nor of me—and certainly not of the signs or name of the Galilean."

"But the sign of the cross? You said it made the daemon flee."

"It was not fear that made him flee. By your action, the daemon discerned a lack of your faith in the gods of the Old Religion. I fear you have offended them by this sign of disbelief. It was this that made the entity flee."

Julian dropped his head. "Then I have failed both you and myself."

Maximus patted Julian's back. "It may not be too late. Let us try once more. If you show yourself to be penitent, the daemon may give you another chance to prove your faith in him and the other gods."

The sorcerer and Julian retraced their path into the old temple and down the winding staircase to the pit. Maximus relit the torches and once again brought Julian to the edge of the abyss. "Courage, Prince," he said, as he proceeded to repeat the incantations.

Maximus had not yet completed the incantations when the temperature within the cave dropped.

Julian grimaced. "There is a foul stench in the air," he whispered. "I smell sulfur."

A gust of air issued from the mouth of the hole, yet the surface of the water remained still.

Julian pointed into the pit. As before, a shadowy, manlike form rose out of the water without causing a ripple. The light from the torches around the cave did little to illuminate it. The shadow floated upward until it came to hover over the mouth of the abyss. Taking definite shape, there appeared a human torso and arms and then the hindquarters, legs, and cloven feet of a goat. Last of all, the head materialized. It had a grotesque face of a man while two large horns protruded from just above its forehead. The eyes burned like hot, glowing embers.

The sorcerer fell to his knees in worship. Julian followed his example.

"It is Pan!" said Maximus.

The image of Pan dissolved. As it did, it transformed into another spectral form. Over the mouth of the abyss stood an attractive young man wearing a plumed Roman helmet and red tunic. He carried a cornucopia in one hand and an upright spear in the other.

Maximus grasped Julian's wrist. "It is one of the Genii! The guardian spirit of Rome."

"Who has summoned us?" asked the specter. Its voice, deep and raspy, echoed in the cave.

Maximus threw back his scarlet hood. He clasped the medallion about his neck. "Servants of the gods!"

The daemon's eyes fixed on Julian. "Flavius Claudius Julianus, hail!"

Julian lowered his head at the sound of his name, touching his forehead to the floor as he shook. "I seek to know the will of the gods," he asked, his voice trembling.

"You have found favor with the gods," said the daemon. "We have determined that you will become Emperor."

"Emperor?"

The specter gave a single nod.

"What would you have me do to serve you?"

"You must not allow the Church of the Galilean to prevail over us. The gods will make you Emperor for this purpose. Do not fail us."

Julian lifted his head and gazed into the eyes of the daemon. "It will be as you say. I will not fail you."

"Farewell, Prince!" said the specter as it descended back into the pit. With its departure, the chill in the air and the foul stench vanished.

***

It was after sunrise when Julian, Maximus, and Priscus reentered the gates of the city of Caesarea Philippi, near the Sanctuary of Pan. Merchants had already opened their shops and inhabitants proceeded about their daily business.

"Could it be possible I am destined to become Emperor?" muttered Julian as they made their way through the stone-paved streets of the city. "I do not see how it can come to pass."

"Trust in the gods, Prince," said Maximus. "The gods have bestowed a great honor and responsibility upon you."

Julian paused when he saw something up ahead. His face turned white. A squad of men and horses waited on the road ahead. The soldiers wore the black of imperial guardsmen.

"What is it, Prince?" asked Priscus.

"There—up the street," said Julian. "A troop of cavalry is outside my villa. They are here to arrest me! The Emperor knows what we have seen and done. He has spies everywhere. Sorcery is punishable by death!"

"They know nothing—we were alone," said Maximus. "Come, let us proceed with confidence. Do not show your fear, lest it betrays guilt."

The three continued down the street. As they drew nearer to the front gate of the villa, Julian's pace slowed, his steps hesitant.

"You there!" said one of the soldiers standing guard.

"Me?" said Julian, his voice quivering.

"Yes," said the soldier as he approached the three. "Are you Prince Julian?"

Julian's eyes darted from side to side, looking for a path to escape if necessary.

"Prince Julian?" the soldier asked again.

Julian nodded.

"Follow me."

"Where are we going?"

"There is someone here to see you," said the soldier. "Follow me."

The soldier led Julian and his companions into the atrium of the villa where several more soldiers stood near a small, shallow pool beneath the open air. In the center of the pool stood a three-foot-tall statue of Pan surround by several nymphs. From the mouth of the god water shot up into the air and fell back into the pool with a steady gurgle.

Seeing the fountain of Pan, the prince thought back to the specter he had seen just a few hours before. His heart beat faster. *They must know what I've done and seen.*

"Prince Julian?" asked a centurion, wearing a helmet with a black, transverse crest.

Julian, clutching his hands together against his chest, nodded. "What . . . what is this about?" he asked, sweat appearing on his brow.

The centurion opened the heavy door to the dining room. He gestured for Julian to enter. "In here, Prince."

Julian hesitated.

Maximus stood beside him. "Show not your fear, Prince," he whispered.

Julian entered the dining hall followed by his two companions. Though familiar with the room, the prince trembled upon seeing the walls which were painted with vivid scenes of Pan dancing or playing his flute in various settings in the wild. His mind flashed back again to the apparition which appeared to him as Pan above the pit.

In the center of the room was a long, low table around which a half dozen couches were arranged. Upon the table bowls of fruit and platters of meat were set out.

"There you are, Julian!" called out a familiar voice.

The prince turned toward the voice and at once caught sight of a head covered in curly, yellow hair. The young man wore a leather cuirass over a white tunic with purple trim. Julian recognized him at once. It was Gallus, his half-brother, reclining at the table for breakfast. Seated beside him was Captain Marcus Scudillo of the Imperial Guard.

Gallus grinned. He sprang up and rushed over to embrace Julian. He held Julian's face in his hands. Gallus chuckled. "Your beard is fuller now. You are a man, now!"

"What are you doing here?" asked Julian, both stunned and relieved at the sight of his brother.

Gallus cocked his head back. "What sort of greeting is that, little brother?"

"Last I heard, you were in Caesarea Maritima tending to the

affairs of the province now that the Jewish rebellion had ended," said Julian.

Gallus released Julian from his bear hug of a grip. "There I was until word came you were here in Caesarea Philippi—of all places." The Caesar strolled over to double doors now opened wide to the fresh air. There he stood looking out over the villa grounds, dotted with fountains and statuary predominated by the figure of Pan. Mount Hermon loomed overhead. In the sunlight, his blonde hair seemed almost like gold. "It is said the fallen angels described by Enoch first came down to our world on this mount." He faced Julian. "Your studies take you to the oddest places, brother. We arrived late last night, but you were not here. We were told you were gone for the evening. I had hoped to visit with you for at least the evening before leaving this morning."

"You leave so soon?" asked Julian.

"I must."

"If I had known beforehand, I would have been here to greet you."

Gallus observed Maximus and Priscus standing at the door. He squinted at them with suspicion. "You keep strange hours, Julian. Brother, where were you with your friends until such an early hour?"

Julian's face turned red. "Ah . . . I . . . we, I mean—"

"The fault for our late return was mine alone, Caesar," said Maximus, coming to the aid of the prince. "We were studying the heavens and the stars into the early hours."

Gallus raised an eyebrow. "The heavens and the stars. Is that so?"

"Debating the views of Aristarchus and Ptolemy regarding the nature of the cosmos."

Gallus stepped past his brother. He stood before Maximus and Priscus. "Wait outside," he ordered them. The two bowed and backed out of the room. When they had left the hall, Gallus closed the door behind them, leaving Julian and Marcus in the room with him.

"I would have been here to greet you," said Julian. "But how could I have known of your coming?"

Gallus placed an arm around his brother. "You could not have known of my coming. My journey is of an urgent and confidential nature."

"You said you planned to leave this morning. Surely, you will stay now that I am here."

Gallus walked over to the table. He poured himself wine and drank. "I must go to Mediolanum."

"What matter can be so urgent that you cannot stay here even a day longer? Does this involve me?"

Gallus laughed. He filled a second cup with wine. "You have always been the nervous, indecisive sort, little brother. Do not be anxious." He handed one of the cups to Julian. "I have good news to relate to you."

"Good news?"

Gallus walked over to Marcus. He placed his arm around the shoulders of the captain. "My good friend of many years, Marcus, has brought me excellent news."

"Tell me, brother," said Julian. "Do not keep me in suspense."

The Caesar leaned against the frame of the door which looked out over grounds and the foot of Mount Hermon. "It has happened just as I foretold to you. Think back to my wedding day in Constantinople and my appointment as Caesar in the East. Remember, I told you that being named Caesar might one day lead to greater things."

"I do," said the prince now joining him at the door.

Gallus pulled a document from the inside of his cloak. "Only two days ago, Marcus brought this letter from the Emperor." He handed it to Julian, who read it aloud:

> "To Flavius Claudius Constantius Gallus, Caesar
>   Greetings and Salutations Dearest Cousin and Brother, who assists me in governing our Empire. We hope this letter finds you and Our sister, Constantina, well. We have hitherto been distracted by the war against the Usurper Magnentius. However, We can now happily inform you that the war against the Usurper has recently been concluded by Our great victory at Mons Seleucus. We also delight in your own report which has reached Us of your great victory over the rebellious

Jews.

The Empire now being once again united, there is need to establish civil order and security for the welfare and prosperity of all. As Our predecessors in Our office have understood, it is a difficult task for one man alone to rule such an extensive realm. Therefore, We wish to meet with you to discuss the governance of the Empire and your elevation to higher authority. Please come at once to Mediolanum so that we might discuss this urgent matter. For the moment, it is best to keep this matter confidential.

> Flavius Julius Constantius
> Augustus et Imperator"

Julian looked up from the letter. "What does it mean?"

"That Constantius intends to make me co-Emperor with him!" said Gallus. "What else could it mean. It is the only possible explanation."

Marcus sprang from his seat. "It can only mean that. What higher authority can there be, but co-Emperor?"

Julian laughed. "Indeed, that must be it!" The prince took a long sip from his cup. *What amazing news. Long ago, my father and older brother killed by order of Constantius. Now, Gallus is to be named an Augustus! Vindication for our family, at last.*

"That is why I am here," said Gallus. "I sent Constantina ahead of me as soon as we received the news. I resolved to find and share this news with you personally, little brother, before I left for the Mediolanum." The Caesar embraced his brother once again. "Our fortunes have changed much since our youth. Who could have imagined that I would one day be an Augustus—and you the brother of one!"

They laughed together.

Gallus turned and grabbed a purple cape that had been draped across the back of a chair. He fastened it to the shoulders of his cuirass. "But now, I must leave."

"Stay a day at least!" urged Julian. "Let us celebrate your good fortune."

"There is a long trip ahead of me."

"We must meet the imperial delegation in Poetavium within the month," said Marcus. "Emperor Constantius is a stickler for punctuality."

Gallus embraced Julian. "We shall celebrate upon my return to Constantinople."

They walked out of the Villa together to a clear, sunny day. A line of soldiers formed an honor guard, saluting their Caesar as he passed. When they exited the gate to the street, they found a squadron of cavalry lining the street before them. Citizens of the city stood on the sidewalks on either side, vying to catch a glimpse of a Caesar. Above them to their right, Mount Hermon towered above them. Gallus strode to his white horse and mounted. He glanced down at Julian and grinned. "Fear not, brother. I leave a Caesar. I return an Augustus." He spurred his horse onward, followed by Marcus and the rest of the cavalry escort.

Julian watched as the column disappeared down the road. He turned to find Maximus and Priscus with him. "My brother is to be named an Augustus."

"Remember, the words of the daemon?" asked Maximus. "You are to be Emperor. Perhaps the elevation of Gallus will be the means by which this comes to pass."

***

Gallus and his escort traveled northward into Anatolia. Crossing over the Bosporus into Constantinople, they passed through the provinces of Thracia, Moesia, and Pannonia until at last entering Noricum. There they came to the city of Poetavium and its fortress where they were to meet the Emperor's delegation.

As the sun began to set, Gallus, with Marcus riding along by his side, led the cavalry escort through the gate into the fortress of Poetavium. The clattering of hooves echoed throughout the stone courtyard as they entered.

Gallus raised his arm. "Column halt!" he ordered, bringing the riders to a rest behind him.

A senior officer from the fortress, with a full beard, a round, burly chest, and wearing a blue cape and crested helmet approached. "Hail, Caesar!" he said, saluting Gallus. "Tribune

Barbatio, commander of the Thirteenth Legion, at your service."

"Greetings, Tribune," said Gallus. He took off his purple-crested helmet to wipe the sweat from his forehead. "We have ridden long and hard."

"I have been instructed to see to your every comfort, Caesar, until the arrival of the imperial delegation," said Barbatio. "You and your officers shall sleep and dine in the Praetorium. My centurions will see to the housing of your men."

After a short rest in their quarters, Gallus, three of his officers, and Marcus took their places in the dining hall in the Praetorium. There they found themselves sitting alone, amidst several empty tables.

"Where are the officers of the Thirteenth Legion?" asked one of Gallus's officers.

Gallus reclined at his seat at the head of the long, oaken table. "We arrived late. Perhaps they have eaten already."

Marcus stood before a large stone fireplace. He walked to the sturdy table and poured two cups of wine.

"These are rather spartan quarters," said Marcus. He glanced at his surroundings. A high fireplace stood set in each of the four walls of the hall. A dozen tables spread about the room stood empty and deserted. Above the large fireplace nearest them, as tall as a man, there hung the shield of the Thirteenth Legion, which bore the emblem of a lion. The flames roared high, as the burning wood crackled. In the shadows of the flickering light, Marcus saw the same shield ringing the walls. These shields appeared to bear the same emblem, but each an older design reaching back hundreds of years. So too, ringing the walls, were statues of gods and emperors of old.

Marcus sat down to the right of Gallus, who rested with his eyes shut. He placed a cup of wine before the Caesar.

Hearing the click of the cup set before him, Gallus opened his eyes which he then fixed on the shield above the fireplace. "Marcus, fate has destined that we are here in Poetavium," he said as he reached for his wine. "Did you know it was here, almost three hundred years ago, that Vespasian was first raised on a shield by his legionaries and hailed as Emperor?"

"I did not," said Marcus, as he took a sip from his wine. He watched as a half dozen slaves entered the hall. They carried platters of carved beef, cheese, and bowls of fruit, which they set out along the table. They then placed plates before the Caesar and the officers.

Gallus smiled. He reached forward and dished himself out several slices of meat. "That is not the only coincidence, dear friend. Like me, Vespasian had fought against a Jewish rebellion before arriving in this city. Both of us stopping here. One named Emperor here while the other pauses on his way to be named Emperor."

"Destiny," said Marcus.

"You have been a good friend, Marcus. I shall not forget it. If Constantius will part with you, I will make you the commander of my imperial guard."

"I would be honored," said Marcus. He then stood and raised his cup. The flames and shadows danced on the stone walls around the hall, casting an eerie light. "A toast!" he said. Gallus's officers from the escort arose, holding their cups high. "To Gallus, a new Vespasian!"

"To Gallus, a new Vespasian!" shouted the officers.

The echoes of the toast had just faded away when the doors to the hall burst open. Two dozen legionaries rushed into the room and surrounded the table. Their spears pointed inward at the half dozen diners.

Gallus glared at the legionaries holding their spears toward him. He jumped to his feet. "What is the meaning of this! Put down your spears. Do you even know who I am?"

Gallus's own officers likewise protested. "Lay down your weapons. This is a Caesar!"

The legionaries did not respond to Gallus. They stared back at him with cold eyes.

Marcus addressed the soldiers. "You heard Caesar. Stand down."

Tribune Barbatio entered the dining hall followed by Commander Arbitio and Eusebius—the Grand Chamberlain—and an agent of the court named Apodemius.

Gallus furrowed his brow. "Arbitio ... Eusebius ... you must be part of the imperial delegation sent to greet me. Tell these legionaries who I am. I am a Caesar! Command them to put their spears down at once."

Arbitio smirked. "There is no mistake. We know who you are." He turned to Barbatio. "Arrest him."

Marcus, wearing puzzlement on this face, looked to Arbitio. *What is happening?*

Upon Barbatio's signal, two of the legionaries seized the Caesar while another disarmed him.

Gallus struggled against them. He managed to free an arm. He reached into his cloak and pulled out a letter. Clutching it, the Caesar waved it about in the air. "Read this! It is from Constantius!"

Arbitio raised his eyebrows, feigning surprise. "Oh . . . a letter from the Emperor?" he asked, his tone betokened a feigned interest.

"It explains everything."

The commander plucked the document from the Caesar's hand. He walked across the room to stand by the fireplace. He read the letter by the light of the flames. "Oh, this?"

Gallus nodded. He quit struggling against the men who held him fast. "Yes. Now you understand. You know why the Emperor sent for me." His back stiffened as he regained his composure. He tilted his head back, assuming a dominant air. "Have these men release me at once," he said in a commanding voice.

Arbitio held the document close to the fire until a small flame appeared at the end of it.

"What are you doing? That is a letter from the Emperor. I am to be elevated to co-Emperor!"

Eusebius snickered. "Oh dear . . . was it?"

The commander watched the flames creep down the note. He tossed it into the fireplace.

The color drained from the Caesar's face. "The Emperor ordered this?"

"Constantius never intended to make you co-Emperor," said Arbitio with a sneer. He gestured to the legionaries holding Gallus. "Take him away."

"Wait!" shouted Gallus as he was being dragged away. "What of my wife? Where is Constantina? She can intercede with the

Emperor on my behalf!" His face wrinkling and quivering with terror and desperation, he stared at this friend. "Marcus, find my wife! She will intercede with Constantius on my behalf! Help me. I beg you!"

Marcus stood where he had, dumbfounded at all that had transpired. Filled with pity for his friend, he reached out a hand as if to help. He was cut short by the Grand Chamberlain.

"Most unfortunate," said Eusebius. "She died a week ago of the fever . . . while on her way to Mediolanum."

"You killed her!" shouted Gallus. He glared at Marcus. "Did you have a hand in this?"

Marcus wanted to speak, but his trembling lips could only form the word no. Gallus's officers stood motionless and speechless, fearing their own fates might be tied to that of their Caesar.

"That is enough for now," said Arbitio.

"What have I done?" screamed Gallus as he was dragged away, his plaintive pleas echoing along the stone corridors.

"What do we do with his officers and escort?" asked Barbatio.

Arbitio stood beside Marcus, who continued to hold the wine cup with which he had toasted Gallus. "Marcus is with us," said Arbitio. "Release the rest outside of the city." He looked at the other officers of the escort who had served with Gallus. "The fate of Gallus is beyond your power to alter. Consider yourselves fortunate you will not share his fate. Go. Return to your units in the East." Barbatio and his legionaries led these officers out of the hall.

Arbitio and Eusebius sat down to help themselves to the food and wine which had been set out. Marcus remained frozen in place at the table where he had been all along, contemplating all that had happened.

The commander took a bite of meat. He looked up at Marcus as he chewed. "Sit, Captain, please. You are safe."

Marcus sank into his chair.

"You performed your task well," said Arbitio. He added wine to the cup Marcus held. "You delivered the letter."

Eusebius laughed. "And he delivered Gallus."

Marcus's hand trembled as he held his cup.

"I think the captain is confused," said Eusebius as he chewed a piece of beef.

Arbitio poured himself a wine. "Gallus exhibited an ambitious nature, which concerned Constantius."

"But the letter?" asked Marcus. "Constantius was to make Gallus co-Emperor."

"A ruse, Captain," said Eusebius. "Gallus would not have delivered himself into our hands if he suspected the Emperor's concerns. He might have led a rebellion, another civil war."

Arbitio stabbed a piece of cheese from a platter with the point of his knife. He held it up and examined it. "We dangled the cheese before him."

Marcus lowered his head. "Gallus was the mouse, and I the cheese," he muttered. He took a drink.

"Feeling remorse?" said the commander. "Guilt?"

"I am accustomed to battle, not intrigue," said Marcus. "Gallus is a friend." Marcus fixed his eyes on Arbitio. "You knew that."

Arbitio laughed. "Knew that? I *counted* on it. Why do you think I chose you to deliver the letter to Gallus?"

"He would not suspect a trap."

"Precisely," said the commander as he saw the troubled expression on Marcus's face. "But do not worry, we will not execute him without an investigation and trial."

Eusebius nodded. "We will first question him to discover his coconspirators. We will try him, then we will execute him. After all, we are not barbarians."

Arbitio locked eyes with Marcus. "Remember where your loyalties lie in this world. We did this on behalf of our lord, Constantius Augustus."

Eusebius raised his cup. "To our lord, Constantius Augustus!"

"Our lord, Constantius Augustus!" said Arbitio doing the same. He paused before putting the cup to his lips, waiting on the captain to join the toast. "Captain—to our lord, Constantius Augustus," said the commander, his tone firm and insistent.

Marcus raised his cup. By the flickering light of the flames, in the dancing shadows against the wall across the room, he discerned the horned head of the god Pan. He drank until he had emptied the cup.

Chapter 18

The Fate of a Caesar

(Pula)

Gallus sat on a stool, his hands and feet in iron shackles. The floor and surrounding walls, all bare stone, were cold and stark. His muscular physique gone, the rag of a tunic he wore appeared oversized on his thin and fragile frame. The Caesar's hair, once thick and yellow, was now unkempt and riddled with streaks of gray. He sat ten feet from a heavy table of oak. Across it sat his judges—Arbitio, Eusebius, and Barbatio. Behind them stood Marcus, wearing the black tunic, cape, and plumed helmet of the imperial guard.

"Flavius Claudius Constantius Gallus, please rise," said Eusebius dressed in a white toga with red trim.

Gallus rose to his feet. His movement slow and weak. He hung his head, keeping his eyes to the cracked, stone floor. *So, now we come to it.*

"You have been accused of unlawful imperial ambition and conspiracy to seize the throne of the East," said Eusebius. The Grand Chamberlain held a scroll bearing the charges, but he did not need to read them. He knew them by heart. He stared at the Caesar with a cold smirk. "By order of the Emperor, you were brought here to Pula several weeks ago. You have been investigated and tried for these crimes. Under questioning, you have named dozens of coconspirators. Now, we, your judges, appointed by the

Emperor for this purpose, have reviewed the evidence against you and find you—guilty."

Gallus collapsed back on to his chair. The chains clinked against the stone as they struck the floor. His shoulders slumped forward. Tears welled in his eyes. *There is no hope. All is lost.*

"Have you anything to say before sentence is pronounced against you?" asked Eusebius.

Gallus's shoulders started to rise and fall, as he wept and laughed together. *I don't know, what is there left to say?* "I appeal to my kinsman—the Emperor."

The Grand Chamberlain placed the scroll down. He tapped a thin, delicate finger on the table. "No appeal is possible."

Gallus looked at his judges with dark eyes and a sullen face. "Words would be useless. This verdict was decided long before—and in a place far from here."

"Very well. Having been found guilty, you are hereby condemned to death. The execution will be carried out tomorrow morning at dawn."

Captain Marcus led the prisoner back to his cell.

Gallus laughed to himself as the heavy door closed behind him.

"Destiny flirts before she destroys."

Marcus peered through the small, barred window of the door. "Caesar?"

"In Poetavium I thought my destiny to be that of Vespasian. Now, we are in Pula."

"I do not understand."

"Pula, Marcus. Pula was the site of the trial of another Caesar. Perhaps within these same walls. Thirty years ago, Emperor Constantine had his son Crispus tried and executed for conspiring against him."

Marcus lowered his eyes. "I had nothing to do with this."

"My downfall?"

"I am a soldier—not an executioner."

"I must admit it was a deft piece of deception," said Gallus. He chuckled. "It was beyond the ability of my cousin Constantius to have thought of it. His way is brute force. He killed my father and kinsmen to secure the throne of the East. No . . . I see the hand of Arbitio or Eusebius in this. It is more their style." He smiled a crooked grin at Marcus. "If you stay in the imperial service, you will learn much from them. If you want to survive, you must."

Marcus pursed his lips.

"Cheer up, Marcus," said Gallus. "I know you had no part in it. You did not have it in you, then. Beware, lest you become accustomed to the company of treacherous men. Their perfidy will infect you—if it does not kill you. Ambition and lust for power was my folly. I forgot the jealousy of the Emperor." He held up his hand. "Farewell, friend."

***

Marcus poured himself a wine as he sat alone at the long table in a dark dining hall. The flames ebbed away in the large, stone fireplace. He sipped his drink. As he leaned his head back to drain the cup, the flickering light revealed the statue of Pan in a niche in the wall. He averted his eyes from its lifelike gaze. He poured himself another drink. He glanced up but recoiled in horror. Directly across the table from him sat Pan, who pounded hard on the tabletop as he laughed and stared into the captain's soul. Marcus screamed.

The captain sat up in his bed in a cold sweat. He looked about his surroundings and saw he was not back in the dining hall in the fortress of Poetavium. Instead, he was in a cramped officers' quarters in Pula. It had been a nightmare. There was a loud pounding at his door. He stumbled out of bed.

Marcus turned up a lantern. In the improved lighting, he again glanced about the small room encased in stone blocks to be sure all had been a dream. There beside his bed, placed upon a stand, rested his black uniform and helmet. *It was only a dream.* The hinges creaked as he opened the wooden door to the hall. Before him in a cold, dank hallway of stone stood a young centurion holding a torch, waiting to speak with him. "What is it?" asked Marcus.

"A rider just arrived with a message," said the centurion, who wore a black tunic and crest. "It is from the Emperor. I could not find Commander Arbitio."

Marcus took the letter. "How many hours until dawn?"

"Less than an hour, sir."

"Let me see this." The captain read the letter by the light of the lantern on the table. An empty wineskin lay on the bed. When he had finished reading, he grinned. "How long until dawn did you say?"

"Perhaps an hour, sir."

"Then I must hurry!" said Marcus as he rushed to dress.

***

The sun appeared over the horizon behind Eusebius and Arbitio as they left the Praetorium and headed for the prison-house. Barbatio, leading a squad of his legionaries and an executioner carrying a large axe, followed along. The heavy, echoing footfalls upon the stone pavement broke the morning silence. From the heights of the courtyard, they could see the blue water of the Adriatic port below. The first few fishing boats of the day were putting out to sea.

Eusebius, who wore a blue toga and a wide golden sash, brought a hand to his mouth as he yawned. "Why are executions at dawn?"

"You need not have gotten out of bed," said Arbitio. The commander wore an armored cuirass with a black cape attached to it.

"I like to see plots through to their conclusion. I would not have missed this for the world."

Arbitio quirked a smile. "You are to be admired for your thoroughness."

"Yes, I am thorough, but sometimes events intervene to disrupt even the best of plans."

"What do you mean?" said Arbitio as he stopped as they neared the prison house, constructed of large blocks of white travertine. Outside, several legionaries stood guard.

"I was not expecting that the Emperor would require that I come on this errand. When we finish with this business here, we must return to Arles. Silvanus will have used this time to further ingratiate himself with the Emperor. If we are not quick about it, he will get himself named to a high and profitable office in the West, which I hoped to win for you."

"Silvanus is a man with grand ambitions," said Arbitio. The

301

black plume of the commander's helmet swayed in the morning breeze from the sea.

"I suspect he entertains the thought of marrying into the imperial family one day and becoming a Caesar—or something greater," said Eusebius. "Come to think of it, you should have set your sights long ago on Princess Helena rather than on the daughter of Florentius. The princess would be a more profitable venture for you."

Arbitio chuckled. "My dear Eusebius, we are on our way to execute Gallus—a Caesar, mind you! Neither his blood relation to the Emperor nor his marriage to the Emperor's sister could save him. Why would I fare better? Like you, I am greedy, ambitious and lacking in most virtues—but the one virtue I have is knowing my limitations."

Eusebius laughed, harsh and ironic.

"I am content with our mutually profitable schemes," said Arbitio. "But, regarding the daughter of Florentius, one day I will have her."

They continued on their way, leading the legionaries and executioner until they reached the doors to the prison house. Marcus met them as they entered the building. He saw the heavyset executioner who, dressed in a simple gray tunic and cap, rested the blade end of the axe on the ground by his side. Marcus lifted his arm from under his black cape, holding the letter from Constantius. "This letter has just arrived from the Emperor. He has repented of his decision. Gallus is to be spared."

Arbitio frowned. "Gallus to be spared?" The commander closed the door to the prison house to give the senior officers privacy, leaving the legionaries and the executioner outside in the courtyard.

Marcus read the letter aloud to Arbitio, Eusebius, and Barbatio.

> "By this letter, we make known our merciful command that the life of our cousin and brother, Flavius Claudius Constantius Gallus, Caesar, be spared. No harm is to come to him. Further, We command that Gallus be brought before us at once."

The captain handed the letter to Arbitio. "Signed . . . Flavius Julius Constantius—Augustus et Imperator."

Eusebius cocked his head back. "Impossible!"

Arbitio took off his helmet. He raised an eyebrow as he read the document. He handed it to Eusebius.

"Why the change of heart?" asked Eusebius after he had read it. He shook his head in disappointment.

"Who cares?" said Marcus. "They are cousins by blood . . . brothers by marriage. The reasons matter not—we have an order from the Emperor."

Arbitio took the document from Eusebius. "Marcus is right. We have an order from the Emperor." He glanced at Eusebius and Barbatio. "The timing could not have been more favorable for Gallus."

The four proceeded down the steps into the dungeon, the air growing cooler the farther they descended. The gaoler who guided them lit torches set into the walls along the way. The sound of dripping water echoed in the dark halls. When they came at last to Gallus's cell, Arbitio dismissed the two gaolers on duty outside of the cell. "You are no longer needed here."

Gallus peered through the window of his cell door. "Is it time?"

Marcus rushed to the door. He smiled. "No, my lord, I have good news for you. You are to be spared and brought back alive to the Emperor. He desires to show mercy."

Gallus gripped the bars with both hands. "Is this a cruel joke?"

"No! I speak the truth."

"How is this possible?"

"A message arrived this morning from the Emperor," said Arbitio. "It commands that your life be spared and that we bring you back to the Emperor."

Tears welled in Gallus's eyes.

The captain retrieved the keys from a hook on the wall. He unlocked the door and pushed it open.

Gallus stepped out of the cell. His ragged tunic hung loose over his thin frame. He trembled. "Is this really so? Dare I believe it? When I awoke this morning, fate had me dead this day. Now, I have my life back again. Truly, fate is fickle." He stood before Arbitio, Eusebius, and Barbatio. His smile faded away. His back stiffened as he stared at them, his eyes now cold and angry. "If it is ever within my power again—your deeds will not go unpunished. You tortured me to extract the names of many innocent men—my coconspirators! It mattered not if they were guilty or not. These are men from whom you planned to extort payments to save their lives. My cousin will hear of how you treated me."

"Fate may be fickle, Caesar—but it does not make mistakes," said Eusebius as he gave a single nod as a signal to Tribune Barbatio.

The tribune drew his sword and plunged it deep into Gallus's chest. Convulsed in pain, Gallus stared in shock at the sword. Spitting up blood, the Caesar collapsed. The captain caught him as he fell and eased him to the floor. As Marcus knelt beside him, Gallus breathed his last with a loud, anguished gasp.

His face red with rage, Marcus yelled at Barbatio. "We were to spare his life!"

"Gallus was a threat to the Emperor," said Eusebius.

"A threat to the Emperor?" asked Marcus. "The Emperor wanted him brought to Arles—alive!"

"Very well then—he was a threat to *us*."

"Us?"

"Gallus would never have forgotten his imprisonment and torture. You heard him yourself. He would have sought revenge if the Emperor ever restored him to higher office. He might have someday turned the Emperor against us."

"The Emperor will be angry when he hears his message was ignored," said Marcus. "You will be punished, regardless."

"The message arrived too late," said Arbitio.

The captain stood, clenching his fists at his sides. "But it did not!"

"That is what we will tell the Emperor," said the commander, seemingly bemused by the captain's reaction. "No good will come of telling the truth at this point. We are all in this together."

"We? *Together?*"

Arbitio nodded. "If the Emperor does not receive a unanimous report, there will be an investigation. Who knew what? Who said what? Who did what? It would be the word of one against many. This sort of thing can get very unpleasant. I have seen it before."

"An investigation would be messy," agreed Eusebius, his words as slick as mud. "The word of the Grand Chamberlain, the Commander of the Imperial Guard, and the word of a legionary commander . . . all against the word of a captain?"

Arbitio turned to Barbatio. "What happened here?"

The tribune snickered. "It was very unfortunate. Tragic. The letter from the Emperor arrived moments too late."

"There will be no investigation, Captain Marcus," said Arbitio. "When we return, we will all tell the Emperor the letter arrived too late. Service to the Emperor can at times be messy. It is a hard, but necessary, lesson for you to learn."

"Public service can lack . . . a certain . . . moral definition," said Eusebius.

Arbitio put his helmet back on and tied the chin strap. "Marcus, it is a good lesson for you to learn, now, early in your career, and to keep it in mind as you strive to advance to higher ranks. In fact, you performed quite well on this mission. Upon our return, I will personally recommend to the Emperor that he promote you to tribune. You have shown great promise."

Eusebius nodded. "And I will second that recommendation. Your career ahead looks to be a bright one, Marcus." He turned and departed in the company of Barbatio.

The captain looked down at the lifeless body of Gallus, the sword protruding from his chest. He turned pale.

Arbitio paused at the door before leaving. He smirked. "Captain, see to the arrangements for his burial—with full honors. He was a Caesar after all." The commander started to leave but stopped a second time. He looked at the body of Gallus on the floor. "Oh, Marcus, do not forget the sword. Barbatio will want it back."

Chapter 19

The Dungeons of Arelate

(Arelate, Fall, 353 AD)

Emperor Constantius reclined in a chair behind a large desk in an office chamber in the prefect's palace in the city of Arelate. A marble bust of his father, Constantine, sat upon a marble pillar beside the desk. Racks full of ancient scrolls lined the walls from floor to ceiling. Behind Constantius, light streamed in through the glass windows. The Emperor was flanked by his court bishops Valens and Ursacius to his left, and the Grand Chamberlain Eusebius to his right. Standing before the Emperor, across the broad desk made of oak, stood two bishops in ankle-length black robes.

"O Emperor, these are the newly arrived legates of Pope Liberius, Bishop of Rome," said Valens. "It is my honor to present to you bishops Vincent of Capua and Marcellus of Campanis."

The two bishops across from Constantius bowed.

"My Emperor, greetings and health to you," said the older of the papal legates, the gray-haired Vincent. He gestured toward his younger, bearded colleague. "I and Bishop Marcellus, convey to you the salutations of Pope Liberius, Bishop of Rome, for whom we have the privilege of serving as his ambassadors to you."

"Your excellency, Vincent, your name and reputation proceed you," replied Constantius. The Emperor looked at the bust of Constantine beside him. "You sat with the great Hosius as a president at the Council of Nicaea, called by my father and Pope Sylvester."

"You are too kind, sire," replied the old bishop with a bow of his head. "My lord, if I may go straight to the point. His excellency, Valens, says we are newly arrived, but truth be told, we have been waiting for an imperial audience for over a month after our arrival in Arelate." He glared at the Grand Chamberlain and the court bishops.

"My apologies for the delay, but I have been busy with matters of governance following the end of the war," said Constantius without conviction. *I wanted you to wait for my own reasons.* "But, pray, continue."

"As you may recall when you were in Rome, Pope Liberius requested that there be a synod to treat of matters related to the Faith, regarding the false doctrine of the Arians, that has reentered the Empire and the Church," said Vincent. "Pope Liberius asked us to convey to you his suggestion that this council be held in the city of Aquileia so that it might be more easily attended by the bishops of Italy."

Constantius smiled. *Why, so he will have more of his own bishops there? I want the attending bishops to reflect my wishes, not his.* The Emperor shook his head and shrugged. "That will not be possible. I have already sent invitations for bishops from the surrounding provinces to gather here in Arelate."

The legates looked to each other, unable to disguise their dismay at the Emperor's response.

"Very well, my lord," said the younger, dark-haired legate, Marcellus. "Pope Liberius in his instructions to us foresaw this possibility. However, while Arelate is acceptable, the Bishop of Rome wishes that the council reaffirm the creed of the Council of Nicaea."

Valens cleared his throat to gain the Emperor's attention. "If I may, my lord."

"Yes, of course, your excellency," said Constantius. "Proceed as you see fit."

"Complaints continue to be heard from the East and Alexandria regarding Athanasius," said the red-bearded Valens.

"What sort of complaints?" asked Vincent, incredulous.

307

"There have been many," said Valens. "It has been said that his election was invalid and that it was purchased with bribes. Furthermore, Athanasius has overthrown altars and broken a sacred chalice. Also, it has been long alleged that he has sold corn, intended for widows, for his own profit."

"Athanasius has also been accused of murder," added the portly Ursacius.

Vincent shook his head. "Your excellencies cannot be unaware these charges have been investigated and judged to be false by several councils in both the East and in Rome itself. All these charges are slanderous and malicious. You level an accusation of murder against Athanasius. But surely you are aware the man alleged to have been murdered was hidden from authorities and was later found to be quite alive."

"Athanasius has been slandered by his many enemies because he is faithful to the creed of Nicaea, because he defends the truth Jesus Christ is of the same substance of the Father," said Marcellus.

"Athanasius is too uncompromising, insisting as he does on this formulation that Christ is 'of the same substance' of the Father," said Ursacius, tapping his fingers on his large belly. "He is too much of a rigorist. There are other formulas of faith, less divisive, allowing each to believe as he will."

"Believe as he will?" said Vincent. "Truth is truth for all, not according to each. What formula are you suggesting?"

"It might be said, for example, that 'the Son resembles the Father in all things,'" said Ursacius.

"*Resembles* the Father conveys a different meaning than *consubstantial*, or *of the same substance of the Father*," replied Vincent. "You have laid bare the need for this council to confirm the faith of Nicaea, to clarify and dispel confusion, lest the use of soft words muddle a meaning that should be clear, or God forbid, allow more than one meaning. The unity of the Church cannot be defended where heresy is entertained or introduced through ambiguity."

Ursacius cocked his head back. "You are suggesting I am a heretic?"

"Not at all, your excellency," said Vincent. "I merely hoped to underline the danger in our present age. We must be careful in our creeds to choose precisely those words that best convey the True

308

Faith. Various creeds have arisen in recent times in the East. It would be wise if this upcoming council in Arelate repeat the agreed upon creed of Nicaea."

"We can address the content of the creed in this council," said Valens. "But we must also deal with the case of Athanasius."

"What must be dealt with?" asked Vincent. "Two councils, one in Rome, have already declared Athanasius innocent of the crimes you have alleged against him."

"There are other accusations," said Valens.

"What other accusations?"

"Newer ones," said Ursacius, pulling a scroll from the inside of his black robes. "Serious accusations."

"More false charges against Athanasius," scoffed Vincent. "It is clear for all to see. By accusing and convicting Athanasius, his enemies seek to discredit the Catholic creed of Nicaea which declared Our Lord, Jesus Christ, consubstantial with God the Father."

The Emperor thumped his open hand down upon the table, rattling it and knocking over a cup of water. He glared at the papal legates, who, recoiling at the outburst, took a step back from the table. "Yes, new accusations!" shouted Constantius, his face red with rage. "Accusations that must be heard and judged by the bishops now gathering in Arelate." He turned to Ursacius. "Read them, your excellency."

Ursacius smirked at the papal legates as he unrolled the scroll and began to read from it. "First, this last Easter, Bishop Athanasius held divine services in Alexandria in an unconsecrated church. Second, what is worse, he encouraged the Emperor's late brother, Constans, at the time he reigned as Emperor in the West, to oppose Constantius. And, third, after Constans was murdered, Athanasius wrote a letter, friendly in tone, to the usurper, Magnentius, soon after his reign began."

The papal legates were about to give a response to the accusations when a court attendant entered the chamber and handed the Emperor a note. "Excellent," said Constantius upon reading it. His dour expression melted away into a cheerful one. "The Grand Chamberlain and Commander Arbitio have returned from Pula." He pushed back his chair and stood. "I go to meet

309

them. Your excellencies shall remain and make preparations for the council." Constantius paused when he reached the door. He fixed his attention on the papal legates, Vincent and Marcellus. "This council must address these accusations against Athanasius, especially those involving treasonous acts against me. Is that understood?"

The papal legates, still quaking from the Emperor's outburst, bowed. "Yes, sire."

***

Marcus, with his helmet beneath his left arm, paced back and forth before the empty throne, his steps upon the marble floors echoing in the hall of the prefect's palace. His black tunic and cape were dusty from a long, hard ride. Several yards away, Commander Arbitio and the Grand Chamberlain, Eusebius, observed the captain with seeming amusement. They quirked their eyebrows and whispered between themselves, but Marcus did his best to ignore them. The walls along the length of the small hall were adorned with pilasters and statues of Roman emperors of long ago. Two slaves lit the lamps as the sunlight coming through the windows behind the throne receded.

"Are you nervous, Captain?" asked Eusebius.

Marcus stopped pacing. He squinted at the eunuch. *I should say something. This is not right. Gallus was killed against the Emperor's express orders. Murdered. And I am to be made a party to this?* He opened his mouth to say something to the Grand Chamberlain, then remembered his commander, Arbitio, standing feet away. He pursed his lips and continued pacing.

Eusebius sauntered over to the empty throne. "There is no need to worry, Captain. Is that not right, Arbitio?"

Arbitio studied a map on a table off to the side. "Quite right. There is no need to be nervous. We all know the truth. The message that might have saved Gallus arrived too late."

"That was very unfortunate," said Eusebius as he ran his finger along the wooden arm of the throne. "Marcus, you will learn to live with such tragedies and complexities which are a part of life in the imperial court."

Marcus stared at the Grand Chamberlain. *Is it he I hold in contempt, or is it myself?*

Arbitio's steps echoed in the shadowy hall. He came up beside Marcus. "I know exactly how you feel, Captain. You can run from it, or you can embrace it. I did. To do so is necessary if you want to remain in the imperial court."

"And one's conscience?" asked Marcus.

"You cannot be too rigid," said Arbitio. "With time, difficult decisions will become less so. You will see." The lean commander slapped Marcus on the back. "Then one day, you will feel nothing at all."

Marcus turned his head to his commander. *The commander's eyes were cold and black. What should I do? I do not want to end up soulless like Arbitio and Eusebius.*

A side door to the hall burst open as a couple of Imperial Guardsmen in black entered.

"It's the Emperor," said Arbitio, donning his black-crested helmet.

Marcus put on his helmet and stood at attention as Constantius came into the room followed by several other guardsmen.

"I just learned you all had returned from Pula," said the Emperor excitedly as he hurried to Eusebius, who stood by the throne. Constantius, smiling, glanced about the room, as if looking for someone. "I trust you all had a safe journey."

Arbitio bowed. "A safe but tiring one, sire."

"But where is my cousin Gallus?" asked the Emperor. His smile began to fade. The travelers from Pula remained quiet. Constantius faced Marcus. "Has Gallus already retired for the evening?"

Marcus bowed his head. "No, sire."

"We bear tragic tidings, my emperor," interjected Arbitio.

Constantius's jaw tightened. "What tragic tidings?" he asked, the timbre of his voice suggesting he had now guessed the answer. He stumbled over to the throne and sank into it. "Tell me all relating to Gallus."

Arbitio approached the throne. "My lord, we diligently carried out all of your instructions regarding Gallus, to the letter. Gallus was transported to Pula for trial. There he was executed according to the sentence you had passed upon him."

The Emperor raised a hand to his forehead.

Marcus clenched his jaw. *He must be told the truth.*

"But what of my letter commanding his life be spared?" asked Constantius.

"We received it only after your sentence was carried out," said Eusebius. "Captain Marcus can attest to this most unfortunate fact."

The Emperor's attention shifted to the Captain. Marcus held his breath. His heart pounded in his chest. *I must tell the truth. How can I not?*

The Grand Chamberlain hurried to the side of Marcus, sensing doubt in the captain. "But, if I may, sire, I must report this about the captain. His service was exemplary on this mission. Without him, the East might have been lost to you. While the death of your cousin is tragic, you must not reproach yourself for his death. His fate was his own doing. If not for the captain, Gallus might be in the East still, sitting in Constantinople not as Caesar, but as Emperor of the East." Eusebius rested his hand on the captain's shoulder. "In view of all this, I recommend Marcus be promoted to the rank of tribune."

The Emperor lowered his head. "I have suffered the loss of my sister Constantina months ago and to this loss is now added my cousin. Though I mourn his passing, what you say, Eusebius, is true. It is not my fault."

Arbitio bowed. "Absolutely not, great Augustus."

"The blame for his tragic end is his alone," said Constantius.

"Entirely, sire," said Eusebius. "You are blameless."

Constantius nodded to himself. "I will have Bishops Valens and Ursacius offer prayers in the divine mysteries for the souls of Constantina and Gallus."

"A holy and wholesome thought, my lord," said Eusebius. "I will remember them in my own, personal prayers as well."

Marcus squinted at Eusebius. *You murderous hypocrite.*

The Emperor rose from the throne and approached the captain and stood before him. "Though this mission involved an unfortunate tragedy, let it now be said I am grateful to those who serve me honestly and well. Marcus Scudillo, thank you for your faithful service to the throne and the imperial family. In gratitude, I now raise you to the rank of tribune."

Marcus pursed his lips. *I should say something. Tell the Emperor all. Tell him the truth of Gallus's death.* The captain remained silent.

Arbitio laughed as Marcus stood there dumbfounded. "Tribune Marcus Scudillo, say something to the Emperor!"

Marcus's jaw tightened. *Tribune Marcus Scudillo?* He bowed to the Emperor. "You are too kind, my lord." *I couldn't tell him. What would that have accomplished? He might have blamed me.* He felt the pit of stomach sink and the skin on his face grow hot. *What have I done?*

"Tribune, you were a friend of Gallus, true?" asked Constantius.

"Yes, sire," said Marcus. "We trained together."

"Tell me, I must know, Tribune, did Gallus face his death bravely, befitting of one in the imperial bloodline?"

The blood raced through Marcus's veins as the images of Gallus's end repeated in his mind. *Am I to lie and cover up a murder?* He looked away from the Emperor. "He did," he said, just above a whisper.

The Emperor nodded, content. "Excellent. Even if he may have been a traitor, I would have hated to hear otherwise."

"His death, though deserved, was nobly faced," said Eusebius. "His funeral procession and burial were magnificent, my lord."

Arbitio nodded. "Indeed. He was a Caesar after all."

The Emperor gathered up the sleeve of his toga. "So be it. There is nothing more that can be done about Gallus." He turned to Eusebius and then Arbitio. "You both have returned at a fortuitous moment. I will have need of you." He returned to his throne and sat down. "A great victory has been won in the West and a problem in the East resolved. The empire has been unified. I can now turn my attention to matters of the Faith here in the West. Under me, let us now endeavor to unify the Church according to my wishes as well."

***

General Florentius stood beside a table beneath a portico of a peristyle. Set out on the table before him, several silver cups and a jar of wine rested on a large platter left out by a servant. Florentius, selecting two cups, filled them with wine. He emerged from the shade into the sunlight and handed one of the cups to Count Varronius. While the general was dressed in a simple red tunic, the count wore an armored cuirass with a dark-blue cape and tunic. His white-plumed helmet rested on a table to his side.

"Welcome back to Arelate, Varronius, my old friend," said Florentius as he took his place in a chair near to him. The city, located in the Roman province of Gaul, sat beside the Rhone river, which flowed into the city's harbor on the Mediterranean Sea to the south. Florentius glanced about the peristyle. A slight frown passed over his face. "I apologize for the cramped conditions of our temporary quarters within the fortress."

The count waved off the apology. He chuckled. "We are soldiers, used to such small quarters."

"Yes, but perhaps I had become somewhat spoiled. Or rather I should say my wife had become spoiled. Something she does not let me forget. In the first couple years of this campaign, our family enjoyed staying close to the Emperor, owing to Melissa's friendship with the Helena, and to the Emperor's interest in her. But now—"

"But now, because you refused to give Melissa's hand to him, the Emperor has grown cold with you."

"It has not affected Melissa's friendship with the princess—and, thankfully, the Emperor is pleasant toward her." Florentius glanced up at the blue sky as his mind wandered off in thought.

"What is wrong, friend? You seem troubled."

"I am thinking of your son, Lucius. His death is my fault. I should have done more to prevent him from going into battle."

Varronius stood in protest. "Nonsense! My boy wanted to be a soldier. Lucius was never have been at peace, being an observer only as others risked their lives in battle." He strode over to Florentius. "And what might you have done to stop him?" The count snorted. "You might have sat on him! But you could not sit on him forever. He was stubborn like his father and brother, Jovian." Deep wrinkles formed beside the count's eyes as they grew moist. His expression grew tender. "Do not fault yourself, Florentius. I do not, old friend. Not in the least."

Portia could be heard calling from inside the house. "Florentius? Varronius? Where are you?"

"My wife comes," said Florentius, as he wiped a tear away.

Varronius took a long drink from his cup. "Ha! We must not let a woman see that two old soldiers have been crying," he said.

Portia came out into the garden with Melissa. "Ah, there you are! See who I have brought outside with me."

Melissa hurried over to Varronius and embraced him. "It is good to see you, Father."

Varronius smiled. Tears began to well in his eyes again. "I have not seen you since Mediolanum, the night of the betrothal. It cheers my soul to hear you call me *father*. I will forever think of you as a daughter."

Varronius and Melissa sat down on a bench together.

"I am so sorry about Lucius," she said. Melissa's face, devoid of any cosmetics, appeared tired and pale. Her long hair hung down around her shoulders. Though washed, it appeared she had taken neither interest nor time to style it.

"Lucius wrote me of his great love for you," said the count. "Even though he was taken from us too young, it is a great consolation for me knowing what happiness you brought him."

Melissa lowered her eyes. She brought her hands to her face. Tears ran down her cheeks. "Suddenly, I am tired. Excuse me, Count. I must retire to my room." Melissa got up to leave.

Portia frowned. Her hands dropped to her sides in frustration. "You only just came down, my dear!"

The count stood to bid Melissa goodbye. "Do not weep forever. An end must come to all mourning. You will find happiness and love again. You are young—with much life ahead of you."

"That is what I tell her!" said Portia. "But my daughter never listens to me."

"While I have no choice but to listen to you, my dear wife," said Florentius.

Varronius took Melissa's hands into his. "You need a splendid diversion to cheer you." The count smiled. "I have just the idea! The imperial fleet is anchored in the harbor. The Emperor will review the fleet later this week before it sails to winter at Portus. Bishops from all over Gaul, who have just arrived to attend a council in the city, will be there. There will be a great party. You must come with your father and mother. The day after the review, the Emperor will sail on his new imperial galley—the *Ithaca*, the fastest ship in the fleet. I will see you all are invited."

Melissa fought back tears. "I do not think I will be up to it."

The count hugged her. "I understand, my dear. I will not twist your arm." He pulled back and looked into her eyes. "But, will you do me a favor? At least—consider it?"

"I will consider it, father," she said with a weak nod. She stood on her toes to reach up to kiss him on the cheek. She then withdrew from the garden.

Portia watched Melissa disappear into the house. "She has been inconsolable since the death of Lucius. She loved him so. We have been in Arelate for a couple of months. She has hardly gone out at all."

"She needs time, that is all," said Varronius.

Portia shook her head. "No. She needs a push." She tapped a finger to her chin as she thought of ideas.

Florentius glared at Portia. "If a push, it must be a gentle and subtle one."

"Oh, I agree," she said. "Gentle and subtle."

"Neither of which are you capable, my dear."

***

Septimus, wearing a scruffy, light-brown beard, sat on the floor of a prison cell leaning against the stone wall. Beside him, Jason counted the neat rows of scratches he had etched into the stone to mark the days, weeks, and months that had passed. Their hands and feet were bound by shackles.

"We have been in this dungeon for over eight weeks," said Jason, his beard now down to his chest and his hair down to his shoulders and upper back

Septimus glanced about the large cell in which they were held. Morning rays of sunlight streamed through three narrow, barred windows set high into the wall to his right, ten feet above the floor. The light from above provided some relief from the shadow and gloom around him. He grimaced. "Once this room was full." *Fellow officers. Civilians and clerics. Those arrested by agents of Constantius. How many others have come through this dungeon in the past months? Thousands, perhaps. Tried and sentenced to death or exile. Poor Father Paul . . . he was among the first taken away. Never to return. I fear what became of him.* "Now it is just the two of us."

Septimus rose to his feet. He shuffled across the cell, the chains between his feet clinking along the stone as he did. The tribune wore a red tunic beneath a padded gray shirt, which he had worn beneath his armored cuirass at the Battle of Mons Seleucus. So many weeks later, these were now faded and covered in dust and dirt. He peered out the barred window of the cell door.

"We must hold a special place in someone's heart, to be among the last tried," said Jason. He chuckled to himself. "I suspect Emperor Constantius has a special place in his heart for us. He will not have forgotten or forgiven us for burning the bridge over the Drava, nor for the loss of his squadron of cataphracts at Mons Seleucus."

Footfalls and voices echoed in the corridor outside the cell. Angling himself to see as far down the hall as he could through the opening, he saw the dim glow of an approaching torch.

"The gaolers come," whispered Septimus. He shuffled back to Jason and sat on the floor beside him. "We must escape. If they take one of us to the tribunal, we must do as I suggested."

The rattling of iron keys sounded outside the cell door.

Jason tilted his head back and rested it against the stone. He laughed. "That crazy plan?"

"I prefer to call it *audacious*."

Jason shook his head. "You have been talking about it for weeks. It won't work."

The tribune looked around the cell. "Well, if you had agreed to it before now, we might have had others to help. Only we two remain. It is now or never."

Jason paused to think. He then gave a grudging nod. "Very well. I suppose there is no alternative now." He sniffed at the air. "I will gladly risk death and danger, if for no other reason than to escape the horrid smell of this place."

The iron hinges creaked as the heavy wooden door was pushed in. The head gaoler, with a large barrel of a belly, entered the cell carrying a torch. He was followed by two muscular gaolers. The larger of these two wore a patch over one eye. The other had many missing and broken teeth. Each of the three gaolers wore a leather

317

cuirass over a gray tunic and a simple iron helmet.

The head gaoler pointed his two comrades toward Septimus. "That one," he said.

The one-eyed gaoler reached down and yanked the tribune to his feet with one quick move.

As he gained his balance when brought to his feet, Septimus tilted his head back to look up at his one-eyed captor. "Polyphemus, I presume?" he asked with a hint of a mischievous smile.

"Don't mind this one," said the head gaoler pointing a club into the tribune's chest. His eyes cold as he considered Septimus. "Your day of judgment has arrived, Tribune," he said, gloating. Dragging him out of the cell, they slammed the door shut.

Jason rolled his eyes. "It is still a crazy plan. God help us."

***

The two gaolers dragged, pushed, and shoved Septimus along damp corridors and then up a flight of stairs. They brought him to a heavy wooden door and opened it. The tribune squinted, blinded by the bright morning sunlight, as he stepped onto the paved courtyard of a fortress. The footfalls of drilling legionaries and the clatter of horses and riders echoed within the walls. Bordering the courtyard on one side stood a brick wall and the main gate of the fortress, and on the remaining sides were brick buildings, some two to three stories high. The buildings included the Praetorium, barracks, and residences and apartments for senior officers and their families.

Septimus observed a stable stood beside the dungeon house. "That explains the smell," he muttered to himself.

His gaolers led him toward the Praetorium, passing several dozen prisoners shackled together and surrounded by guards.

At once, Septimus recognized many of the prisoners. He tried to pull back against the tug from the gaolers. "Drusus!" he shouted, seeing many belonged to Jason's company of men. "Samson!"

The larger of the two muscular gaolers, who wore the patch over an eye, pushed the tribune through the door into the Praetorium before he could receive a response. "Keep moving," said the gaoler.

Septimus turned to the one-eyed gaoler. "Where are they taking those men?"

The cyclops glanced at his comrade. "Demetrius, this one wants to know where they are taking his friends," he said with a cackle. "Why don't you tell him?"

"They are going downriver to the harbor—to the fleet," said Demetrius with a sinister grin exposing the few teeth he had left his mouth. "It is to be the galleys for that lot. Chained to an oar for the rest of their short lives."

The gaolers brought Septimus to a large room and made him sit on a wooden stool. Sunlight from a window set high in the wall illuminated the floor around the tribune. In the shadows in front of him stood a long table behind which sat three gray-haired judges wearing white togas.

"His name?" asked the seniormost judge, the oldest of the three, sitting in the center. He rapped his fingers on the table, appearing impatient and rushed.

"Gaius Marius Septimus," said the gaoler wearing the patch.

"Also known as 'Romanus'?" asked the judge, now referring to a stack of parchments in front of him. "Is this correct?"

Septimus nodded. He studied the judges. On either side of the senior judge, his comrades seemed equally disinterested in the proceeding. The judge on the left seemed to daydream as he drew pictures on the parchment before him. The judge on the right, who sat with a wine cup in front of him, struggled to keep his eyes open. *There is no mercy to be had from this lot.*

The judge set down the parchment. "You were a legionary commander in the service of the Usurper—otherwise known as Flavius Magnentius. Do you deny this?"

Septimus shook his head.

"Our sources in Rome have provided a report which details your family's wealth and property," said the judge.

"What?" asked the tribune.

"The wealth and holdings of the House of Marius in Italy and Iberia have been forfeited to the Emperor. Land. Cattle. Gold. Silver. All of it."

Septimus sprung to his feet. His face grew red with anger. "It is

319

not all mine. The greatest part of it belongs to my father and my brothers."

The one-eyed gaoler punched the tribune in the stomach. Septimus doubled over in pain and fell to his knees. Septimus struggled to regain his breath. He glared at the cyclops.

"It belongs to the Emperor now," said the judge, his tone cold and devoid of any emotion. "Your wealth, like the wealth of all rebels, will help replenish the imperial coffers."

"My father and brothers have nothing to do with my case!" said Septimus.

The cyclops of a gaoler knocked the tribune to the ground. "Silence!"

"They have *nothing* to do with my case!" shouted Septimus again. As he rose to a knee, the same gaoler struck him down again. His head spinning from the blow, the tribune's jaw tightened as he glanced up at the muscular gaoler who towered above him. *Today will be your day of reckoning, Polyphemus.*

"This tribunal decides who and what is relevant to your case," said the judge. The three judges conferred for a few moments in a whispered conversation. The senior judge then cleared his throat and began to read from a scroll. "This tribunal, constituted by our lord, Constantius, Imperator et Augustus, declares you—Gaius Marius Septimus Romanus—guilty of treason."

"How can it be treason to fight for one's own Emperor?" said Septimus. He looked to each of the three judges in shock and disbelief. "What sort of trial is this? Your sentence was already written out for you to read!"

"Silence!" shouted the judge.

The gaoler knocked Septimus off his chair, sending him again to the floor. He kicked the prisoner. "You heard the judge! Silence!"

The judge continued with the sentencing. "Being found guilty by this tribunal, you and all members of the House of Marius forfeit all properties, wherever they may be found. We deprive you of your military rank and sentence you to perpetual exile from the Roman world. The sentence of exile to be executed as soon as arrangements can be made to transport you to the frontier."

"Wait!" shouted the tribune.

Ignoring Septimus, the judge gestured to the gaolers. "Take him back to his cell."

***

The two gaolers, each holding the tribune by an arm, pushed him out of the Praetorium and down the several steps to the courtyard. The tribune's chains rattled along the stone. As he was pulled along back toward the prison house, Septimus looked for Drusus, Samson, and the other prisoners who he had seen on the way to his trial. His shoulders slumped. They were nowhere to be seen. *They are on their way to the fleet and life in the galleys.*

The one-eyed gaoler cackled. "Looking for your fellow rebels, Tribune?"

"You will not see them again, ever," said Demetrius with a near toothless grin.

As they were about to pass the stable on the way back to the prison-house, they paused. A squad of legionaries passed in front of them, rolling a red carriage out of the stable. Stable hands followed behind them, leading a team of four horses to hitch to the carriage.

Septimus observed a golden eagle painted on the side of the carriage. *The imperial insignia.*

The gaolers retraced their steps into the gloom of the dungeon until they stood with Septimus in the passageway outside of his cell. There they were met by the head gaoler in the gloomy, torchlit hall.

Jason grasped the bars as he peeked through the tiny window of the cell door. "What news, Tribune? Has your time come?"

"Shut up in there!" said the heavyset head gaoler.

The one-eyed gaoler laughed as he and his comrade Demetrius still held tight to the Septimus, who appeared too weak to stand on his own. His legs seemed ready to buckle underneath him.

The head gaoler observed the tribune wincing in pain. "What's wrong with that one?"

"I had to work him over a bit," said the cyclops. "He was a bit insubordinate during the trial, you might say!"

The head gaoler chuckled. He pushed his helmet back off his forehead. "So, what sentence did they give him?"

"Exile for him!"

"Exile?" asked the head gaoler, puzzled and disappointed. He grappled a ring of keys from an iron hook set into the damp stone. "Is that all? I thought for sure it would be death for him."

"A former Roman tribune exiled beyond the frontier?" said Demetrius, again bearing a near-toothless grin. "He will not last long! If the brigands don't kill him, the barbarians will." He saw Jason peeking through the window of the cell door with a smirk. "Your fate will be worse. You will join your comrades in the galleys. The fleet is in the harbor."

Jason squinted to see the tribune. "Is this true?"

Septimus nodded. "Exile for me. The galleys for you and your comrades. I am afraid the *time* we have spoken of has come. We must part."

Jason winked. "Understood."

The head gaoler approached the heavy wooden door of the cell. The rattling of the keys echoed in the dark halls of the dungeon. He glared at Jason whose face still pressed against the small opening. "Get back from the door while I open it, prisoner!"

Jason's head disappeared from view into the shadows.

The gaoler unlocked the door and pushed on it. The door did not budge. "What's this about?" he said. He pushed again but the door did not give an inch. He peered through the window then looked at his comrades, his face turning red. "He is lying on the floor—bracing the door with his legs and feet!" He peered inside the cell. "Move away from the door, if you know what is good for you!"

"If you say so!" called out Jason.

The gaoler tested the door, pushing at it with one hand. It did not open. Muttering curses under his breath, the gaoler walked to the weapons rack. He straightened the helmet on his head, then grabbed a thick, sturdy club. The gaoler thumped it a few times against his open palm. He glared at the door. "It won't be the galleys for you, it will be the sharks. I will turn you into chum myself."

His comrades laughed. "Beat him senseless!"

"Be careful, Jason!" shouted Septimus. "You have made the troll rather mad. He has taken down a club. He will beat you senseless."

The one-eyed gaoler shook the tribune as he held his arm.

322

"Quiet!"

Septimus shrugged. "Sorry! I was only trying to help."

The gaoler returned to the cell door with his club. He backed up several steps, preparing to get a running start at the door.

"Surrender Jason, he is about to force the door!" said the tribune.

"No, never!" shouted Jason. "I do not want to die in a galley. I will not move from the door!"

"I will beat you senseless," said the gaoler. He took another couple of steps backward for good measure and then rushed forward at full speed. He plunged his left shoulder and chest into the heavy door, driving against it with all his might. However, instead of offering resistance at impact, the door gave way and flung open. The momentum of the gaoler carried him into the middle of the cell. "What the—"

Before the gaoler could react or recover his balance, Jason grabbed him by the collar and, as the gaoler screamed for help, rammed him headfirst into the far wall of the cell. The man crumpled to the floor.

The two gaolers holding Septimus glanced at each other wondering what they should do.

"Quick, the Ostian is loose!" the tribune shouted. "He will kill your comrade, save him! Quick!"

The toothless gaoler let go of Septimus and rushed into the cell to help his comrade, too used to taking commands to stop and think. As soon as he disappeared inside, Septimus turned against the remaining gaoler who held his other arm. He tackled the hulking man, driving him into the stone wall with a thud. The gaoler's iron helmet toppled off his head, striking the floor with a loud clank, the echo resounding in the dungeon.

The cyclops grabbed hold of the tribune by his padded shirt. Lifting him off the floor without effort, he hurled Septimus across the narrow corridor. The tribune's chains rattled against the stone as he slid down to the floor. The twin of Polyphemus sneered. "Didn't get enough earlier, did you, Tribune?"

Septimus stared back at the cyclops, who, turning his back on the tribune, headed toward the weapons racks, a few yards down the corridor. Helpless, Septimus looked about for something to use as a weapon. *The helmet!* The tribune grabbed the gaoler's helmet that lay on the floor. Springing to his feet, he took several steps, and with his hands still in manacles, threw the helmet at the gaoler, striking him in the back of the head. The cyclops did not even flinch.

The tribune watched as the helmet struck the gaoler's head, then bouncing to the ground, it rolled across the stone floor. Without even bothering to turn to face Septimus, the cyclops shook his head dismissively.

"Uh oh," muttered Septimus.

The gaoler reached for a club on the rack. His feet chained, the tribune shuffled forward. Jumping onto the gaoler's back, he threw his arms over the cyclops' head. Using the chain between the manacles, he began to choke the gaoler. The cyclops dropped the club as he struggled to pull at the chain now tight around his neck. As his face grew red, he slammed Septimus from side to side against the walls of the corridor, but the tribune held on tight for his own life. At last, the cyclops, his face now dark purple, fell back onto the floor, pinning Septimus beneath him. The gaoler's body grew still.

Pushing the heavy body to one side, the tribune saw Jason standing over him. Septimus winked. "Told you my 'audacious' plan would work."

Jason shook his head. "There is no earthly reason this crazy plan should have worked, Tribune. None."

Septimus frowned. "Thank you for your faith in me. That hurts."

The two retrieved the keys and unlocked their shackles. They chained and gagged the guards, and closing the door, locked them inside the cell.

"I saw your comrades," said Septimus. "Drusus and Samson were among them."

"Where?" asked Jason. "When?"

"In the courtyard, an hour ago. They are to be taken to the river and then on to the harbor."

"I cannot let that happen!"

"Nor will I abandon them to such a fate, if it be within my strength to prevent it."

Jason glanced down the dungeon corridor. "What then—what is the rest of your escape plan?"

Septimus shrugged. "I do not know. I did not think we would get this far."

***

Melissa lay on her bed. Without a candle lit and with shutters closed, the room was swamped in darkness. There came a soft knock at the door.

"I am resting," groaned Melissa.

There was another knock, this time more insistent.

"I am napping. Go away!"

"Open this door," came a muffled shout from the other side. It was Princess Helena.

Melissa hurried across the room. She unbolted the door. The princess entered the bedchamber, breezing past her.

"Good morning, Princess. I did not realize it was you at first."

Helena walked around the apartment. The princess frowned. "Good morning, you say? It is so dark in here, how can you even tell the time of day?" She threw open the shutters and the door to the balcony. The bright light of day washed into the room. "Morning? My dear, it is past noon."

The princess strolled about the room, inspecting it. Melissa's sketch of Rome rested on a stand. "This is the same piece you began in Rome? The same piece I saw in Mediolanum?"

Melissa nodded.

"You have made no progress in all this time," said the princess. "Tell me . . . are you Penelope awaiting her Odysseus? Do you undo your work in the late watches of the night, all to thwart your many suitors?"

Melissa sank into a chair. Her shoulders slumped as she lowered her head.

Helena hastened to her side. She crouched beside Melissa and placed an arm around her. "I am sorry. It was a bad joke. I know you are sad, and here I am making jokes about Penelope and Odysseus. Forgive me!"

The princess pulled a chair next to Melissa and sat. "I know you still grieve for Lucius. However, many weeks have passed since his death. I recently saw the count. The poor man also grieves the loss of Lucius. Nice man that he is, he is concerned more for you than for himself."

Melissa looked at her hands. She rubbed and wiped at them as if trying to wash something off of them. "My father . . . mother . . . and the count . . . they all think I cry out of sadness for the loss of Lucius."

"Do you not?"

Melissa shook her head. "It is remorse. Shame. Guilt. Whatever one might call it."

"Guilt? Over what?"

"Guilt over not having loved Lucius at all," said Melissa. "I did not believe we were meant to be together. No, that is not it. I did not want us to be together. He was a good man. So, everyone told me. Whilst he lived, those who I trust and respect insisted he was a man of character. A devout man. He told me that he loved me." Tears welled in her eyes. "Why was that not enough for me? I grieve, but not because I loved Lucius. I grieve because I did not love him and still do not. Not even now in death."

"You are just confused," said the princess. She held Melissa's hand.

"Do you not see? I did not love him. *That* is what killed him. I killed him."

"Nonsense!" said Helena. "His death was not your fault."

Melissa's fingernails bit into her palms as she squeezed her hands into fists. "It was. My distance and coldness toward him are what pierced his heart. This killed him as much as any mortal wound did that horrible day at Mons Seleucus."

"Oh, my dear, you do not know that!"

"Perhaps not by any clear word or sign, but in my heart, I know it to be true with certainty," said Melissa. "He knew he did not have my love. I was cruel. I was indifferent and cold and never tried to conceal this hard truth from him. Out of spite against my father, who contracted a marriage against my wishes, I did not wish to veil it from him. He, not they, became the object of my scorn. I had wished that my indifference would lead Lucius to lose heart and abandon our engagement. Instead, it only seemed to light the desire of his broken heart to try all the more. Father has never spoken of it, but I believe it was out of a forlorn hope that he volunteered for the battle, thinking it might win my respect, if not my love. I sent him to his death."

Helena embraced Melissa. "Do not reproach yourself with such harsh accusations."

"I was cruel. So cruel, that I am undeserving of any man's devotion or love ever again."

"Lucius was a brave and honorable man," said Helena. "You would have come around to it and learned to love him in time, had he lived. I know it. But Lucius is now dead and buried. He would not want you wallowing over him like this. You will have love and devotion one day."

The princess stood. She reached down and, grabbing Melissa by her hands, pulled her to her feet. "Get up!" she said, her tone firm and resolute. "One must not wallow away the days, lingering over past regrets or mistakes that are now beyond one's ability to repair."

Helena led Melissa out onto the balcony which overlooked the fortress courtyard. Above, the sun shone down from a clear blue sky. Below, a dozen legionaries marched to the gate for the changing of the watch. "Arelate may not be Rome or Constantinople or even Mediolanum—but it is a lovely city, and it is a lovely fall day. My brother says the court will move back to Mediolanum after the new year." She glared at Melissa. "You have not seen much of this city. There is a stadium. A theater for plays and orations. A hippodrome. You have seen none of it! I have gone on far too long, letting you wallow and hide in your despair. No more!"

The princess pointed to the courtyard below them. "Do you see the horses and carriage across the courtyard?"

Melissa nodded. There at the steps of the Praetorium rested a red carriage emblazoned with the imperial insignia. Stable hands worked to hitch a team of four black horses to it. A squad of a dozen mounted riders wearing the black of the Imperial Guard waited close by.

"I have ordered a carriage from the stable to take you and me on a tour of the city this afternoon," said Helena.

The princess dragged Melissa back inside the room. "Come,

dress in something pretty, and fix your hair!" she commanded. "I promised the count—and your mother—that I would help you escape from this self-made dungeon of yours. We will see the city this afternoon. Later on today, we will go to the harbor to watch a naval review. My brother wants to show off his new galley—the fastest in the fleet, he says!"

"I don't know," said Melissa.

Helena scowled at her. "I will not take no for an answer! I know you love the water. Do not even dare pretend you do not want to go."

Melissa smiled limply. "Okay."

"Besides, Tribune Marcus Scudillo is just back from a trip to the east," the princess added. "He expressed an interest in escorting us—once I mentioned you would be coming!"

"Marcus?" she asked as if she had not heard the name in a long time. "He is a tribune now?"

Helena laughed. "You would have known all about his promotion if you had not been living such a secluded life of late. There are many things for you to catch up on, but I must spoon-feed them to you, otherwise, your head might burst if you were to ingest them all at once!"

Melissa hugged Helena. "You are a dear friend."

Helena giggled. "Do not think so highly of my motives in getting you out and about. I also have a selfish motive. There will be many handsome officers at the naval review—such as Claudius Silvanus. But I cannot go alone." Helena placed her arm around Melissa's waist. They walked out onto the balcony. "We will have such fun today, Melissa—I just know it!"

Chapter 20

The Ithaca

Helena strolled arm in arm with Melissa across the fortress courtyard. A squad of legionaries drilled under the watchful eyes of a centurion. Shouts, the clank of armor, and marching echoed within the fortress. The two women walked toward a carriage parked outside of the Praetorium. An escort of a dozen horsemen waited in front of the carriage, and an officer stood beside it.

The princess, wearing a long red tunic with a purple girdle about her waist, gave Melissa a slight nudge with her elbow. "There is Tribune Marcus."

Melissa observed Marcus standing near the carriage, attired in a breastplate and helmet which glittered in the sunlight. Chatting with one of the dozen riders of the escort, he had not yet seen them as they crossed the courtyard toward him.

"I haven't seen him for a couple of months, not since our arrival in Arelate," she said.

"Apparently, Marcus was on a mission of some sort—very secretive," said Helena. "My brother promoted him when he returned to Arelate a few days ago. Now that Marcus is back, he seems different. He has changed."

"Different? How so?"

The princess tilted her head to one side as she thought for the moment. "I cannot put my finger on it. Something happened to him. His mind seems elsewhere. He seems sadder." She glanced at Melissa from the corner of her eyes. "He now reminds me of the

329

mood you have been in." Helena winked at her friend. "Perhaps seeing you will cheer him up. Perhaps it might cheer *you* up."

Melissa lowered her eyes, her shoulders drooped slightly. "I am not ready for romance, Princess." *I don't know if I will ever be, now or ever.*

"Princess Helena and Lady Melissa!" said Marcus as the two women neared. His face lit up upon seeing Melissa. He took off his helmet. He stood back as he studied Melissa who wore a yellow tunic with a green girdle about her waist. Her long brown hair was gathered in a bun, from which several curls hung down upon her bare collarbones. "You look well, Melissa."

Melissa gave a slight bow of her head. "It has been quite some time since we have seen each other."

"Quite some time," said Marcus. "I hope it will not be so long until the next time."

"Oh, I told Melissa your wonderful news," interjected the princess. She nudged Melissa again with her elbow. "Did I not?"

"Yes, I understand you were promoted to tribune," said Melissa. "All for what you did on some mysterious mission for the Emperor."

The smile faded from Marcus's face. He averted his eyes for a moment, glancing down at the stone pavement. "Thank you, Lady Melissa." He placed his helmet back on. "But come. Your carriage and escort are at your service." He assisted the women as they climbed into the open carriage, which had two rows of benches behind the perch for the drivers.

"Melissa has not been well," said Helena. "A tour of the city and a ride down to the harbor for the naval review might help her feel better."

Marcus saluted the princess. "I shall lead your escort, personally."

Helena smiled. "Why don't you join us, Tribune? Ride with us in the carriage. You must sit next to Melissa and tell her all you know about the city."

Marcus grinned. "It would be an honor to do so."

"Excellent!" said Helena. "Then it is settled."

Marcus looked at the empty perch. He shook his head. "I am still waiting on the carriage drivers. Excuse me while I check to see what happened to them and inform the escort of the route we are to take." Marcus left the women alone in the carriage as he walked to the head of the escort column.

Melissa rolled her eyes at the princess. "Seating Marcus and me together. You can be worse than my mother sometimes!" she whispered. "Have I ever told you that?"

Helena giggled. "Yes, you have."

Melissa smiled to herself as she glanced at the blue sky. *Yes. Going for a peaceful ride on a beautiful day is just what I needed.* She looked out over the team of black horses. In front of them was a squad of mounted riders. Marcus stood before the decurion at the front of the column of men and horses.

"You will lead the escort," Marcus informed the decurion. "I will ride in the carriage with the ladies." He saw perch was still empty. He frowned. "Where are the drivers for this carriage?"

The decurion pointed toward the stable sixty feet away. "I saw two drivers step into the stable a few minutes ago."

Marcus strode toward the stable to find them when he saw two soldiers exiting it. "You two!" he shouted. "Come over here. I need drivers for this carriage."

The drivers looked at one other, seeming to hesitate. After conferring in a quiet discussion, they approached and hurried past Marcus, keeping their heads down and away from him.

Marcus scowled. "Hurry up about it or I will have you both flogged!" he yelled after them.

Melissa watched as the drivers hustled over and climbed into the carriage's perch. The two turned and saluted the ladies. They appeared disheveled and hurriedly put together in their uniforms. Their leather cuirasses and blue tunics were ill-fitting. The driver seated on the left of the perch had a scruffy beard that was visible beneath the cheek guards of his helmet. His face was grimy and beads of sweat ran down his face. The driver on the right wore a long, matted beard down to his chest. His long, black hair flowed out from under his tightly fitting helmet, reaching down to his shoulders.

"They are rather unkempt for soldiers," Helena whispered to Melissa. She brought a hand to the side of her nose and turned her head to her shoulder. "Unshaven. I dare say they have not bathed in quite some time."

The soldier on the left of the perch, seeming impatient, grabbed hold of the reins to the team of horses. He looked over his shoulder at the women. "Where to, my ladies?"

"The princess and I want a tour of the city," said Melissa.

"Right away!" said the driver. He prompted the horses forward, turning them hard to the left to avoid the cavalry escort. The suddenness of the movement threw the women back in their seats as the carriage lurched ahead.

Accustomed to the noise and echoes of the busy courtyard and focused on giving his instructions to the decurion, Marcus failed at first to notice the moving carriage. "Lady Melissa has not seen the city, so I want to take her by the . . ." he began to tell the junior officer before his voice trailed off into silence. Looking past the decurion, he saw the carriage heading toward the gate which opened to the city.

Marcus lowered his eyebrows. "Good Lord, what are they doing?" he muttered. "Hold on, what are you doing?" he called out to the driver. He hurried after the carriage. "I will have them flogged," he said to himself as the drivers drove the carriage onward, oblivious to his command. The carriage picked up speed. "Hold on there!"

The princess and Melissa, hearing the shouts from Marcus, turned to see him striding after them at a brisk pace. He waved his arms. "Stop!"

Helena tapped the driver holding the reins on the shoulder. "Excuse me, driver, should we not wait for the tribune?"

"Right away!" said Septimus. However, instead of pulling the horses to a halt, he urged them on to a trot.

Melissa glanced back, a confused expression upon her face. Marcus had paused in his pursuit of the carriage just as loud and frantic shouts rose up from the prison house. *What is happening?* Gaolers and legionaries emerged from the entrance to the dungeons. "Prisoner escape!" they shouted. "Two prisoners have escaped!"

"Prisoner escape?" gasped Melissa, as she blessed herself with a sign of the cross as she continued to observe the scene unfolding behind them. "Did you hear that, Princess?"

Helena clasped her hands together and grinned. "How exciting! An escape!"

Behind, two men, dressed only in their undergarments, stumbled out of the stable with their hands tied behind their backs and rags stuffed in their mouths. Melissa gasped and her gaze darted to Marcus. His eyes opening wide, he now ran after the carriage, now only fifty feet away from the gate. "Close the gate!" he shouted. "Close the gate at once! Prisoner escape! Close the gate!"

Melissa now faced forward as they began to move even faster. The officer of the watch at the gate called out to them as the carriage neared. "What is going on back there?"

"Two dangerous prisoners have escaped!" said the one holding the reins, as they began to pass through the gate. "They are loose in the fortress. We must get the ladies to safety. The tribune wants the gate closed after we pass!"

"Right away!" said the officer, who did as he was told.

Melissa clasped a hand to her heart, unable to speak.

Marcus arrived at the gate just as it shut before him. "Open the gate . . . open the gate!" he shouted. He pulled a nearby rider off his horse. After Marcus mounted it, he beckoned to the cavalry escort to join him. "The Princess and Lady Melissa have been abducted. Find that carriage! Split up and search the city! They cannot have gone far!"

As soon as the carriage cleared the gate, the driver urged the horses on as fast as he dared down the stone-paved streets. Making several tight turns down side streets, he pulled the carriage to a stop into a narrow alley.

The princess and Melissa turned around and glimpsed a troop of cavalry gallop as it passed by the entrance to the alley.

Melissa trembled as a realization suddenly dawned upon her. She reached and grasped Helena's hands. "I think we have been abducted!" she whispered.

The princess nodded with a broad grin. "Yes—I think so too!"

Melissa's jaw dropped. "Princess!"

"Is it not thrilling?"

The long-bearded soldier nodded to the driver. "The riders have passed."

The driver started the team of horses in motion. Reaching the end of the alley, they turned down a larger street. He handed the reins to his long-bearded companion to his right. He spun around in the perch to face the women. The clopping of hooves and the rattling of wheels upon the stone echoed along the street, which was clear of other traffic, as carts were not allowed into the city until after dark. Pedestrians about their day's business, seeing the imperial insignia on the carriage, stepped aside and bowed as it passed.

Helena raised her eyebrows as she looked upon Septimus. She put her lips to the ear of Melissa. "Is he not handsome? Look at his blue eyes or are they grey? Just like an emperor of old!"

He saluted the women. "Tribune Gaius Marius Septimus at your service, ladies." He patted his fellow escapee on the shoulder. "And this is my traveling companion—Jason."

Melissa put her mouth to Helena's ears. "We must not tell them who we are. We should say nothing about ourselves. God knows where they would take us—or what they might do to us."

"Quite right, Melissa!" Helena whispered with a nod. She then looked up at Septimus on the perch. She smiled at him. She presented her hand—palm down—to her captor, offering him the opportunity to kiss it. "My name is Helena. I am an imperial princess. Sister of Emperor Constantius."

Melissa cocked her head back as she glared at the princess. "Helena!"

Septimus smiled. He took the hand of the princess and kissed it.

The princess gazed at her captor. Rolling her eyes to one side, she gestured with her head toward Melissa. "Tribune Marius, meet my friend, Melissa, daughter of General Florentius—a very, very important general."

"Princess!" Melissa gasped. She folded her arms. "I will not let him kiss my hand, Helena—because he is *abducting* us!"

The princess winked at Septimus. "We both might fetch a dear ransom!"

"So, one of you is the sister of Emperor Constantius and the other the daughter of General Florentius? In truth, it is a small world. I have had occasion to meet them both."

There came a clatter of hooves from the road behind them.

"Jason, go!" said Septimus as four riders raced after them. "Imperial Guardsmen!"

The Ostian whipped the reins against the horses. "Yah!" The carriage lurched forward, throwing the women back in the seats.

"Faster!" said Septimus. He stepped down from the perch. The carriage hit a bump as Jason brought the team of horses to a gallop. Septimus stumbled toward Melissa before he caught himself—his face inches from hers. Each beheld the other. She closed her eyes. Expecting that his purpose was to steal a kiss from her, she winced and crinkled her face, as though tasting something awful. Several moments passed. She opened one eye. She opened the other. He was gone. Melissa turned and saw Septimus was now in the back of the carriage, struggling with one of the Imperial Guardsmen who had jumped from his horse onto the back bench. The two men fell down upon it, the guardsman atop the tribune with his hands at his throat. Septimus reached down and drew forth the soldier's sword. Using the end of the hilt, Septimus struck the guardsman on the side of his helmet, knocking it off. He continued to pound the side of the guardsman's face until he released his grip on the tribune's neck.

Melissa and Helena clung to each other for mutual protection as they watched. The two men wrestled for the sword, both now standing on the back bench. The guardsman managed to steal the sword back. Septimus held tight to his opponent's wrists, straining to keep the sword from slitting his throat. Changing tactics, the guardsman pulled back with all his might to free his wrists and hands to wield the sword. As the guardsman yanked his arms and body away from Septimus, the tribune simply let go. The guardsman's own momentum carried him backward until he tumbled off the moving carriage, sending the poor soul flying into a fruit stand on the side of the street as they passed by it.

Septimus gave a quick nod to the women. "Do not worry. We will let you go as soon as it is safe to stop."

"Safe for us—or for you?" shouted Melissa.

"Both—I hope!" said Septimus.

The women screamed as the other two guardsmen leapt onto the carriage from their galloping horses. The first pulled himself onto the driver's perch and wrestled Jason for control of the reins and the horses, while the other grabbed Septimus from behind and began to choke him. The clatter of hooves and the rattle of rolling wheels echoed down the streets of Arelate. Mixed with these sounds came the screams and shouts of "Get out of the way!" and "Watch out!" as pedestrians, shop owners, and street performers ran for cover. Some ducked into doorways while others jumped through the first-floor windows of shops and residences. The carriage careened from one side of the street to the other, hitting the curb one moment and sideswiping a merchant stand the next— sending fruit, vegetables, and fish sailing into the air.

Another imperial guardsman leapt onto the carriage and fell across Melissa's lap. She brought her hands to her cheeks. She shrieked. Red-faced and apologetic, the guardsman stood to his feet before the women, trying to keep his balance as the carriage swayed and rattled as it rolled along. "I am so sorry, my ladies. Pardon me. But have no fear. You will soon be safe!" He saw Septimus win the struggle against one of his comrades who, thrown to the street, tumbled along for several yards. Seeing this, he stepped up to the bench on which the women were seated. Standing between Melissa and Helena, he pulled his sword—ready to stab the unaware tribune in the back.

"Watch out!" Melissa screamed.

Hearing the warning cry, Septimus turned and saw the guardsman towering above him. "Thanks!" he shouted to Melissa.

Melissa glared at Septimus, her expression one of disgust. "I was not warning you!" She pointed to the soldier between her and Helena. "I was warning him!"

The guardsman paused. He raised a puzzled eyebrow as he glanced down at Melissa. "Warning me of what?"

Melissa pointed toward the street ahead. The guardsman turned to look, but before he could react, the carriage passed beneath the low arch of a footbridge that crossed over the street. In an instant, with a dull and sickening thud, the soldier was gone—swept off the carriage as it passed through the archway. Septimus went to the rescue of Jason, who still grappled with a guardsman. Tossed from the careening carriage by the tribune and Jason, the uninvited passenger landed in a dung-cart along the side of the road.

Tribune Marius took the reins and turned down another street and slowed the team of horses to a slow walk.

Melissa scowled at Septimus. "You are safe. Now let us go."

Helena grabbed Melissa's arm. "No, not yet! This is too much fun!"

Jason surveyed the street and shook his head. "Uh oh."

"What is it, Jason?" asked Septimus.

The Ostian gestured to the right side of the carriage where a wall towered over them and the length of the street. "The fortress."

Septimus lowered his head. He blushed as he shook his head. "Great Achilles' heel! We are back where we started.

"The horses knew where home is!" said Melissa with a gloating laugh.

"That is it, then," said Jason. His shoulders slumped. "We are done for."

The tribune lifted his head and gazed at the street ahead. "The bridge is up ahead. We can cross the Rhone and escape."

Listening to their conversation, Melissa looked toward the bridge ahead. The first fifty feet of the bridge projecting from the bank was of stone and cement. At the end of this length, loomed a fortified tower of stone and red brick that rose from the midst of the river. The tower housed a drawbridge that connected the shore to a wooden bridge high over the river which was built atop specially constructed pontoon boats tethered by strong lines to pylons upriver. Melissa smirked as she saw a half dozen mounted Imperial Guardsmen standing watch at the drawbridge. *They will not escape.* "I think I see Marcus at the bridge!"

"We cannot go that way," said Jason, seeing the way blocked.

Melissa leaned forward, her head between Septimus and Jason. "Ha! Now you will be caught. Tortured. Hung. Beheaded. Burnt alive. Or, whatever cruel thing that they do to awful people like you who deserve the cruel things that are done to them! But whatever horrible cruelty it might be, I am sure it will not be half as horrible or nearly as much as you deserve."

Melissa cocked her head back in surprise. The tribune gathered the reins into his hands with a tight grip. *What is he doing?*

Jason swept his long black hair back from his face. "What are you doing?"

Septimus urged the horses on to a trot. "The drawbridge is still down."

Jason squinted at the tribune with one eye. "Are you crazy?"

Septimus clenched his jaw. He turned to the Ostian. "I prefer *audacious*." He shouted at the horses and whipped the reins to bring the team to a full gallop, sending Melissa flying back into her seat.

Hearing the commotion and clatter, one of the guardsmen at the bridge pointed at the oncoming carriage. "Sir! Look!"

"Raise the drawbridge!" Melissa heard Marcus shout. "Raise it! Raise it now!"

The slaves within the tower's gear house, urged on by the whips of the foreman, turned the great winch to raise the drawbridge.

Melissa saw the drawbridge rising. Grabbing hold of the tribune's shoulder with her left hand and Jason's with her right, she pulled herself to her feet and kept her balance. "Are you crazy?" she yelled above the clopping of hooves and speeding wheels upon the stone and the rattling and shaking of the carriage.

The carriage reached the first length of the bridge. The Imperial Guardsmen and their horses had positioned themselves to block the path to the bridge. However, startled by the din of the onrushing horses and carriage, their own horses panicked. The horses reared up and bucked off their riders. A couple of the riders toppled over the side of the bridge into the river below with a loud splash.

The team of horses pulling the carriage along with them raced up the drawbridge. The princess screamed. Melissa, still holding tight to the tribune's and Jason's shoulders, glanced back at her friend to see Helena holding her arms outstretched above her head as she squealed in joy and excitement. With their speed and momentum, and unable to stop, the horses continued up and over the edge of the rising drawbridge—now nearly a half dozen feet off the pontoon bridge—and leapt. The horses and carriage sailed into the air in an arc. Melissa's feet lost contact with the floor, as she seemed to float. The pit of her stomach rose into her chest. She saw the other bank of the river with its own drawbridge tower. Then, as the carriage angled downward behind the horses, she saw the bridge fast approaching.

"Ah!" Melissa yelped as her body flew as the horses landed on the bridge, their legs nearly buckling as they did. A moment later, the carriage crashed hard and sudden, impacting the bridge at a steep angle. Melissa tumbled forward. There came two loud thuds in rapid succession, punctuated by a piercing snap of splintering wood. All went dark for Melissa, though she heard the clattering of the horses now on the wooden deck of the bridge and felt the rattling of the wheels as the carriage was pulled along. There then came another snap of wood, after which the momentum of the carriage began to slow. All the while, the clatter of the galloping horses grew more and more distant. At last, she felt the carriage come to a stop. No longer did she hear the clopping of hooves, only the gentle rush of the river against the pontoon boats upon which the bridge rested.

Shrouded in a fuzzy, brown haze, Melissa lay on her back, her legs elevated. A wave of anxiety swept over her. *I can't see! Have I been blinded?*

"Are you okay?" came a man's voice, full of concern. It sounded only vaguely familiar, but warm and comforting.

Melissa brought her hands to her eyes to feel them. Her bun had come all undone and her long brown hair now covered her face. She parted it. She exhaled a sigh of relief. *There is the blue sky! I can see!* Rolling her eyes to the right, she looked up into a scruffy beard and a pair of blue-gray eyes staring back at her. The man smiled. Melissa smiled back as she gazed into his eyes. *Such a lovely color. What a handsome face.* Then she remembered. *The escape! The abduction! The chase!* Melissa glanced from side to side. She had landed in the lap of Septimus, who had caught her in his arms as she had fallen forward. "Ah!" she shrieked as she scrambled to her feet, pulling herself free from his arms. She brushed down her ankle-length tunic, which had gathered above her knees during her fall.

Melissa brushed her hair back over her shoulders as she glanced about. *What happened?* It soon became clear to her. The team of horses was gone, galloping free across the lowered drawbridge on the far shore after the hitch had snapped off after the impact. The horseless carriage had rolled on with the momentum it had left, slowing as it went on wobbling wheels, coming to a stop one hundred and fifty feet from where it landed, two-thirds of the way across the bridge. Then she remembered something else. *The princess!* Frantic, she turned around.

Helena, the imperial tiara hanging crooked over her forehead, held her hands above her head as she grinned. "That . . . was . . . fantastic!"

Melissa glowered at her. *We've been abducted!*

Septimus took a deep breath and blew out the air as he exhaled. He turned toward Jason. He gave him a single nod. "That went surprisingly well."

As if on cue, all four wheels collapsed into a heap at the same moment, dropping the carriage to the deck of the bridge with a thud as they did.

As the carriage dropped and crashed to the bridge, Melissa lost her balance and fell over to one side. She found herself once again in the arms of Septimus, sitting upright on his lap with her arms around his shoulders, their faces and lips inches apart. She paused to listen to the clinking of the metal chains and gears of the drawbridge whence they came. A similar noise came from the other shore, where there was another drawbridge. "One drawbridge rises . . . the other lowers. Soon Marcus Scudillo will have you in chains."

Melissa squinted at him with cold, green eyes, their arms still around each other. She smirked. "You are trapped, Tribune. You cannot escape across the drawbridge ahead because even now they raise it." Septimus placed his hands about Melissa's waist and lifted her as he stood. Melissa tilted her head back to gaze into his eyes, even as her arms were still around his neck.

"Then, my lady, forgive me if I must take my leave," said Septimus. He turned and stepped from the carriage to survey his options for escape. He glanced to both ends of the bridge, then down and upriver. He locked eyes with Jason who had stepped down from the perch. They nodded and smiled at one another.

Jason ran to the end of the pontoon bridge that was closest to them. He glanced back toward Septimus. "Come on, Tribune!" he said as he climbed down over the edge and disappeared. Septimus began to walk hurriedly toward the edge of the bridge.

Helena climbed out of the remains of the carriage. She worked on straightening the tiara in her now disheveled hair as she ran after the tribune and pulled at his tunic to stop him. "Are you finished abducting us? You are not going to force us to go with you?"

"Princess!" said Melissa, as she caught up to her. "Do not give him ideas!"

Septimus faced Helena. He smiled. "Princess, neither of you were abducted. The carriage was handy. You ladies had the misfortune to be in it when we borrowed it."

He saluted and bowed to the women. "Princess Helena. Lady Melissa. I hope your hair and clothes have not been terribly mussed by this adventure. When you think of all the bad things that happened today—the abduction, the chase, jumping the drawbridge, and the danger of it all—please remember there were some positives."

"Positives?" demanded Melissa. "What positives?"

Septimus winked at her. "You did have your tour of the city." The clatter of hooves on the drawbridge drew their attention.

Helena grabbed Septimus by the hand, as he was about to turn away. "Wait!" she said. She flung her arms around him. She planted a long kiss on his lips. They stood two yards from the end of the bridge.

Melissa's jaw dropped. *She's kissing him.* "Helena! Remember yourself, Princess." She scrunched her eyebrows, as she placed her hands on her hips. *That should have been me, not her!* She bit her lower lip. *Wait, what am I thinking! Kiss him?*

"Farewell, ladies," said Septimus, as Marcus and the guardsmen hurtled toward them, less than fifty feet away.

Tribune Marius took a running jump off the end of the bridge. Melissa shrieked. *What is he doing? He will perish!* To Melissa's amazement, when she thought he would plummet the thirty feet into the river, a vessel passed through the opening left by the raised drawbridge. Septimus had waited and timed his jump to grab hold of the vessel's mast which rose a dozen feet higher than the deck of the pontoon bridge. He clung to the mast as he collided into it, wrapping his arms and legs around it. As the ship cleared the bridge, Septimus glanced back at the women. He bowed his head and saluted them one last time.

Melissa and Helena sighed together in relief.

At that moment, Marcus rode up and jumped off his horse. He hurried to the women. "Ladies! Are you all right?"

The princess and Melissa stood at the railing of the bridge. They faced south, watching the vessel as it continued downriver. The princess sighed. "Yes, we are all right," she said, dreamy-eyed.

Marcus leaned against the railing. He observed the vessel and chuckled. "They will not get far."

"Why is that?" asked Helena.

"Two reasons," said Marcus. "First, the river leads to the harbor where the entire fleet is anchored."

"And the other reason?" asked Melissa.

Marcus grinned. "They have landed on a prisoner transport with two dozen gaolers and legionaries aboard."

***

Jason climbed down over the side of the bridge. There he waited on top of one of the pontoons upon which the bridge rested. The vessel's crew shipped the oars to create clearance on each side of the craft as it drifted between the pontoon on the left and the concrete footing of the tower on the right. Sailors used wooden poles to keep the vessel centered as it went through the opening.

Scanning the vessel as it began to drift past him, he saw the deck crowded with perhaps a hundred men, seated in groups of ten. He cocked his head back in surprise. *Drusus! Samson!* There in the midst of one of the groups of men near center deck were his friends. *If the ship passes, they will be beyond my ability to save them.* Without another thought, the Ostian ran across the deck of the pontoon and leapt onto the passing vessel, landing at the feet of several oarsmen chained to a bench with a loud thud.

"Grab him!" shouted a gravelly voice from the deck a few feet above the rowing pit.

Jason scrambled to his feet as two legionaries set upon and took hold of him by the arms. They brought him out of the pit onto the deck. The men seated in groups of a ten were chained together, as were the several dozen men in the rowing pits on either side of the deck. Among the men on the deck were Drusus and Samson, as well as many of his Jewish comrades who had served with him under Magnentius. He heard "It's Jason!" spread in hushed tones from group to group as all eyes and attention on the vessel turned

342

toward him.

The two legionaries brought Jason before a one-armed gaoler, holding a rolled-up whip in his hand. The gaoler looked Jason over from head to foot. His attention lingered on the loose-fitting cuirass with an outline of a horse embossed across the chest. He took note of Jason's long black hair and beard, matted and unwashed. He shook his head. "What sort of soldier are you?"

Several legionaries and a gaoler, attracted to the commotion, ran over to them, their feet pounding on the wooden deck.

One of the legionaries holding him observed his cuirass. "He is a cavalryman."

"That's right," nodded Jason, at a loss of what else to say.

"What is your business aboard this ship?" the one-armed gaoler asked.

"Um, well," Jason said with a stutter. *I did not think this through.*

The one-armed man tapped the whip against Jason's chest. "Seems suspicious to me." He then gestured to the legionaries holding Jason. "Let's bring him to the officers. Let them decide what to do with him!"

"You are making a mistake!" Jason protested as he struggled to free himself. However, the two gaolers who had hold of him were too large and too powerful. They dragged him through the midst of the seated prisoners, bringing him before a centurion standing beside the mast.

"This soldier jumped on the ship back at the bridge," said the one-armed gaoler.

The centurion, wearing a transverse-crested helmet with alternating bands of white and black feathers, rested the end of his vine staff against Jason's chest. "Who are you, and what are you doing here?"

"It is an inspection," said Jason, with an unconvincing lilt in his voice that sounded more like a question than a statement.

"An inspection?" the centurion replied. He cackled in disbelief. He pushed back his helmet from his forehead. He raised an eyebrow.

Jason cleared his throat. "Yes—an inspection," he said in a dramatic voice. He glanced around at the prisoners. "There are criminals aboard the ship. Dangerous ones." He bent down and pulled at the chains of one prisoner, pretending to test the strength and security of the links. "Yes, yes—I can tell this chain is very secure. Well done." He looked around at the growing number of gaolers and legionaries surrounding him. "Where are the keys? Are they in a secure place?"

"They are secure," said the centurion, rattling a large ring of keys hanging on a hook from his belt.

The Ostian smiled. "Yes, I see." *Now I know where the keys are.*

"All right, what is this all about," shouted a voice approaching from the stern. The group of legionaries and gaolers around Jason parted. The captain of the ship, wearing a broad-brimmed hat, pushed his way through to the centurion and Jason next to the mast. "What is all this commotion about?"

"This man just jumped onto the boat as we passed through the bridge," said the centurion. He chuckled. "He said he is inspecting the ship." The legionaries around laughed.

The captain glared at the intruder. "I have never heard of anything like this on a prisoner transport." He leaned forward and studied Jason's face. "This is more than suspicious. What sort of inspection?"

Jason opened his mouth to give an answer. Nothing came out. He had run out of ideas. *Yes, should have thought this through. Looks like the galleys for me, too. At least I will remain with my friends.*

"Well—what sort of inspection?" said the insistent captain.

It was then Septimus appeared. Sliding down a rope from the top of the mast, he landed on his feet beside the astonished captain. The tribune cocked his arm back and punched the captain square in the face, sending the sailor into a couple of legionaries who all together tumbled backward into the rowing pit. Septimus nodded his head. "A surprise inspection."

Seizing the moment as all stood stunned at what just happened, Jason grabbed the keys from the belt of the centurion and tossed them to the waiting hands of Drusus. No sooner had Jason thrown the keys then he was grabbed from behind by the centurion, who began to choke him with his vine staff. A great shout went up among the prisoners as they cheered on the mutiny. Jason struggled to free himself; the two stumbling about the deck. As they came close to a group of chained men, one of the prisoners, grabbing hold of a couple of the leather straps hanging from below the centurion's cuirass, pulled him down to the deck. The prisoners around began to pummel the centurion. Wherever a gaoler or legionary was within reach on the vessel, other prisoners tripped or tackled them, doing whatever each could to win control of the ship. Drusus, after unlocking his shackles with the key, set about doing the same for his comrades and the other prisoners. As more prisoners were freed, they rushed to the aid of Septimus and Jason and soon the outnumbered crew and captors were subdued. When the fight was over, the ship was under the command of Tribune Marius.

Standing at the bow of the vessel, Septimus slapped Jason on the back. "All things considered, that escape when surprisingly well," he said with a smug smile.

Laughter drifted forward from the stern. Freed prisoners gathered around Samson, cheering him as he tossed the remaining gaolers overboard, one by one.

Jason raised an eyebrow. "All things considered, Tribune? Consider this. *Nothing* was planned beyond the initial breakout. The carriage. The drawbridge. The boat which just happened to pass with our comrades on it—at the *precise* moment we needed it. It is beyond serendipity. We could not have planned this outcome had we wanted to do so!"

"Okay. Fortune did smile upon us—a *bit.*"

"Do not give thanks to cold impersonal destiny."

"As Father Paul would say, 'If God is with us, who can be against us?'"

"That sounds right," said Jason as he looked downstream. Ships of the Roman fleet, anchored in the harbor, came into view. "What tricks do you have now, Tribune? We cannot outrun imperial galleys in this boat."

Septimus surveyed the boat and crew. Observing the pile of Roman helmets and uniforms piled on the deck, he picked up the centurion's helmet. He put it on his head and tied it on. He nodded to himself with a smile. He looked at the Roman fleet, a twinkle in his eye. "If this boat is not fast enough—let us pick a faster one."

***

Emperor Constantius, senior members of the imperial court, and other guests took their places on a reviewing stand which, set on a terrace, looked out on the harbor of Arelate. The guests included bishops from the surrounding provinces invited to the upcoming council. Musicians played in the background while servants circulated amongst the guests carrying platters of food and cups of wine.

Inviting the papal legates to sit at his right hand, Constantius sat down on his portable throne. "The war is over. It is a beautiful day by the sea. Let us have fun!"

At his word, flag bearers signaled to the fleet to commence the review. Members of the court cheered and applauded as galleys rowed past the reviewing stand in single file. The Emperor consulted with Count Varronius and other senior fleet commanders, who stood behind his chair, to learn the name and details of each ship as it sailed by.

Princess Helena and Melissa arrived on horseback under the watchful eye of Marcus and an escort. The women hurried up the steps to the terrace level. Helena glimpsed her brother on the reviewing stand. "My brother is smiling. I have not seen him this happy in some time." She pulled Marcus and Melissa aside. "For the moment, let us say nothing about what happened to us today."

"Why not?" asked Melissa. *Of course, the Emperor must hear of this!*

"Look at my brother," said the princess. "He smiles. He is in a good mood today. Hearing that his sister was abducted would send him into a furious rage. He has such a frightful temper. This party would be ruined." She grabbed two cups as a slave girl passed by with a platter of wine. She handed one to Melissa, who took it with reluctance. Helena took a long sip from her own. "I want to enjoy the rest of the day!"

"I must tell the Emperor at once!" said Marcus, his tone firm and insistent. "His sister—a princess—and a daughter of an important general were abducted." The tribune fidgeted in embarrassment as he continued. "What is more, I saw the prisoner take liberties with you that he should not have taken."

"You will do what I command," said the princess, scrunching her eyebrows as she lowered her voice. "And, another thing

346

Marcus—you will report *nothing* about the kiss to my brother. The escaped prisoner is in enough trouble. I will not add a harmless kiss to his list of crimes. Do you understand?"

Marcus's eyes widened. The princess had never used such a stern tone with him before. He bowed. "Yes, Princess—if that is your wish. My report can wait 'til later. By now the two prisoners have surely been recaptured and are in chains aboard the transport ship. I suppose there can be no harm in waiting."

Helena turned to Melissa and winked at her. "You must obey my command, as well. Remember, I am a princess!"

Melissa replied with a grudging, reluctant nod. "Okay. Not a word—for now."

"My dears—your hair . . . your clothes!" called out Portia, as she and Florentius strolled over to greet them. Portia looked at the two young women from head to foot. She gasped. You both look a little worn! What on earth happened to you?"

"We had something of an adventure getting here!" said Melissa, as her mother attempted to pat down her frazzled hair that had been hastily tied together in a single tail after coming undone on the bridge.

"An adventure?" asked Florentius.

The princess elbowed Melissa. She smiled at Florentius. "General, we had a carriage problem."

"A carriage problem?"

Melissa held a hand to where she had been elbowed. She glared back at Helena. *I am not going to lie to my parents.* "Yes, a *carriage* problem. Something to do with the wheels. We had to come part of the way by horse."

The princess took Melissa by the hand. "Excuse us, General, and Lady Portia," said Helena as she led her friend away. "We would like to see the ships. Come along, Melissa!"

Florentius held his wife's hand. "You girls are acting a bit odd. Like you are hiding something."

"Does it matter?" asked Portia. "Melissa appears happy. Happier than she has been in a long time."

Melissa shrugged off the comments as she hurried away with Helena.

Soon, she and Helena found a place to stand along the terrace railing where they had a good view of the harbor. Surveying the terrace, Melissa spied the Emperor seated on his portable throne. There beside him sat her friend Aurelia. She felt a knot grow in her stomach. *Aurelia with the Emperor?* "Princess, Aurelia seems to be sitting very close to your brother, does she not?" asked Melissa.

Helena giggled. "Remember I said there were things which might make your head burst if I told you? If you had gotten out more these last months, you might have guessed this bit of news." Helena put her lips to her friend's ear. "My brother will take Aurelia Eusebia to be his bride."

Melissa's eyes opened wide. "Aurelia married to Constantius? She is to be an empress?"

The princess nodded. "They began to grow close in Rome about the time you returned to Mediolanum with your parents."

Melissa lowered her head. "Suddenly, I feel old." *What might have been had I not been betrothed to Lucius? Might that have been me sitting beside the Emperor and not Aurelia? But it is not like I loved the Emperor.*

Helena giggled. "Well, I feel young—I was kissed today!"

Melissa lifted her head. "*You* were kissed? Ha! You kissed *him* is more like it."

"Well, *maybe* I did. Just a little."

Melissa nodded. "Yes, you did! Just a little! But do not forget he is an escaped criminal. A condemned man."

"It was wonderful all the same," said the princess, dreamy-eyed. "But you had your chance. You were in his arms in the carriage on the bridge."

Melissa brought her hands to her face, the skin growing warm, as she remembered his face inches from her own. *His voice and his eyes.* "I must admit to something. When we were on the bridge, and I saw you kiss him, I felt jealous."

"Really? Jealousy?"

Melissa nodded. "I do not know why."

"Excellent!" said the princess.

"Excellent? What do you mean?"

"It means you *can* find love! Therefore, you can have him. I want you happy."

Melissa blushed deep red. "I can have *him*? That criminal?"

"Yes. My brother would never let me marry such a man."

Melissa laughed. "But my parents would? What do you think of them to say such a thing? What do you think of me? Heaven knows what that man did to deserve prison. He could be a thief . . . a murderer, or worse!"

"That is not what I meant," said Helena with a giggle. "I have told you before—Constantius will one day arrange my marriage for the *good of the empire* or something like that." She sighed. "That day will come. But, when it does, I will still have the happy memory of today." She giggled. "Since I cannot have him, with an unburdened heart, I give him to you."

"Thank you, Princess, for permitting me the rights to such a rogue!" Melissa said with a bow. They laughed. "But it matters not. We will never see nor hear of that rogue ever again—thank God."

"Helena and Melissa—I see you are finally here!" said Constantius as he approached them with Aurelia hanging onto his arm. Aurelia wore a long blue tunic trimmed with gold, that was a bit too tight for her plump figure. "Melissa, you two know each other, I believe."

Aurelia leaned against the Emperor's side. She stole a glance at Melissa's messy hair and her wrinkled tunic. "Hello, Melissa," she said as she ran a hand across the gold necklace that hung around her bare neck and then with the same motion touched her hand to the side of her head, displaying the matching earrings and bracelet about her wrist. She barely disguised a triumphant smirk as she wagged her head. "I have not seen you for some time. There is *so* much to tell you."

Melissa squinted at Aurelia. *You always wore too much red, drawing attention to your fat cheeks.* "I have not been well. But feel much better now."

"Tomorrow I will take out my new galley for a sail," said Constantius. "Helena and Melissa, you both must come along to keep Aurelia company. Smaller than a normal galley, it is sleek and swift. The fastest ship in the fleet they tell me."

There came applause from the guests as another galley passed in front of the reviewing stand. It moved with grace as it slid through the water, the oars cutting into the water and pulling the vessel forward with each stroke. Members of its crew hurried along the deck and up the mast to unfurl the sail and to set it.

The Emperor raised his eyebrows. He grinned. "Oh look! See how fast that one goes." Constantius beckoned to Varronius. "Count, pray tell, what ship is that?"

"That is your personal galley, my lord. The *Ithaca*."

"Look everyone!" said the Emperor as he shouted to all on the terrace. "Come look! My personal galley—the *Ithaca!*"

A cheer went up from the terrace. Three hundred court officials, officers, wives, bishops, and other guests rushed to line the edge of the terrace, two to three people deep. Several thousand citizens from Arelate, who had come out to picnic along the shore of the harbor, watched the imperial fleet pass in review, joined their voices to the cheers. All, great and small alike, waved to the crew of the *Ithaca* which was less than two hundred feet offshore. "Look— they wave back!" exclaimed Aurelia.

"I did not realize the *Ithaca* would sail during the review," said the Emperor. "I thought we were saving her for tomorrow."

"That was my understanding as well, my lord," said the count. "Seeing the ship now, I assumed you had ordered it to participate in the review."

"I gave no such order."

"Oh look—it is moving very fast!" said Aurelia. "It is so sleek and beautiful. What a marvelous vessel!"

Constantius kissed Aurelia on the cheek. He smiled. "Yes, my dear." He watched for several minutes as the galley turned and headed toward the mouth of the harbor. He turned to Varronius. "Count, the other galleys in the review turned around by this point."

"Yes, my lord."

Constantius furrowed his brow. "Then, why is my galley not turning around like the others? Where is it going?"

Varronius beckoned to one of his young naval aides for the answer. "Where is the Emperor's galley heading?"

"My lord, I do not know how the ship is even underway," said the young officer, his voice trembling. "Most of the crew aboard the *Ithaca* are on shore leave. There only a skeleton crew aboard her today."

The cheers and applause for the *Ithaca* grew as it continued to pull further away.

350

Constantius turned red. "Why is my ship not coming back?"

The guests on the terrace sensed a change in the Emperor's mood. The cheers, laughter, and even the music trailed away into silence.

"Why is my ship not coming back?" Constantius shouted. "Someone tell me!"

Marcus stepped forward. "I think I know why, sire."

"Why?"

Marcus lowered his head. "It has been stolen. Pirated."

The Emperor's jaw dropped. "*Ithaca* . . . stolen?" He glanced back at the harbor. The galley, at full sail, was now in the open sea, heading south. He glared at Marcus. "My ship—pirated?"

"My lord, two prisoners escaped from the dungeons this afternoon," said Marcus, sheepishly. "They commandeered a carriage—the princess and Melissa were in it when this happened. We gave chase, but the prisoners escaped. They jumped aboard a transport ship that was carrying galley slaves to the fleet. The transport's crew included many gaolers and legionaries. I cannot imagine how, but the prisoners must have seized control of that ship and then pirated your galley."

"After them," barked the Emperor. "I want those pirates brought before me!"

Naval officers scrambled from the terrace down to the docks. Horns blared, sounding an alarm to recall crews from shore leave.

Constantius turned his attention to the princess and Melissa. "You two were abducted? Why did you not inform me at once?"

"We just couldn't bear to tell you and break your festive mood," said the princess.

"It must have been awful for you both!" said the Emperor.

"It was horrid," said Helena, feigning a pout. She brought her hands to cover her face as if to cry. Turning her head to one side, she peeked at Melissa through her fingers and smiled. "Do you not agree, Melissa?" she asked with a wink.

Melissa bit her lip as she nodded. "Yes . . . it was horrid." She turned away to face the sea, resting her hands on the railing. Melissa watched the *Ithaca* recede into the distance. "It was absolutely horrid," she whispered to herself. Then she smiled.

INDEX OF CHARACTERS

Anicetus: Husband of Marciana the Elder (Lady Tertia). Father of Lady Marciana the Younger (Lady Marciana Quarta).

Arbitio: Commander of the Imperial Guard. Close confidante and coconspirator of the Grand Chamberlain Eusebius in various enterprises. Rumors claim as a younger officer he secured the imperial throne of the East for Constantius by organizing the massacre of members of the imperial family who were potential claimants to the throne.

Arius: A priest from Alexandria who originated the heresy (ARIANISM) named for him, which claimed Jesus Christ was not consubstantial (of the same substance) with God the Father; and so is not co-eternal with Him. The Council of Nicaea in 325 AD condemned Arius and his doctrine.

Athanasius: As a young deacon, he took part in the council of Nicaea. He was an able and visible defender of the Catholic faith against the Arians, incurring their enmity. Later named Bishop of Alexandria, which in importance was second only to the Apostolic See of Rome, Athanasius was a staunch defender of the faith of the Nicene Council. Deposed from and restored to his see many times by successive emperors, he once fled to Rome seeking the protection of Pope Julius and Constans (brother of CONSTANTIUS), Emperor of the West. Constantius later restored Athanasius to his See in Alexandria to keep the peace with Constans, who favored the Catholic faith. Constantius harbored resentment against Athanasius, believing the bishop had turned his brothers against him and for the fact he stood in the way of compromise with the Arians.

Aurelia (Flavia Aurelia Eusebia): Daughter of Flavius Eusebius who held various offices during the reign of Constantius. Friend and sometime traveling companion of Princess Helena and Melissa.

Camilia: Wife of Senator Gaius Marius.

INDEX OF CHARACTERS

Cassius: Legionary commander of the Third Italica before Gaius Marius Septimus (Romanus). Tribune Cassius was killed during an ambush in the streets of Rome by Nepotian's gladiators.

Constans (Flavius Julius Constans Augustus): Youngest of Emperor Constantine's three sons. Following the death of Constantine, his three sons divided the empire between themselves. Constantine II ruled the provinces of Spain, Gaul, Britain, and the westernmost reaches of North Africa. The youngest brother, Constans, received Italy, Illyricum, and parts of Northern Africa, while Constantius received the empire in the East, including Anatolia, the Levant, and Egypt. While Constantius favored the Arians, Constans accepted the Nicene faith. When Constantius deposed Bishop Athanasius, Constans gave the bishop haven in the West. Constantius forever blamed Athanasius for turning his brother against him. Constans lost his life in a revolt in 350AD which led to General Magnentius being named Emperor of the West. His death precipitated the Roman civil war between the Eastern and Western Empires.

Constantine (Flavius Valerius Aurelius Constantinus Augustus): Constantine was the fifty-seventh emperor of the Roman empire. He along with his co-emperor legalized the Christian religion after the Battle of the Milvian Bridge (313 AD). Defeating his imperial rival, Licinius, in a civil war, Constantine united the throne of the two empires in 324 AD. With Pope Sylvester, he called the Council of Nicaea and defended its edicts. His first son was Crispus, born of a concubine, Minervina, before his conversion. He married Fausta who gave him five children: Constantina, Constantine II, Constantius II, Constans, and Helena. Constantine ordered the execution of Crispus and Fausta, who he believed had plotted against him. Constantius died in 337 AD.

Constantina: Emperor Constantine's eldest daughter. Emperor Constantine married her off to her cousin Hannibalianus, who Constantine made king of the Pontic tribes. After the death of Constantine, rumors claim Constantius ordered the death of Hannibalianus and other kinsmen to eliminate potential rival claimants to the imperial throne. Constantius later married off

353

Constantina to his cousin Gallus when he elevated him to the rank and position of Caesar.

Constantius (Flavius Julius Constantius Augustus), aka Constantius II: He was the second oldest of Constantine's three sons. Following Constantine's death in 337 AD, his three sons and a nephew (Dalmatius) divided the empire amongst themselves. Constantine II ruled the provinces of Spain, Gaul, Britain, and the westernmost reaches of North Africa. The youngest brother, Constans, received Italy, Illyricum, and parts of Northern Africa, while Constantius received the empire in the East, including Anatolia, the Levant, and Egypt. Their cousin Dalmatius, granted the title of Caesar by their father, ruled over Thrace, Greece, and Macedonia. Rumors claim Constantius secured the imperial throne of the East by ordering the massacre of members of the imperial family he viewed as potential rival claimants to the throne. The religious policy of Constantius sought a compromise creed with the Arians who rejected the Nicene Creed.

Cornelius: A legionary in the Third Italica.

Cyprian: Marciana's older brother.

Domitia: The daughter of Anicetus and Marciana the Elder (Lady Tertia). The eldest sister of Marciana Quarta, Domitia became a Vestal Virgin known for her dour appearance and personality, and love of wine. According to an ancient custom, she was chosen by lot at the age of six from among the daughters of the noblest Roman families to enter the Temple of Vesta and become a priestess. The same custom which chose Domitia exempted her younger sister, Marciana, from ever having to become a Vestal Virgin herself. Noting that the dour and unattractive Domitia entered the temple and the beautiful Marciana was spared this fate, the single noblemen of Rome joked amongst themselves in whispers: *Vestae vincere. Romae lucrum*—"Vesta's win is Rome's gain."

Drusus: A close friend of Jason and Samson. He volunteered to join Jason's company of Jewish recruits for the war against Constantius and Gallus. Jason's father tasked Samson and Drusus to keep his son safe.

Eumaeus: Long-time servant to the household of Senator Marius.

Eusebius the Eunuch: Grand Chamberlain in the court of Constantius. He was the chief political aide to Constantius and had Arian sympathies. A close associate of Arbitio, Commander of the Imperial Guard, they used their positions to exact bribes and payments from office seekers.

Eusebius of Myndus: Philosopher and instructor of Julian in Pergamum.

Florentius (Flavius Florentius): Military advisor and chief of the Emperor Constantius's military planning staff, a task he assumed during the reign of Constantine. He served as a naval officer during the civil war between Constantine the Great and Licinius, taking part in the Battle of the Hellespont, during which he first came to the attention of Constantine, and in the Battle of Chrysopolis. Married to Lady Portia, he is the father of Melissa and several sons studying and training in Caesarea and Antioch. Florentius is a friend of Athanasius and Count Varronius. He is one of the few Catholics in the court.

Gallus (Flavius Claudius Constantius Gallus): The son of Julius Constantius. His father and a brother were killed in the massacre after the death of Constantine, some say by order of Constantius. Gallus and his half-brother Julian are all that remains of the male members of their family. Having elevated Gallus to the position of Caesar, Emperor Constantius gave his own sister Constantina in marriage to Gallus as war loomed with Magnentius in the West. The Emperor appointed Gallus to rule the East while the Emperor led the war against the Western Empire. Gallus is a friend of Marcus Scudillo, a captain in the Imperial Guard with whom he underwent military training.

Hannibalianus (Flavius Hannibalianus): Cousin and first husband to Constantina. Killed during the purge following the death of Constantine.

Helena: Daughter of Constantine and sister of Emperors

Constantius, Constans and Constantine II. Her best friend is Melissa, who she has known since the time they were small children.

Jason: The son of a Jewish merchant with a small fleet of ships that sailed out of Ostia. When a Jewish rebellion in the East broke out against Constantius and Gallus, he gathered a group of friends from Ostia and Rome to fight with the Western Emperor Magnentius against the Eastern Army, hoping to aid their people.

Julianus (Flavius Claudius Julianus) aka Julian: Born 331 AD. Half-brother of Gallus. His father and an older brother were killed during the massacre following the death of Constantine. He was a cousin to the Emperor Constantius.

Leontius: Military tribune and friend of Gaius Marius Septimus. Suffering a grievous wound in the Battle of Rome, Septimus saved his life as they fought Nepotian and his army of gladiators. At the onset of the civil war, Marcellinus appointed him commander of the Garrison of Rome to maintain the loyalty of the city to Magnentius.

Liberius: Pope and Bishop of Rome. He was elected pope following the death of Pope Julius in 352 AD.

Longinus: Held the senior rank of "First Centurion" of the Third Italica Legion. He is a Christian. Others are uncertain of his age though he is believed to have been near fifty years old at the start of the war with Constantius. He entered the legions in his teens and is a veteran of thirty years. He fought in the civil war against Licinius and took part in the Battle of Chrysopolis (324 AD).

Lucius (Captain): Served as an assistant and aide to Florentius on the emperor's military staff. Son of Varronius, and brother of Jovian, an officer serving in the army in the East. He experienced a crippling leg injury in training which left him unable to remain an active officer in the cavalry.

Magnentius (Flavius Magnus Magnentius): Declared emperor by the troops who murdered Constans. Constantius calls him "the Usurper."

INDEX OF CHARACTERS

Marciana Tertia (the Elder): Lady Tertia was the wife of Anicetus and mother to Marciana Quarta.

Marciana Quarta (the Younger): Daughter of Anicetus and the elder Marciana. Engaged to Gaius Marius Septimus. Considered the most beautiful young woman in Rome.

Marcellinus: Appointed Magister Officiorum (Master of offices) under Emperor Magnentius of the Western Roman empire. Although a Christian, he was a long-time friend of Senator Marius and mentor to the senator's son, Septimus.

Marcus Scudillo (Marcus): A captain of the Imperial Guard who served under the command or Arbitio. He was a close friend of Lucius, Prince Gallus, Princess Helena, and Melissa.

Marius (Senator Gaius Marius): Roman Senator and father of Septimus. Senator Marius owned several large estates in Italy and Spain that were managed by his older sons. The House of Marius boasted a long line of illustrious ancestors including generals, senators, and consuls, going back to the days of the Roman Republic.

Maximus (of Ephesus): A pagan philosopher who studied in Pergamum in the school of Aedesius. Despite his philosophic training, he devoted his time to studying and practicing the black arts of the occult, including divination and magic. He became Julian's instructor and mentor.

Melissa: Eldest child and only daughter of General Flavius Florentius and Portia. She was a lifelong friend of Princess Helena, who she knew since they were toddlers. They were schooled together by the same tutors in the imperial court. Melissa's parents hoped to arrange a marriage between Melissa and Lucius, the son of their dear friend Varronius.

Nepotianus (Flavius Julius Popilius Nepotianus Constantinus): He was a nephew of Constantine. After Emperor Constans was killed and Magnentius declared Emperor in the West, Nepotian raised a small army of gladiators in the city of Rome and declared himself Emperor. The uprising was put down by General Marcellinus, who led a small force of infantry (under Cassius and Septimus) and cavalry (under Claudius Silvanus and Leontius). Nepotian was killed in the battle.

Paul (Father Paul): Priest who served as the unofficial chaplain of the legion known as Third Italica, manned by Christian legionaries. Known to the clergy of Rome, including several popes, he was assigned to the spiritual care of the legion by Pope Julius, the immediate predecessor of Pope Liberius. Loved by the legionaries in his care; he was over forty years of age.

Portia: Wife of Flavius Florentius and mother of Melissa and several boys away in military training in Antioch and Caesarea Maritima.

Priscus (of Epirus): Pagan philosopher and fellow student and friend of Julian.

Samson: The nickname of one of Jason's protectors, given to him for his size and strength reminiscent of the biblical character. His true name and history were unknown to even his closest friends. He was believed to be forty years of age.

Silvanus (Claudius Silvanus): A senior military tribune commanding several cavalry squadrons and legions, under the command of General Marcellinus.

Septimus (Gaius Marius Septimus Romanus): Son of Senator Gaius Marius and Lady Camilia. As a youth and son of a leading Roman noble, he lived as a hostage among the Alemanni tribes. Later, as a Roman officer, he served with the legions in Gaul. As second in command of the Third Italica legion, he marched with the legion to Rome to put down the insurrection of Nepotian the Usurper. When the legion's commanding officer (Cassius) was killed in an ambush, Septimus rallied the legionaries to defeat a larger force comprised of gladiators. He was acclaimed "Romanus" by his troops on the spot, an agnomen later confirmed by the Roman Senate. He was later promoted to commanding officer of the Third Italica at the suggestion of Marcellinus and with the consent of Emperor Magnentius and the Roman Senate. He

358

became engaged to Marciana the Younger soon after meeting her at the foot of the Virgo Acqua near the Tre Vie.

Ursacius: Bishop (Singidunum) with semi-Arian sympathies. Theological adviser to Constantius. Opponent of Athanasius.

Ulysses: The gray warhorse of Tribune Gaius Marius Septimus Romanus. Septimus acquired the horse from a less-than-reputable trader who exaggerated the animal's pedigree and intelligence— facts Septimus refused to acknowledge. Septimus delighted in training the horse but was more often than not disappointed in the results. He maintained that the horse was clever and was therefore hard to train. Others maintained the horse was stupid and that the tribune's efforts to train it were wasted at best and possibly dangerous to himself.

Valens: Arian bishop (Mursa) and theological adviser to Constantius.

Varronius: Held rank of count while also being an admiral in the imperial fleet. He was a longtime friend of Florentius and his wife Portia. He is the father of Lucius and Jovian.

Map of the Roman Empire (351 AD)

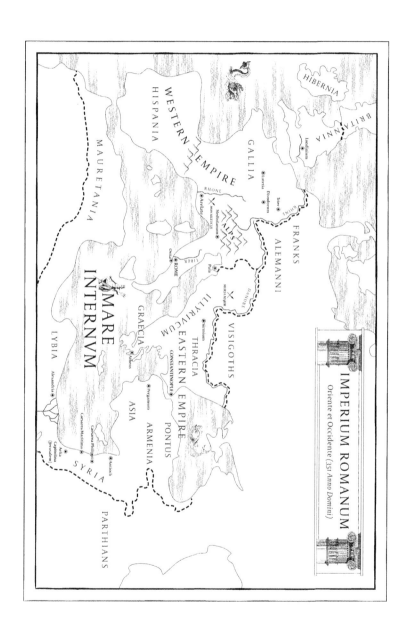

ABOUT THE AUTHOR

Steven O'Reilly writes on Catholic and general Christian apologetics topics. He has written articles for *This Rock* and currently writes for his own Internet blog.

He graduated from the University of Dallas with a Bachelor of Arts in Economics. He also received a Master of Science in Management from the Georgia Institute of Technology.

He served in the Central Intelligence Agency and currently works in private industry. He and his wife, Margaret, have four sons (Patrick, Peter, Brian, and Kevin). The author and his wife live in the Atlanta area. He can be contacted at StevenOReilly@AOL.com.

Printed in Great Britain
by Amazon

38337424R00208